# Killer of Men

# Killer of Men

CHRISTIAN CAMERON

First published in Great Britain in 2010 by Orion Books,
an imprint of The Orion Publishing Group Ltd
Orion House, 5 Upper Saint Martin's Lane
London WC2H 9EA

An Hachette UK Company

1 3 5 7 9 10 8 6 4 2

Copyright © Christian Cameron 2010

A CIP catalogue record for this book is
available from the British Library.

ISBN (Hardback) 978 0 7528 9858 2
ISBN (Export Trade Paperback) 978 0 7528 9859 9

Typeset by Deltatype Ltd, Birkenhead, Merseyside

Printed in Great Britain by CPI Mackays, Chatham ME5 8TD

The Orion Publishing Group's policy is to use papers that
are natural, renewable and recyclable products and
made from wood grown in sustainable forests. The logging
and manufacturing processes are expected to conform to
the environmental regulations of the country of origin.

www.orionbooks.co.uk

*For the Plataeans*

These were urged on by Ares, and the Greeks by flashing-eyed Athena, and Terror, and Rout, and Discord that rageth incessantly, sisters and comrades of Ares, killer of men.

Homer, *Iliad* 4.440

# Glossary

I am an *amateur* Greek scholar. My definitions are my own, but taken from the LSJ or Routledge's *Handbook of Greek Mythology* or Smith's *Classical Dictionary*. On some military issues I have the temerity to disagree with the received wisdom on the subject. Also check my website at www.hippeis.com for more information and some helpful pictures.

**Akinakes** A Scythian short sword or long knife, also sometimes carried by Medes and Persians.

**Andron** The 'men's room' of a proper Greek house – where men have symposia. Recent research has cast real doubt as to the sexual exclusivity of the room, but the name sticks.

**Apobatai** The Chariot Warriors. In many towns, towns that hadn't used chariots in warfare for centuries, the *Apobatai* were the elite three hundred or so. In Athens, they competed in special events; in Thebes, they may have been the forerunners of the Sacred Band.

**Archon** A city's senior official or, in some cases, one of three or four. A magnate.

**Aspis** The Greek hoplite's shield (which is not called a hoplon!). The *aspis* is about a yard in diameter, is deeply dished (up to six inches deep) and should weigh between eight and sixteen pounds.

**Basilieus** An aristocratic title from a bygone era (at least in 500 BC) that means 'king' or 'lord'.

**Bireme** A warship rowed by two tiers of oars, as opposed to a *trireme*, which has three tiers.

**Chiton** The standard tunic for most men, made by taking a single continuous piece of cloth and folding it in half, pinning the shoulders and open side. Can be made quite fitted by means of pleating. Often made of very fine quality material – usually wool, sometimes linen, especially in the upper classes. A full *chiton* was ankle length for men and women.

**Chitoniskos** A small *chiton*, usually just longer than modesty demanded – or not as long as modern modesty would demand! Worn by warriors and farmers, often heavily bloused and very full by warriors to pad their armour. Usually wool.

**Chlamys** A short cloak made from a rectangle of cloth roughly 60 by 90 inches – could also be worn as a **chiton** if folded and pinned a different way. Or slept under as a blanket.

**Corslet/Thorax** In 500 BC, the best *corslets* were made of bronze, mostly of the so-called 'bell' *thorax* variety. A few muscle *corslets* appear at the end of this period, gaining popularity into the 450s. Another style is the 'white' *corslet* seen to appear just as the Persian Wars begin – re-enactors call this the 'Tube and Yoke' *corslet* and some people call it (erroneously) the *linothorax*. Some of them may have been made of linen – we'll never know – but the likelier material is Athenian leather, which was often tanned and finished with alum, thus being bright white. Yet another style was a tube and yoke of scale, which you can see the author wearing on his website. A scale *corslet* would have been the most expensive of all, and probably provided the best protection.

**Daidala** Kithairon, the mountain that towered over Plataea, was the site of a remarkable fire-festival, the *Daidala*, which was celebrated by the Plataeans on the summit of the mountain. In the usual ceremony, as mounted by the Plataeans in every seventh year, a wooden idol (*daidalon*) would be dressed in bridal robes and dragged on an ox-cart from Plataea to the top of the mountain, where it would be burned after appropriate rituals. Or, in the *Great Daidala*, which were celebrated every forty-nine years, fourteen *daidala* from different Boeotian towns would be burned on a large wooden pyre heaped with brushwood, together with a cow and a bull that were sacrificed to Zeus and Hera. This huge pyre on the mountain top must have provided a most impressive spectacle; Pausanias remarks that he knew of no other flame that rose as high or could be seen from so far.

The cultic legend that was offered to account for the festival ran as follows. When Hera had once quarreled with Zeus, as she often did, she had withdrawn to her childhood home of Euboea and had refused every attempt at reconciliation. So Zeus sought the advice of the wisest man on earth, Kithairon (the eponym of the mountain), who ruled at Plataea in the earliest times. Kithairon advised him to make a wooden image of a woman, to veil it in the manner of a bride, and then to have it drawn along in an ox-cart after spreading the rumour that he was planning to marry the nymph Plataea, a daughter of the River God Asopos. When Hera rushed to the scene and tore away the veils, she was so relieved to find a wooden effigy rather than the expected bride that she at last consented to be reconciled with Zeus. (Routledge *Handbook of Greek Mythology*, p.137–38)

**Daimon** Literally a spirit, the *daimon* of combat might be adrenaline, and the *daimon* of philosophy might simply be native intelligence. Suffice it to say that very intelligent men – like Socrates – believed that god-sent spirits could infuse a man and influence his actions.

**Daktyloi** Literally digits or fingers, in common talk, 'inches' in the system of measurement. Systems for measurement differed from city to city. I have taken the liberty of using just one, the Athenian units of measurement.

**Despoina** Lady. A term of formal address.

**Diekplous** A complex naval tactic about which some debate remains. In this book, the *Diekplous* or through stroke is commenced with an attack by the ramming ship's bow (picture the two ships approaching bow to bow or head on) and cathead on the enemy oars. Oars were the most vulnerable part of a fighting ship, something very difficult to imagine unless you've rowed in a big boat and understand how lethal your own oars can be – to you! After the attacker crushed the enemy's oars, he passes, flank to flank, and then turns when astern, coming up easily (the defender is almost dead in the water) and ramming the enemy under the stern or counter as desired.

**Doru/Dory** A spear, about ten feet long, with a bronze butt spike and a spearhead.

**Eleutheria** Freedom.

**Ephebe** A young, free man of property. A young man in training to be a *hoplite*. Usually performing service to his city and, in ancient terms, at one of the two peaks of male beauty.

**Eromenos** The 'beloved' in a same-sex pair in ancient Greece. Usually younger, about seventeen. This is a complex, almost dangerous subject in the modern world – were these pair-bonds about sex, or chivalric love, or just a 'brotherhood' of warriors? I suspect there were elements of all three. And to write about this period without discussing the *eromenos/erastes* bond would, I fear, be like putting all the warriors in steel armour instead of bronze …

**Erastes** The 'lover' in a same-sex pair bond – the older man, a tried warrior, twenty-five to thirty years old.

**Eudaimonia** Literally 'well-spirited'. A feeling of extreme joy.

**Exhedra** The porch of the women's quarters – in some cases, any porch over a farm's central courtyard.

**Helot** The 'race of slaves' of Ancient Sparta – the conquered peoples who lived with the Spartiates and did all of their work so that they could concentrate entirely on making war and more Spartans.

**Hetaera** Literally a 'female companion'. In ancient Athens, a *Hetaera* was a courtesan, a highly skilled woman who provided sexual companionship as well as fashion, political advice, and music.

**Himation** A very large piece of rich, often embroidered wool, worn as an outer garment by wealthy citizen women or as a sole garment by older men, especially those in authority.

**Hoplite** A Greek upper-class warrior. Possession of a heavy spear, a helmet, and an *aspis* (see above) and income above the marginal lowest free class were all required to serve as a *hoplite*. Although much is made of the 'citizen soldier' of ancient Greece, it would be fairer to compare *hoplites* to medieval knights than to Roman legionnaires or modern National Guardsmen. Poorer citizens did serve, and sometimes as *hoplites* or marines, but in general, the front ranks were the preserve of upper class men who could afford the best training and the essential armour.

**Hoplitodromos** The *hoplite* race, or race in armour. Two *stades* with an *aspis* on your shoulder, a helmet, and greaves in the early runs. I've run this race in armour. It is no picnic.

**Hoplomachia** A *hoplite* contest, or sparring match. Again, there is enormous debate as to when *hoplomachia* came into existence and how much training Greek *hoplites* received. One thing that they didn't do is drill like modern soldiers – there's no mention of it in all of Greek literature. However, they had highly evolved martial arts (see *Pankration*) and it is almost certain that *hoplomachia* was a term that referred to 'the martial art of fighting when fully equipped as a *hoplite*'.

**Hoplomachos** A participant in *hoplomachia*.

**Hypaspist** Literally 'under the shield'. A squire or military servant – by the time of Arimnestos, the *hypaspist* was usually a younger man of the same class as the *hoplite*.

**Kithara** A stringed instrument of some complexity, with a hollow body as a soundboard.

**Kline** A couch.

**Kopis** The heavy, back-curved saber of the Greeks. Like a longer, heavier modern Kukri or Ghurka knife.

**Kore** A maiden or daughter.

**Kylix** A wide, shallow, handled bowl for drinking wine.

**Logos** Literally the 'word'. In pre-Socratic Greek philosophy the word is everything – the power beyond the gods.

**Longche** A six to seven foot throwing spear, also used for hunting. A *hoplite* might carry a pair of *longche*, or a single, longer and heavier *dory*.

**Machaira** A heavy sword or long knife.

**Maenad** The 'raving ones' – ecstatic female followers of Dionysus.

**Mastos** A woman's breast. A *mastos* cup is shaped like a woman's breast with a rattle in the nipple – so when you drink, you lick the nipple and the rattle shows that you emptied the cup. I'll leave the rest to imagination…

**Medimnoi** A grain measure. Very roughly – thirty-five to a hundred pounds of grain.

**Megaron** A style of building with a roofed porch.

**Navarch** An admiral.

**Oikia** The household – all the family and all the slaves, and sometimes the animals and the farmland itself.

**Opson** Whatever spread, dip, or accompaniment an ancient Greek had with bread.

**Pais** A child.

**Palaestra** The exercise sands of the gymnasium.

**Pankration** The military martial art of the ancient Greeks – an unarmed combat system that bears more than a passing resemblance to modern MMA techniques, with a series of carefully structured blows and domination holds that is, by modern standards, very advanced. Also the basis of the Greek sword and spear-based martial arts. Kicking, punching, wrestling, grappling, on the ground and standing, were all permitted.

**Peplos** A short over-fold of cloth that women could wear as a hood or to cover the breasts.

**Phalanx** The full military potential of a town; the actual, formed body of men before a battle (all of the smaller groups formed together made a *phalanx*). In this period, it would be a mistake to imagine a carefully drilled military machine.

**Phylarch** A file leader – an officer commanding the four to sixteen men standing behind him in the *phalanx*.

**Polemarch** The war leader.

**Polis** The city. The basis of all Greek political thought and expression, the government that was held to be more important – a higher god – than any individual or even family. To this day, when we talk about politics, we're talking about the 'things of our city'.

**Porne** A prostitute.

**Porpax** The bronze or leather band that encloses the forearm on a Greek *aspis*.

**Psiloi** Light infantryman – usually

slaves or adolescent freemen who, in this period, were not organised and seldom had any weapon beyond some rocks to throw.

**Pyrrhiche** The 'War Dance'. A line dance in armour done by all of the warriors, often very complex. There's reason to believe that the *Pyrrhiche* was the method by which the young were trained in basic martial arts and by which 'drill' was inculcated.

**Pyxis** A box, often circular, turned from wood or made of metal.

**Rhapsode** A master-poet, often a performer who told epic works like the *Iliad* from memory.

**Satrap** A Persian ruler of a province of the Persian Empire.

**Skeuophoros** Literally a 'shield carrier', unlike the *hypaspist*, this is a slave or freed man who does camp work and carried the armour and baggage.

**Sparabara** The large wicker shield of the Persian and Mede elite infantry. Also the name of those soldiers.

**Spolas** Another name for a leather *corslet*, often used for the lion skin of Herakles.

**Stade** A measure of distance. An Athenian *stade* is about 185 meters.

**Strategos** In Athens, the commander of one of the ten military tribes. Elsewhere, any senior Greek officer – sometimes the commanding General.

**Synaspismos** The closest order that *hoplites* could form – so close that the shields overlap, hence 'shield on shield'.

**Taxis** Any group but, in military terms, a company; I use it for sixty to three hundred men.

**Thetes** The lowest free class – citizens with limited rights.

**Thorax** See *corslet*.

**Thugater** Daughter. Look at the word carefully and you'll see the 'daughter' in it …

**Triakonter** A small rowed galley of thirty oars.

**Trierarch** The captain of a ship – sometimes just the owner or builder, sometimes the fighting captain.

**Zone** A belt, often just rope or finely wrought cord, but could be a heavy bronze kidney belt for war.

# General Note on Names and Personages

This series is set in the very dawn of the so-called Classical Era, often measured from the Battle of Marathon (490 BC). Some, if not most, of the famous names of this era are characters in this series – and that's not happenstance. Athens of this period is as magical, in many ways, as Tolkien's Gondor, and even the quickest list of artists, poets, and soldiers of this era reads like a 'who's who' of Western Civilization. Nor is the author tossing them together by happenstance – these people were almost all aristocrats, men (and women) who knew each other well – and might be adversaries or friends in need. Names in bold are historical characters – yes, even Arimnestos – and you can get a glimpse into their lives by looking at Wikipedia or Britannia online. For more in-depth information, I recommend Plutarch and Herodotus, to whom I owe a great deal.

Arimnestos of Plataea may – just may – have been Herodotus's source for the events of the Persian Wars. The careful reader will note that Herodotus himself – a scribe from Halicarnassus – appears several times ...

**Archilogos** – Ephesian, son of Hipponax the poet; a typical Ionian aristocrat, who loves Persian culture and Greek culture too, who serves his city, not some cause of 'Greece' or 'Hellas', and who finds the rule of the Great King fairer and more 'democratic' than the rule of a Greek tyrant.

**Arimnestos** – Child of Chalkeotechnes and Euthalia.

**Aristagoras** – Son of Molpagoras, nephew of Histiaeus. Aristagoras led Miletus while Histiaeus was a virtual prisoner of the Great King Darius at Susa. Aristagoras seems to have initiated the Ionian Revolt – and later to have regretted it.

**Aristides** – Son of Lysimachus, lived roughly 525–468 BC, known later in life as 'The Just'. Perhaps best known as one of the commanders at

Marathon. Usually sided with the Aristocratic party.

**Artaphernes** – Brother of Darius, Great King of Persia, and Satrap of Sardis. A senior Persian with powerful connections.

Bion – A slave name, meaning 'life'. The most loyal family retainer of the Corvaxae.

Briseis – Daughter of Hipponax, sister of Archilogos.

Calchas – A former warrior, now the keeper of the shrine of the Plataean Hero of Troy, Leitus.

Chalkeotechnes – The Smith of Plataea; head of the family Corvaxae, who claim descent from Herakles.

Chalkidis – Brother of Arimnestos, son of Chalkeotechnes.

**Darius** – King of Kings, the lord of the Persian Empire, brother to Artaphernes.

Draco – Wheelwright and wagon builder of Plataea, a leading man of the town.

Empedocles – A priest of Hephaestus, the Smith God.

Epaphroditos – A warrior, an aristocrat of Lesbos.

**Eualcidas** – A Hero. Eualcidas is typical of a class of aristocratic men – professional warriors, adventurers, occasionally pirates or merchants by turns. From Euboeoa.

**Heraclitus** – circa 535–475 BC. One of the ancient world's most famous philosophers. Born to aristocratic family, he chose philosophy over political power. Perhaps most famous for his statement about time, 'You cannot step twice into the same river'. His belief that 'strife is justice' and other similar sayings which you'll find scattered through these pages made him a favorite with Nietzsche. His works, mostly now lost, probably established the later philosophy of Stoicism.

Herakleides – An Aeolian, a Greek of Asia Minor. With his brothers Nestor and Orestes, he becomes a retainer – a warrior – in service to Arimnestos. It is easy, when looking at the birth of Greek democracy, to see the whole form of modern government firmly established – but at the time of this book, democracy was less than skin deep and most armies were formed of semi-feudal war bands following an aristocrat.

Heraklides – Aristides's helmsman, a lower class Athenian who has made a name for himself in war.

Hermogenes – Son of Bion, Arimnestos's slave.

**Hesiod** – A great poet (or a great tradition of poetry) from Boeotia in Greece, Hesiod's 'Works and Days' and 'Theogony' were widely read in the sixth century and remain fresh today – they are the chief source we have on Greek farming, and this book owes an enormous debt to them.

**Hippias** – Last tyrant of Athens, overthrown around 510 BC (that is, just around the beginning of this book), Hippias escaped into exile and became a pensioner of Darius of Persia.

**Hipponax** – 540 BC–c. 498 BC. A Greek poet and satirist, considered the inventor of parody. He is supposed to have said 'There are two days when a woman is a pleasure: the day one marries her and the day one buries her'.

**Histiaeus** – Tyrant of Miletus and ally of Darius of Persia, possible originator of the plan for the Ionian Revolt.

**Homer** – Another great poet, roughly Hesiod's contemporary (give or take fifty years!) and again, possibly more a poetic tradition than an individual man. Homer is reputed as the author of the *Iliad* and the *Odyssey*, two great epic poems which, between them, largely defined what heroism and aristocratic good behavior should be in Greek society – and, you might say, to this very day.

Kylix – A boy, slave of Hipponax.

**Miltiades** – Tyrant of the Thracian Chersonese. His son, Cimon or Kimon, rose to be a great man in Athenian politics. Probably Miltiades was the author of the Athenian victory of Marathon, but Miltiades was a complex man, a pirate, a warlord, and a supporter of Athenian democracy.

Penelope – Daughter of Chalkeotechnes, sister of Arimnestos.

**Sappho** – A Greek poetess from the island of Lesbos, born sometime around 630 BC and died between 570 and 550 BC. Her father was probably Lord of Eressos. Widely considered the greatest lyric poet of Ancient Greece.

Simonalkes – Head of the collateral branch of the Plataean Corvaxae, cousin to Arimnestos.

**Simonides** – Another great lyric poet, he lived circa 556 BC–468 BC, and his nephew, Bacchylides, was as famous as he. Perhaps best known for his epigrams, one of which is:

> Ω ξεῖν᾽, ἀγγέλλειν Λακεδαιμονίοις ὅτιτῇδε
> κείμεθα, τοῖςκείνωνρήμασι πειθόμενοι.
> *Go tell the Spartans, thou who passest by,*
> *That here, obedient to their laws, we lie.*

**Thales** – circa 624 BC–c. 546 BC The first philosopher of the Greek tradition, whose writings were still current in Arimnestos's time. Thales used geometry to solve problems such as calculating the height of the pyramids in Aegypt and the distance of ships from the shore. He made at least one trip to Aegypt. He is widely accepted as the founder of western mathematics.

**Theognis** – Theognis of Megara was almost certainly not one man but a whole canon of aristocratic poetry under that name, much of it practical. There are maxims, many very wise, laments on the decline of man and the age, and the woes of old age and poverty, songs for symposia, etc. In later sections there are songs and poems about homosexual love and laments for failed romances. Despite widespread attributions, there was, at some point, a real Theognis who may have lived in the mid-6th century BC, or just before the events of *Killer of Men*. His poetry would have been central to the world of Arimnestos's mother.

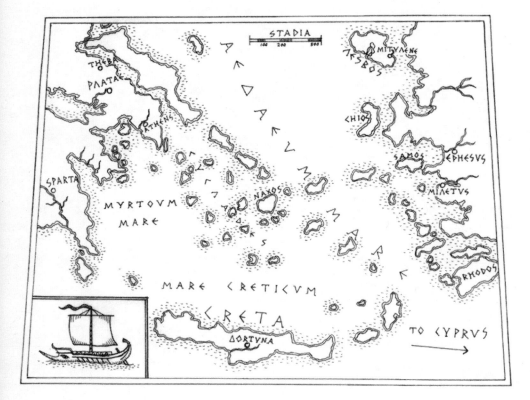

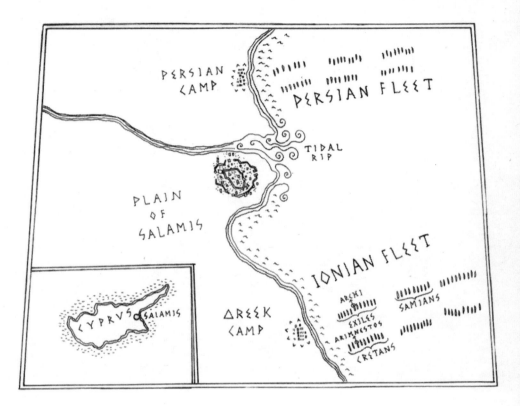

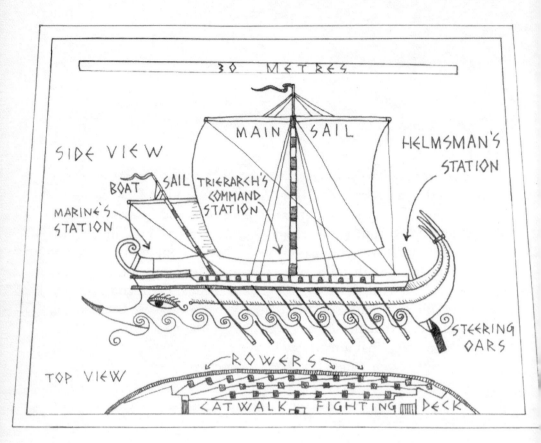

30 METRES

SIDE VIEW

MAIN SAIL

HELMSMAN'S STATION

BOAT SAIL TRIERARCH'S COMMAND STATION

MARINE'S STATION

STEERING OARS

TOP VIEW

ROWERS

CATWALK FIGHTING DECK

It may seem odd to you, *thugater*, who has only known me as an old man, and an aristocrat, that I was once young and poor. And indeed, when the singers rise to sing of our ancestors, and men say that we are descended from Heracles and Zeus, I always laugh in my gut, because when I was young the smell of sheep dung was more common in our house than the smell of incense, and my mother's hands were red and hard, despite her high birth and constant complaints.

But you, who have soft hands and whose only work is the loom, should know that those days were happy days too. And that it is worth knowing that a man can live as happily on a farm in Boeotia as in a city in Asia. Life is not all rose water and porphyry.

Listen then. And may the Muses aid me – I am old, and my memory may lose the furrow where the plough should go. I pour this libation to Heracles, my ancestor, who endured the twelve labours, and to all the jealous gods, who gave me this good life, despite famine and peril, and a long war.

# Part I

## *The Lovely Bloom of Youth*

As long as some mortal has the lovely bloom of youth, he plans with a light heart many things that are never to be fulfilled.

Simonides, fr. 20

# I

The thing that I remember best – and maybe it's my first memory, too – is the forge. My father, the smith – aye, he farmed too, because every free man in Boeotia counted his wealth in farmland – but Pater was the bronze-smith, the best in our village, the best in Plataea, and women said that he had the touch of the god upon him, because he had a battle wound that made him lame in his left foot, and because his pots never leaked. We were simple folk in Boeotia, not fancy boys like Athenians or joyless killers like the men of Sparta – we valued a man who made a pot that didn't leak. When Pater pounded out a seam, that seam held. And he liked to add more – he was always a man to give more than he got, so that a housewife who paid him ten hard-won drachmas and a bowl of potted rabbit might find that Pater had put a carefully tooled likeness of Demeter or Hecate beneath the rim of the pot, or worked her name into the handle of the cauldron or tripod.

Pater did good work and he was fair. What's more, he had stood his ground twice in the storm of bronze, so that every man knew his measure. And for all that, he was always ready to share a cup of wine, so the front of the smithy had become a gathering place for all the men of our little village on a fair day when the ploughing was done – and sometimes even a singer or a minstrel, a *rhapsode*. The smithy itself was like a lord's hall, as men brought Pater their quarrels – all except his own bloody family, and more of that later – or came to tell him their little triumphs.

He was not much as a father. Not that he hit me more than a dozen times, and every one deserved, as I still remember. I once used my father's name to buy a knife in the *polis* – a foolish thing, but I wanted that knife. It broke in my hand later – yet another tale, lass – but I meant no harm. When Pater learned that I had pledged his name for a simple blade he'd have made me himself, he struck me with the whole weight of his fist. I cried for a day from the shame.

He had the raising of us all to himself, you see. My mother was drunk from the time I first remember her – drinking away the forge, Pater would say when the darkness was on him. She's your grandmother, lass – I shouldn't speak ill of her, and I'll try to tell her true, but it's not pretty.

She was the daughter of a lord, a real lord, a *basileus* from down the valley in Thespiae. They met at the Great Daidala in the year of the Olympics, and the rumour of my youth had it that she was the wildest and the most beautiful of all the daughters of Apollo, and that Pater swept her up in his great arms and carried her off in the old way, and that the basileus swore a curse on their marriage.

I respect the gods – I've seen them. But I'm not one to believe that Hera comes to curse a woman's womb, nor Ares to push a spear aside. The gods love them that love themselves – Mater said that, so she wasn't a total failure as a mother, I reckon. But she never did aught to love herself, and her curse was her looks and her birth.

She had three children for Pater. I was the middle one – my older brother came first by a year, and he should have had the smithy and maybe the farm besides, but I never faulted him for it. He had red hair and we called him 'Chalkidis', the copper boy. He was big and brave and all a boy could want in an older brother.

I had a sister, too – still do, unless Artemis put an arrow into her. My mother gave her the name of Penelope, and the gods must have been listening.

I know nothing of those first years, when Pater was as handsome as a god, and Mater loved him, and she sang in the forge. Men say they were like gods, but men say a great many things when an event is safely in the past – they tell a lot of lies. I'll no doubt tell you a few myself. Old man's prerogative. I gathered that they were happy, though.

But nothing ended as my mother expected. I think she wanted something greater from my father, or from herself, or perhaps from the gods. She began to go up in the hills with the maenads and ran wild with other women, and there were words in the forge. And then came the first of the Theban years – when the men of Thebes came against us.

What do you know of Thebes? It is a name in legend to you. To us, it was the curse of our lives – poor Plataea, so far from the

6

gods, so close to Thebes. Thebes was a city that could muster fifteen thousand hoplites, while we could, in an emergency and freeing and arming our most trustworthy slaves, muster fifteen hundred good men. And this is before we made the Great Alliance with Athens. So we were a lonely little polis with no friends, like a man whose plough is broken and none of his neighbours have a plough to loan.

They came at us just after the grain harvest, and the men went off to war. Whenever I hear the *Iliad*, thugater, I weep when I hear of mighty Hector's son being afraid of his father's shining helmet. How well I remember it, and Pater standing there in his panoply, the image of Ares. He had a bronze-faced shield and a splendid helmet he had forged himself from one piece of bronze. His horsehair plume was black and red for the smith god. He wore a breastplate of solid bronze, again of his own making, and thigh guards and arm guards of a kind you scarcely see any more – aye, they were better men. He carried two spears in the old way, and long greaves on his legs, and when he stood in the courtyard with the whole panoply he gleamed like gold.

Mater was drunk when she poured the libation. I can see it in my head – she came out in a white *chiton*, like a *kore* going to sacrifice, but the chiton had purple stains. When she went to bless his shield she stumbled and poured wine down his leg, and the slaves murmured. And she wept, and ran inside.

So Pater went off to fight Thebes, and he came back carried by two men on his *chlamys* and his spears, and his shield was gone. We lost. And Pater lost most of the use of his left leg, where Mater spilled the wine, and after that there was nothing between them but silence.

I suppose I was five. Chalkidis was six, and we lay in the loft of the barn and he whispered to me about Pater's part in the battle and about our cousins – the grandsons of Pater's father's brother. Aye, thugater, we count such relations close in Boeotia. Pater had no brothers – his father must have read Hesiod one too many times – and this batch of surly cousins were the nearest relations I had on Pater's side. On Mater's side they scarcely allowed that we were kin – until later, and that's another tale, but a happier one.

My brother said that Pater was a hero, that he'd stood his ground when other men ran, and he saved many lives – and that when the Thebans took him, they hadn't stripped him, but ransomed him like a lord. I was young and I knew nothing of ransom, only that Pater, who towered over me like a god, was unable to walk and his mood was dark.

'The other Corvaxae were the first to run,' Chalkidis whispered. 'They ran and left Pater's side open to the spears, and now they slink through the town and fear what Pater will say.'

We were the Corvaxae – the men of the Raven. Apollo's raven. Look up, lass – there's the black bird on my *aspis*, and may the gods send I never feel it on my arm again! You know what the sage says – count no man happy until he is dead. I pour a libation in his memory – may his shade taste the wine.

The black bird is also on our sails and on our house. I was five – I knew little of this, except that I knew that Pater told me it was a good omen when a raven landed on the roof of the smithy. And our women were Corvaxae, too – black-haired and pale-skinned, and clannish. No man in our valley wanted to cross my mother, or my sister, in their day. They were Ravens of Apollo.

And the truth is that my story starts in that fight. It is from that day that the other Corvaxae turned against Pater, and then against me. And from that day that the men of Plataea decided to find a new way of keeping their little town free of Thebes.

It took Pater almost a year to get to his feet. Before that year, I reckon we were rich, as peasants in Boeotia measured riches. We had a yoke of oxen and two ploughs, a house built of stone with a tower, a barn that stood all weather and the smithy. Pater wore the full panoply when the muster was called, like a lord. We ate meat on feast days and we had wine all year.

But I was old enough to understand that at the end of that year we were not rich. Mater's gold pin went, and all our metal cups. And my first bad memory – my first memory of fear – is from that year.

Simonalkes – the eldest of the other branch of the Corvaxae, a big, strong man with a dark face – came to our house. Pater had to walk with a crutch, but he rose as fast as he could, cursing the slaves who helped him. My brother was in the *andron* – the men's room – pouring wine for Simon like a proper boy. Simon put his feet up on a bench.

'You'll be needing money,' Simon said to Pater. Not even a greeting.

Pater's face grew red, but he bowed his head. 'Are you offering me aid, cousin?'

Simon shook his head. 'You need no charity. I'll offer you a loan against the farm.'

Pater shook his head. 'No,' he said. If Pater thought that he was hiding his anger, he was wrong.

'Still too proud, smith?' Simon said, and his lip curled.

'Proud enough to stand my ground,' Pater said, and Simon's face changed colour. He got up.

'Is this the famous hospitality of the Corvaxae?' Simon said. 'Or has your whore of a wife debased you, too?' He looked at me. 'Neither of these boys has your look, cousin.'

'Leave my house,' Pater said.

'I came to tender help,' Simon said, 'but I'm met by accusations and insults.'

'Leave my house,' Pater said.

Simon hooked his fingers in his belt and planted his feet. He looked around. 'Is it *your* house, cousin?' He smiled grimly. 'Our grandfather built this house. Why is it *yours*?' Simon sneered – he was always good at sneering – and snapped his fingers. 'Perhaps you'll marry again and get an heir.'

'My sons are my heirs,' Pater said carefully, as if speaking a foreign language.

'Your sons are the children of some strangers on the hillside,' our cousin said.

Pater looked as angry as I'd ever known him, and I'd never seen two grown men take this tone – the tone of hate. I'd heard it from Mater in the women's quarters, but I'd never heard it rise to conflict. I was afraid. And what was I hearing? It was as if cousin Simon was saying that I was not my father's son.

'Bion!' Pater shouted, and his biggest slave came running. Bion was a strong man, a trustworthy man with a wife and children who knew he'd be freed as soon as the money came back, and he was loyal. That's right, thugater. Melissa is Bion's granddaughter, and now she's your handmaiden. She's never been a slave, but Bion was once. As was I, lass, so don't you wrinkle your nose.

'You'll be even poorer if I have to kill your slave,' Simon said.

Pater thumped one crutch-step closer and his heavy staff shot out and caught Simon in the shin. Simon went down and then Pater hit him in the groin, so that he screamed like a woman in childbirth – I knew that sound well enough, because Bion's wife provided him with a child every year.

9

Pater wasn't done. He stood over Simon with his staff raised. 'You think I'm afraid of you, you coward!' he said. 'You think I don't know why I'm lame? You ran. You left me in the bronze storm. And now you come here and your mouth pours out filth.' He was panting and I was more afraid, because Simon was wheezing, down on the floor, and Pater had hurt him. It was not like two boys behind the barn. It was *real*.

Simon got himself up and he pushed against Bion. 'Let go, slave!' he croaked. 'Or I'll come back for you.' He leaned against the doorway, but Bion ignored him, linked an arm under his chin despite his size and dragged him from the room.

All the *oikia* – the household, slaves and free – followed the action into the courtyard. Simon wouldn't stop – he cursed us, and he cursed the whole oikia, and he promised that when he came into his own he'd sell all the slaves and burn their houses. Now I know it for what it was – the blusterings of an impotent but angry man. But at the time it sounded like the death curse of some fallen hero, and I feared him. I feared that everything he said would come to pass.

He said that he'd lain with our mother in the hills, and he said that Pater was a fool who had risked all their lives in the battle and who sought death rather than face his wife's infidelity. He shouted that we were all bastards, and he shouted that the basileus, the local aristocrat, would come for the farm because he was jealous of Pater.

And all the time Bion dragged him from the yard.

It was ugly.

And when he was gone, Pater wept. And that made me even more afraid.

It seemed as if the roof had fallen in on our lives, but it was not many weeks later when Pater brought the priest to the forge, all the way from Thebes. He rebuilt the fire and the priest of Hephaestus took his silver drachma and made a thorough job of it; he used good incense from the east and he poured a libation from a proper cup, although made of clay and not metal as we expected. Because Chalkidis and I were old enough to help in the forge, he made us initiates. Bion was already an initiate – Hephaestus cares nothing for slave and free, but only that a craftsman gives unstintingly to his craft – and he advanced a degree. It was very holy and it helped to make me feel that my world was going to be restored. We swept the forge from top to bottom and Pater made a joke – the only one I can remember.

'I must have the only clean forge in all Hellas,' he said to the priest.

The priest laughed. 'You took that wound fighting us last year,' he said. He pointed at Pater's leg.

'Aye,' Pater allowed. He was not a man given to long speeches.

'Front rank?' the priest asked.

Pater pulled his beard. 'You were there?'

The priest nodded. 'I close the first file for my tribe,' he said. It was a position of real honour – the priest was a man who knew his battles.

'I'm the centre man in the front rank,' Pater said. He shrugged. 'Or I was.'

'You held us a good long time,' the Theban said. 'And to be honest, I knew your device – the raven. Apollo's raven for a smith?'

My father grinned. He liked the priest – a small miracle in itself – and that smile made my life better. 'We're sons of Heracles here. I serve Hephaestus and we've had the raven on our house since my grandfather's grandfather came here.' He kept grinning, and just for a moment he was a much younger man. 'My father always said that the gods were sufficiently capricious that we needed to serve a couple at a time.'

That was Pater's longest sentence in a year.

The priest laughed. 'I should be getting back,' he said. 'It'll be dark by the time I see the gates of Thebes.'

Pater shook his head. 'Let me relight the fire,' he said. 'I'll make you a gift and that will please the god. Then you can eat in my house and sleep on a good couch, and go back to Thebes rested.'

The priest bowed. 'Who can refuse a gift?' he said.

But Pater's face darkened. 'Wait,' he said, 'and see what it is. The lame god may not return my skill to me. It has been too long.'

The fire was laid. The priest went out into the sunshine and took from his girdle a piece of crystal – a beautiful thing, as clear as a maiden's eye, and he held it in the sun. He called my brother and I followed him, as younger brothers follow older brothers, and he laughed. 'Two for the price of one, eh?' he said.

'Is it magic, lord?' my brother asked.

The priest shook his head. 'There are charlatans who would tell you so,' he said. 'But I love the new philosophy as much as I love my crafty god. This is a thing of making. Men made this. It is called a lens, and a craftsman made it from rock crystal in a town in Syria.

It takes the rays of the sun and it burnishes them the way your father burnishes bronze, and makes them into fire. Watch.'

He placed a little pile of shavings of dry willow on the ground, then he held the lens just so. And before we were fidgeting, the little pile began to smoke.

'Run and get me some tow from your mother and her maidens,' the priest said to me, and I ran – I didn't want to miss a moment of this *philosophy*.

I hurried up the steps to the *exhedra* and my sister opened the door. She was five, blonde and chubby and forthright. 'What?' she asked me.

'I need a handful of tow,' I said.

'What for?' she asked.

We were never adversaries, Penelope and I. So I told her, and she got the tow and carried it to the priest herself, and he was tolerant, flicking her a smile and accepting the tow with a bow as if she were some lord's kore serving at his altar. And all the time his left hand, holding the lens, never moved.

The light fell in a tiny pinpoint too bright to watch, and the willow shavings smoked and smoked.

'I could blow on it,' I said.

The priest looked at me strangely. Then he nodded. 'Go ahead,' he said.

So I lay down in the dust and blew on the shavings very gently. At first nothing happened, and then I almost blew them all over the yard. My brother punched me in the arm. The priest laughed.

Quickly, I ran into the shop, where Pater stood by his cold forge with a distant look on his face, and I took the tube we used for controlling the heat of the forge – a bronze tube. I ran back into the yard, put the end of the tube near the pinpoint of light and gave a puff, and before my heart beat ten times, I had fire.

The priest wasn't laughing any more. He lifted the tow, put the flames in the midst and caught the tow, so that he seemed to have a handful of fire, and then he walked into the forge at a dignified pace, and we followed him. He laid the fire in the forge under the scraps and the bark and the good dry oak, and the night-black charcoal from mighty Cithaeron's flanks. The fire of the sun, brought down from the sky by his lens, lit the forge.

Pater was not a man easily moved, but he watched the fire with a look on his face like hunger in a slave. Then he busied himself managing the fire – the hearth had been cold for a long time, and he needed coals to accomplish even the slightest work. So my brother and I carried wood and charcoal, and the priest sang a long hymn to the smith god, and the fire leaped and burned through the afternoon, and before long there was a good bed of coals.

Pater took down a leather bag full of sand from his bench, and he had Bion cut him a circle of bronze as big as a man's hand. Then, with that hungry look, he took the bronze in his great hand and set the edge to the leather bag. and after a brief pause his rounded hammer fell on the bronze in a series of strokes almost too fast to see.

That's another sight I'll never forget – Pater, almost blind with his lust to do his work, and the hammer falling, the strokes precise as his left hand turned the bronze – strike, turn, strike, turn.

It was the bowl of a cup before I needed ten breaths. Not a priest's holy cup, but the kind of cup a man likes to have on a trip, to show he's no slave – the cup you use to drink wine in a strange place, that reminds you of home.

Outside, the shadows were growing long.

In the forge, the hammer made its muffled sound against the leather. Pater was weeping. The priest took the three of us and led us outside. I wanted to stay and see the cup. I could already see the shape – I could *see* that Pater had not lost his touch. And I was six or seven and all I wanted was to be a smith like Pater. To make a thing from nothing – that is the true magic, whether in a woman's womb or in a forge. But we went outside, and the priest was holding the tube of bronze. He blew through it a couple of times, and then nodded as if a puzzle had been solved. He looked at me.

'You thought to go and fetch this,' he said.

It wasn't a question, so I said nothing.

'I would have thought of it too,' my brother said.

Penelope laughed. 'Not in a year of feast days,' she said. One of Mater's expressions.

He sent a slave for fire from the main hearth in the kitchen, and he put it in the fireplace in the yard. That's where Pater kindled the forge in high summer when it was blinding hot. And he blessed it – he was a thorough man, and worth his silver drachma, unlike most priests I've known. Blessing the outdoor hearth was something Pater hadn't even considered.

Then he built up his little fire and the three of us bustled to help him, picking up scraps of wood and bark all over the yard. My brother fetched an armload of kitchen wood. And then the priest began to play with the tube, blowing through it and watching the coals grow brighter and redder and the flames leap.

'Hmm,' he said. Several times.

I have spent much of my life with the wise. I have been lucky that way – that everywhere I've gone, the gods have favoured me with men who love study and yet have time to speak to a man like me. But I think I owe all of that to the priest of Hephaestus. He treated all of us children as equals, and he cared for nothing but that tube and the effect it had on fire.

He did the oddest things. He walked all over the yard until he found a whole straw from the last haying, and he cut it neatly with a sharp iron knife and then used it to blow on the flames. It gave the same effect.

'Hmm,' he said.

He poured water on the fire and it made steam and scalded his hand, and he cursed and hopped on one foot. Penelope fetched one of the slave girls and she made him a poultice, and while she nursed his hand, he blew through the tube on the dead fire – and nothing happened except that a trail of ash was blown on my chiton.

'Hmm,' he said. He relit the fire.

Inside the forge, the sound had changed. I could hear my father's lightest hammer – when you are a smith's child, you know all the music of the forge – going *tap-tap*, *tap-tap*. He was doing fine work – chasing with a small chisel, perhaps. I wanted to go and watch, but I knew I was not welcome. He was with the god.

So I watched the priest, instead. He sent Bion for a hide of leather, and he rolled it in a great tube, and breathed through it on the fire, and nothing much happened. He and Bion made a really long tube, as long as a grown man's arm, from calf's hide, and the priest set Bion to blow on the fire. Bion did this in the forge and he was expert at it, and the priest watched the long tube work on the fire.

'Hmm,' he said.

My brother was bored. He made a spear from the firewood and began to chase me around the yard, but I wanted to watch the priest. I had learned how to be a younger brother. I let him thump me in the ribs and I neither complained nor fought back – I just stood watching the priest until my brother was bored. It didn't take long.

My brother didn't like being deprived of his mastery. 'Who *cares*?' he asked. 'So the tube makes the fire burn? I mean, who cares?' He looked to me for support. He had a point. Every child of a smith learned to use the tube – as did every slave.

The priest turned on him like a boar on a hunter. 'As you say, boy. Who would care? So answer this riddle and the Sphinx won't eat you. *Why* does the tube air make the fire brighter? Eh? Hmm?'

Pater's hammer was now going *taptaptaptaptaptap*.

'Who cares?' Chalkidis asked. He shrugged. 'Can I go and play?' he asked.

'Be off with you, Achilles,' the priest said.

My brother ran off. My sister might have stayed – she had some thoughts in her head, even as a little thing – but Mater called her to fetch wine, and she hurried off.

'May I touch the lens?' I asked.

The priest reached up and put it in my hand. He was down by the fire again.

It was a beautiful thing, and even if he said it had no magic, I was thrilled to touch it. It brought fire down from the sun. And it was clear, and deep. I looked at things through it, and it was curious. An ant was misshapen – some parts larger and some smaller. Dust developed texture.

'Does it warm up in your hand when you bring down the sun?' I asked.

The priest sat back on his heels. He looked at me the way a farmer looks at a slave he is thinking of purchasing. 'No,' he said. 'But that is an excellent question.' He held up the bronze tube. 'Neither does this. But both make the fire brighter.'

'What does it mean?' I asked.

The priest grinned. 'No idea,' he said. 'Do you know how to write?'

I shook my head.

The priest pulled his beard and began to ask questions. He asked me hundreds of questions – hard things about farm animals. He was searching my head, of course – looking to see if I had any intelligence. I tried to answer, but I felt as if I was failing. His questions were hard, and he went on and on.

The shadows grew longer and longer, and then my father started singing. I hadn't heard his song in the forge in a year – indeed, at the age I was at, I'd forgotten that my father *ever* sang when he worked.

His song came out of the forge like the smell of a good dinner, soft first and then stronger. It was the part of the *Iliad* where Hephaestus makes the armour of Achilles.

My mother's voice came down from the exhedra and met Pater's voice in the yard. These days, no one teaches women to sing the *Iliad*, but back then, every farm girl in Boeotia knew it. And they sang together. I don't think I'd ever heard them sing together. Perhaps he was happy. Perhaps she was sober.

Pater came out into the yard with a cup in his hand. He must have burnished it himself, instead of having the slave boys do it, because it glowed like gold in the last light of the sun.

He limped across the yard, and he was smiling. 'My gift to you and the god,' he said. He handed the cup to the priest.

It had a flat base – a hard thing to keep when you round a cup, let me tell you – with sloping sides and a neatly rolled rim. He'd riveted a handle on, simple work, but done cleanly and precisely. He'd made the rivets out of silver and the handle itself of copper. And he'd raised a scene into the cup itself, so that you could see Hephaestus being led to Olympus by Dionysus and Heracles, when his father Zeus takes him back. Dionysus was tall and strong in a linen chiton, and every fold was hammered in the bronze. Heracles had a lion skin that Pater had engraved so that it looked like fur, and the smith god was a little drunk on the happiness of his father's taking him back.

The priest turned it this way and that, and then he shook his head. 'This is king's work,' he said. 'Thieves would kill me in the road for a cup like this.'

'Yours,' Pater said.

The priest nodded. 'Your gifts are unimpaired, it seems,' he said. The cup was its own testimony. I remember the awe I felt, looking at it.

'Untouched by the rage of Ares,' Pater said, 'I owe more than that cup, priest. But that's what I can tithe now.'

The priest was visibly awed. I was a boy, and I could see his awe, just as surely as I had seen Simon's fear and rage. It made me wonder, in a whole new way, who my father was.

Pater summoned Bion, and Bion poured wine – cheap wine, for that's all we had – into the new cup. First the priest prayed to the smith god and poured a libation, and then he drank, and then Pater drank, and then Bion drank. Then they gave me the cup, and I drank.

'Your boy here has a gift too,' the priest said, while the wine warmed our bellies.

16

'He's quick,' Pater said, and ruffled my hair.

First I'd heard of it.

'More than quick,' the priest said. He drank, looked at the cup and held it out to Bion, who filled it. He started to pass it back and Pater waved at him.

'All servants of the smith here, Bion,' he said.

So Bion drank again. And let me tell you, when the hard times came and Bion stayed loyal, it was for that reason – Pater was fair. Fair and straight, and slaves know. Something for you to remember when you're tempted to a little temper tantrum, eh, little lady? Hair in your food and piss in your wine when you mistreat them. Right?

Anyway, we drank a while longer. It went to my head. The priest asked Pater to think about moving to Thebes – said Pater would make a fortune doing work like this in a real city. Pater just shrugged. The joy of making was washing away in the wine.

'If I wanted to be a Theban,' he said, 'I'd have gone there when I was young.' He made the word *Theban* sound dirty, but the priest took no offence.

And then the priest turned back to me.

'That boy needs to learn his letters,' he said.

Pater nodded. 'Good thing for a smith to know,' he agreed.

My heart soared. I wanted nothing – *nothing* – more than to be a smith.

'I could take him to school,' the priest said.

Pater shook his head. 'You're a good priest,' Pater said, 'but my boy won't be a *pais* in Thebes.'

Again the priest took no offence. 'You won't teach the boy your-self,' he said. No question to it.

Pater looked at me, nodded, agreeing. 'No,' he said. 'It's my curse – I've no time for them. Teaching takes too long and I grow angry.' He shrugged.

The priest nodded. 'There's a hero's tomb with a priest up the mountain,' he said.

'Leitos,' Pater said. 'He went to Troy. Calchas is the priest. A drunk, but a good man.'

'He can write?' the priest asked.

Pater nodded.

The next morning, I rose with the sun to see the priest go. I held his hand in the courtyard while he thanked the god and Pater for his cup, and Pater was happy. He reminded Pater that I was to learn to write, and Pater swore an oath unasked, and the thing was done. I wasn't sure what I thought about it, but that was Pater's way – a thing worth doing was done.

The priest went to the gate and blessed Bion. Pater took his hand and was blessed in turn. 'May I have your name, priest?' he asked. Back then, men didn't always share their names.

The priest smiled. 'I'm Empedocles,' he said.

He and Pater shook hands the initiates' way. And then the priest came to me. 'You will be a philosopher,' he said.

He was dead wrong, but it was a nice thing to hear at the age of six or seven, or whatever I was.

'What's your name?' he asked.

'Arimnestos,' I answered.

# 2

It must seem strange to you, sitting in Heraklea, where we rule Propontis as far as the wild tribes, that in Boeotia two towns a day's walk apart could be inveterate enemies. It's true – we told the same jokes and we worshipped the same gods, and we all read Homer and Hesiod, praised the same athletes and cursed the same way – but Thebes and Plataea were never friends. They were big, dandified, and they thrust their big noses in where we didn't want them. They had a 'federation', which was a fancy way of saying that they would run everything and the old ways could go to Tartarus, and all the small poleis could just obey.

So I was five, or perhaps six, when Pater went away and came back wounded, and the men of Thebes had the best of it. They didn't harry our orchards or burn our crops, but we submitted and they forced little Plataea to accept their laws.

And there it might have remained, if it hadn't been for the Daidala.

You think you know all about the Daidala, my dear – because I am master here, and I make the peasants celebrate the festival of my youth. But listen, thugater – it was on the slopes of Cithaeron that Zeus first feared to lose the love of his wife, Hera. She left him, for he is a bad husband, and he cheated on her – and you must tell me, should your husband ever forsake your bed. I'll see to it that he returns, or he'll wear his guts for a *zone*.

At any rate, she left him, and when she was gone, as is the way with men, he missed her. So he asked her back. But when you are a god, and the father of gods – aye, or when you are merely a mortal man and full of your own importance – it is hard to ask forgiveness, and harder still to be refused.

So Zeus went into Boeotia, and in those days there were kings. He found the king – a Plataean, of course – and asked him for advice.

The king thought about it for a day. If he had any sense, he asked his own wife. Then he went back to mighty-thewed Zeus, and he no doubt shrugged at the irony of it all. And he said, 'Mighty Zeus, first among gods and men, you can win back beautiful cow-eyed Hera if you make her jealous, by making her think that you intend to replace her for ever.' So he proposed that they make a wooden statue of a beautiful kore, a maiden in a wedding gown. And that they take it to the sacred precincts on the mountain, and imitate the manner of men and women going to a wedding.

'Hera will come in all her glory to destroy her usurper,' the king said. 'And when she sees that it's nothing but a billet of wood, she'll be moved to laughter. And then you'll be reconciled.'

Perhaps Zeus thought it was the silliest plan he'd ever heard, but he was desperate. To an old man like me, it seems a deeply cynical plan. But for all that, it worked. The wedding procession wound up the hillside, and Hera came and destroyed the statue with her powers. Then she saw that she had merely burned a piece of wood, and she laughed, and she and Zeus were reconciled, and celebrated their eternal marriage again.

So every town in Boeotia used to take turns to celebrate the Daidala – forty-eight towns, and in the forty-ninth year, the Great Daidala, when the fires burned like the beacons burned when the Medes came. And they would compete to celebrate with the best festival, the largest fire, the finest ornaments on the dresses, the most beautiful kore. But as Thebes's federation gained power, so Thebes took over the festivals. They would allow no rival, and the Daidala was celebrated only by Thebes – and little Thespiae and our Plataea. Only our two little states dared to insist on our ancient rights.

Now, when the men of Thebes bested us that time, our leaders signed their treaty, accepted their laws and accepted the federation, the way a poor man accepts a bad sausage in the market when he dares not haggle. But the treaty said nothing about the Daidala. And Plataea's turn was coming – her first turn to celebrate the festival in nigh on fifty years.

For a year after the battle, men said little about it. But then the Plataean Daidala was just a few years away – and towns worked for years to make the festival great. So it was that not long after the priest came to our house – this is how I remember it – and the forge fire was relit, men started to come back to the forge. First they came to have their pots mended, and their ploughs straightened, but soon enough they came to talk. As the weather changed, and Pater worked outside, men would come as soon as their farm work was done – or before – and they would sit on Pater's forging stumps, or recline against the cow's fence or her shed. They would bring their own wine and pour it for each other or for Pater, and they would talk.

I was a boy, and I loved to hear men talk. These were plain men, not lords – but not fools, either. Even here in this house I hear the life of the rustic made a thing of fun. Perhaps. Perhaps there are boors who think more of the price of an ass than of a beautiful statue. What of it? How many of these philosophers could plough a straight furrow, eh, girl? There is room in the world for many kinds of wisdom – that was the revelation of my life, and you should write it down.

Hah! It is good to be lord.

At any rate, by the end of the day we'd have the potter, Karpos, son of Phoibos, the wheelwright, Draco, son of Draco, the leather worker, Theron, son of Xenon, some of their slaves and a dozen farmers in the yard. And they would debate everything from the immortality of the gods to the price of wheat at the market in Thebes – and Corinth, and Athens.

Athens. How often in this story will I mention her? Not my city, but crowned in beauty and strong, in a way Plataea could never be strong – yet capricious and sometimes cruel, like a maiden. As you will be, soon enough, my dear. Athens is now the greatest city in the world – but then she was just another polis, and outside of Attica, men paid her little heed.

Yet she was starting to learn her power. I must weary you with some history. Athens had been under a tyranny for forty years – the Pisistratidae. Some say that the tyrants were good for Athens, and some say they were bad. I have friends of both groups, and I suspect the truth was that the tyrants were good in some ways and bad in others.

While the tyrants were lording it over Athens, the world was changing. First, Sparta rose to power, initially by crushing the cities nearest to her, and then by forcing the rest of their neighbours into a set of treaties that compelled them to serve Sparta. Now, in the Peloponnese – everywhere else, too – only men of property fought in the battles. Slaves might throw rocks, and poor farmers might throw a javelin, but the *warriors* were aristocrats and their friends.

Armies were small, because there are, thank the gods, only so many aristocrats in the world. But when Sparta created her 'League', she changed the world. Suddenly the Peloponnese could field a bigger army than anyone else. Spartans are great warriors – just ask them – but what made them dangerous was their *size*. Sparta could put ten thousand men in the field.

The other states had to respond. Thebes formed her own league, the Federation of Boeotia, but other states had to find another way to provide that manpower. In Plataea, we took to arming every free man. Even so, we could never, as I have said, muster more than fifteen hundred armed men.

In Athens, the tyrants kept their armies small. They did not permit men to carry arms abroad, and when they had to fight, they hired mercenaries from Thessaly and Scythia. They didn't trust their people.

Don't fool yourself, honey. We're tyrants, too.

At any rate, while I was a boy, the Pisistratidae fell. The survivors ran off to the Great King of Persia and Athens became a democracy. Suddenly, in a day, Athens had the manpower to field a big army – ten thousand hoplites or more. The Athens of my boyhood was like a boy who has just developed his first muscles.

You've stayed awake through my history lesson – that fellow who is courting you must be having his effect. The point is – there is a point, honey – that for the first time, Athens was feeling strong, and she was suddenly open as a market for the Plataeans, just over the mountains and guarding the pass to Thebes. Some of the richer farmers had learned that if they carted their olive oil and grain and wine over the mountain to Athens, they fetched a *much* better price than they got in the market of little Plataea – or in the market of mighty Thebes.

I longed to go to Athens. I dreamed of it. I had heard that the whole city was built of Parian marble. Lies, of course, but you have dreams of your own – you know what dreams are like. And we heard that the Alcmaeonidae were building the new Temple of Apollo at Delphi of marble – it had never been done before – and it was a marvel. Draco the wheelwright, as close to a good friend as Pater had, went on a pilgrimage to Delphi and came back singing of the new temple.

Bah, give me that wine cup and never mind an old man's digressions. Anyway, the talk that summer was of the Daidala and the price of grain.

Epictetus was the richest of the local farmers. He'd been born a slave and made all his wealth from his own sweat, and he might have been old Hesiod reborn. A hard man to cross. But he'd just made the trip to Athens the year before and he swore by it. I remember the day that he pulled up with a wagon full of hired hands.

'This is the party?' he said. He had a grim, deep voice.

'No party here,' Pater said. He was making a cauldron, a deep one, and the anvil sang with every stroke as he bent the bronze to his will. 'Just a bunch of loafers avoiding their work!'

There were twenty men around the forge yard, and they all laughed. It was mid-afternoon, and there wasn't a lazy man there. They had a skin of last year's wine, the good purple stuff that our grapes make at home, dark as Tyrian dye.

Epictetus got off his wagon and his hired men climbed down. It was a high wagon – Draco's best work, the kind that would carry five farms' worth of grain. He had a grown son – Epictetus son of Epictetus – who was a shadow beside his hard-working father.

'Bring our wine, son,' the father said, and then he walked into the yard.

It was quite the event, because Epictetus *never* came to loaf in the forge yard. He said that a man had but one life, and any time he wasted counted against him with the gods. He was the only farmer in Boeotia who owned four ploughs. He only needed two, but he built the other two – just in case. He was that sort of man.

So he came into the yard and Pater sent me for a stool from the kitchen. It was like one lord visiting another. I fetched a stool, and Epictetus – the son – poured wine from a heavy amphora for every man in the yard. I had a taste of Pater's. It was not cheap.

Epictetus looked around. 'I've picked the right day,' he said. He nodded. 'I have a thought in my head and I can't get it out. I wanted to talk to the men – the real men – without giving myself away to the Theban bastards in town.'

Pater handed Bion the new cauldron. 'Punch her for rivets,' he said. 'Did you pour me a new plate?'

Bion nodded. He was better at casting bronze even than Pater. 'Smooth as a baby,' he said.

'He'll be a rival to you when you free him,' Draco said.

'No,' Pater said. He pulled his leather apron off and tossed it to another slave. Then he poured some water over his head, wiped his face with a rag and walked back. 'It is good to see you in my yard, and a guest is always a blessing,' Pater said, and poured a libation. 'I always have time to listen to you, Epictetus.'

Epictetus bowed. He rose, as if speaking in the assembly. And in a way he was, for in the yard were the leaders of what might have been called the 'middling' sort – the men who supported the temples and shrines, who served in war. There were some aristocrats, and two very rich men, but the men in our yard were – well, they were the voice of the farmers, if you like.

'Men,' he said. How imposing he was! Tall, strong and burned so dark that he looked like mahogany. Even at fifty, he was someone to be reckoned with. 'Men of Plataea,' he began again, and suddenly I knew that he was nervous. That made me nervous, too. Such a strong man? And rich?

'Last year I went to Athens,' he said. 'You know that Athens has overthrown the tyrants. They are gone – fled to the Great King in Persia, or dead.' He paused and smiled a little. 'But you know all this, eh? I'm a windbag. Listen. Athens has money – their silver owls are the best coin in Hellas. And they have an army – they muster ten *thousand* hoplites when they go to war.' He looked around, took a sip of wine. 'They have so many mouths to feed in their city that they need our grain. Aye – they import grain all the way from Propontis and the Euxine!'

Men shifted restlessly.

'I'm no hand at this. So here's what I'm trying to say. We cannot fight Thebes alone. We need a friend. Athens should be that friend. They need our grain.' He shrugged. 'I talked to some men in Athens. They talk to farmers as if they were men of substance, in Athens. Not like some bastards I've known, eh? And the men I talked to were very interested. Interested in being friends.'

He looked around.

I remember that I found the idea so exciting that I thought I might burst. Athens – glorious Athens, as an ally?

Which goes to show what you know when you're seven years old. The rest of them shuffled their feet and looked at the ground.

Draco shrugged. 'Listen, Epictetus. Your idea has merit – and it's time we started to talk about these things. No man here will deny that we need a friend. But Athens is so *far*. Over the mountains. Five hundred stades as the raven flies – more for a man and a cart.'

Myron, another farmer, leaned forward on his heavy staff. 'Athens would never send their phalanx over the mountains to protect us,' he said. He had a scar on his thigh from the same fight where Pater had been made lame. 'We need a friend with five thousand hoplites who will stand their ground beside us, not a friend who will come and avenge our corpses.'

Epictetus nodded to Myron – they had each other's measure, those two. 'It might be true,' he said. 'But we need a friend far enough away that he won't force us to be more than just an ally.' He looked around. 'Like Thebes and the so-called federation.'

All the men spat at the mention of Thebes.

Myron nodded. 'That's sense. How about Corinth?'

Evaristos, the handsomest of the men, shook his head. 'Corinth is too close and has too many ships and too few hoplites. And no need for our grain. And loves Thebes too well.'

Draco held out his cup to one of our slaves. 'A splash more, darling,' he said. 'What of Sparta? They've an army worth something, or so I hear.'

'Ten times the distance as Athens,' Epictetus said.

'I know,' Draco said. 'I made my pilgrimage last year to Olympia—'

'We know!' many of the men called, tired of Draco's endless travel tales.

'Listen, you oafs!' Draco shouted. They jeered him with humour, but then they were silent. He went on, 'Sparta is not like us. Their citizens – all they do is train for war.'

'And fuck little boys,' Hilarion put in. If the least rich of the farmers, he was the most cheerful and the best with a crowd. And the least respectful of authority. He shrugged. 'Hey – I've been to Sparta. Women there are lonely.'

Draco glared at Hilarion. 'Whatever their personal foibles, gentlemen, they're the best soldiers in Greece. And they don't farm, or make pots, or work metal. They fight. They can march here, if they have a mind to. Their farms will be tilled whether they march or not.'

'Their wives are lonely whether they march or not,' Hilarion added. 'Maybe while they march to save us, I'll just slip over the isthmus and visit a few of them.'

Pater spoke for the first time. 'Hilarion,' he said softly. He met the younger man's eyes, and Hilarion dropped his.

'Sorry,' he said.

Pater walked into the middle of them. 'My sense of what you say,' he began, 'is that you all support the idea of finding ourselves a foreign friend.'

They looked at each other. Then Epictetus stood and emptied his cup. 'That's the right of it,' he said.

'But none of us knows what will suit us – Athens or Sparta or Corinth – or perhaps Megara.' Pater shrugged. 'We're a bunch of

Boeotian farmers. Epictetus here has at least been to Attica, and Draco's been to the Peloponnese.' He looked around. 'Who would *want* to be our friend?'

Epictetus winced, but said nothing.

'If we trained harder, our men could beat the Thebans!' said Myron's son, a fire-breather called Dionysius. 'And then we'd have no need of these foreigners.'

Myron put a hand on his son's shoulder. The boy was only just old enough to take his stand, and hadn't been there for the defeat. 'Boy, when they bring five thousand against our one thousand,' he said, 'there's no amount of training that will help us. No man here cares a tinker's damn how many we kill – only that we *win*.'

The older men nodded agreement. The *Iliad* was a fine story for children, but Boeotian farmers know just what war brings – burned crops, raped daughters and death. The glory is fleeting, the expense immense and the effect permanent.

They talked more, but that's how I remember it – the day the idea was born. In fact, it was just grumbling. We all hated Thebes, but they weren't hurting us any.

Epictetus stayed to dinner, though. And he offered to carry the cream of Pater's work over the mountains to Athens – and back, if it didn't sell. And Pater agreed. Then Epictetus commissioned a cup. He'd clearly seen the priest's cup and wanted one for himself.

'A cup I can drink from, in the fields or at home,' he said.

'What do you want on it?' Pater asked.

'A man ploughing a field,' Epictetus said. 'None of your gods and satyrs. A good pair of oxen and a good man.'

'Twenty Athenian drachmas,' Pater said. 'Or for nothing, if you carry my goods to Athens.'

Epictetus shook his head. 'Twenty drachmas is what you're worth,' he said. 'And I'll carry your goods anyway. If I take it as a gift, I owe you. If I pay you, you owe me.' That's the kind of man he was.

Pater worked like a slave for the rest of the summer, making finer things than were his wont. He made ten platters, the kind gentlemen served feasts on, and he made more cups, including the fanciest of the lot, with a ploughman, for Epictetus. And he made a Corinthian helmet – simple in design but perfect in execution. Even in the summer of my seventh year, I knew perfection in metal when I saw it.

Pater had no patience in him to teach the young, but he let me put it on my head. He laughed. 'You'll be a big man, Arimnestos,' he said. 'But not yet.'

He made bronze knives for me and for my brother, fine ones with some work on the backbone of the blade and horn scales on either side of the grip.

I worked like a slave that summer, because we were poor and we had just Bion's family as slaves – and Bion was far too skilled to waste his time putting air on the fire or punching holes in leather, or any of the other donkey work. And though my brother was too small to plough, he ploughed anyway, with help from Bion's son Hermogenes. Together they made a man.

Occasionally men like Myron would appear out of the air and take a turn at the plough, or repair a wheel, or perhaps sow a field. We had good neighbours.

When I wasn't in the forge, I was in the fields too. I loved that farm. Our land was at the top of a hill – a low hill, but it gave a view from the house. In the paved yard, where men stood to talk, you could see mighty Cithaeron rising like a slope-shouldered god, and you could see the walls of our city just across a little valley. Up on Cithaeron, we could see the hero's tomb and the sacred spring, and if we looked towards Plataea, we could see the Temple of Hera clear as a lamp in a dark room. The trees of Hera's grove were like spears pointing up the hill at our little acropolis, even though they were stades away. We had an apple tree at the top of the olive grove, and I went up and trimmed the new growth in the spring and again in the autumn. We had grapes on the hillside, and when we had no other work to do, Hermogenes and Chalkidis and I would build trellises to carry the vines.

There was a small wood by the stream at the base of the hill, and the old people had dug a fish pond. I could pretend that we were great lords, with our own hill fort and our own woods for hunting, although we didn't have an animal larger than a rabbit to hunt. But there's no memory dearer to me than walking home from the agora in Plataea with Bion – we must have just sold some wine, or perhaps some oil, and I was allowed to go to town – walking home past the turning where our road went down to the stream and then up the hill to our house, and thinking, this is my land. My father is king here.

Most nights, unless Mater was raving drunk, we'd meet in the courtyard after dinner and watch the sun set. We had a swing in the courtyard olive tree. Pater showed me the grooves in the branch that bore it, sunk into the wood the way chariot wheels will cut ruts even in stone. The swing had been on that tree for many lives of men.

It may sound dull to you, dear, but to watch a sunset from a swing on your own land is a very good thing.

It must have been after the festival of Demeter – because all the harvest was in – that Epictetus arrived with his wagons. He had two. No one else we knew had two wagons.

'Well?' he said, when his wagons were in the yard.

Pater and Bion had all the bronze laid out, so that our courtyard looked as if it had been touched by King Midas.

Epictetus walked around, handled everything and finally nodded sharply. He picked up his cup – snatched it up – and then looked at Pater for confirmation that it was, indeed, his.

'Don't get many requests for a plough and oxen,' Pater said.

Epictetus looked at it, then hefted it in his hand.

Bion stepped forward and poured wine into it. 'You have to feel it full,' he said with a smile.

Epictetus poured a libation and drank. 'Good cup,' he said. 'Pay the man, boy,' he said to his son.

'I'd rather have it in bronze, from Athens,' Pater said.

'Less a quarter for cartage?' Epictetus asked.

'Less an eighth for cartage,' Pater said.

Epictetus nodded, and they both spat on their hands and shook, and the thing was done. Then the hired men loaded all the work of a summer and the big wagons rolled away down the hill.

I was old enough to know that all of Pater's stock of bronze was rolling away in those carts. He had nothing left but scraps to make repairs. If robbers took Epictetus on the roads, we were finished. I knew it.

And I felt it over the next weeks. Pater was a fair man, but when he was dark, he hit us, and those weeks were dark. One afternoon he even hit Bion – savagely. And I dropped a fine bowl and he beat me with a stick. He beat my brother when he caught him watching the girls bathe, and he raged at us every day.

Mater was sober. It has an odd sound to it, but it was as if she knew she was needed. So she stopped drinking and did housework. She read aloud to us every day from a stool by her loom, and she was very much like the aristocratic lady she'd been born to be.

I loved her stories. She would tell us the myths of the gods, or sing pieces of the *Iliad* or other stories, and I would devour them the way my brother devoured meat. But when she was done, and the magic of her voice faded, she was just my dull and drunken mother, and I couldn't like her. So I went back to the fields.

It was in those weeks that I went into Plataea with Bion and pledged the family's credit to an iron knife. Only the gods know what I was thinking – a little boy with an iron knife? Who had a perfectly good bronze one on a thong round his neck? Children are as inscrutable as the gods.

Pater beat me so badly that I thought I might die. I see it now – I had pledged money he didn't have. And we were at the bottom. All our harvest and all our work was off at Athens, or lost on the road. I see it now, but at the time, it hurt me far more than just a beating. I decided that night, tears burning down my face, that he wasn't really my father. No man could treat his *son* that way.

That was a deeper pain than any blow. I still bear it.

The next day he apologized. In fact, he all but crawled to me, making false jokes and wincing when he touched my bruises, alternating with making light of my injuries. It was a strange performance, and in some way it was as confusing as the heavy beating.

And then he recovered. Whatever *daimon* was eating his soul, he rose above it. It was three weeks or more after Epictetus had left, and he was a week overdue. Pater came out into the vineyard with us and started building trellises – work he never did – as if it was the most natural thing in the world. He didn't complain, and he didn't hit anyone, and we worked steadily all day under the high, blue skies of autumn. The grapes were almost ripe and the trellises creaked. Bion and I were both physically wary of him – we had bruises to prove that we had the right – but he passed no reproof harder than a look. My brother fell on a vine and wrecked an hour's work, but Pater merely shook his head and took up his light bronze axe. He went off to the wood to cut more supports, and sent my brother to the river to cut reeds.

It was an autumn day, but hot. Beautiful – you could see the stream glinting, and the line of the Oeroe river down the valley. I sweated through my chiton and stripped it off to work naked, which meant a slap from Mater if she caught me, but she wasn't likely to come out to the vineyard.

Bion had brought a bucket of water from the well. He offered me the first dipper – I was the only free man on the hilltop. But I'd learned some things, even at that age.

'I'll drink last,' I said.

I saw a spark in Bion's eye, and knew I'd hit that correctly.

I remember that, and the beauty of the day, but most of all I remember that Pater came for us. He didn't have to, you see – he was down at the wood, and he'd have seen Epictetus's wagons turn off the road. He might even have seen them three stades away, or farther. And as the master, and the man with so much to lose, it would have been natural for him to take his axe and go down to the yard and leave us to work on the hilltop. But he didn't. He came up the hill, hobbling quickly.

'Come with me,' he said. He was terse, and all of us – even Bion – thought that there might be trouble.

We put our tools down and followed him through the vineyard to the house.

Pater said nothing, so we didn't either. We came into the yard and only then could we see the hillside and hear the wagons in the lane.

I couldn't see my face, but I could see Hermogenes. He flashed his father a smile of utter joy. He said, 'You'll be free!', which meant nothing to me at the time.

Epictetus was driving his own oxen on the wagon. His son was beside him, and he had two of his hired men in the box, but the second wagon was gone – and the smiles must have been wiped from every face in the oikia. Even the women were leaning over the rail of the exhedra.

Epictetus the Younger leaped down and ran to the heads of the oxen, and he flashed Pater a smile – and then we knew.

As old Epictetus got down, he couldn't keep the smile off his own face.

Then the hired men got down, and they threw heavy wool sacks on to the ground. They made a noise – like rock, but thinner – copper, I knew from the sound. And then tin wrapped in leather from far, far to the north.

Epictetus came forward with his thumbs in his girdle. 'It was cheaper to buy copper and tin than to buy ingots of bronze,' he said. 'And I've watched you do it. If you don't like it,' he raised an eyebrow, 'I'll lend you the wagon to get it back.'

'Cyprian ingots,' Pater said. He had the heavy wool bags open. 'By Aphrodite, friend, you must drive a fair bargain if all this copper and tin is mine for twenty drachmas less an eighth for cartage.'

Epictetus shrugged, but he was a happy man – a man who'd done another man an unanswerable favour. 'Fifty drachmas of silver less an eighth cartage,' he said. 'I spent thirty of your profits on new material. It seemed like sense.'

Pater was kneeling in the copper like a boy playing in mud. 'I owe you,' he said.

Epictetus shrugged. 'Time you made some money. You're too good a man to starve. You know how to work, but not how to be rich.' He held out a bag. 'Three hundred and seventy-two silver drachmas after my cartage and all that copper.' He nodded. 'And there's a man coming to see you about a helmet.'

'From Athens?' Pater didn't seem to know what was being said, so he fixed on the idea that the man from Athens was coming. 'Three *hundred and seventy drachmas?*' he said.

He and Epictetus embraced.

That night, Mater and Pater sang together.

They were a remarkable couple, when sober and friends to each other. You'll never credit this, Thugater, but you'll find it hard enough when you are my age to look back and see your father and mother clearly, and if Apollo withholds his hand and Pluton grants fortune enough that I live to see you with children at your knee – why, then you'll remember me only as an old man with a stick. Eh? But I love to remember them, that day. In later years – when I was far away, a slave – I would think of Pater dressed in his best, a chiton of oiled wool so fine that every muscle in his chest showed, and his neck, like a bull's, and his head – he had a noble head – like a statue of Zeus, his hair all dark and curled. He always wore it long, in braids wrapped around the crown of his head when he was working. Later I understood – it was a warrior's hairstyle, braids to pad his helmet. He was never just a smith.

And Mater, when sober – it is hard for a child to see his mother as beautiful, but she was. Men told me so all my childhood, and what is more embarrassing than other men finding your mother attractive? Her eyes were blue and grey, her nose straight, her face thin, her cheekbones high and hollow – I often wonder how many Mother Heras in the temple were carved to look like Mater. She would come down in a dress of Tyrian-dyed wool with embroidery – not her own, Athena knows – and she was trim and lithe and above all, to me, sober.

The next day, Pater freed Bion. He offered him a wage to stay, and sent for the priest from Thebes to raise Bion to the level of a free smith. Bion and Pater dickered over the price of his family and Pater settled on two years' work at the forge. Bion accepted and they spat on their hands and shook.

The following day, Pater came to me where I was sweeping. 'Time to go to school,' he said. He didn't smile. In fact, he looked nervous. 'I'm – sorry, boy. Sorry I beat you so hard for a drachma knife.' He handed it back to me – he'd confiscated it *and* the bronze one he'd made for me. 'I made you a scabbard,' he said.

Indeed he had. A bronze scabbard with a silver rivet decoration. It was a wonderful thing – finer than anything I owned. 'Thank you, Pater,' I mumbled.

'I swore an oath that if we made it through the summer ...' He paused and looked out of the forge. 'If we made it through the summer, I'd take you up to the hero's shrine and pay the priest to teach you.'

I nodded.

'I mean to keep my word, but I want you to know that – you're a good – worker.' He nodded. 'So – put your knife round your neck. Let's see it. Now go and put on a white chiton as if you were going to a festival, and kiss your mother.'

Mater looked at me as if I'd been dragged in by the dogs, but then she smiled. Today she looked to me like a queen. 'You have it in you to look like a lord,' she said. 'Remember this.' She held up her mirror, a fine silver one that hadn't been sold while we were poor, with Aphrodite combing her hair on the back. I saw myself. It wasn't the first time, but I still remember being surprised at how tall I was, and how much I really did look like my idea of a lord – fine wool chiton, hair in ringlets and the knife under my arm. Then she offered me her cheek to kiss – never her lips and never a hug – and I was away.

I walked with Pater. It was thirty stades to the shrine of our hero of the Trojan War, and I wasn't used to sandals.

Pater was silent. I was amazed that he hadn't sent Bion or someone else, but he took me himself, and when we had climbed high enough up the flank of the mountain to be amidst the trees – beautiful straight cypress and some scrubby pine – he stopped.

'Listen, boy,' he said. 'Old Calchas is a worthy man, for a drunk. But he – that is, if you want no part of him, run home. And if he hurts you, I'll kill him.'

He held my shoulders and kissed me, and then we walked the rest of the way.

Calchas was not so old. He was Pater's age, and had a fuller beard, with plenty of white in it, but he had the body of an athlete. He didn't look like a drunk. I fancied myself an expert – after all, I knew every stage of Mater's drinking, from red-rimmed eyes and foul breath to modest bleariness. Calchas didn't show any of that. And he was *still*. I saw that at once. He didn't fidget and he didn't show anxiety.

But it was his eyes that held me. He had green eyes – as I do myself – and I'd never seen another pair. They also had a particular quality – they seemed to look through you to a place far beyond.

I know, dear. My eyes do the same. But they didn't then.

I don't think most of the farmers of the valley of the Asopus knew what Calchas was. They thought him a harmless priest, a drunk, a useful old man who would teach their sons to read.

It is almost funny, given what Plataea was to become, that in all the valley, there wasn't a man hard enough to look the priest in the eye and see him for what he was.

A killer.

I lived with Calchas for years, but I never thought of his hut beside the spring and the tomb as *home*. From the edge of the tomb I could see our hill rising thirty stades away, and when I was homesick I would climb the round stones to the top, lie on the beehive roof and look across the still air to home. And often enough he would send me back on errands – because we paid him in wine and olive oil and bread and cheese, and because he was a kind man for all that his eyes were dead. He'd wait until I cried myself to sleep a few nights, and then he'd send me home on an errand without my asking.

That whole first autumn, I learned my letters and nothing else. For hours every day, and then we'd scour his wooden dishes and his one bronze pitcher, a big thing that had no doubt been a donation in the ancient past. He didn't speak much, except to teach. He simply taught me the letters, over and over again, endlessly patient where Pater would have been screaming in frustration.

I'd like to say that I was a quick learner, but I wasn't. It was early autumn, and everything was golden, and I was an outdoor boy caught in his lessons. I wanted to watch the eagles play in the high air, and the woods around the shrine fascinated me, because they were so deep and dark. One day I saw a deer – my first – and then a boar.

I felt as if I had fallen into the land of myth.

Travellers sometimes came over the mountain to the shrine. Not many, but a few. They were always men, and they often carried weapons, a rare sight down in the valley. Calchas would send me away, then he'd sit with the men and drink a cup of wine.

They were soldiers, of course. Soldiers came to the shrine from all over Boeotia, because the word was that the shrine and the spring provided healing to men of war. I think it was Calchas who healed them. He talked and they listened, and they went away lighter by a few darics and some care. Sometimes he'd get drunk afterwards, but mostly he'd go and say some prayers at the shrine of the hero, and then he'd make us some barley gruel.

His food was terrible, and always the same – black bread, bean broth without meat, water. I've lived in a Spartan mess group and eaten better. At the time I cared little. Food was fuel.

Calchas had fascinating things in his hut. He had an aspis as fine as Pater's – a great bowl of bronze and wood, with a snake painted in red and a hundred dents in the surface. He had a sword – a long sword with a narrow blade, nothing like Pater's long knife. He had a dull helmet – a simple one, not a fancy Corinthian like Pater's – and his cuirass consisted of layers of white leather scarred and scuffed and patched a hundred times without a scrap of bronze to brighten it. He had a fine hunting spear, beautifully made by a master, with a long tapering point of steel, chased and carefully inlaid in the Median style, and a bow of foreign work with a quiver of arrows.

He was content to let me touch it all, which I was never allowed with Pater's kit. All except the bow.

So naturally, I had to steal the bow.

It wasn't hard. His hut had one piece of ornamentation – a window made from panes of horn pressed thin and flat. It let light in, in the winter, and it was beautifully crafted, the gift of some rich patron. It was made to pivot on a pair of bronze pintles cunningly fashioned. Calchas used to laugh about it. He called it the 'Gate of Horn' and said all his dreams came through it – and he also called it the 'Lord's Window'. 'A foolish thing to have in a peasant's hut,' he said, although that window alone allowed me to read in the winter.

I had soon learned that I could get in and out of that window. I whittled a stick with my sharp iron knife so that I could prise the window open from outside. I waited till he was drunk, then got in and took the bow and quiver and ran off up one of the hundreds of paths that led from the clearing by the spring. I found my way to a small meadow with an old stump, spotted on an earlier ramble, and my

34

adventure came to an end when I tried to string the bow. I spent the afternoon striving against the power of a man's weapon and I failed.

So I carried the bow and quiver back down the mountain and sneaked them into his hut, returning the bow to the peg where it hung.

After lessons the next day, I said, 'Master, I took your bow.'

He was putting away the stylus and the wax sheets he made. He turned so fast that I flinched.

'Where is it?' he asked.

'On its peg,' I said. I hung my head. 'I couldn't string it.'

I never saw his hand move, but suddenly my ear hurt – hurt like *fire*. 'That's for disobedience,' he said calmly. 'You want to shoot the bow?'

'Yes!' I said. I think I was crying.

He nodded. 'I'm sending you for more wine,' he said. 'When you come back, perhaps we'll make a bow you can shoot.' He paused. 'And we'll do the dances. The military dances. Now, what letter is this?' he drew one, and I said 'Omicron.'

'Good boy,' he said.

My ear still hurt, all thirty stades home.

My brother was working in the forge, and he didn't like it. It's odd, being brothers. We were alike in so many ways – and we were always friends, even when we were angry – but we wanted different things. He wanted to be a warrior, a nobleman with a retinue and deer hounds. He wanted the life Mater wanted for him. And all I wanted to be was a master smith. Irony is the lord of all, honey. I got what he wanted, and he got a few feet of dirt. But he was a good boy, and he was in the forge doing the job that I would have sold my soul to do. That's the way of it when you are young.

I showed Mater my letters and sang her the first hundred lines of the *Iliad*, which Calchas had also taught me, and she nodded and kissed my cheek and gave me a silver pin.

'At least one of my sons will grow up a gentleman,' she said. 'Tell me of this Calchas.'

So I did. I told her all I knew about him, which proved, under her Medusa-like glare, to be little enough. But she smiled when I said he ate black bread and bean soup.

'An aristocrat, then,' she said happily. Not my idea of an aristocrat, but Mater knew some things better than her eight-year-old child.

I stayed at home for two days while Pater gathered some wine. I helped in the forge and saw that my brother had already learned a few things. He'd made a bowl from copper and he was scribing it with a stylus – just simple lines, but to me it looked wonderful.

He pulled it from my hand, threw it across the forge and burst into tears. And we embraced, and swore to swap when Pater and Calchas wouldn't know. It wasn't an oath either of us meant – we knew we'd never fool an adult – and yet it seemed to comfort us, and I've long wondered about which god listened to that oath.

There were changes. Mater was better – that was obvious. The house was clean, the maids were singing and my sister smiled all the time. We had a new slave family – a young man, a Thracian, and his slave wife and their new baby. He didn't speak much Greek, and Bion didn't like him, and the man had a big bruise on his face where someone had knocked him down *hard*. His wife was pretty, and men in the forge yard watched her when she served them wine. Not that Pater allowed anything to happen. That's where you *really* betray your slaves, thugater. But I get ahead of myself.

The talk in the forge yard was louder than when I'd left, even two months before, and it was cold outside, so there was a fire in the pit. Skira – the Thracian's wife – served wine with good grace, and her husband worked the bellows while Bion made a pot. The men in the yard talked about Thebes and plans for the coming Daidala. It was just three years away. Pater was suddenly an important man.

We had a donkey. We'd never had a donkey before, and Pater said he'd send Hermogenes with the donkey to carry the wine for me. That sounded good.

But the donkey and the wine and Hermogenes took time to prepare, and it became clear that I wasn't going back to Calchas on the second day, either. Which was fine by me. The 'loafers' were all gathered. Draco had built Epictetus a new wagon, and had it standing by the gate ready for delivery. It was even taller, broader and heavier, the wheels just narrow enough to fit in the ruts of the road. We were all admiring it when a stranger turned into our lane from the main road. He was riding a horse, as was his companion.

I think, honey, because you know a world where every man of substance has a horse, that I have to stop here and say that though I'd seen horses by the age of eight, I'd never touched one. No one I knew had a horse. Horses were for aristocrats. Farmers used oxen. A rich farmer might have a donkey. Horses did nothing but carry men, and farmers had legs. I don't think ten families in Plataea owned a horse, and there were two of them coming up our lane.

They had cloaks and boots, both of them. They were clearly master and man – the master had a chlamys of Tyrian red with a white stripe, and a chiton to match, milk white with a red stripe at the hem. He had red hair like my brother but even brighter, and a big beard like a priest. He wore a sword that you could see, even at the distance of a horse's length, was mounted in gold.

All conversation stopped.

Listen, thugater. In the Boeotia of my youth, we bitched quite a lot about aristocrats. Men knew that there were aristocrats – we had our own basileus, after all, although he didn't have a gold-mounted sword, I can tell you. And local men knew that Mater was the daughter of a basileus. But this was the genuine article. Frankly, he looked more like a god than most statues I'd seen. He was the tallest man there by more than a finger's breadth. And I knew nothing of horses, but his big bay looked like a creature out of story.

I still think of that man. I can see him in my mind's eye. I'll tell you a truth – I worshipped him. I still do. Even now, I try to be him when I'm 'lording it' over some court case or petty tyrant.

Even his servant looked better than we did – in a fine chlamys of dark blue wool with a stripe of red and a white chiton. He didn't have a sword, but he had a leather satchel under his arm and his horse was as noble as his master's.

And yet, this god among men slipped from his horse's back and bowed. 'I seek the house of the bronze-smith of Plataea,' he said politely. 'Can any of you gentlemen help me?'

Myron bowed deeply. 'Lord,' he said, 'Chalkeotechnes the smith is working. We are merely his friends.'

The red-haired god smiled. 'Is that wine I see?' he asked. 'I'd be happy to pay for a cup.'

None of my family was there. I stepped forward. 'No guest of this house should pay for his wine,' I said in the voice of a boy. 'Pardon, lord. Skira, a cup and good wine for our guest.'

Skira scampered off, and the red-haired man followed her with his eyes. Then he looked at me. 'You are a courteous lad,' he said.

Boys don't talk back to lords. I blushed and was silent until Skira came back with a fine bronze cup and wine. I poured for the man, and he cast much the same look over the cup as he did over Skira.

He drank in silence, sharing with his man. Some of the loafers began to talk again, but they were subdued in his presence, until he slapped the wagon. 'Nice,' he said. 'Nice and big. Well made.'

'Thanks,' Draco said. 'I made him.'

'How much for the wagon?' the man said.

'Already sold,' Draco answered in the voice of a peasant who knows that he's just lost the chance of a lifetime.

'So build me another,' the man said. 'What did you charge for this one?'

'Thirty drachmas,' Draco said.

'Meaning you charged fifteen, doubled it for my gold-hilt sword, and you'll be happy to make me two wagons like this for forty.' The man smiled like a fox, and I suddenly knew who he must be. He was Odysseus. He was like Odysseus come to life.

Draco wanted to splutter, but the man was so smooth – and so pleasant – that it was hard to gainsay him. 'As you say, lord,' Draco said.

And then Pater came.

He still had his leather apron on. He came out into the yard, saw the wine in the man's hand and flashed me a rare smile of reward.

'You wanted me, lord?' he asked.

'Do you know Epictetus?'

'I count him a friend,' Pater said.

'He showed me a helmet in Athens. I rode over the mountain to have you make me one.' The man was half a head taller than Pater. 'And greaves.'

Pater's brow furrowed. 'There are better smiths in Athens,' he said.

The man shook his head. 'I don't think so. But I'm here, so unless you don't like the look of me, I'd thank you to start work tomorrow. I have a ship to catch at Corinth.'

'Won't the captain wait for you, lord?' Pater asked.

'I am the captain,' the man said. He grinned. He had the happiest smile I'd seen on a grown man. 'I sent them round from Athens.'

I don't think any of us had ever seen a man rich enough to *own* a ship before. The man held out his hand to Pater.

'Technes of Plataea,' Pater said.

'Men call me Miltiades,' the lord said.

It was a name we all recognized, even then. The warlord of the Chersonese, his exploits were well known. For us, it was like having Achilles ride through our gate.

'Oh, fame is a fine thing,' he said, and his servant laughed with him while we stood around like the bumpkins we were.

Pater made him a helmet and greaves, right enough. And Miltiades stayed for three days while Pater did the work and chased and repoussed stags and lions on to his order. I saw the helmet often enough in later years, but I didn't get to stay to see it made. I was shipped back to dull old Calchas with the wine.

I did carry with me one gem. That night, my brother and I lay on the floor in the room over the andron and listened to the men talk – Miltiades and Epictetus and Myron and Pater. Miltiades taught them how to have symposia without offending – taught them some poetry, showed them how to mix their wine, and never, ever let on that he was slumming with peasants. It's a fine talent if you have it. Men call it the common touch when they are jealous. There was nothing common with Miltiades. He was, as I said, like a god on earth for the pleasure of his company and the power of his glance. He gave unstintingly of himself and men loved to follow him.

He talked to the men about alliance with Athens. I was eight years old, and I understood immediately that he didn't need a new helmet. He probably had ten helmets hanging from the rafters of his hall in the Chersonese. Mind you, as it turned out, he wore that helmet for the rest of his life – so he liked it. And it always put me in mind of my father, later, and what my father might have been.

Aye, those are tears, little lady. We're coming to the bad part.

But not yet. Aye. Not yet. So we listened as they talked – almost plotted, but not quite. The talk was pretty general and never got down to cases. Miltiades told them how valuable an alliance with Plataea could be to the democrats in Athens, and how much more they had in common. And they listened, spellbound.

And so did I.

Then, late in the evening – I think I'd been asleep – Miltiades was making a point about trade when he stopped and raised his *kylix*. 'I drink to your son Arimnestos,' Miltiades said. 'A handsome boy with the spirit of a lord. He guested me and sent a slave for wine as if he'd hosted a dozen like me. I doubt that I'd have done half as well at his age.'

Pater laughed and the moment passed, but I would have died for Miltiades then. Of course, I almost did. Later.

And the next day I went back to my priest on the mountain, and it seemed as if all hope of glory was lost.

# 3

I spent the winter with Calchas. He made me a bow. It wasn't a very good bow, but with it I learned to shoot squirrels and threaten songbirds. And he took me hunting when the winter was far enough along.

I still love to hunt, and I owe it to that man. In fact, he taught me more than Miltiades ever did about how to be a lord. We went up the mountain, rising before the sun and running along the trails through the woods after rabbit or deer. He killed a wolf with his bow, and made me carry the carcass home.

The thing I remember best from that winter is the sight of blood on the snow. I had no idea how much blood an animal has in it. Oh, honey, I'd seen goats and sheep slaughtered, I'd seen the spray of blood at sacrifice. But to do it myself . . .

I remember killing a deer – a small buck. My first. I hit it with a javelin, more by luck than anything. How Calchas laughed at my surprise. And suddenly, from being *big*, at least to me, it seemed so small as it lay panting in the snow with my javelin in its guts. It had eyes – it was alive.

At Calchas's prompting, I took the iron knife that I'd earned with a beating, and I grabbed the buck's head and slashed at its throat. It must have taken me eight or ten passes – the poor animal. May Artemis send that I never torment a creature like that again. Its eyes never left me as it died, and there was blood *everywhere*. It flowed and flowed over me – warm and sticky and then cold and cloying, like guilt. When you get blood under your nails, you can only scrape it out with a knife, did you know that? There's a moral there, I suspect.

And I was kneeling in snow – cold on bare knees. The snow filled with the blood like a brilliant red flower. It transported me. It seemed to me to carry a message. There's a philosopher teaching at Miletus these days who says that a man's soul is in his blood. I have no trouble seeing it.

Yes – the story.

I learned letters, day by day and week by week. When I could make out words on papyrus, the rhythm of our days changed. We would hunt until the sun was high in the sky – or just walk the woods – climbing up and up on Cithaeron until my legs burned as if the fire of the forge was flowing in my ankles, and then back down to the hut to read by the good light of day. And every day we did the dance – the *Pyrrhiche*. First naked, and then in armour when I was older.

It was a good life.

By spring, I was bigger and much stronger, and I could go out in snow wearing a chiton and come back with a rabbit. I understood the tracks animals made in the snow and what they meant, and I understood the tracks men made on paper and what *they* meant. Once I got it, I got it – I may have been the slowest starter in the history of reading, but after the first winter, I had Hesiod down pat and was off on the *Odyssey*. Of course it is easier to read a thing when you've listened to the story all your life – of course it is, honey. But I loved to read.

When the snow had gone from the hills and the sun grew warm, Calchas stopped hunting. We'd eaten more meat than I'd ever had in my life, but he said that spring was sacred to Artemis, when animals came down from the high places to mate. 'I won't kill again till the feast of Demeter,' he said. And his lip curled. 'Unless it's a man.'

Oh, yes.

The man he killed came to rob us. It was six months since I'd been home and Calchas had me running every morning before the sun was up, running and running on the trails behind the shrine. So I was running when the thief came, and the first I knew was when I came back into the clearing, naked and warm, and found Calchas with a sword in his hand. The thief had a *machaira*, a big knife or a short sword, depending on how you saw it. From where I stood, it was huge.

'Stay well clear, boy,' Calchas called out to me.

So I ran around the man. He sounded desperate. 'Just give me the *money*,' he said.

'No,' Calchas said. He laughed.

I was getting a chill. It wasn't summer, and I was naked. And the man with the sword had the same desperation in his voice I had heard from Simon.

Calchas backed away to the tomb and the thief followed him. 'Just give me the money!' he shouted.

Calchas sidestepped the thief's clumsy advance. Suddenly the thief had his back to the tomb. 'Just give me—' he asked, and he sounded as if he was begging.

Calchas raised his sword. 'I dedicate your shade to the hero Leitos,' he said. And then the thief's head fell from his shoulders, and blood sprayed.

I had seen Calchas kill animals, and I knew how deadly he was. So I didn't flinch. I watched him arrange the corpse so that the rest of the blood poured out on to the beehive of the tomb. A man has even more blood than a deer.

I went in and put some clothes on and my hands shook.

Later we buried the corpse. Calchas didn't pray over it. 'I sent him to serve the hero,' Calchas said. 'He needs no prayers. Poor bastard.' He and I buried the thief by digging with a pick and a wooden shovel, and in the process of burying him I realized that there was a circle of graves around the tomb.

Calchas shrugged. 'The gods send one every year,' he said.

That night he got very drunk.

Next day I ran and played all day, because he didn't get up except to warm some beans.

But the third day, when I came back from running, I asked him if he'd teach me to use the sword.

'Spear first,' he said. 'Sword later.'

I'm telling this out of order, but I have to say that the only problem I had with Calchas and lessons was that, once I had my nine-year-old growth spurt, he wanted me. As soon as he put his hands on me, that first day, teaching me the spear, I knew what he wanted.

I didn't want it. There are boys who do, and boys who don't. Right? Girls the same, I imagine. So I kept away from his hands. He could have forced himself on me, but he wasn't that way. He just waited, and hoped, and whenever he touched my hips or my flanks, I'd either flinch or go still. He got the message and nothing had to be said.

It was a shame, in a way. He was a good man and an unhappy one. He needed friends, drinking companions and a life. Instead, he taught a boy who didn't love him and listened to the sins of wandering mercenaries. I have no idea what he had done or where, but he had condemned himself to death.

Sometimes good people do sad things, honey. And when a person decides to die, they die. I believe that Calchas lived a little longer to teach me. Or maybe I just like to think that.

Summer came, and I went home to help bring in the barley. I could read, and Calchas sent me home with a scroll to follow while I was away from him – the ship list from the *Iliad*. And I told him that Mater had scrolls of Theognis, and he asked me to borrow them for him.

My house was different.

Pater was rich. No other way to put it. We had three slave families tilling. I was almost superfluous to reaping, although I put in one hard day setting the sheaves. Mostly I read aloud to Mater, who was the friendliest I can ever remember her. She was drunk when I arrived, and ashamed of her state. But she sobered up by the next morning and bustled about the place. The irony of it was that she could, by then, have acted like a lady. There were six or seven slave women – I didn't even know their names. There was a new building in the yard – a slave house.

My sister had changed. She was seven, and sharp-tongued, busy teaching her elders their business. She had a fine pottery-and-cloth doll from the east that she treasured. She sat in the sun and told me stories of her precious doll Cassandra, and I listened gravely.

My brother worked the forge and resented it, but his body was filling out. He already looked like a man – or at least, he looked like a man to me. He wasn't interested in anything I could tell him, so I left him alone. But on my second evening, he gave me a cup he'd made – a simple thing with no adornment, but the lip was well turned and the handle well set.

'Pater put in the rivets,' he admitted. Then, with a shrug, 'I can probably do better now.' He frowned, and looked away.

I loved it. I imagined drinking with my own bronze cup by a stream, up on the mountain. 'Hephaestus bless you, brother!' I said.

'So you like it?' he asked. Suddenly he was my brother again. The next day was like the old days and the resentment was gone, so that I was able to show him a better way to fling a javelin and he loved it, and he took me into the shop and showed me how he raised a simple bowl. We'd come a long way as a family, when my brother could work a sheet of carefully pounded-out copper without permission from Pater. In fact, Pater came in, looked at his work and ruffled his hair. Then he turned to me.

'How are your letters, boy?' he asked. 'Your mother claims you can read.'

Odd how fast the mind works when fear comes in. For one moment, I thought that I would impress him – and then I thought that perhaps that would be an error, because my days on Mount Cithaeron would end, and there would be no more rabbit hunts in the dawn. And in that one burst of thought, I understood how much I had become separated from the world of the forge.

But, of course, the desire to please Pater won out.

'I can read the *Iliad*, Pater,' I said. 'And write all my letters.'

Pater handed me a piece of charcoal and a flat board he white-washed and used for designs. 'Write for me. Write, "This cup is of Miltiades and Technes made him".'

I thought for a moment, and then, somewhat daring, I changed the words so that I needed only two.

I wrote in a clear hand, like a good craftsman. I knew that Pater would engrave the words if mine were good enough. Two words – Greek is a splendid language for ownership. 'OF-MILTIADES BY-TECHNES', I wrote.

Pater examined it. He could read, albeit slowly. Then he smiled.

My brother winked at me, because we could count those smiles on our fingers, they were so few and so valuable.

'Mmm,' he said. He nodded, then scribed it on copper – twice, to be sure. Then he put it on a cup he had, around the base. He used a very small chisel – a new tool, and clearly expensive, with a fine handle – to work the letters deeply. Chalkidis and I watched together until he was done.

'Chalkidis pounded the bronze to sheet,' Pater said. 'I made the cup. You provided the letters.' He nodded, obviously satisfied. 'He will like this.'

Pater had a standing commission, making armour and fancy table-ware for Miltiades. Pater wasn't alone – Miltiades bought Draco's wagons almost as fast as he could build them. They might have asked themselves why an Athenian aristocrat didn't buy these things closer to home, but they didn't.

Mater did. She mentioned it at least twice a day.

'Your father is rushing to his doom,' she said. 'Miltiades is as far beyond your father as he is beyond – me.'

Sober, Mater's intelligence was piercing and cruel. Sadly, the gods made her so that she was only happy when she was lightly drunk – witty, flirtatious, clever and social. But sober she was Medea, and dead drunk she was Medusa.

I read to her, and she lent me her book of poems and said that she would come and visit. 'I like what I hear of your Calchas,' she said. 'Has he made love to you yet?'

She was born of aristocrats, you see. And that was the way, even in Boeotia – men with boys, and women with girls. At least, in the aristocracy.

I blushed and stammered.

'So he hasn't. That's good. You wouldn't like it, would you?' She said this stroking my cheek – scary itself, in a way. She never touched us.

'No,' I said.

'No.' She was sitting on her *kline*, a low bench like a bed. She reclined, pulling her shawl about her. 'When that urge comes on you, tell me, and I'll buy you a slave for it.'

I had no notion what she was talking about, any more than I understood what Calchas wanted, except as a vague fear. And in many ways, I liked Calchas better than I liked Mater.

I found that I was eager to get back to the shrine. I said my good-byes with more relief than longing. Hermogenes came back with me. We had a good walk.

'I'll be free next year,' he said wistfully.

'Let's pretend you're free now,' I said. 'You can use the practice.'

He looked at me. 'How do I pretend to be free?' he asked.

I laughed. 'Calchas tells me that we all pretend to be free,' I said, a typical boy trying to sound as adult as his teacher. 'But you can meet my eyes when you talk, and tell me to fuck off when I make you angry. Come on – pretend!'

Hermogenes shook his head. 'You've never been a slave, Arimnestos,' he said. 'No one *pretends* to be free. And I guarantee you that no free man *pretends* to be a slave.'

We arrived at the shrine near nightfall. Hermogenes stayed the night and we took him hunting in the morning. He was an excellent rabbit killer, trained by hunger, and he quickly won Calchas's praises. I was jealous. Names flew, and some nine-year-old punches.

In the midst of a flurry of blows, I called him a slave and he stopped moving.

I never saw the blow from Calchas. It caught me in the ear and knocked me flat.

'Are you a gentleman?' he asked me, from the advantage of six feet of height. 'You invited him to be a free man. You asked him to trust you. Then – you called him a slave. Can you keep your word?'

I was resentful, but I wasn't a fool. Pain has a remarkable effect on boys. I sat up. 'I apologize, Hermogenes,' I said formally. 'I meant it – only as a hateful word, like "bastard".' I tried to grin it off.

Calchas shook his head. 'That's a worthless apology, young man. You must never call a bastard "*bastard*" or a slave "*slave*" unless you want to fight to the death. Trust me – I'm a bastard. I know.'

We ended up apologizing to each other, very formally. There was some silence and some walking apart.

Calchas laughed, called us girls and led us up the mountain after a deer. It was late, but the Lady of Animals sent us a good buck, and Hermogenes and I ran him down with javelins, Calchas working carefully through the trees to push the deer back on our weapons, and we killed when the sun was almost in the treetops. Then Calchas made Hermogenes cut the buck's throat and anointed him with blood on his face, as he had with me.

'Arimnestos says you are to be a free man,' Calchas said. 'You must learn to look other men in the eye. And to think of them like this,' and he pointed at the corpse of the deer. 'Slave or free, a man is nothing but a pile of bones and flesh with blood in the middle.'

Hermogenes didn't say anything, but he embraced me and when he went to leave, we clasped hands as if we were men. We sent Hermogenes home with a haunch of venison and a couple of rabbits, which no doubt made him a hero to his family. Hermogenes and I date our friendship from that morning. But I had to be a slave before I learned how true Calchas's words were.

In the Boeotia of my youth, we were poor men, and though we thought we knew the world, we knew little of what passed beyond our town and our mountain and our river. These were the borders of our lives.

Festivals came and passed, and sowing, and reaping, and I was getting older. Hard men came to the shrine and Calchas sat up the night with them. The second year, one tried to rape me, and Calchas killed him. I was well-nigh paralysed with fear, although I managed to bite his hand so hard he screamed. After that, I was more wary of the hard men.

I spent more and more time practising for war. Calchas was a warrior – I had realized that, although I couldn't put a day to the thought. All the men who came were fighters, too. It was as if they belonged to a guild, just like the smiths or the potters, which was odd, because in the Boeotia of my youth, every free man had to be a warrior, but no man I knew actually liked it. Like sex and defecation, it was something every man did but only boys talked about.

What a pretty blush.

So I trained with him. I wasn't always aware that he was training me. He had exercises for every hour of the day, and many of them were remarkably like work – gathering firewood, breaking it in the breaking tree, chopping the bigger pieces into firewood lengths for the hearth with a sharp bronze axe and then splitting them. This task could consume as much time as Calchas wanted it to consume – we needed wood, come winter. And the use of the axe taught me many things – that, just as with smithing, precision was more valuable than raw strength, for instance. That the ability to hit twice in exactly the same place was better than hitting once in two different places. Ah, my dear – you will never fight a man wearing bronze. But you must accept the word of an old man – you can kill a man right through his expensive bronze helmet if you can hit the very same place often enough.

Calchas was no *hoplomachos* – not just a fighting master. He didn't have a special dance to teach, nor were his lessons about the sword as organized as his lessons in writing. Rather, we'd be deep in a passage of the *Iliad*, and he would look up and make such a comment as I just made.

'Arimnestos?' he'd say. 'You know that if you hit a man often enough in precisely the same place in the helmet, his helmet will give way? And you'll spill his brains?'

I'd look at him, trying to imagine it. And then we'd go back to the *Iliad*.

There is a passage, late in the poem, when Achilles is still sulking and Hector rages among the Greeks. And several of the lesser heroes form a line, lock their shields and stop Hector's rush. I remember him singing that whole passage softly. The autumn light came in strongly through our horn window and dust motes floated in the shaft of light. When this happened, I liked to imagine that the gods were with us.

Calchas looked up, into the shaft of light, and his eyes were far away. 'That's how it is, when the lesser men seek to stop the better. You must lock your shield with your neighbour's, put your head down and refuse to take chances. Let the better man wear himself out against your shield. Poke hard with your spear to keep him at arm's length and refuse to leave the safety of the shield wall.' He shrugged. 'Pray to the gods that the killer finds other prey, or trips and falls, or that your own killers come and save you.'

'But you were one of the better men,' I said. 'You were a – a killer.'

Suddenly his eyes locked with mine and I could see him in his high-crested helm, his strong right arm pounding a lesser man's shield down, down, until he made the killing cut. I could see it as if I was there.

'Yes,' he said. 'I was a killer of men.' Then his eyes slipped away. I knew where he was – he was on a battlefield. 'I still am. Once you have been there, you can never leave.'

# 4

A sowing and a reaping, and another year. Animals died under my spear. I read all of Theognis from Mater's book and came to appreciate that grown men had sex with boys and grew jealous when they took other loves. And that aristocrats could be ill-tempered and avaricious like peasants.

You should read Theognis, my sweet. Just to understand that being well-born is a thing of no value.

I read Hesiod, too. I knew much of him by heart by now, of course. In Boeotia, he is our own poet, and we spurn mighty Homer so that we can love Hesiod better. Besides, his poems are for us – farmers. Is Achilles really a hero? He's as much of a bitch as Theognis, to my mind. Hector is the hero. And even he would not have made much of a farmer – well, perhaps I do mighty Hector wrong. Given a month of rain, Hector would not surrender or sulk in his barn.

I was bigger. I was stronger. I could throw a javelin farther and better than any boy my age in the valley, and Calchas was talking about the boys' games at places like Olympia.

Across the river, the farm grew richer. Every grape vine was trellised and trimmed, the apple trees had supports on the branches and all the new growth was excised in spring by what seemed to me to be a phalanx of slaves.

Miltiades' money could be seen everywhere in our community. Myron had two ploughs. Epictetus's younger son, Peneleos, went with the great man to fight, and his father bought a second farm for his older son. There was talk of his older son wedding Penelope when she turned twelve or thirteen.

Hermogenes was freed and joined his father as a man who worked for wage. All their family was freed now, and Bion made himself a helmet and a great bronze shield and was welcomed into the *taxis*. Not all freed men were so welcomed – but Bion was a special case.

I went with my brother and Hermogenes to watch the men dance at the festival of Ares. All of them had practised the dances since they were old enough to learn – twelve or thirteen, in most cases. And my father had done well by Bion, teaching him – something that I knew Pater did only with the quickest of learners. So Bion did not humiliate himself, although as a newly freed and enfranchised man, there were farmers eager to see him fail.

That's how men are, honey. Don't you know? With peasants, it is the same in Asia and Aegypt and Boeotia. They think there is much evil in the world and little good, and that one man's gain is another's loss. If Bion was free, then a free man would become a slave. So they whispered.

I watched them dance. I had seen it before – it was magnificent and made my blood run fast, two hundred men in bronze and leather, swaying in line, turning around, thrusting with their spears, parrying with their shields.

Two years and more on the mountain and I knew those moves better than the dancers. I watched with a critical eye – and, honey, there is nothing more critical than a boy of eleven.

It was also my brother's first year in the dance. He was well kitted, with a fine Corinthian helmet and a big shield to keep him safe in the storm of bronze. I watched him dance and thought he did it well enough, but the boy in me couldn't avoid criticism, so that night I asked him why he didn't change the weight on his feet when he went from defence to attack.

Of course he had no notion of what I was talking about, but only heard his younger brother finding fault. We wrestled in the barn – to a draw. I was weaker, but I knew quite a bit more. There's a lesson there, too. All my skill – and I had quite a bit of skill already – was not enough to match his longer reach and his smith's strength.

And even with my blood up, I wasn't fool enough to put a finger in his eye.

But the next day, he cut two poles and asked me to show him what I meant. So I showed him as Calchas showed me – how the movement of your hips reinforces the push of the spear or the rise of the shield. Chalkidis was no fool. No sooner did he see, than he was asking questions. And he took his questions to Pater. Pater came and watched us.

His eyes narrowed. 'I sent you up the mountain to learn to read and write,' he said. 'What is this?'

I was proud of my martial skills, so I showed him. I showed him the guards that Calchas taught and the spear attacks. I could hit my brother at will, although when I had the weight of a real aspis on my shoulder, I could barely move.

Pater shook his head. 'Foolishness,' he said. 'All you should do is keep your place in the shield wall. The rest is madness. The moment you lunge, the enemy to your right plunges his spear in your thigh. Or your neck. Every attack you make leaves your shield side un-covered.' He shook his head. 'Calchas must stop teaching you this nonsense.'

'He is a great warrior,' I said hotly.

Pater looked at me as if really noticing me for the first time. 'There are no great warriors,' Pater said. 'There are great craftsmen, great sculptors, great poets. Sometimes, they must put a spear on their shoulder. But nothing about war is great.' Pater looked across the valley, towards the shrine. 'Your teacher is a broken man who keeps a shrine about which no man cares a whit. He teaches boys to read and he nurses old hatreds. I think that it is time I brought you home.'

'Many men care about the shrine!' I said. There were tears in my eyes.

Pater dusted his hands. 'Come,' he said.

We walked to the shrine. I argued, and Pater was silent. When we arrived, Pater ordered me to collect my things. And he went and spoke to Calchas alone.

I still know nothing of what they said to each other, but I never saw a frown or a harsh word. I collected my javelins, my spear 'Deer Killer', my scrolls and my bedroll. I put them on the donkey and went to kiss Calchas goodbye. He embraced me.

'Time for you to go out into the world,' he said. 'Your father is right, and I have probably filled your head with nonsense.'

I knew that he would be drunk before we walked to the base of the mountain. But I smiled and kissed him on the lips – which I had never done.

On the way down the path, I stopped. 'He will die without me,' I said. I was eleven going on twelve, and the world was much less of a mystery to me than it had been. 'By leaving, I am killing him!'

Pater embraced me. I think it is the only embrace that I remember.

He held me for a long time. Finally, he said, 'He is killing himself. You have your own life to lead.'

We walked home, Pater silent, me crying.

I went back to working the forge, although I now lagged far behind my brother. I read to my mother, who fussed over my hands and bellowed abuse at Pater about how his noble son was being forced to peasant work.

Pater ignored her.

I lose track of time, here. I think it was the same summer as I left Calchas, but it might have been the next. They were golden summers, and the wealth of Plataea came in with the grain. We sold much of our grain in the markets of Attica, and now that we were the richest peasants in Boeotia, our fathers plotted how to spend our wealth on the greatest Daidala in history.

Men came to the yard of the smithy and leaned against the new sheds, or sat on the stools that now littered the yard, drank Pater's excellent wine served by a pair of pretty slaves and planned the Daidala. There was no other discussion that summer, for the next spring was the moment when we would watch the ravens on the hillside, choose our tree and set in motion all the traditions and customs and dances and rituals that would lead us to a successful festival – a festival that would cause other men across Boeotia to envy our wealth and curse us. Or rather, that was the plan.

For before the summer was old enough for the barley to lose its green, the word came to our valley that the men of Thebes were preparing the Great Daidala, and had ordained that Plataea was but a community of Thebes and not a free city. What's more, Thebes had voted a great tax to be placed on us to 'support the festival'.

I had missed two years of talk in the courtyard, but little had changed. The speakers wore a better quality of cloth, but they were the same men – solid men, who were a little richer but had no toleration for fools. Myron was not the richest, but he tended to speak for Pater's friends in the assembly, and there was talk of making him *archon* instead of the old basileus. The old basileus was now poorer than Pater. The world was turning on its head.

The word of the Theban tax goaded them even more than the word that we would not host the festival. Peasants *hate* it when other men take their money. I know that hate. Steal the money of a slave and look at his eyes. That is the look of a peasant who is taxed.

Simon had joined the men in the yard. I wasn't there when he moved back into our lives. It seems odd, after all that happened, but peasants quarrel as much as aristocrats and then settle their differences or simply move on. Simon came back, and I continued to hate him, but Pater treated him with courtesy and all was well.

It was Simon who said the words on everybody's mind.

'We should fight,' Simon said.

Every man in the yard sipped his wine and nodded.

'We should ask the Spartans for an alliance,' Draco said.

Epictetus the Younger spent more time in the yard than he should have, but he was rich enough already that slaves did all the farm work for him, and he wandered about with a body slave like a lord. It made his father frown, but his farm ran well enough and he was growing into a big man who spoke well and would fight in the front rank. He stood up. 'We should offer alliance to Athens,' he said. 'Miltiades is a friend of every man here.'

Draco shook his head. 'Miltiades is our friend, but he's almost an exile this year. They refused to let his ships land last autumn. Men say he'll make himself tyrant of Athens. He's no help to us. Besides,' and Draco looked around as if expecting enemies to leap from behind the forge, 'Sparta is ready to make war on Thebes.'

'Once we take it to the assembly, Thebes will know what we are about,' Myron said.

Pater stood forward. I remember him from that afternoon, how dignified he was and how proud I was that he was my father. He looked around the circle of men. 'What if we decide on a thing, here in this yard,' he said, 'and then Myron travels around and talks quietly to other men of substance?' He paused, and fell silent. He was never a man for big talk.

Myron nodded. 'We might call it something different. We might call it the "salt tax".'

It took a moment to explain to Draco, who could be slow, and to my brother, who had no notion of the duplicity an assembly could practise.

But that's what they did. They called the alliance with Sparta the 'salt tax' and Myron went from oikia to oikia around the whole polis, so that when they went to the assembly where the Thebans waited, and voted for a salt tax, the Thebans were suspicious but nothing could be proven.

Then the farmers sent Draco, Myron and Theron, son of Xenon, one of our richest men, and he sold his leather armor as far away as Peloponnese. His son began to wear Spartan shoes and Myron's son began to puff out his chest and speak of buying himself a horse. Epictetus came by and frowned.

'We owe Miltiades better than this,' he said. 'We should send him word.'

Pater shrugged. 'He is an exile in a barbarian land,' he said.

Epictetus looked around the yard. 'His money bought everything here.'

'Send word to your son, then,' Pater said. 'Miltiades has a factor at Corinth. I have a shipment of armour for him. I'll send word to him. But Draco has the right of it. Miltiades is our friend and our benefactor, but he has no power in Boeotia.'

'Uhh,' Epictetus grunted.

Pater sent my brother with the armour to Corinth. He came back with some fine pottery and a new donkey and a small pile of silver coins. He was proud of himself – he'd been far from home, over the mountains, and returned without incident.

Pater nodded, and sent him back to the forge. I suppose it was a form of compliment that Pater always assumed that we would succeed at anything he assigned us. But an actual compliment would have gone a long way.

The message must have carried, though, because just after the feast of Demeter, the great man himself came up the lane, riding another magnificent horse. He wore a golden fillet in his hair and he looked even more like a god.

The thing that made him stand out to me this time was that I could see he'd been trained the same way I had. I could see it in how he stood and how he walked. I still did the exercises that Calchas had taught, and twice I'd gone deer hunting alone, and once killed a deer. I'd taken Calchas wine. He ruffled my hair and said little. I left offerings at the shrine when he wasn't there – or perhaps he was there, lying drunk on his pallet and waiting for me to go away.

At any rate, Miltiades came and stayed the night, and Pater invited Epictetus, along with Myron's son Dionysius and my brother. I was too young for the *andron*, but I served the wine.

They spoke of politics, about Athens and Sparta and Thebes.

'Our friend Draco has it wrong,' Miltiades said. 'Sparta is not going to make war on Thebes. Sparta is making an alliance with Thebes to isolate Athens.'

I thought that the red-haired man was angry, but hiding it well.

Dionysius was braver, or more foolish, than the older men. 'What do you care, sir?' he asked. 'Athens has exiled you.'

Miltiades leaned back on his kline. I was filling his cup and he put a hand on my hip. 'You fill out well, boy,' he said. 'Who taught you to move like a gymnast? You make the other boys look like farm workers.'

I froze. I knew that touch.

Pater laughed. 'He's as much a farm worker as the rest,' he said, and Miltiades laughed with them, aristocrat that he was. Then he shrugged. 'City politics can't be so different in Plataea and Athens,' he said. 'I'm an exile, but I will always be a man of the city. I have a settlement of my own, and colonists, every man of whom is a citizen somewhere else – by the gods, I have some of your own young men! And we are still loyal to our homes. Would you want me to convince your sons to be my citizens rather than Plataeans?'

They nodded. We all understood him.

'So I watch out for the good of Athens,' he went on. 'Athens needs Plataea. Plataea needs Athens. Sparta will take your alliance – and later he'll shove it up your arse.' His crudity hit them hard. He was a brilliant speaker, capable of using all words, big and small, rough and elegant, and he could modify his text to his audience, a wonderful talent. But most of all, he was a charismatic man. Later I saw him in an assembly of thousands, and his words carried an army. At close quarters, he was as deadly in argument as he was in combat.

Epictetus frowned. 'What do we do, lord? We did not seek to displease you.'

Miltiades shook his head. 'My fault for not voicing my desire openly. I shouldn't have made you guess. I'm not usually so coy. I want this alliance. I want Plataea welded to Athens with bonds of bronze and iron.' He grinned his infectious grin. 'Well, we'll see. Your embassy will be back soon enough. Doubtless the Spartans will accept and shaft you later, but perhaps I can speak sense into you before that.' He laughed. 'I'll go and visit the old soldier on the hill. Calchas. Do you know him?'

Pater glanced at me. 'He was my son's tutor,' he said.

Miltiades gave me an appraising glance. 'Really? Old Calchas took you on? What did he teach you?'

'Reading,' Pater said quickly.

'Hunting,' I said, before I knew what I was saying.

Pater frowned, but Miltiades smiled. 'You hunt? Take me in the morning, lad. We'll have a fine time.'

'He is my son,' my father said carefully.

'I understand,' Miltiades answered.

We went up the mountain together. I rode his horse, my arms around his waist and a bundle of javelins in my fists. I showed him my prize spear and he looked it over carefully and admitted that it was a fine one for a lad my age. I realized that I was striving for his approbation with every breath. I never wondered why his slave had stayed on the farm, or why he didn't lend me his slave's horse, although, in truth, I probably couldn't have ridden her.

It took us less than an hour to cross the valley and mount the slopes to the shrine. We rode into the green meadow and dismounted. I ran to the door of the hut, but Calchas didn't answer my knock. The sun was just rising, and Miltiades was fully active – he was never a sluggard, even with a skinful of wine.

He had a fine canteen, covered in leather, and he spilled a libation to the hero. Then he tethered his horse and we went up the trails behind the tomb at a run. He was in magnificent shape – I've seldom seen a man with a better command of his body – and we ran six or seven stades without stopping, until we were high in the oak forest.

'I thought we might catch up with the old bastard,' Lord Miltiades said. He was scarcely panting.

'No tracks on the trail,' I said. I was breathing hard.

Again, the lord looked at me carefully. 'Good eye,' he said. 'Can you find me a buck, lad?'

So we moved quietly across the mountainside. It took me an hour to get the spoor of an animal, and another hour – the sun was getting too high – to put the small buck between us. I charged it, yelling hard, and it broke away from me, running for its life right at the Athenian.

But I hadn't seen the other buck. He was a magnificent animal, as big as a small horse, and in autumn he'd have carried a rack of antlers big enough to sell. Even in high summer he had started his horns. He rose out of a tangle of brush, crashed shoulder to shoulder with the younger buck, spilling him and saving his life, and sprang. His leap was so high and so hard that Miltiades stood with his mouth open, his javelin cocked and forgotten in his hand, as the buck sailed over his head.

We didn't touch either animal. Miltiades slapped me on the back. 'You can stalk,' he said. 'Not your fault I missed my throw, boy. And what an animal! Artemis held my hand – I felt her cool fingers on my wrist, I swear. That beast must be her special love.'

We walked down the mountain together. The sun was too high to try again. I potted a rabbit foolish enough to sit in the middle of the trail eating a leaf, and Miltiades praised my throw, sweet praise such as I never received at home.

Yet he was not just a flatterer. He made me throw for him six or seven times, and he adjusted my body each time, correcting my tendency to advance my right foot too much, and there was none of the urgency to his touch that I'd felt with Calchas. He taught well, and when he threw his own spear, a heavy *longche* that I would be hard-pressed to toss across the meadow, he threw it as Zeus on high throws a bolt of lightning.

I was worshipping him by the time we returned to Calchas's hut and the shrine.

'I wanted to see him,' Miltiades said.

'I'll fetch him out,' I said, bold as brass. 'Lord, he may be a little drunk.'

Miltiades laughed. 'You fetch him out of there,' he said. 'I'll sober him up – or give him some decent wine, better than the piss you peasants drink.'

It was the first time I'd heard Miltiades speak ill of us. He could only guard his tongue so long.

Ah, listen, honey. He was not a bad man, as powerful men go. He saved Greece. He was good to me. But he was used to the finest horses, the most beautiful women. It was our foolishness that made us think he was happy to drink sour wine with peasants in Boeotia.

I climbed in through the window of horn. I'd done it dozens of times – once to steal the bow. I told you that story.

As soon as I got it open – the stick I'd whittled to prise the window open was still leaning where I'd left it – flies came out, buzzing like some evil thing. In Canaan, men call the lord of the dead the 'Lord of the Flies'. It was just like that – as if all the flies made a single creature and moved with one will.

I dropped from the sill into the room, and it smelled of old leather and bad food. At first I thought he had gone, leaving a rotten haunch of venison and an old brown cloak on the deer's carcass in the middle of the floor.

But, of course, he was there.

The details came to me one at a time, although I think I understood as soon as the flies buzzed past me in the window. The odd shaft of light over the deer carcass was shining on the sword. The sword was stuck, hilt first, into the floorboards. There was no deer carcass.

Calchas had wedged his sword into the floor and fallen on it. He had done it so long before that the brown cloak was just his hair and the last of his skin over his bones.

How long since I had crossed the valley and left a sacrifice at the tomb? How many times had I come when he already lay here, dead? I wonder, in a way, if I had already known, because I had said my goodbyes and I didn't weep. I went to the door, unbarred it and found the bronze-shod shovel Pater had made for him with his athlete's pick. I carried them out into the yard and went straight to the tomb. Miltiades called something but I didn't listen. Instead, I began to dig.

I didn't see Miltiades go to the hut, but I know that before the sun rose much higher, he was at my side, his lord's hands digging in the earth with mine. We did a proper job.

'Not much to burn,' Miltiades said, when I began to pile up the winter's supply of wood in the yard. It was old wood, and a little rotten. He hadn't cut more, nor had he burned much, last winter. This was the wood I had cut while training.

I piled it high. I was tempted to burn the cottage, but I knew that another man would come to mind the tomb. Why ruin it for him?

Then I went in and spread my cloak on the floor. I lifted his corpse and put it gently on the good wool. Some pieces of him fell away. I was not squeamish. I filled my cloak and carried him into the yard. I put copper coins in the empty sockets of his skull and set the bag of my cloak and his bones on top of the woodpile, then Miltiades got a flame going with his fire kit.

'He was a great warrior,' Miltiades said. 'Twice he saved my life in the haze of battle. Once he saved my ship. And he could sing poetry like a bard. He was a gentleman like the heroes of old. May his shade go with theirs, to the island of the blessed, for he was all the old virtues together in one man.'

Then I wept. I said a few halting words, and the flames rushed up and consumed him.

But he lives in my words, honey. Honour him. He made me. In

a way, he made you. Because he put the skill of arms in me, and because of him, I am not dead.

His death was the beginning of everything that went wrong.

Miltiades and I went back home. You might think that I'd have shouted at Pater, but I didn't. Pater knew – that is, he knew when we were riding away, the day he took me from Calchas. He knew what would happen, and he told the truth. We didn't kill him. We were like a sword left lying in a tavern, and then used in a murder. We were the instruments of his death.

I think some of Calchas passed through the skin of my hands and into my heart. I think I became a man while I carried his body, light as dried bone, out to the yard to burn him on his pyre. Is that just memory playing tricks?

Mater had never met him, but she wept for him, nonetheless – odd, in a way. He had no use for women, and yet a woman who had never known him mourned him. Somehow, it was fitting.

We kept a three-day vigil at our home, as if he'd been family, and Miltiades joined in – or led us – and that bound him to us even more, and us to him. He sat with Mater and read to her and told her she was beautiful. She drank a little and flirted harmlessly.

Then Draco and Theron came back, riding donkeys.

They came into the yard, failure written on their bodies like words on papyrus. Draco dismounted first and he didn't meet Miltiades' eyes, but told the story simply and quickly. The Spartans had derided the three of them, called them peasants and rebels, and told them to take their petty attempts at democracy to Athens, where such things are welcome.

Draco wasn't a broken man, but he was changed by the experience. He was used to being taken seriously, and he'd been treated like a boor and a dolt. He complained long and hard. Indeed, for the rest of his life, he complained of the treatment he received in Sparta.

Myron came later. He complained less, but his resentment was hotter. Perhaps, as a farmer and not a craftsman, and as a member of an old family that claimed descent from the gods, he actually thought of himself as an aristocrat. Anything is possible. But the insults of the Spartans made his blood boil. The difference was that he never spoke of it again. Neither did Theron. For other reasons, as you shall see.

Epictetus followed, and then the archon himself. He had a horse, although it looked like a sorry beast beside the fine mounts Miltiades had brought.

Mater wanted to know who had arrived, and I went up to the women's quarters to tell her.

'Your father is about to find out why a man like Miltiades has cooled his heels for five days in our house,' she said. 'Will you grow to be a man like him? Like Miltiades? Or just another good craftsman like your father? Poor man. I led him to this. I couldn't just be the wife of a smith, and now we're about to be part of a political game.' She gulped wine. 'I should fall on a sword like your teacher. He knew what he was about.'

I sighed and left her.

I served the wine that night, when they decided to send the 'salt tax' to Athens. Miltiades sent his slave with them and stayed with us, well over the border from his home city.

We didn't have to wait long.

The events of that summer were like one of the storms that roll down the valleys of Boeotia. First you see the storm – the black clouds rising like the strongest towers, spiralling up over the mountains – and then you hear the thunder. And when the thunder comes, honey – you run, or you get wet. At first it seems very far away – a murmur on the far horizon, and perhaps a prayer to the storm god. Then, before you know it, unless you are in the barn or house, you'll be wet through your cloak and chiton in an instant, as the lightning flashes every few heartbeats and crashes to earth – sometimes all around you – and the wind rips branches from the trees and the end of the world seems just one bolt away.

When the men of Plataea sent Myron to Athens, the storm was still a tower of darkness on the horizon, and we were blinded by our own desires. But the desires of men are nothing when the gods send a storm. The first drops of rain were falling, and only Miltiades knew how big the storm was. And he didn't tell us.

Athens sent a deputation back in a week, riding on horses over the trade road. They brought a decree welcoming Miltiades back and they brought us a treaty. The men of Plataea signed the treaty, promising to stand by Athens, and Athens promised the same. The men of the city went to the Temple of Hera and swore together in the sacred precincts. Pater went, and my brother. I was too young.

It was a magnificent summer. I remember them coming back from the temple, all the men of our valley in their long clothes – chitons and the big cloaks we wore then. They made a beautiful procession. I thought that this must be how the king of Persia looked.

The sun was high and the sky had the magnificent blue that is so hard to remember on a rainy day like this. We were all proud that Athens wanted us. And the men from Athens acted as if we were men of worth.

I remember that time as happy. Perhaps it is just by contrast with what came after.

The men of Athens went home and Miltiades went with them. Pater went back to work on an order for spear points. Draco went up the mountain with both his sons to cut oak for wheel rims. Myron went home to watch his slaves reap his barley.

I began to form my first cup.

It wasn't going badly when the Athenian herald rode up the valley, summoning us to war.

Two weeks. That's how long we had before the storm broke.

I never doubted that I would go with the men. I went as a shield-bearer, of course – a hypaspist – I was too young to fight as a hoplite. These days men take slaves, but in those days, it was more acceptable to take boys just short of manhood to carry your equipment.

Hermogenes went for his father and I went for my brother. My father took a slave.

We never thought to refuse the Athenians. And aside from my mother, who wept and railed against the fates, there were few who saw how completely the Athenians had duped us. They were not saving us. We were marching to protect them. But no one said so.

We took less than a week to muster. We might have mustered faster, but our farmers needed to get their crops in. It was already known in the polis that Thebes intended revenge – that we were viewed as rebels. They might come and burn our crops if we didn't bring them in. It was bad enough leaving grapes on the vines and olives on the trees.

I have no idea whether any man suggested that we either forget our alliance with Athens or simply send a minimum of men. We were proud peasants, and we sent the whole of our muster over the mountains. Men like Myron worked like slaves to get their harvest in. I remember working in the fields with Hermogenes and our slaves, already feeling like a man at war. I drank wine with the men in the evening and hoped that they would present me with an aspis and put me in the taxis. Farmers freed slaves to fill out the ranks, but I was not invited.

We went across the mountains after the feast of Demeter. We marched up the same road that passed the shrine, and every man in the ranks touched the tomb, and I thought of Calchas. We'd heard that the Spartans and all their Peloponnesian allies had marched around the south end of the mountain and entered Attica. Boys like me feared that we would be too late.

War is something a man should want to be late for. We crossed into Attica, and the Spartans were sitting across the stream from the tower at Oinoe, a fortification the tyrants of Athens had built against this very kind of war. Of course, Sparta had been an enemy of tyranny – but when the Spartans saw how strong the new Athens was going to be, they became enemies of democracy as well. Nation states are always that way, honey. They have no more morality than a whore in the Piraeus looking to score some wine. Anything to get what they want.

Ares, how we feared the Spartans. Cleomenes, their king, a famous man, had with him only a thousand Spartiates – the Spartan citizens, and there were six thousand Athenian citizens. But he made up the numbers with 'allies', cities of the Peloponnese that had to fight when Sparta said fight.

And how the Athenians cheered us, although we brought just a thousand hoplites. They gave us the honour of the left end of the line. The position of highest honour is the right flank. If the right gives way, an army is done – dead. Miltiades' father, also called Miltiades, held the right of the line with the senior tribes of Athens. They looked magnificent, with cloaks of tapestry-woven wool, and the whole front rank had bronze breastplates like heroes. Every man had a horsehair plume in his helmet. They made us look like farmers.

Hah! We *were* farmers. Half our men had leather caps. Only the front rank had helmets, and half of them were open-faced war hats. My father was one of only a dozen fighters with bronze panoply, and not all our front rank even had leather to cover their bodies. A couple of men wore felt.

Hermogenes and I were *psiloi*. That meant that we were to run close to the enemy, throw rocks at them and goad them into action. Sometimes psiloi just yelled insults. It was all rather like something religious. Psiloi rarely harmed anyone.

I had six good javelins – quite a few for a boy my age, but then none of the others, slave or free, had spent two years on the mountain hunting deer. I gave three to Hermogenes.

Myron's youngest son Callicles was our leader. He was a year older than me, and bossy. I was used to my brother, who would listen to any argument I made and judge it on its merits. Slow and careful and totally solid, my brother. Callicles had none of those qualities. My halting attempts to tell him that I knew a lot more about this game than he did led to him putting an elbow in my nose. He caught me by surprise and had me on the ground in an instant. I broke free before he could hurt me – but I chose to obey.

We camped for two days, watching the Spartans. The alignment meant that if we fought, we'd be the ones facing the Spartiates. They'd be on the right of their line, and we'd be on the left or ours. There was some talk, but none of the men had much time for us boys except my brother. He told me how scared he was.

'I feel like I'm going to die,' he said. 'I'm cold all the time. I'm going to be a coward, and I hate it!'

I hugged him. 'You'll be brave!' I told him. 'Just don't be too brave.' I grinned and gave him Calchas's advice, which must have sounded foolish from a beardless boy. 'Stay in the shield wall and don't let anyone over your shield,' I said.

He laughed at me, despite his fear. 'I'm in the sixth rank,' he said. 'Safer than we are in a storm at home!' He laughed, but then he was serious. 'We're going to form deep, to slow the Spartans down,' he said. 'Pater says if we form a dozen deep, we'll stand longer.'

It sounded like sense to me. Still does.

In those days, honey, men didn't fight as they do today. Well – the Spartans did. They were orderly and careful, but most men didn't even form a proper phalanx with ranks and files – something every city does today. No, back then, we were still like the war bands of the lords in the *Iliad*. Men would cluster around the leaders like trees around a spring, and if a leader died, all his men would run.

But my father paid attention to things he saw and heard, and it was he who had suggested that the men of Plataea should each have a place – a rank and a file – and should practise in those places, the way the Spartans and the best of the Thebans did – their *apobatai*, the elite fighters, who had once been the charioteers. And now Pater had ordered them to fight in a very deep order – in those days, twelve deep was twice as deep as most men fought.

63

But I digress, as usual. I could tell that my brother was afraid. I wasn't afraid. I thought that it would be like deer hunting. I imagined that I'd run around the flank of their line and throw my javelins into this packed mass, killing a Spartiate with every cast. Calchas had told me the truth about war, but my ears had been closed.

It may sound odd to you, but I took quite a shine to young Callicles. He was arrogant but he was older, and that matters to peasants. And when he saw how far I could throw a javelin – he only had one – he treated me differently. In an afternoon of rock- and javelin-throwing on the height beside the tower, I became his second man, his phylarch, and we copied our elders, speaking at length about our 'tactics'. As boys will, we made the other boys do as we did, and we practised running and jumping and throwing javelins and rocks. Most boys merely had rocks. The slaves hung back.

Fair enough. It wasn't their fight. Those who had been freed had everything to gain by fighting well, but those who were still slaves had no interest in the fight at all. They sat around until we yelled at them, and then the older ones were slow and so obviously unwilling that they poisoned our confidence. These men were masters of avoiding work, and a couple of teenaged boys were nothing to them. These were men who were used to dealing with the wrath of Pater or Epictetus the Elder.

By the third day, it looked to all of us as if there would be no fight, and the Athenians heaped praise on us. Just by coming, we'd given the Peloponnesians pause. Now they were outnumbered. And, it appeared, they'd expected the Thebans to join them, but the Thebans weren't there yet. Or weren't coming at all.

I'll have a lot to say about war, honey. I may put you to sleep with it for a month while I weary you with my story. And one thing I'll say a thousand times is that every army has its own heart, its own soul, its own eyes and its own ears. In that army, that Peloponnesian army, they didn't really want to be in Attica. They were all too aware that the Spartans were only there to support their alliance with Thebes, and the Spartans, as was their way, had shown their lack of interest by sending only a token force under the junior king.

As they did again later, against the Medes. Never trust a Spartan, honey.

Anyway, they should have known that the bloody Thebans were coming. They were a hundred stades away or less. Ares must have laughed.

Cleomenes finally committed to fight because the Peloponnesians were starting to leave him. Allies were freer in those days. They told the king of Sparta what they thought, and then they marched away. Not many of them, but enough to make old Cleomenes decide to fight before he had no army at all.

We knew that the Thebans were coming. It was said around every fire. The Athenians and all the farmers of Attica – they had farmers too – were already looking over their shoulders and doubting the new leaders that they'd elected. But Miltiades and his father were everywhere – even among us – putting bars of iron into the spines of every man. Miltiades even came and watched our boys practising. He praised my javelin throw, and an hour later his slave came and gave me a pair of spears with blued steel heads – even now, the memory of them makes me smile. They were fine weapons. I thought my spear Deer Killer was a fine weapon – it had a bronze head made by Pater with its name engraved on the spine – but it was crude next to these, with their red hafts and their blue-black heads.

I kept Deer Killer and the gifts and gave my other javelins to other boys. Callicles took the best and gave his own to the poorest.

Three javelins for the richest boys. A hemp sack full of rocks for the poorest. What fools we were. And our fathers were being matched against the red cloaks of Sparta.

The day dawned. I slept well enough, unlike my father, my brother and most of the other Plataeans. The heralds had been exchanged the night before. By the time we ate our barley porridge, Miltiades the Elder had made his sacrifices. He found them auspicious.

I'm sure they were auspicious for Athens.

I had never seen a phalanx form. Pater was one of the chief officers of the Plataeans and he walked up and down, forming men into their place in the ranks, his black and red double crests nodding as he walked, and he looked as noble and as deadly as any Spartiate. I marvelled at his performance – he knew who was steady and who had nerves, and he placed them as gently as possible, avoiding any form of insult. I was proud that he was my father. Still am.

I saw that Cousin Simon was in the sixth rank. What fool of a polemarch had ever put him in the front for the last battle? He was green already! In the middle, he'd be safe and he wouldn't hurt anyone.

Then I saw that he was one man to the right of my brother.

Chalkidis looked worried, but he waved. He was the only man in the sixth rank who had greaves and a fine helmet. That's what you get when you are a bronze-smith and the son of a bronze-smith. He had his helmet tipped back on his head, the way you see the goddess Athena in her statues. And he managed a solid smile for me. I pushed through the ranks and hugged him, leather cuirass and all. I was jealous, but he looked magnificent and he was still a head taller than me, and suddenly all I wanted was for him to succeed and be a hero, and when we were done embracing, I hurried to the roadside shrine and poured a little of Pater's honeyed wine on the statue of the Lady and prayed that he would be brave and succeed in battle.

I had no doubts that he'd be brave.

Before my first battle story is told, I think I have to speak about courage, honey. Are you brave? You don't know, but I do. You're brave. And when it's your turn to face the woman's version of the bronze storm – when a child comes from between your knees into the world – you may scream, and you may be afraid, but you'll do it. You'll get it done. No one expects you to like it, but all your friends, all the womenfolk who've borne their own children, they'll crowd around you, wiping your brow and telling you to push.

It's the same for men. No one is brave. No one really, deep down, wants to be Achilles. What we all want is to live, and to be brave enough to tell our story. And older men who've done it before will call out and tell the younger men to push.

The thing is, hardly anyone is such a coward as to stand out. You are there with the whole community around you. Courage is asking a girl to marry you, alone against her parents. Courage is standing before the assembly and telling them they're a pack of fools. Courage is fighting when no one will ever see your courage. But when the phalanx is locked together, it's hard to be a coward.

Fucking Simon. He was no coward in other ways, but when the phalanx formed, he lost his wits. Gods, how I still hate him.

Our phalanx looked a poor thing next to the Athenians. They had blue and purple and bright red and blinding white, and we had all the homespun colours of peasants. Pater had a good cloak, and so did a dozen men – all Miltiades' friends. The son of the basileus's sister looked as good as the Athenians. The rest – even some of the better men – looked drab and dun.

We formed our boys in a thin line in front of our fathers. We saw the Athenian psiloi. They were a poor show compared to us – all slaves, and half of them didn't even have rocks. So we joked that there was one thing we did better than the men of Athens.

We were still forming when the Spartan helots came across the ground at us. They had rocks in bags, and they threw hard. I caught one on my shin and I fell. That was the glory of war. Just like that – the first rock, and I was down.

Two or three of us fell, and the rest of the boys ran like deer on the mountain. I hadn't even had time to think about how I might be a hero. I hadn't even thrown a spear. But my pater was right there, so close I could almost touch him, and I was not going to run. Besides, as I got up, I found that I couldn't. My shin hurt too much and there was blood.

The helots were almost close enough to touch, too. In fact, two of them had just begun to lob rocks at our phalanx. They ignored me.

I killed the one closest to me. Deer Killer knocked him flat, just as she had done a dozen times to deer.

That got their attention. A rock came so close that it brushed my ear like the whisper of a god, telling me that I was mortal. I planted my feet, ignoring my shin, and a beautiful blue-tipped spear killed a second helot. They *died*. This is no boyish boast. We were as close as your couch and mine, honey – and I threw to kill.

They broke. They were slaves, and like our slaves, they had nothing to gain from bravery. They didn't even care about avenging their comrades. Slaves have no comrades. They turned and fled as our boys had just moments before.

That's when I learned that Calchas had come into my body when I burned his corpse, because when they fled, I killed another. I liked it. I cocked back my arm and threw my spear into the back of a fleeing slave *and I liked it*.

Then I hobbled forward and retrieved my javelins.

Behind me, the left-most Athenians and the right-most Plataeans were cheering. They were cheering me. It went to my head like unwatered wine.

The other boys came back fast enough. They weren't cowards. They just hadn't understood the game.

We still didn't understand. Callicles slapped my back and we ran forward together. I tried to angle across the Spartan front, because I knew we'd be safer on the flank, but I was slowed by my shin.

When I looked up, the Spartans terrified me. It's not like being in the phalanx, out there in the middle between the armies. And the Spartans – they all look the same, with matching shields of bronze, like the richest Athenians, and with almost identical helmets. I actually wondered who made all those helmets. They looked very fine. And they scared me.

But I couldn't flinch now. Although a curious reaction hit me – I still remember it. I felt cold as I hobbled forward and I began to shake. Then the other boys began to throw. We were too far away and Callicles started to yell like a real officer, pushing them forward. He turned his back on the Spartans and yelled at us to come on, come on, throw from closer.

I was near him when I saw the Spartan file-leader call an order and four hoplites burst out of the front of the shield wall. They came so fast, they were like javelins themselves. They were all athletes in high training, of course, not boys. I knew from the first long leg kicking that they were faster than I was when I wasn't injured. There were only four of them against thirty of us.

Callicles died first. The fastest Spartan singled him out. I remember that the Spartan had a smile on his face under the helmet. I screamed at Callicles to run, but the fool stood his ground and threw my second-best spear, and the Spartan ducked his head and it passed him. He never even slowed, and his long *doru* went into Callicles above the groin and drove out of his back like some wicked growth, and then there was an explosion of blood, front and back. I'd seen it a hundred times hunting. Callicles was a dead boy.

All four of them killed a boy, like farmers cutting weeds. The leader killed a second boy next to Hermogenes.

Hermogenes fell to the ground without being touched, and then used his javelin to trip the lead Spartan. He went down in a clatter of armour, but he was up in less time than it takes to tell the sentence. Yet he was off balance and he was using his shield hand to push himself off the ground. Calchas had taught me better than that.

It was my worst throw of the day. I was terrified and elated at the same time, and my Deer Killer went into his left arm behind his shield, pinning the arm against the shield back. And he couldn't get it out.

The others stopped to help him, because he was bellowing, and *then* Hermogenes grabbed me and helped me run.

By all the gods, my thugater – I thought those were my last moments, and when we were clear of the Spartans, I vowed that

I would never, ever put my body in front of the phalanx again. I vowed it like a drunkard vowing not to drink.

Hermogenes and I got clear of the right flank. We had no idea where the other boys were. Then we lay down in the grass and heaved. Ares! We were alive. Wait until you bear a child, honey – you'll feel the same rush of *eudaimonia* unless Artemis comes for you. Avert!

But when we looked up, the Spartans were charging.

They came forward to the music of pipes. And all the giants going to war with Father Zeus couldn't have looked more dangerous or noble.

The rest of the Peloponnesians hesitated, and the Athenians came forward cautiously, but they came on, and the Plataeans weren't cowards. They went forward into the Spartans.

The two lines hit each other like – well, like two phalanxes coming together. Imagine every cook in this town with every bronze kettle and a wooden spoon flailing away at it. Imagine every man bellowing with all his might. That is the sound of the storm of bronze, the battle line.

Hermogenes and I watched from the safety of the far right. And we saw what happened when the Spartiates hit our fathers.

They reaped them like wheat, that's what happened.

What made the reputation of Plataea was not that our men were great fighters – at least, not that day. What forged our reputation for ever was that our men wouldn't run. But Hermogenes and I watched men die. It was horrible – and awe-inspiring. The two blocks of spearmen crashed into each other at the same speed, and not a man flinched. Spartans tell me that they remember that day well – because so few foes withstand the impact, yet the men of Plataea slammed in, aspis to aspis. And then the killing started.

We watched as the helmet plumes in the front rank went down. It took only seconds and it seemed as if the whole front rank was gone. And then the Plataeans gave ground – grudgingly – but they lost ten steps.

I think it was Pater who stopped it from being a rout. Pater gave ground, but Bion says he killed a man – a spear thrust to the throat against a Spartiate file-leader. Then he and Bion pushed into the gap and Bion says they each took a man down. No one cares in the heat of a fight whether you kill your man as long as you put him down.

In that little eddy of the overall whirlpool of Plataean defeat, the

Spartans hesitated. How often did men push through their front rank? I think it was Pater. I could see the plume on his helmet when the others, like Myron's, were gone. And then the file-closers planted their feet and pushed at the back of the Plataean lines, and suddenly the Plataeans weren't moving back – they were standing firm.

But some of the Spartans had broken through the front ranks, where men were capable and expected to fight. Soon they were pounding the rear ranks to ruin, killing like the machines that they were.

A few men broke from the rear of our phalanx and ran – and Simon must have been one of them. But elsewhere, our neighbours closed their files and shocked the Spartans who'd broken their ranks, crushing them like insects, stabbing them front and rear. There's a reason why breaking ranks is punishable by law, and a reason why veterans call it foolish. The Spartans thought that we'd break – but we didn't, and their young men died.

Who knows how long the men of Plataea would have held the Spartans? Another fifty heartbeats, perhaps. Perhaps less. The Spartans were going to win. The miracle of Ares is that our men stood their ground at all. They held for the time a goat takes to birth a kid – the time it takes a smith to make a sheet into a bowl with a few quick blows of skill.

But the Peloponnesians didn't know any of this. What they saw was that the Athenians outnumbered them, and that their precious masters were being held up by a bunch of farmers from Boeotia.

The allies broke like songbirds faced with an eagle. They broke before the Athenians even hit them. They ran before the spears crossed, and not one of them stood. The Spartan king cursed, no doubt, and then backed his phalanx away, step by step. Unbeaten. Virtually victorious. But they backed away, and the Plataeans had *just barely* clung to their formation. From where we stood, Hermogenes and I knew that more men had started to flee from the back of our deep block. But enough stood to hold on.

*Just barely.*

Plataea was never the same.

No one cheered.

I've been on a hundred fields, honey. I've won against the odds and seen black defeat, but that's the only time I've seen men so shattered *by victory* that they couldn't cheer. Nor did they pursue. The men of

Plataea shifted and recovered their ranks, because they were good men, and then they stood, silent, awed by their own success. Then some of the fallen began to stand up – Myron got to his feet, bleeding from a thigh, the red coming in little spurts where something big had been cut.

Let me tell you how it is in the line, honey. When you go down – and you can fall just because you lose your balance – why, then you won't ever get up in that fight. Against honourable men, if you stay down and pull your shield over your body, no one will kill you just for sport. Maybe they will strip your armour if they win, but no one will kill you. You hope.

Anyway, Myron stood and began to sing. He sang the 'Ravens of Apollo' from the Daidala and all the voices of Plataea took it up, boys and men. We all knew it. It was an odd song for a battlefield – the song men sing while they wait for the ravens to pick us a tree to make the statue of the fake bride. Who knows why Myron chose that song?

Across the field, the Athenians were slowing. They'd never reached the Peloponnesians, and now, ranks untouched, they were coming to a halt and heads were turning to look at us.

Just two stades away, the Spartans halted in perfect order, covering their camp.

The Plataeans kept singing.

Then Cleomenes made a mistake. He didn't trust the Thebans, and his Peleponnesian allies were running all the way back to their homes. And the Plataean farmers were singing as if they could stop the Spartans every day, for ever. That song had more effect on the battle than Pater's stand, honey. That song was defiance of a different sort. Whether it was true or not, the 'Ravens of Apollo' told Cleomenes that there were men opposing him who would not flinch if he came on again. And if we held him for a hundred heartbeats, then all the hoplites in Attica would be in his flank.

Cleomenes sent a herald. He requested a truce to collect his dead.

By our law of war, this ended the battle and allowed the defeated free passage home. And it meant that, whatever the Thebans might do, the Spartans were done.

What changed our world was that Cleomones sent the herald to *us* rather than to the Athenians. That was respect. They knew they were the better men, and men who are better are never petty. They respect accomplishment, and they respected that we *tried*.

So their herald came and he walked towards Pater. Pater looked around, but the archon was dead and Myron, who had started the song, was down again – sitting on a rock, supported by his sons. Pater had two wounds on his sword arm; I had his helmet under my arm and he was pouring his canteen over his head.

'Hey!' Bion called. 'Hey – look sharp, Technes! The herald is coming.'

Pater looked up, and there was the Spartan, resplendent in his scarlet cloak, with a heavy bronze staff to show his status. He bowed.

Pater returned his bow, head dripping water. I remember how the water from his canteen mixed with the blood on his hands and arms.

'Cleomenes, King of Sparta, requests your permission to retrieve and bury his dead,' the herald intoned.

Pater didn't smile. I did – I was wearing a smile as big a wolf's. Hermogenes had his father's aspis on his own arm and he was grinning like a fool. Bion was grinning too. But Pater simply nodded.

'Our archon is dead, and our polemarch is badly wounded.' Pater turned to the Plataeans. 'Am I in command?' he asked.

Again there was no cheer – just a soft grumble. But every man in the first two ranks nodded. So Pater turned back to the herald.

'The Plataeans grant the truce,' he said. No mention of himself or his own name. Oh, he made me proud.

And with those words, the Battle of Oinoe came to an end. The Athenians killed a hundred Peloponnesians, more or less – the slow ones, I assume, since the Peloponnesian allies didn't linger to fight. They put up a magnificent trophy on the Acropolis, a chariot and a set of slave fetters, to celebrate their victory over the Spartans. The Medes later pulled it down and took the bronze, but the base is still there with eight lines of verse. They don't mention us. But on the day, they treated us like heroes come to earth. Miltiades ran up, his plume nodding, and embraced Pater and then every man he could find. His investment had paid off.

Men began to trickle off the ground. We had our dead to bury, and the Spartan helots were coming for their own.

We had forty-five dead. Seven of them died in the week after the battle, so on that morning, we had thirty-eight bodies. And one of them was my brother. He lay with his face to the enemy, a Spartan spear in his right side under his sword arm. He fell clutching the spear, and the other fifth- and sixth-rankers brought the Spartan down and killed him because my brother held that spear point with his dying hands.

I wept. Pater wept. Bion and Hermogenes wept, and Myron and Dionysius wept. We all cried.

The Spartans had nine dead. Two more died later – so we lost forty-five to their eleven. If you want to understand the heart of phalanx fighting, honey – and I can see you don't – you need to see that Pater killed three of those Spartans and that our whole thousand lived or died by the actions of a few valiant men. Myron didn't give a foot of ground. Bion followed Pater into the hole Pater made. Epictetus and his son gave ground, but then they locked their shields with men in the second rank and held the rush, and Dionysius killed a Spartan in the fifth rank when they broke through. Take away any of those actions and the result is different.

Karpos, our best potter, died, and Theron, son of Xenon, who made all the harnesses and wineskins and much of the armor the men wore. Pater said he was the first to die, a Spartan spear in his throat at the first contact, and he didn't live to see Cleomenes come to us for truce – after refusing our embassy.

We buried the dead – the boys and the slaves did the work. The men sat and drank. They had endured the storm of bronze for the time it takes a man to run the stadion, and they were exhausted.

That night it rained. We were wet and cold, but Pater came and wrapped his arms and his heavy Thracian cloak around me. He was still crying, but he held me tightly, and after a while I slept.

The rain stopped, and I was cooking eggs – I'd purchased a Boeotian hatful from a shy girl who had crept into our camp with the dawn. I used Pater's money, and his flash of a not-quite-smile told me I'd done right. I had a fine bronze *patera* with the figure of Apollo as the handle. It wasn't Pater's work – it was his father's work, and the planishing on the pan was like a reminder of greater days. If we'd lost, it would have been loot for a Spartan.

Miltiades came to Pater with a wagon. He had a dozen Athenians with him, important men with Tyrian purple in their cloaks. Pater was eating a bowl of eggs with a scrap of stale bread.

'Technes of Plataea, all Athens mourns your losses.' Miltiades bowed.

He had a priestess of Athena with him, and she was dressed, even at that hour, in the whitest chiton I'd ever seen, with gold thread in the hems. Bumpkin that I was, I couldn't take my eyes off her.

Pater had a mouth full of egg. He swallowed. His eyes were red from weeping, and he wore a damp *chitoniskos* of linen that had once been off white and neatly pleated, and was now grey with age and shapeless. There were slaves in our force who dressed better than Pater.

He rose to his feet. 'I was not chosen in the assembly to lead the men of Plataea,' he said formally. 'But until the assembly chooses another, I accept your words on behalf of all the men of our city.'

Miltiades spread his arms wide. It was interesting to watch him be a public man – I had only seen him at close range. He was about twenty-five then. Just coming into his powers.

'Plataea brought one eighth of the force we had to face the Peloponnesians,' Miltiades said. 'We offer Plataea one quarter of all that we took with our spears, and we call you the bravest of the allies.'

The wind ruffled their cloaks. Pater said nothing, but the men of Plataea behind him were gathering, and they began to shout – approval, almost a cheer. Then the priestess stepped forward and she chanted a prayer to the Lady, and all the men present joined her. Then she purified us, for killing. She was good – her voice was gentle and firm, and every man felt better for her words, and the spirit of the goddess that we call the Lady and Athenians call Athena was on all of us.

Miltiades invited Pater and Myron to attend him at a meeting of the commanders. I found Pater my best chlamys, and I put it on him with a gold pin from the loot. Pater was above such things, but Myron gave me a nod of approval. No one wanted Pater to look like a ragman in front of the Athenians.

The two of them came back before the sun was high, and their faces were strained, and Pater had black marks in the corners of his eyes. Pater ignored my questions, and sent me and Hermogenes and every other boy we could find to assemble all the Plataeans.

There were only a thousand hoplites and another thousand boys and slaves. We assembled before the birds stopped singing. We were on the hilltop by the old fort, and Pater and Myron carried spears, as if they, jointly, were Speakers. Pater nodded at Myron, and Myron held up his spear.

'Men of Plataea!' he said. He was leather-pale. He'd lost quite a

74

bit of blood, and he walked carefully where the Athenian doctor had burned the wound near his groin. He might have been a walking dead man, if the deadly archer willed it. But Myron had the courage that allows a man to go about his business, even with a wound. 'The archon died serving the city. We have no new archon and we have no *strategos*.'

'Who cares?' someone called. 'Let's go home. We can debate in the assembly!'

'Men of Plataea,' Myron said. His voice was quiet, but men were silent to listen to him. 'The army of Thebes is a day's march away, and the men of Athens call on us to stay and fight.'

That was greeted with a wave of grumbles and muttering.

Pater stood forth. He held up his own spear. 'Don't be fools!' he shouted. 'We fight them tomorrow with Athens by our side, or we face them in a month at home, alone.' That shut them up. Then Pater nodded. 'We stopped Sparta!' he said. 'What has Thebes got?'

Now they cheered. Everyone hated Thebes. Sparta was a noble and scary monster from travellers' tales, but Thebes was the familiar enemy.

Myron pointed at Pater. 'I move that Technes of the Corvaxae be strategos.'

They didn't roar. Pater had none of the magnetism that can make men love you. But every hand went in the air.

Myron nodded to Pater. Pater pointed his spear at Myron. 'I move that Myron of the house of Heracles be archon of the Plataeans until we stand in the assembly.'

And so it was done.

Before the day was another hour older, the shield-bearers were packing. We had donkeys now – dozens, as part of the spoils of the Peloponnesian camp. I was trying to figure out a foreign pack frame on a stubborn beast when Pater's hand fell on my shoulder.

'Take your brother's armour,' he said. 'And take Hermogenes as your shield-bearer. You will stand with the men tomorrow. No more playing with the boys.'

And just like that, I was a hoplite.

# 5

We marched east, across Attica, and the Thebans retired before us, confused by this turn of events. I sweated in my brother's armour, and Pater adjusted it at an Attic forge, borrowing tools to change the waist of my brother's bell corslet and the pinch of his greaves. His helmet fitted me very well.

Pater wept while he worked.

By the third day, we thought that the Thebans would melt away, and then we had word that there was yet another army coming – from Euboea. The Euboeans hated Athens. Truth to tell, Athens is arrogant and most cities hate her.

Then Miltiades' father showed why he was a strategos to be reckoned with. He woke us four hours before dawn, and we left our fires burning and the slaves and boys to watch them, and we marched east and then north. Men who travelled said we were somewhere near Tanagra. I only knew that the weight of my dead brother's arms, his panoply, was the same as the weight of a five-year-old girl, and I was carrying it over a mountain.

Miltiades the Elder had a good plan – to march around the Thebans and catch them napping, and force them to fight, cut off from the Euboeans. But the Thebans were no fools. They had spies and scouts, and their slaves probably traded food with our slaves. They knew we were coming, and they marched in the dark, too, determined to ambush us on the flanks of Mount Parnes. And as with most battles, neither plan bore the least resemblance to the mess that followed.

Plataeans were the left of the army, and this meant that we were the rearguard – the last men to march. Crossing the flank of Mount Parnes on goat tracks, we marched in double file – two wide. It took hours to go a few stades, and where I trudged, we seemed to stop more than we walked.

By the luck of tribe and farm, I walked next to Simon. No one had mentioned that he had run from the Spartans. I didn't even *know* that he had run – only two or three men had broken, and while I was pretty sure he was one, he wore a plain old helmet with no crest and he had no blazon on the leather face of his shield – like most of our men. Now he walked beside me, and we did not talk.

He was much taller and broader than me. Indeed, I was thirteen, and too young to stand the storm of bronze, but I think that Pater felt that we needed to make up the holes in our phalanx. Who knows what he thought? He never discussed such stuff with me. At any rate, Simon was a head taller and much heavier with muscle. And in the dark, on the flanks of Parnes, I learned what he really was.

His spear-butt flashed in the moon and I ducked. And then he used his hip and almost pushed me off the trail – and off the mountain.

Calchas, dead Calchas, saved my life. Rough-housing with a bigger, stronger man had taught me many tricks. I swayed, armour and all, and got my feet planted. Simon kept right on walking, and the man in the file behind me cursed.

That was the first of three times he tried to trip me, and once I think he meant to put his spear-butt through my eye. But I was wary, and after the third time, someone in the file – we were all neighbours, and Myron's Dionysius was right ahead of me – someone said something to our phylarch, old Epictetus, and he trotted back and asked Simon what he was doing.

Simon flashed me a smile. 'I'm just clumsy,' he said. 'And this boy can't really carry the weight of his panoply.'

Epictetus peered at me. I had my helmet up on my head and I was sweating like a deer bleeding out. I tried to grin.

'Too heavy for you?' he asked.

'No,' I said. 'Simon's a bastard.'

Epictetus shot him a glare. 'Yep,' he said. Most of our file laughed. 'Watch yourself, Simon. I'm watching you.'

That's when I think Simon decided to kill us. Right there on the mountain. Up until then, I think he just hated us quietly. But I called him a bastard, and old Epictetus agreed, and everyone laughed, and the fates spun.

We were the last. Miltiades and his tribe were the first. And the Thebans were waiting in ambush. It should have been a disaster.

There's no better position for a phalanx than catching your opponent strung out over a goat track.

But the Thebans moved late, and they were late straggling into their ambush site. Hoplites don't usually ambush each other. Maybe they felt unmanly. Who knows what a Theban thinks? At any rate, they fucked it all up.

The result was that their men blundered into Miltiades in the dark. Instead of an ambush, we had a mob fight in the first light.

The first I knew was that the files started to move faster, and then they stopped, and then we could hear it – fighting. One battle made me an expert. But this didn't sound like the fight with the Spartans. This sounded like Chaos come to earth, and it was.

Neither side ever got a phalanx formed. That's what everyone remembers about the Battle of Parnes. Our files and theirs poured into each other in the scrubby, broken ground on the northern shoulder of the mountain, and the push of men behind kept adding fighters. It was so dark that, with your face inside your helmet, you couldn't be sure of the man on your right or left unless you tapped their shield with your own. Twice, Epictetus stopped us without orders and formed our files up close. He was doing what he knew how to do – forming the block that would keep us safe. But both times the path soon narrowed to nothing again and we had to file off.

An hour after we first heard the fighting – exhausted with the fear of waiting and the fatigue of marching – we rounded a bend and saw the fight. The sun was a red ball on the horizon to the east, and we caught glimpses of the sea to the north as the trail climbed and dipped, and then the fight was right there, a spear's throw away.

I could see Pater's double plume. He was standing still, shield against his knees, arms crossed.

The valley was full of men locked in combat, and it was a swirl of death. Because the armies had never formed, no man had a front or a back, and there was no safety and no shield wall.

The Athenians were begging us to come on, COME ON! And still Pater looked out over the valley. I, for one, was in no hurry to plunge into that maelstrom.

And then Pater made his decision. I could see it in the set of his shoulders and the movement of his back. He made his decision and we were moving – not down into the battle, but across the hillside to the north. Pater began to run, and the files ran after him.

It might seem a simple thing, to lead a thousand men around a battle that is only two stades or so wide. One man can run the stade in the time another man sings a song, but a thousand men take a hundred times longer, or so it seems when the fate of your city rests on the outcome. And we were scared, honey. We'd been promised a stratagem and an easy fight, and this was chaos and death.

Pater ran north and the files followed him. Just over the brow of the low hill where you first see the polis at Tanagra in the distance, he turned west, halted and ordered the files to form. That was easy. He'd picked a piece of flat ground, and each file ran up, directed by their phylarch and Pater's spear, and they halted to the left of the file before them, so that in the time it took the sun to rise a finger's breadth, the phalanx was formed, minus the cowards and the men who couldn't make the run.

I made it.

Simon didn't. I wonder what he might have done had he made it to the front, but the run left him behind. About sixty men stayed in the rear. This always happens. So the phylarchs say a few words to the men who make it to the fight, and then they close the files.

Suddenly I was in the fourth rank. My hand was cold and clammy on Deer Killer. I had a heavy javelin to go with her, and that's all I had. I had no sword. On the other hand, I had armour like the best men.

Epictetus put me in the fourth rank because, in his opinion, I was more fit for combat than the eight men behind me. He was right. But at the time I thought him a monster for putting me so close to the front.

I was one file from the far right. Bion was my file-leader, and Pater was about a spear's length away when we closed our ranks and files in the *synaspismos*.

Then we sang the Paean. Usually men sing it before they charge, but not always. I don't know what happened to the Paean at Oinoe – whether I have forgotten it, or whether we didn't sing it. But I was *in* the phalanx at Parnes, and I remember singing, roaring my fear out inside the bronze helmet that my brother had died wearing.

In the closed ranks, you are three feet from the men on either side, so that the rim of your shield can just touch if you move to tap them – something men do all the time as they wait. You start a few feet from the men in front and behind, but as a fight goes on, everything closes in. Well, that's what usually happens. You end up in a tight-packed mob that pushes together and sees only with the eyes of the front rank. In that fight, I had no idea what was happening in front of us from the moment that our files closed up. I could see Dionysius's leather-clad back, and I could see Pater's plumes and the rim of my own aspis.

We pushed forward.

We marched together to the sound of the Paean. We had a slight hill behind us and we went down the hill and then our front slammed into the fight. Friends? Enemies? The front of a phalanx has no allies. We went down into the fight, and the only sign I had that Pater was facing death was an increased pressure on my shield.

But they melted in front of us. I stepped over a man who was down. I looked down – hard enough in a helmet – and saw his eyes peeking over the rim of his shield, and the black blood on his legs. I let him live, and so did everyone else.

We started to plough through the maelstrom. Dust rose with the sun, and the battle was *not* ending. We pushed forward a step at a time, and I was hot and miserable, my spear held point-up so that it wouldn't foul the men ahead of me. Sometimes the man behind me – a middle-aged farmer from two farms beyond us, a bitter man named Zotikos – pushed too hard, and I was sandwiched between the curved front of his aspis and the curved back of my own. I was too small for this, and it hurt.

Zotikos always apologized to me every time he slammed in. 'Sorry, kid!' he'd grunt. 'No good at this shit!' He was pale with fear – but he pushed.

I know – now – what happened in the front rank, but at the time I knew nothing except that Pater was alive, because I could see his plumes and hear his voice. And we should have been winning an easy victory – we were the only formed troops on the field, and the Thebans were outnumbered.

Maybe they were stubborn Boeotians, just like us.

Maybe the phalanx isn't as important as men think. To be honest, I've seen unformed mobs stop a phalanx several times. Only Ares knows. We pushed forward and our front-rankers stabbed with their spears, Athenians rallied on our right and Thebans melted away, and then, suddenly, we stopped.

Calchas was right – it is the killers who are dangerous. The rest of war is very like a sport. Like pushing and pulling and spear-fencing all together. But when the killers come, it is nothing like a sport.

I don't know who they were. A brotherhood? Some men who had trained together as boys? Or more likely, a band of aristocrats. They had good armour and they knew their business. Perhaps they were mercenaries. At any rate, they hit our phalanx when we were tired and lazy and confident that nothing would stand against us. Epictetus went down and, as I raised my head to look, Dionysius took a blow to the helmet and down he went.

And just like that, I was in the front rank, facing a killer. I had all the time it took him to push past Dionysius to see that he was clad from head to foot in bronze, with thigh guards and arm guards and knuckle guards like a professional, and he had a bronze-faced shield and a heavy spear and a double plume of red.

*You must lock your shield with your neighbour's, put your head down and refuse to take chances.* That's what Calchas said.

When you are faced with a killer in the bronze storm, there are two things that tempt you. One is to run. That way lies instant death. The time to run has long passed when the man in bronze is at the end of your spear. The other temptation is to attack. This is a twin child born of the same parent – fear. You attack to prove to yourself that you are not afraid, and because you have no real hope. Or to get it over with. I have seen lesser men kill greater, but it doesn't happen often, so the second is as hopeless as the first, although it makes a better story for your mother. Because you'll be dead.

Calchas's way is the way that takes care, and time, and discipline. But as Dionysius fell, his aspis fouled the killer's spear and I got a breath to think.

I backed one step and shoved my aspis *high* and hard against the man next to me. He was Eutykos, a young man from a good family. Later on we were friends, and I loved his sister. I'd met her, of course, at festivals, and she was pretty – but at thirteen you don't look at girls as much as you should. Hah!

So I locked my shield with Eutykos and the killer's doru crashed into my aspis – high. He was going for my helmet, but I had tucked my head so that only the top of the helmet came above the rim of my aspis. He swung again and his doru glanced off my helmet, but I had no crest to catch the point and he lost his balance and crashed against me, breast to breast.

Old Zotikos stood his ground. He threw his shoulder against my back and held me against the killer's shove, bless him. And he went one better. While the killer rained blows of his spear on my head and aspis, Zotikos rammed his spear into the killer's shield, full force.

I got to breathe.

Eutykos poked at him, too.

On my left, Straton, Myron's older son, locked his aspis against mine.

Only then did I realize that the voice shrieking 'Lock up!' was mine.

Now the killer was facing three men – six, really, because none of our followers flinched – and the spear points were coming for him.

Locked up and secure, we began to kill him. I have no idea who got him. Later, my spear point was bloody and the blood dripped down the shaft and over my hand. But Zotikos also had blood on his and so did Straton. Perhaps we all took him. It doesn't matter. No man – no man born of women – can face six steady hoplites, even if they are so scared that shit runs down their legs.

That one fight was the battle, for me. I'm sure that other men did great deeds, and I am sure that the prize of honour went to Miltiades the Younger, who cut a red swath through the Thebans and broke their centre. His sword was like a thunderbolt, so men said.

I never saw him. By Ares, I didn't even see Pater, and I could have touched him with my spear point.

But I saw the killer, and I held my ground.

Still makes me smile, honey.

And then the Thebans broke and we ran them down.

I killed some poor exhausted sod who begged me to spare him. But he didn't drop his sword and I was too tired to take a chance. Hard to tell what was in my head. I asked his shade for pardon the next day. I think that if he'd let the sword go, or stopped waving it, I'd have let him live. When the pursuit starts, the shield wall collapses, winner or loser, and every man fights on his own. Eutykos stuck by me, but none of the rest of my file-mates were anywhere to be seen, and we picked up prisoners and fought our last fight in the middle of a thousand screaming Attic farmers. Some brightly armoured aristocrat knocked me flat and another yelled 'Can't you see the yokel is a Plataean?' and they ran off elsewhere.

We had no dead. Dionysius was deeply unconscious, and he slurred his words for ten days and missed the third fight, but he lived to thank me for covering his body. That's what his father thought I did, and it saved my life later.

We picked up our wounded and treated them as best we could. The Athenians had taken it much worse. They had hundreds of dead.

The Thebans had more. The north end of the valley was carpeted with Theban dead. We stripped them with gusto. Their herald came and they made their submission, and Myron hobbled off – Pater couldn't even walk, he was so tired – and on that very spot on the south bank of the Asopus, the boundaries of free Plataea were settled between archons and heralds, a deputation of Corinthians – neutrals, and honest men – settling the matter and guaranteeing it.

Myron was no fool – by settling the borders and not making high demands, he ensured that the treaty would last, and he ensured that he would be elected archon. And by enlisting the arbitration of Corinth, he won us another ally.

As I said, we stripped their dead. Our boys and slaves brought the camp up, and we loaded carts with Theban camp furniture and Theban armour. Pater got quite a bit – he was strategos.

A tribunal met and discussed Simon. He was not the only man to miss the fight, but he was no man's friend and his cowardice was a public disgrace. Even other men who had missed the fight – too tired to keep up, they claimed – complained about him.

Simon spoke well enough in his own defence. And he knew, as we all knew, that we still had to fight the Euboeans. So he asked that he be allowed to fight in the front rank.

The phylarchs discussed it and refused, but they put him in the second rank, behind Bion. Two men in front of me. To earn back the respect of other men.

After the tribunal, Pater told me that he'd asked that I have that spot. And so the gods speak to us, thugater. If I had stood there – well, I would be a bronze-smith in Boeotia and you would never have been born.

I was tired after the fight and I slept before the light failed, but the next day I was full of energy. That's how it is for the young, honey. You recover fast. Pater and Epictetus and Myron took much longer.

We sent the spoils home over Cithaeron and marched east, into the rising sun, to fight the Euboeans. It was insane – three battles, in a week. Ah, you brighten – you've *heard* of the 'Week of Three Battles', eh?

I was there, honey. And after the first two, the Plataeans thought that they were gods. And the Athenians the same. I said that every army has a heart, a soul, eyes and ears. After the Thebans, that army was *as one*. We were still Atticans and Boeotians, Athenians and Plataeans, but we shared water and wine and jokes.

Not one of us doubted that we would rout the Euboeans.

They were soft. Their days of greatness were in the past and they had hoped to ride on a chariot of war driven by Thebes and Sparta. Now their mighty allies were gone, and their army marched back out of Boeotia, over the bridge at Chalcis, and stood waiting for us.

It was just seven days since the Spartans had sent their herald to Pater when we marched over the bridge around midday. We did it well – we'd been together for two weeks and by Greek standards we'd become veterans. I was in my *second* fight as a hoplite and my shin still hurt from the rock a week before. And I could see Simon, two places in front of me, as we closed our files to the right.

The Euboeans formed very close and stood with their shields overlapping, awaiting our charge. They didn't come forward, and to me, at thirteen, they didn't look soft at all.

We marched in easy, open order until we were a stone's throw away. If they had any psiloi, they didn't come out. Neither did ours.

Then we closed. We closed by doubling our files from the rear, so that seventh-rank men became front-rank men – the 'half-file' leaders. This was the closest order. I remained in the fourth rank, and Zotikos was now in the front. He swore and complained and grumbled as we closed, and Bion told him to keep it clean for the gods, and Zotikos said something under his breath and older men laughed.

Now we were a spear's throw from them. We were locked up in the same close order. We were on the left, and again we were facing the cream of their warriors – the men with the best armour, the right of their line.

Pater stood clear of our line. It was the only time I ever heard him speak before a fight, at least for so long. 'We're going to walk forward in time to the Paean, just as we did at Parnes. And when we hit their shield wall, we push straight on. Use your shoulders. Their line is thin, and they are already afraid. We have faced Sparta. We have nothing to fear here.'

Men beat their spears on the face of their shields.

Miltiades came running down the face of the army. When he was in front of the left-most Athenians, he raised his spear.

'Sing!' he called, even as an enterprising Euboean threw a spear at him.

Insults were called. We ignored them, although they were so close we could see faces, shield devices, bad teeth and good teeth. Pater started the song and every voice picked it up. We sang the first verse standing and then the whole army – Athenians and Plataeans – moved forward.

Perhaps our line wasn't perfect, but I remember it as perfect. And when we were a spear's length from the Euboeans, I knew we'd won. A veteran at the age of thirteen, I knew as surely as if Athena sat on one shoulder and Ares on the other that the men of Euboea would break when our shields hit theirs.

We must have had a bow in our line – because Pater and Bion hit them a heartbeat before the rest of the line, or perhaps the Euboean line had a curve in it. We hit, and the front opened like a door. Pater's helmet flashed in the brilliant noontime sun, and his plumes shone like the wings of some god-sent bird, and we gave a great shout as the aspides clashed and their line broke up the way a pot breaks when dropped on flagstones from a height.

Even as the Euboeans broke, I saw Pater fall. I saw the way his head turned, and I saw that he fell forward as if pushed, and I know now as if I had seen it that Simon had stabbed him in the back, under his back plate. But I couldn't see, and battle deprives a man of many of his wits. All I thought at the time was that Pater was down, though the battle was already won.

*Pater was down.* Somehow I got my legs on either side of his chest and stood my ground, because the Euboeans weren't beaten. Their front ranks crumbled but then stiffened, much as ours must have done against the Spartans, and they came back at us like men. I saw Simon with a short sword in his hand, dripping blood. He was green, his lips were white with fear and his eyes met mine.

I didn't see it – oh, I'll tell it in its place. But that's when the Euboeans counter-attack struck, and I wasn't in the fourth rank any more, because I wouldn't give over Pater's body. I had no idea if he was alive or dead, but I stood my ground like a fool, and then, in that moment, I found out why old men and poets call it the *storm of bronze.* I got my dead brother's aspis up, and the hammering knocked me down over Pater – I was too small to stand the pressure of ten or fifteen weapons beating against my shield.

But other Plataeans crowded in around me. They saw who was down and they were men, too. They pushed and killed. I could smell the copper of blood, the heavy waft of excrement that men release when they go down, the cardamom and onions they'd eaten for lunch. I got a knee under me and pushed my spear under the press and felt the soft, yielding resistance of flesh as I cut some poor bastard's sinews.

Then I took my first wound. It's this one, see? And it saved my life, as you'll hear. Right through the top of the thigh, honey – some big bastard stood over me and pushed his spear right down over my aspis. It didn't cut the muscle, praise to Ares, but I went down, blood spurting between my fingers, with Deer Killer forgotten in the Euboean grass. I fell on top of Pater.

I made the mistake of falling forward over my shield, and some Euboean bastard hit me on the head.

When I awoke, I was rolling in my own filth and vomit, wearing the shackles of a slave.

# Part II

## *Some Made Slaves*

War is the king and father of all, and some he shows as gods, others as men; some men are freed, and some are made slaves.

Heraclitus, fr. 53

# 6

Hard to imagine what that awakening was like for me.

I had a fever. My wound was oozing pus – not that I knew that yet, I was off my head. And I had never been on a ship. I had no idea why I was wet, why the world swayed, why it was so cold.

It didn't take me long to know, to *know*, honey, that I was dead and in Tartarus for some forgotten sin. I didn't *think* that I was dead. I *knew* it. I flailed and swallowed my own filth. I was shackled under a rowing bench in the bottom rank of rowers. No one expected me to row – only free men rowed, back then – but I was shackled flat with eight other slaves, destined for market. Not that I understood. I knew nothing.

I went down again.

I awoke a second time when a tall man poured water over me while another man held his nose. They looked at the pus – that's when I saw my leg, red and angry and inflamed – and flinched. The tall man with the pointed beard prodded my leg and I was gone again.

I surfaced a third time in a pen, somewhere in Asia, I learned. I wasn't shackled, but my thigh still bled pus like a boy's spots. I had a fever like a child. And the other slaves – there were hundreds – avoided me as if I had the plague. For all they knew, I did. Slaves don't help each other, honey. That lesson hits you right away, when you go from the brotherhood of the phalanx to slavery.

I was never completely out again. I raved – and no one bought me. I wasn't worth an obol. The wound on my thigh wept pus, as they say, and because of it, no one buggered me, not even the sick bastards who live at the bottom of the muck of the slave trade. No one made me play their flute, or any of the other things they do to slave boys and girls. You ever wonder why Harmonia flinches every time you move your hand, honey? You don't want to know.

89

Have you seen the kind of slaves who sit in corners rambling, talking crazy, and never raise their eyes? No – you haven't. I never buy 'em, not even for rough work. People can be broken, just like toys.

I missed being broken because I was so disgusting. Bless the Lord of the Silver Bow and his deadly arrows. His ravens sit on my shield to this day because of that beautiful, stinking pus. I watched it – they raped a boy until he stopped complaining just a spear's length from where I lay. He was Thracian, and he got up silently from their abuse and killed himself, ripping his guts out with a stick, but few are so determined. Honey, you have no idea what a person can put up with, what depth of cowardice we discover when, by small surrenders, we can stay alive. Eh?

Oh, yes. Me, too. I'm sure I'd have given in. I was just a boy, and unlike the brave Thracian, I was utterly disoriented. I couldn't imagine how I'd come to be a slave, and I couldn't get my feet under me, so to speak, and I had a wound.

The slaves themselves prey on the weak. Oh yes! No honour among slaves. I had no food – ever. No honest boy came and brought me bread. They ate my gruel and my soup, and one day I awoke to find two bigger boys discussing my squalor and deciding I wasn't worth 'a fuck' – pardon me, honey, but they meant it. And then they pulled up their rags and pissed on me.

This is harder for you than the death of Pater, isn't it? Hard to picture the noble aristocrat as a victim, your own father with boys raining yellow urine in contempt. Hard to imagine me as a worthless slave. The dishonour. The shame. Eh?

Listen, honey – you know what Achilles says? *Better to be the slave of a bad master than King of the Dead.* Right? I was *alive*.

I told you that I tell the truth, at least as I remember it. Who is this fellow you've brought to listen to me? You look like an Ionian, young man. Well – eat well. You are my guest, and guest-friendship still counts for something, eh?

Odd as it sounds, I've always thought that the urine saved me. Being pissed on. It made me angry, and I think it washed the wound. Persians and Aegyptians use piss that way. Maybe not. Maybe the Deadly Archer simply looked the other way and I healed.

But, by the Lady, I was weak. I was so weak that I couldn't stand. I hadn't eaten for two weeks at least. I didn't even know where I was, but I knew that I was angry, and I wasn't going to die so that they could defecate on my corpse. I decided that I had to eat. And to eat,

I had to fight off all comers and take food. The thing is, I couldn't fight. I could barely drag myself to the place where the food trough was filled. The boys who ate the most food were bigger, tougher, and none of them had a wound.

I'd like to say that I thought of something noble, like the Plataeans at Oinoe. They didn't win by fighting better. They merely refused to break. Fair enough. But I didn't really have a thought in my head. I was an animal. I decided that if I could endure pain, I could eat. I noticed that other slaves tried to take their food off into a corner and eat, like animals on a kill ripping a haunch and running. But it occurred to me in my feverish desperation that I could simply eat while they beat me. I'd tear food out of their hands and put it in my mouth. I've seen a starving cat do the same, on a wharf in Aegypt.

That was my plan, and it worked well enough.

It only worked because they feared the guards.

We had Scythian guards. Now that I know the Sakje better, I suspect that few, if any, were actually Sakje. They were probably a rabble of Persian bastards, half-Medes, half-Sakje and Bactrians. Scum. But armed scum, soldiers with bows.

They didn't do a lot, except prevent escape and punish us if we hurt each other too much. After all, we were worth money. But they watched us with the lazy, amused contempt of the better man for the worse. All free people know they are better than slaves. Slaves have no honour, no beauty, no dignity, nothing that makes them worth knowing. Why? It's all taken from them with their freedom, that's why. The ones who might have had dignity kill themselves.

They watched us for entertainment. They loved it when we fought, and they would wager money on their favourites.

One old fellow had wagered money that I would live. I figured it out from listening to him argue – he felt that I'd already beaten the odds. So the first day that I decided to eat, when I grabbed bread from the trough and stuck it in my mouth, and when a bigger man hit me with his fist, I kept eating.

I took a blow to the head, and my nose broke, and blood sprayed.

I kept eating.

Then the cage opened and the old Sakje waddled in and kicked my tormentor in the head.

I ate his food, too. While he lay unconscious, I ate it all.

The next morning, he was groggy. I ate his food again. His partner, one of the boys who had pissed on me, hit me in the face, where my nose had been broken, and I vomited from the pain. Then I picked up my bread and ate it. Disgusted yet?

In the evening, I felt better, despite the inflammation of my whole face. I got to the food trough and waited.

When the bread loaves began to fall into the trough, I waited for the food mêlée to begin and then I punched the biggest boy in the ear. Down he went. Once he was down, I kicked him in the head and took his bread. While I ate, I kicked him again and hurt my foot.

The next morning, the other slaves gave me space at the trough. My guard laughed when he saw me. Later I heard him demand payment, but the other soldier told him I would be dead before the end of the day. He said this in Ionian Greek, a variant on our language – well, you know, honey. And this fellow you brought with you grew up with it, so I won't bore you with how it still sounds alien to me now.

It didn't take long to realize that my two tormentors were planning to kill me. Murder was not so infrequent in the slave pens. I watched them from under my hair – my lank, filthy hair, full of bugs – and saw they were together. I had united them. Or perhaps they were allies before my coming, although, as I say, such alliances are rare for slaves.

Of course, they were waiting for my Scythian to go off duty.

I watched them, and I waited, and I tried to plan. But I was still wounded, and I was still weak, and they were bigger and tougher and there were two of them.

I was beginning to think of attacking them – if only to get it over with while my Scythian was on duty – when the cage opened and a priest came in. He was fat, and clean, and his eyes were sharper than Deer Killer.

Six of the archers came in behind him. He began to gesture with his staff, and the men and boys he pointed out were taken.

I was the last to be chosen.

Someone was purchasing a packet of slaves – ten or twelve in a single lot. I was being used to make weight, which meant that somebody was getting swindled. I was as likely to die as live.

Slave traders. The very lowest form of life, eh?

We were fettered together by the necks and wrists and marched off up the road. I had no idea where I was, and no idea where I was going, and I didn't care. I had already surrendered. I might not have broken yet, but I was breaking, because I had no one to talk to and no one to care about. I plodded along behind another man, as close as if we were file-mates in the phalanx, and I didn't know his name.

On the other hand, neither of the boys who had wanted me dead were in the purchase. I was going to live, if I could just get through the walk to wherever we were going.

I had thought that the trip over Parnes was the hardest thing I would ever do, marching with all the weight of my brother's armour, but this was far tougher, although the pace was gentle enough. I was touched with the whip only once – for falling – and otherwise we were fairly treated.

We walked some stades. Perhaps my fever was still on me, but I scarcely remember a moment of it. I knew we were by the sea, or perhaps a great river. I assumed we were in Euboea.

For the first time, I wondered how I had come to be a slave, when none of the other men were Plataeans or even Athenians. And as far as I could remember, we were winning the battle when I fell. But that made no sense.

The farther I walked up a long river valley in the brilliant noon sun, the more unlikely it was that I was in Euboea. For one thing, except for the old bridge, Euboea is an island. It has neither great mountains nor a huge river. I was walking along a great river, deep enough to carry a warship with three tiers of oars. It flowed out of a pair of mighty mountains in the purple distance, or so it seemed when I raised my head and looked around.

When we stopped at a well and the guards paid silver for water, the people were small and brown. Not much browner than I was myself, but brown with that flawless skin that marks Lydians and Phrygians – not that I knew that then. And of course our guards were Scythians. I'd seen Scythians in pictures, and Pater had fought some, and Miltiades had fought thousands and run away from others – a story he loved to tell.

As we walked, and my thigh throbbed, I saw that there were trees I didn't know, and the goats were different.

I kept walking. What could I do?

We walked up that valley for a day. I've ridden the distance in an hour – the guards must have had orders to go easy on us – but I never expected to live.

We had a meal of gruel and bread in a village on the flank of a mountain, still above the beautiful river. I squatted next to the safest-looking male.

'Are we in Asia?' I asked.

He looked startled when I spoke. He chewed bread, and his eyes flicked around as he considered his answer. Finally, he nodded. 'Yes,' he said. He pointed up the valley, where something winked like fire. 'Ephesus,' he said.

I was such a bumpkin that I had never heard of Ephesus. 'What's Ephesus?' I asked.

'You are a fool,' he said. And turned his back.

We walked on in the cool of the evening, and before true night fell, we were in the streets of a city more beautiful than anything I had ever seen in Boeotia or Attika. The streets were paved in grey stone. There was a temple that rose from the peak of the acropolis over the town, and it was made of marble. It looked like a house of the gods, and the roof was gold – that was the 'fire' I had seen ten stades away. The houses were brick and stone, every one of them bigger than anything at home. Water flowed from springs through fountains.

It was like a mortal going to Olympus. I had never seen anything like it, and I gaped like the barbarian I was.

The people were tall and handsome, and they looked like Greeks – dark hair, straight noses, fine-breasted women and strong men, with a proportion with fairer skin and red and blond hair. They were taller and more handsome than Boeotians, but not a different race.

I felt even dirtier.

The guards moved us carefully from square to square so that we didn't offend the citizens as they strolled through the cool evening air. But several men and at least one woman stopped to look at us.

Women in Boeotia seldom leave their own farms. I was not used to seeing a half-clothed woman in her prime gawping at slaves and mocking the guards. I stared at her.

She turned and stared back, and then her hand moved and she tried to strike me. I moved my head.

The man with her stopped. He was examining the older man who had called me a fool. Now he turned and looked at me. He was even taller than the other tall men, with the muscles of an athlete and the chiton of a very rich man.

He looked at me for a moment and then threw something at me.

It was a nut. He had been eating nuts, and he threw hard.

I caught it.

He nodded, whispered something to the beautiful woman at his side and turned away. Then the guards moved us on, up the acropolis and into a slave barracks at the bottom of the temple district.

In the morning, I was sold to the man who had thrown the nut. He came in person to collect me. I had no idea what he saw in me, any more than I knew why I was a slave, but the man obviously saw something he liked and bought it – or rather, his beautiful wife did. Later, I came to know that he was simply that way, and his life of random acquisition had probably saved my life and my spirit, for the slaves who went to the temple sometimes became priests, but those who didn't died of the work. The rest of the parcel I came up with carried mud bricks for the new priests' barracks for two years. Back-breaking labour in the sun.

A priest told me that my new owner's name was Hipponax, and that I should call him Master and avert my eyes. Hipponax put his carnelian seal on a clay tablet, grabbed me by the neck and hustled me out of the slave barracks. At the portico of the great temple, he stopped and looked me over. Then he made a face. 'Well,' he said, 'you were cheap.' He laughed. 'Aphrodite's tits, boy, you stink. Let's get you a doctor.'

We walked down from the acropolis, past the magnificent steps to the Temple of Artemis and into the lower temple precinct, where he took me to the Temple of Asclepius. We don't even have Asclepius in Boeotia. He's a healing god.

I was there for three days. They cleaned my leg and poured wine over it twice a day and wrapped it in bandages. I was bathed and fed well – coarse food, but there was barley bread, pork and lots of onions, and I ate like a horse.

Let me give you, in a sentence, the difference between Ephesus and Plataea. At the Temple of Asclepius, I was housed in the precinct of slaves. I thought I was living with aristocrats. My bed had linen sheets and a white wool blanket, and they gave me a linen chiton to wear as if it wasn't worth more than my best spear. I was waited on by free men and women until I was healed. Imagine!

Most of the other men in my ward were victims of old age, and most of them were Thracians. In fact, the overwhelming number of slaves in Ephesus were Thracians, blond men and women with robust bodies and big heads. And I didn't have a word in common with them.

On the third day, my new master came and fetched me. I was clean. All my hair had been cut away and my head shaved. I thought it was a condition of servitude, but it turned out that they did it to rid me of lice. They shaved my pubic hair, too. That worried me. Easterners were notorious for their sexual licence.

I wore my linen chiton when I followed my master on to the street. The sun, reflected from marble and pale grey stone, blinded me. I had a crutch and I hobbled along behind him as best I could.

We walked down just one level of the town. The acropolis was at the top, and then the temples, and then – the rich.

He took me into the main entrance of his house, and it was so magnificent that I stopped behind him and looked.

In the entranceway, under the gate that led from the street to the courtyard, there was a fresco of the gods sitting in state, painted in colour on the plaster. On either side, carved as if from life, there was a maenad on my right and a satyr on my left. Once I walked two more steps under the portico and into the courtyard, I saw that every column was a statue of a man or a woman, each standing like slaves awaiting service, holding the roof, and under the arches there were more painted scenes – scenes from the *Iliad* and scenes of the gods. Zeus ravished a very willing Europa, and the only cowlike thing about her was her eyes. Achilles held his arms high in triumphant revenge, and Hector lay at his feet.

'Welcome,' my master said. He smiled. 'Let's have a look at you.'

He pulled my chiton off. The beautiful woman came out into the courtyard, followed by two female slaves. All three of them were perfumed, and all three were wearing garments better than Plataea's finest wedding dress. The lady had gold earrings and a necklace as broad as a soldier's girdle that seemed to be tied with the knot of Heracles in gold, although I didn't think that was possible. I caught her name from my master – she was Euthalia, and that name was right for her, for she was beautiful and well-formed, and child-bearing had not touched her, except to give her the strength of face that most matrons get when they have had the rearing of a child.

I took the knot of Heracles as a sign. Heracles was the family patron, and there was his sign in the home of my master. Heracles had been a slave. I took it as a sign and I still think it was.

They ran their hands over me and played games. The slave girls fetched a ball and threw it at me. I caught it. The man nodded. Then

96

he swung a stick at me – slowly, but with some force. I moved. I ducked. I ducked a blow *and* caught a ball without dropping my crutch.

Finally, the man nodded. 'What do you know of horses?' he asked.

'Nothing,' I said.

Both Master and Mistress looked disappointed. 'Nothing? Speak the truth, boy.'

I shook my head. 'I have touched a horse,' I said.

That made Mistress smile. 'He could be taught,' she said.

'He will be too tall soon,' Master said. 'But it is worth a try.' He put a finger under my chin and raised my face, the way a man does with a shy girl. 'What's your name, boy?'

'Arimnestos,' I said. 'Of Plataea.'

'You're a Greek,' he said.

'Yes, master,' I answered.

He shook his head. 'Well, I'm glad to have a Greek slave, but the man who sold you is a fool. You were a free man, weren't you? And you were trained to be an athlete.' He glanced back – he *almost* treated me as a person and not a household object. 'I am Hipponax. You've heard of me?'

'No, master.' I hung my head. He had expected me to know of him. He had expected me to know of horses, too.

I had never thought of Calchas's training as training for sport. 'I was trained to hunt and fight,' I said. 'Master.'

He pursed his lips and looked at Mistress.

She smiled back at him. It was good to see them together, they were so much of one mind. 'Don't be offended because a slave does not know your poetry, dear. He can't read, after all.'

I wondered if I was foolish to brag about my skills – but I did not want to go back to the priests. And they seemed like good people.

'I can read and write,' I said.

'You can read and write Doric?' master asked. 'Or Ionic? Or both?'

'I can read the *Iliad* and the *Odyssey* and Alcaeus and Theognis,' I said.

Mistress smiled broadly. 'I think you owe me a new robe of my own choosing, dear. Oh, that Daxes will be so *angry*.' She clapped her hands. Then she came and ran a hand down my flank, and I shivered, and she laughed. 'You can fight, catch a ball and read. Fine accomplishments for a young man. But your name is barbarous. I think we shall call you Doru. A spear – a Dorian. An intrusion to our family.' She smiled at me and turned back to Master. 'I am going to try and spend a few useful hours accomplishing something at my loom.'

Master kissed her shoulder. It was a shock – everything was a shock, but his casual, open affection wasn't something I had ever seen Greek people do. 'I can think of another role for him, if he can hunt and fight,' he said, 'and read.'

'As can I. But let's have him put to the farm with some reins in his hand first,' she said. 'And he can always drive for Archilogos if he can't last a race.'

'So he can, my dear. Your usual splendid eye for good muscles.' He turned back to me. 'Arimnestos, we are sending you to learn to be a charioteer. Do you think you will like that?'

I might have said many things. Instead, I shrugged. Really – I was ten thousand stades from home and my world was dead. What was I to do? Escape? It never crossed my mind. It sounded better than being pissed on, or hauling mud bricks for priests.

So I went to the farm with an old slave and slept well enough, and in the morning, I started to learn to be a charioteer.

# 7

I was never a great charioteer. I stood at the reins in some races on the farm, and I never won. The truth was that Hipponax had me pegged. As soon as they gave me good food, I grew so fast that I was too heavy for even a four-horse team – in a race. As a military charioteer I would have been like a god, but chariots were hardly ever used in combat any more.

Scyles was my teacher. He was an old man from Mytilene, on Lesbos, and had been a charioteer all his life. I was unsure whether he was a family retainer or a slave – he seemed part of the horse farm, as much a part of it as the old stallions and the young mares.

I will disappoint you again by saying that my slavery was so soft that I enjoyed it, and my door was never locked. Not even the first night! I could have picked up my crutch and hobbled away at any time, and a week later, when I was almost fully healed and the growth began, I could have run.

But run where, my honey? Back to Plataea across the sea? I was in mighty Ephesus in Asia, the slave of a wealthy man. No one seemed to know anything about my home, or even about the war that I'd been in. I asked – I asked Scyles from the first day. He shrugged and said that no one in the real world cared a damn what the barbarians of Athens and Sparta did. He called them bumpkins – clods.

And to be honest, honey, I wasn't really so anxious to get back to Green Plataea.

Sounds shocking, doesn't it? I was a *slave* and I didn't want to return to my homeland and be *free*. But freedom is a word we use too easily. I think now – older and wiser – I can say that I was free for the first time. I was free of my father, who was, in many ways, a cold, unfeeling bastard who seldom had any time for me. There, I've said it. I never mourned him – not really. I was proud of him.

But I couldn't muster much regret that he was dead. And Mater? I wouldn't have crossed Ephesus, wouldn't have walked *down* the steps to the temple, to see her. So – be shocked if you like. I can remember the first night sitting on the cool marble floor of the slave quarters – the *slave quarters had a marble floor*, – and thinking that I must be a poor son because I didn't want to go home. I cried a little. I began to wonder if I was going to be a cold, unfeeling bastard like my father.

And I'll say it again – in Ephesus, no one had ever heard of Plataea. Among a thousand shocks I received that autumn, this had to be the greatest – that to the Greeks of Asia, mighty Athens and military Sparta were clods of no importance. Interesting, too, that this was soon to change. And that I would play my part in making it change. I dare say every man in Ephesus knows where Plataea is now.

Nonsense, I can drink wine at this hour. Wine is always good for a man. Pour it full, there's a dear.

Now – where was I? Ah, yes. Life as a slave. Not a bad life. They called me Doru – all of them, so that for a while I simply forgot my name. As soon as my thigh was healed, I had a training schedule and I was massaged and exercised by professionals. I learned to ride, and to feed horses and to keep them happy.

I never loved horses. I've known a few that were smarter than a rock, but not many. They're stubborn and stupid and not unlike cats, except that cats don't injure themselves the moment you turn your back. At any rate, after two weeks, Scyles said I would never be a charioteer, and he was right, but we kept trying.

I loved to drive. We started with a little pony cart, and I fell off a dozen times trying to make tight corners, but I was healed up by then. And we had exercises – wonderful exercises, like balancing on a board placed across the hollow of a shield, so that the face of the shield was in the dust and you could tilt and fall so easily – we'd fight that way, to practise balance. And the pony cart – I'd ride on the pole, or ride the pony, until I was comfortable anywhere in the cart or out of it. That was Scyles' way. Then we tried a two-horse chariot with real horses, and I broke my arm the first day. That took months to heal, and I spent that time doing exercises and working like a normal slave in the kitchens. Scyles ran a tight farm, and he knew his business. If I wasn't learning my new trade, I could at least run the treadmill that lifted water from the well.

It was while I was healing my arm that I discovered what stallions and mares were born knowing, if you take my meaning. One of the kitchen girls asked me how strong my spear was – all the girls laughed, even the oldsters. And that night she had me. There wasn't a great deal of foreplay, and she laughed at how quick I was – this from a girl no more than my own age. Girls can be cruel.

But we played quite a bit, and I played with other girls, too. Slave girls like to be pregnant – it makes for less work. And it makes the owner a profit, unless he's a fool. We had a rich owner and no one was threatened with being 'sold away', so the girls played. It was as much of an education as the athletic training, in its way.

The truth is, honey, it was a happy time.

There was hardship, and I was aware that I was not free. But I was young, and I had food, sex, challenge – all in all, life was simple and easy. We worked long hours. When we built a structure over the privy, we worked six straight days from dawn until dusk, but when we were finished we had *done* something. Other slaves ploughed, sowed and reaped, and I did some of all of that work once I was healed. We had most of the religious feasts, too. Really, in some ways I did less work than I did later as a free man.

On a farm where everyone is a slave, slavery does not seem so bad.

We did have some troubles. There was a boy I hated. He whined, he was weak, he went out of his way to avoid work and he refused to change. He also peddled tales to the overseers – who was having sex with whom, who had eaten too much, who drank the master's wine. His name was Grigas, and he was Phrygian.

And there was a Thracian boy that I liked, although slaves find it hard to be friends – real friends – because so much of that has been taken from you. But Silkes was a handsome youth, and he was a great wrestler. He'd been taken in a war, and insisted that some day he would escape. He was the first man I heard discuss escape as if it could be done.

One afternoon, we were lying in the horse barn. We'd curried all the hunters and all the chargers and chariot horses and ponies. and now we were flopped on the spare feed straw that lay heaped where Grigas had failed to make neat haystacks.

'So what if you escape?' I asked. 'Where would you go?'

'Home,' Silkes said.

'How?' I asked.

He shook his head. 'I don't know,' he said. 'If I have to walk on water, I'll walk home.' He looked at me. 'Perhaps I'll hunt fish with my spear, and light a fire on floating weed.'

'Now you're just talking foolishness,' I said. 'If they catch you, you won't be brought back here, learning to be a charioteer. You'll end up breaking rocks, or cutting salt, or rowing. Something crappy.'

'So?' Silkes asked. 'It's all slavery. I'm not a slave. I'm a free man.' He rolled towards me. 'You're just a Greek. Slavery is natural for you.'

I broke his nose before he got me in a hold and pounded my head against the barn's wall. And yet, we were not really angry. But we both missed work because we had hurt each other, and because of it, and because Grigas reported us, we were brought before the chief overseer, Amyntas. Amyntas was a Macedonian, and he was a hard man, but fair, we all thought.

He looked us over. 'Why did you fight?' he asked.

I was ready for him. 'Over a girl,' I said. I looked sullenly at Silkes, who glared back.

'Which girl?' Amyntas asked.

'Sandra, in the kitchen.' She and I got along. I knew she wouldn't talk.

He nodded. 'I've heard that you two were discussing escape.' He looked at me. I was a Greek. I didn't flinch.

But Silkes blushed. Amyntas shrugged. 'You are a stupid Thracian. Why did you fight him?'

Silkes looked at me. 'He hit me,' he said. 'And the girl.'

He was the worst liar I'd ever met. No wonder they call Thracians 'barbarians'.

Amyntas nodded again. He had a table in the farmhouse that he used as a desk, and it was piled with scrolls. He pointed at me. 'Five blows with a riding whip,' he said. He pointed at Silkes. 'Ten blows – five for damage to your master's property, and five for attempting to incite escape. You will be punished this evening. Go to work.'

The waiting was the worst – and the humiliation. Everyone came to watch, and Grigas stood at the front, openly gloating.

I took the five blows well enough. I probably cried out, but I didn't scream or cry. Silkes took his ten in total silence.

We were whipped naked. After I took my five, Sandra handed me my chiton.

Grigas laughed. 'I guess we know who has the power here,' he said.

He was too smug. I half-turned, as if to talk to Sandra, and then I hit him with the full force of my fist.

I hurt him, too.

I received ten more blows from the whip.

As Grigas was still unconscious, I felt I had won.

The next morning, I stood before Amyntas, alone. He was behind the desk. I was in front of it. He had a bronze stylus in his hand and two sets of wax tablets open.

'You have injured the slave Grigas,' he said.

'Good,' I said.

He nodded. 'I begin to feel that you are rebellious. Listen to me, young man. Do not choose this road. Master and Mistress have plans for you – plans that will help you all your life. If you choose to be rebellious, I will have to inform them. They will sell you. Is that what you want?'

I kept my eyes down. 'No,' I said.

'You want to rebel. Please do not do it. You dislike Grigas. He is useful to me and I will protect him. You will treat him with respect and that is all. Am I clear?' Amyntas got up.

'Yes,' I said.

'Good. Go back to work,' he said.

That was it. Grigas gloated, and I took it. Silkes was disgusted, and ceased to be my friend. A month later, he ran. I never heard what happened to him. Well, that's not exactly true, but let's save that bit, shall we?

Grigas was still there, though – gloating. He was beginning to have a belly – a fifteen-year-old slave with a belly. And he began to force the girls.

I was healed, and had gone back to riding and driving. I could pretend that I was no longer part of the daily rhythm of the kitchen. What was it to me? But it hurt me, each time I had to turn away from that little worm. Each time I saw him fondle a girl, each time he made a better slave knuckle under.

But I knew that I was not going to be a charioteer, and that put me in a bad position, as a slave. If I failed as a charioteer – and as I say, Scyles knew from the second week that I lacked the love of horses – then I could be resold for another task.

More slaves arrived – a new cook, a pair of horse-breakers and some field slaves. I saw that Grigas was going to own them – that they accepted his vicious authority. And I saw his effect on the place. When I'd arrived, people were, for the most part, happy. No one was happy any more.

I thought it over quite a bit. Scyles caught me at it. One day – late spring, almost a year since I'd become a slave – he watched me for a moment and then shook his head. 'You think too much,' he said.

I nodded, acknowledging that he was right.

'What's the problem? A girl? A boy?' Scyles was all right. He either wasn't a slave or he wasn't part of the hierarchy of the place. Amyntas never tangled with him.

'Grigas is evil,' I said.

Scyles nodded, and looked away. 'So?'

'So,' I said. 'So nothing.' I had learned not to discuss important things, you see.

Scyles was watching a filly. He didn't take his eyes off her. 'Good and evil are words philosophers and priests use,' he said. 'What do you want to do?'

I shook my head in mute negation. I wasn't going to tell him.

'Can I tell you something, lad?' he said, and his voice was kind. 'You won't be a good charioteer.'

'I know,' I said, although hearing it from him had the force of an axe blow.

He nodded. 'Don't be stupid,' he said.

'But he makes things worse for everyone,' I said. 'Not just me. Everyone.'

Scyles scratched his chin and continued to watch the filly. 'Interesting. I barely know him.'

'He's an informer. He forces the girls. He humiliates the men just for fun. The other night he made a farmhand – Lykon, the big one – made him give up the girl he liked. Then he took her. Just like that. That sort of stuff never used to happen.'

Scyles nodded. 'It only takes one,' he said. Then he looked me in the eye. 'Planning to beat him senseless?' he asked.

I sat silently and stared over his head.

Scyles nodded. 'Because if you do that, he'll just report you. He's probably too stupid to understand that you were born free and might choose to accept punishment to hurt him. Born slaves are always mystified by the actions of free men.'

Somehow that speech moved me deeply, perhaps because Scyles identified me as a free man.

'If I do nothing, then I truly am a slave,' I said.

Scyles twitched his lips. 'You are a slave,' he said. 'But—' He looked around. 'Listen, lad. Use your head. That's all I can say.'

I nodded.

And I thought about it some more.

As it turned out, the action was absurdly easy. I over-planned, and then the gods handed me my enemy. A lesson there.

I decided to kill Grigas. Plain, simple murder. Not a fair fight. He had to go, and I decided that I didn't need to be caught to prove to myself that I was a free man.

I decided to drown him in the baths. I made some preparations and I changed my routine so that we would be in the baths at the same time. I was bigger and stronger. I imagined that I would hold him under water. No screams.

Not a bad plan.

We bathed together twice. The second time, he spent the whole bath telling me things that turned my stomach. He had decided that I liked him.

He was a fool.

I stole a small wooden mallet from the wood-shop so that I could knock him unconscious and hid it in the towels and rags by the big wooden tub.

That evening, Master came. He arrived in a four-horse chariot. I was able to drive four horses by this time, and I was impressed at his skill, considering that he was an aristocrat.

He called for Scyles and the two of them had a long talk. They kept looking at me. It made me sad – I really was a slave – to think that I was going to be sold away. I liked the farm, apart from Grigas. And I could tolerate him, now that I held his life in my hand.

Master chatted for some time with Scyles, and then the two came to where I was cleaning tack. Master had some beautiful halters – worked in bronze and silver, fine Lydian work.

'Doru,' he called, and I ran to them.

He nodded to me. 'Scyles says that you will never make a chariot-eer,' he said. 'He says that you can drive and handle horses. That you are safe and unexceptional. And that you don't love horses.'

I stared at the ground. It was all true.

Master raised my chin. 'Mistress and I have another plan for you. My son needs a companion. He is a little younger than you, I think. But you will make a good right arm. So – would you like to come back to the city with me? And try working for my son?'

I had learned a great deal about being a slave on the farm. So instead of sullen silence, I pretended to be delighted. 'Yes, master,' I said, and clapped my hands.

He looked at me a long time, and I wondered if he was fooled. 'Let me see your thigh,' he said. I raised my chiton, and he looked at the wound. It looked then much as it does now – a red fish hook.

After a few moments, he frowned. 'Is there pain?' he asked.

'Just before the weather changes,' I said. 'Otherwise, none.'

He nodded. 'Tomorrow we will go to the city. Say your goodbyes and finish your tasks.'

'Yes, master,' I said. I thought I would never settle Grigas, and the thought made me feel like a failure, but the gods had other ideas.

Sometimes chance – Tyche – is better than any plan of men. I was ordered by the head cook to run to the village market for some rue. I had good legs by then – I think I was a foot taller than I had been at the battles – and I could run. So I set off into the late afternoon with a few obols clutched in my fist.

I got the rue from a peasant woman in a stall covered in hide. Then I turned and ran back to the farm, my legs eating the stades.

I doubt that I was even winded as I passed the barn. And then I heard the sound of a woman crying.

I ran into the barn. I was moving fast. Tyche sat at my shoulder, and there were furies at my back.

Grigas was up in the loft with a girl. He was making the smallest kitchen slut blow his flute. He had her hair— Anyway, that's not a thing to tell you, honey. I ran straight to the ladder and climbed, and I suspect he never heard me. She was doing what she had been made to do, and was crying.

I pushed her aside, broke his neck and threw him from the loft. His head made the sound a wooden mallet makes as it hits the cow's head when the butcher is slaughtering – he hit the stone floor of the barn, but he was dead before he left my hands.

I was eating dinner when they found his body. I laughed. 'Good riddance,' I said, and Amyntas looked at me. I met his eye.

The next day, I drove Master's chariot from the farm up the mountain to Ephesus, proud as a king. I had learned three lessons from the murder – lessons I've kept with me all my life. First, that older people are wise, and you should listen to them. Second, that dead men tell no tales. And third, that killing is easy.

# 8

Hipponax's son was Archilogos. I see you smile, honey. It's true. He was my master and I was his slave. The gods move in mysterious ways.

Archilogos was a boy of twelve years when I was fourteen. He was handsome, in the Ionian way, with dark curly hair and a slim build. He could vault anything, and he had had lessons in many things – sword-fighting, chariot-driving and writing among them.

He was the most Medified Greek I had ever met. He worshipped the Persians. He admired their art, their clothes, their horses and their weapons. He practised archery all the time, and he had a religious regard for the truth, because his father's friend, the satrap, had told him that the only two requirements for being a Persian were that a boy should shoot straight and tell the truth.

I should speak of the satrap. In the sixty-seventh Olympiad, when I was young, Persia had conquered all of Lydia, although they'd effectively had the place many years before – almost fifty. So Ephesus, like Sardis, was part of their empire. They ruled their Greeks with a light hand, despite all the cant you hear these days about 'slavery' and 'oppression'.

Their satrap was Artaphernes. He is so much a part of this story that he will vie with Archilogos for the number of times I mention him. He was a handsome man, tall and black-haired, with a perfectly trimmed beard and bronze skin. His carriage was wonderful – he was the most dignified man I've ever known, and even men who hated him would listen respectfully when he spoke. He had the ear of the King of Kings. Great Darius. He never lied, as far as I know. He loved Greeks, and we loved him.

He was a fearsome enemy, too. Oh, honey, I know.

He was a good friend to Hipponax. Whenever he came to Ephesus

– and that was at least once a year – he would stay with us. And he was a 'real Persian', not a mixed-blood. A noble of the highest sort.

My new master wanted to grow up to be that man.

Artaphernes was in the house when I was brought from the farm. I had driven the chariot and I was flushed with Master's praise – he said Scyles was surely wrong, as I'd scarcely bumped him once in driving up the mountain. Now, this was certainly a bit of foolishness, but flattery was like water to a drowning man when I was a slave. When did you last praise a slave, honey?

Exactly.

The Persian was in the courtyard when I came in. I was dressed in a short wool kilt – like a charioteer. He was wearing trousers and a coat made of embroidered wool and he was reading from a scroll. Master was behind me, giving instructions to another slave, and I was alone, so I bowed and remained silent. I had never seen a Persian before.

The Persian returned my bow. And my silence. After a pause where our eyes met, he went back to reading his scroll.

Master came, and the two embraced.

'Sorry to be absent for your arrival, my lord.' Hipponax grinned. 'You are reading my latest!'

'Why do you do yourself so little justice?' the Persian asked. He had very little accent – just enough to add a tinge of the exotic to his voice. 'You are the greatest living poet, in Greek or Persian. Why do you seek praise in this manner?'

Hipponax shrugged. 'I am never sure,' he said.

The Persian shook his head. 'It is this unsureness that makes you Greeks so different. And perhaps makes your poetry so strong.' He nodded at me. 'This young gentleman has perfect manners.'

Hipponax flashed me a smile. 'He is to be my son's companion. Your praise pleases me. He is a slave.'

The Persian looked at me. 'We are all slaves, under the king. But this one has dignity. He will be good for your son.' He shrugged. 'I had no idea he was a slave.'

As far as I was concerned, Artaphernes could do no wrong.

Then Master took me into the house and brought me to his son. Archilogos was in the back garden, shooting arrows at a target. He had a Persian bow, and the lawn was decorated with arrows.

'You'll have to do better than that if you want to be a Persian,' his father said. I thought that he was not particularly happy to find his son shooting.

Archilogos threw the bow on the ground in anger. Then he looked at me. 'What's he for?' the boy asked. He was a boy to me. I was a grown man, as far as I was concerned.

'Your mother and I have chosen him to be your companion.' Master nodded. 'I give him to you. We call him Doru, but you may ask him his name. He is Greek. He can read and write.'

Archilogos looked at me for a long time. Finally he shrugged. 'I can read and write,' he said. 'Can you shoot a bow?'

'Yes,' I said. Ignoring both of them, I picked up his bow. It was heavier than any I'd shot, but I had all kinds of new muscles. I raised the bow, drew and shot, all in one motion as Calchas had taught me, and my arrow flew true and struck the target – not in the centre, but squarely enough.

Archilogos went and hugged his father.

Who winked at me.

I thought that they were the happiest family I had ever seen. Their happiness helped to keep me a slave when I could have run. They seemed so happy that most of their slaves were happy too. It was a good house, until the disaster came and the fates ordained that they be brought low. I loved them.

That first night, we watched the Persian shoot. He had his own bow, lacquered red and stringed in something beautiful, and he shot arrow after arrow into the target without apparent effort. I had never seen an archer so deadly.

Mistress lay on a kline at the edge of the garden, watching. She shared the kline with Master, and we heard their conversation and their commentary as we shot. The Persian watched them from time to time, and I could see that, whatever his friendship for Hipponax, he found her very much to his taste.

I shot adequately. Artaphernes coached my new master and he shot well enough, and then the Persian ordered one of his troopers, one of the Persian cavalrymen in his escort, to come up and shoot. The man had been down in the lower city, probably up to no good, but he shot with gusto and he shot well, although not quite as well as his lord. And then the soldier gave us pointers. He spoke to me at length about the weight of the bow. I understood from this that my new master needed a lighter bow.

Here's the difference between a slave and a companion. Slaves avoid work. To be a successful companion, you have to work hard.

You have to anticipate your master's needs and fulfil them. No one had to tell me this. I saw it in the way they all behaved.

The truth is that I liked him the moment I met him. And so I wanted to please him. That night, while the Persian lord flirted with Mistress, I went to Master and asked him for the money to buy the boy a lighter bow. He nodded.

'Come with me,' he said, and took me to Darkar, the steward, another Lydian.

'Darkar is the man who controls this house,' Master said. 'I'm lucky he allows me to live here. Darkar, this young man is to be my son's companion.'

I bowed to the steward. He nodded. He was a slave.

'He will need money,' Master said.

Darkar nodded, went into a storeroom and emerged with a purse. He handed it to me. 'Fifty gold darics and some change,' he said. 'You will only be told once. If you steal, you'll be sold. If you don't steal, you'll receive a bonus to put away towards your freedom. Understand?'

I nodded. Fifty darics was the price of a hundred slaves. Or a ship. And he said *eleutheria*, freedom, as if it was a certain thing. 'Master, why do I need so much money?' I asked the steward.

'Never call me master, boy. This is your companion's money. You but carry it for him, and watch it, and count it – treat it carefully, for they never will. Give me a good accounting, and I'll speak well of you. My word caries weight, when it comes time for freedom.'

Freedom!

Of course, in my head, I wasn't really a slave, so I looked at the purse and considered running for a ship.

Ionians. Too much money.

At any rate, the moment I had the purse in my hand, I ran off to the market and bought a good, lightweight bow. I paid well, almost half a daric, and I pocketed the change. What do you think? I knew that they couldn't catch me. I put the change in a jar in the garden. And I had the bow on Archilogos's bed when he awoke in the morning, and forty-nine golden darics left to show on my accounts.

The whole time that Artaphernes was with us, we shot until my fingers bled. That's an expression you hear, but in our case, it was true. First you shoot until your fingertips swell, and after a while they hurt as if stung by ants and they turn bright red. But a pair of boys, each eager for praise and fearing the catcalls of the other, will go right on, until the fingers turn a darker colour, and then the abrasion of the bowstring will break the swollen flesh, and they bleed. And later, if you go back to shooting before the calluses grow, the scabs break and they bleed again. The bowstring of our bow had a brown spot at the draw point from our blood.

Archilogos never tired and never gave up. His whipcord body was proof against fatigue, and he would run and shoot, do lessons and shoot, go to the theatre and shoot. Anything to impress his hero. He'd learned a few lines of Persian poetry and he'd declaim them, hoping that the Persian would overhear.

The Persian had troubles enough without the adoration of the boy. First, it was obvious to me, after the sexual politics of the farm, that the Persian was deeply in love with Mistress, and that she toyed with him. But even that was of little moment next to the greater matters that surrounded us.

It was the years of the seventieth Olympiad. In Greece, the last of the great tyrants had gone and peace began to emerge from her nest. But in Ionia, the tyrants still held sway. Not law-givers, men who make good laws and then relinquish control. I speak here of strong warlords and aristocrats who aped Persian manners and ruled Ionia for their own benefit, not that of their cities.

Hippias, the tyrant of Athens, had been overthrown in my childhood. He had retreated to Sigeum in Asia, a city that his family, the Pisistratidae, ruled in much the same way as Miltiades ruled the Chersonese. Hippias was in Ephesus with his own train of soldiers and courtiers, making noise in the lower city and spending money.

My second night in the household, I heard the satrap at dinner. He was complaining to Hipponax about the Greek lords on their islands, and how their bad rulership reflected poorly on the Great King and would, if left unchecked, lead to revolt.

'And men blame me!' he complained. 'I don't have enough soldiers to punish Mytilene! Or Miletus! And what good would it do me to take them – I would only punish the very men of the city who are treated so ruthlessly by the tyrants I wish to be rid of!' He looked at his host. 'Why are you Greeks so rapacious?'

Hipponax laughed. 'I suspect that the tyrants merely do as they think a Persian would do, lord.'

The satrap frowned. 'I hope that this is humour, my friend. No Persian lord would behave this way. This is weakness. These are rulers who do not trust themselves, nor do they tell the truth to their people or their king.'

Hipponax shrugged and looked at his wife. 'Is it really so bad?' he asked.

The satrap raised a cup of wine. 'It is. And Hippias – this former tyrant – has been at me again and again to take Athens back for him. What does the Great King want with these yokels?' His eyes crossed mine. I lowered my eyes as slaves do, but I couldn't help bridling at the term 'yokel' from a barbarian, even if he was handsome as a god.

Hipponax nodded at me. 'That young man has been a warrior in the west, haven't you, lad? That's a spear scar on your thigh. Go ahead – you may speak.'

I was behind Archilogos's couch, and I was caught with a pitcher of water in my hands – hardly the most warlike pose. 'Yes, master,' I said.

Artaphernes smiled at me. 'You fought for Athens?' he asked.

'I am a Plataean,' I answered. 'We are allies of Athens.'

Hipponax laughed. He meant no harm, I think, but his laugh hurt me. 'See how the westerners are? That's a town smaller than our temple-complex claiming to be the "ally" of Athens, a town so small we could fit five of them inside Ephesus.'

Artaphernes dismissed me with a flick of his fingers. 'I have never heard of your Plataea,' he said. I don't think he meant it unkindly, but the gods were listening. I wish I could say I replied with something witty, or strong. Ha! Instead, I stood like a statue as he went on. 'However provincial Athens is, men here in the islands and on the coast look at the tyrants and talk of rebellion. They have never seen the wrath of the Great King, or how he disciplines rebellion. They are like children.' He drank. 'You know Aristagoras as well as I do. He has taken an embassy to Sparta and Athens asking for fleets and soldiers to raise rebellion against us. And farther from home, men like Miltiades of Athens foment war.'

I leaned forward at the mention of my hero. I hadn't heard his name in a year. It was as if I had been asleep.

'That warlord! What do we care for him? He's just a petty brigand.' Mistress was amused. 'A handsome brigand, I'll allow. A far better man than Aristagoras the windbag.'

'Miltiades has most of the Chersonese in his hand,' the Persian said.

'The Lydian Chersonese?' Mistress asked, alarmed.

Master laughed at her – not mocking, but honest laughter. 'Nothing to be worried about, my sweet. Miltiades has his lair in the Chersonese of the Bosporus – over by Byzantium, north of Troy.'

'He has more men and more ships each year,' the satrap continued, nodding. 'And he preys on us. Soon, I will need to mount an expedition to evict him from the Chersonese, I have so many complaints. But when I go against him, he will counter by pushing Samos or some other island into revolt. He spends silver like water. And these fool tyrants play into his hands!' He drank again. 'And yet – bah – why do I bore you with these matters of governance?'

All of that sounded like my Miltiades. A thumb in every wine bowl. And lots of silver.

Mistress smiled. 'Because we are your friends. And because friends ease each other's burdens. Surely, lord, you can just buy Miltiades? He worships money, or so I understand.'

The satrap shook his head and rolled over on his couch. I thought that his trousers looked ridiculous. Greek men – even Ionians – display their legs to show how hard they exercise. A man in trousers looked like some sort of effeminate clown, but otherwise, I thought him the best figure of a warrior I had ever seen. I understood why Archilogos was so eager to impress him.

He held out his hand for wine. I cut off another house slave and filled it for him, and he flashed me a smile. 'It is not Miltiades who really worries me,' he admitted. 'It is your windbag, Aristagoras of Miletus. My spies tell me he is to speak to the assembly in Athens.'

Hipponax yawned. 'Ephesus can defeat Athens without help from any of the other cities, if it comes to that,' he said.

Artaphernes shook his head. 'Don't be too sure,' he said. 'Their power is growing. Their confidence is growing. I do not want the westerners involved, if there is to be trouble in the islands.'

There was more of the same – indeed, an old man's memory being what it is, I'm not sure that I even have what they said in the right order. But Hipponax and Euthalia took the parts I have given them. They were supportive, loyal subjects of the Great King.

As the companion to Archilogos, I was excused a great many duties in the house, but I was smart enough to know that it was by willingness to work and not by arrogance that I would gain the alliance of the other slaves and the steward. So I put my master to bed and then returned to the andron to help tidy up. It wasn't bad work – there was plenty of wine going around among the slaves, and as long as we didn't chip the ceramics or dent the metalware, Master didn't seem to care much what we did. I took tray after tray down to the kitchens, and then I helped the girls wash the cups in hot water, which was what Cook liked to see.

My young master had a sister I hadn't met yet, named Briseis after Achilles' 'companion'. People choose the oddest names for children, eh, honey? Greece is full of Cassandras – what kind of name is that for a girl? Anyway, her companion was Penelope, the same as my sister, and I met her that night. Penelope was just my age, had red hair like Miltiades and was of the same mind as me – to do some extra work and be seen as a help. So we washed cups and drank wine together, and we talked of our lives. She wasn't born a slave, either. Her father sold her when her family lost their farm. He still came and saw her, though.

I listened, as well as talking. It was a new experience for me, and she commented on it. Emboldened, I tried to kiss her, and I put a hand on her breast, but she slapped my ear hard enough to make me see the stars. Then she flashed me a smile.

'No,' she said. And slipped away.

I liked her. I even liked the slap, and I'll jump ahead of my story to say that I started to make excuses to see her. The house was big, but it wasn't that big – it's just that while Mistress came and went from the women's quarters as she wished, we men weren't allowed there.

I went to bed late and with much to think about.

And in the morning, we went for our lessons to the great Temple of Artemis. It was my first time inside the precinct. I climbed the steps with a certain awe, because they were so high and so much of the precinct was stone. In Boeotia, we put down a couple of courses of stone to raise the building clear of the damp, and then we build the rest in mud brick. But the Ephesian temple was all stone, with marble steps and marble pediments and lintels, and painted statues of Artemis and Nemesis – and Heracles. I think I spoke aloud in wonder to see my ancestor so nobly arrayed in a foreign land, wearing a helmet like a lion's head and holding a club. I touched the statue for luck.

When we reached the top we passed beneath the magnificent portico, into the blinding sunlight of the courtyard, which was paved in pale golden stone. Gold and bronze statues caught the light reflected by the brightly coloured marbles.

Archilogos didn't give it so much as a glance. 'Don't gawp like a peasant,' he said. 'Come!'

He marched me to the steps of the great temple itself. There were dozens of young men there and in the cool space under the columns. Most sat around tutors, but the biggest crowd gathered around a white-haired man who was so thin that his bones threatened to burst from his skin. He wore a chlamys without a chiton, like the young men, but he had an ugly, bony body – except that his muscles stood out like a Boeotian farmer's. He seemed very old to me.

He watched us come, although there were a dozen boys around him on the steps.

'You are late,' he said to my new master.

Archilogos smiled. 'Pardon, master,' he said. 'I should not have waited so long to dip my toe.'

This comment made the other boys giggle. I had no idea why.

The teacher glared at him. 'If you understood what I said,' he commented, 'you would know how foolish that last sally sounded. Why do I teach the young?'

'We pay well?' another wag said.

Boys began to laugh, but he old man had a stick and it smacked into the jokester's shins before he could move.

'I neither accept pay nor do I ask for it,' the teacher said. 'Who are you, boy?'

That last was directed at me. I was not the only companion present. 'I belong to Archilogos,' I said meekly.

He grunted. 'Not in my class, boy. Here, you are your own man. Your own mind. For me to mould as I see fit.' He coughed into his hand. 'What do you know? Anything?'

'No,' I said. 'Nothing.'

He smiled. 'You have a nice combination of humility and arrogance, young man. Sit down right here. We are talking about the *logos*. Do you know of the logos, young man?'

'No, teacher,' I answered.

And so I met Heraclitus, my true master, the teacher of my soul. But for him, I would be nothing but a hollow vessel filled with rage and blood.

At the time, I was enraptured to find another thinker like the priest of Hephaestus from Thebes. This one was even deeper, I thought, and I sat in the shade, my back against a warm marble pillar, and let him fill me with wisdom.

In fact, much of it sounded like gibberish, and it was up to every boy to take what he could from the well, or so Heraclitus told us. On that first day, though, he turned to me, of all those boys. 'So – you know nothing. Are you a hollow vessel? May I fill you?'

I remember nodding and blushing, because other boys giggled and too late I saw the double entendre.

'Bah,' Heraclitus said, and his stick struck a shin. The owner squeaked. 'Sex is for animals, boy. Talking about sex is for miserable ephebes.' He prodded me with the bronze-shot tip of his staff. 'So? Ready to learn?'

'Yes, master,' I said.

He nodded. 'Here is all the wisdom I have, boy. There is a formula, a binding and a loosing, a single, coherent thought that makes the universe as it is, and we who sit on these steps call it the logos.' He prodded me again. 'Understand?'

I looked at him. His eyes were dark and full of mischief, like a boy's. 'No,' I admitted.

'Brilliant!' Heraclitus laughed. 'You may yet be a sage, boy.' He looked around and then back at me. 'Have you heard the phrase "common sense"?' he asked.

'Yes,' I answered.

'Is it, in fact, common?'

I laughed. 'No,' I said.

'Superb!' the old man said. 'By all the gods, you are the pupil I've dreamed about.' He leaned close and poked me with his stick again. 'Which has the truer understanding, lad? Your ears and nose, or your soul?'

I looked around, but all the boys were watching me. 'What's a soul?' I asked. I had heard the word, but seldom as something that could sense.

He stopped poking me. He turned to Archilogos. 'Young Logos,' he said, and suddenly I knew where my young master had got his name, 'how much did your father pay for this slave?'

Archilogos raised his hands. 'No idea, master. But not much.'

Heraclitus laughed. 'Now I know that wisdom can, indeed, be purchased.' He turned back to me and the stick pushed into my ribs. 'Listen, boy,' he said, 'the soul is the truest form of you. It can sense the logos in the same way it can sense when another man lies, if you allow it.'

I considered this. 'What does it sense? If my eyes sense light and my ears sense noise, what does my soul sense?'

Heraclitus stepped back. 'Excellent question.' He walked away a few steps and came back. 'Work on it, and you will be a philosopher. Now we will examine some mathematics. What's your name, boy?'

'I am Doru,' I said.

'The spear that cuts to the truth, I see. Very well. On the feast of Artemis, have prepared an oration on what the soul senses, and how. You may present it to the other boys.' Then he turned away. 'Now. This is a triangle.'

That was our first encounter.

He was always a challenge. If you said nothing, he would hit you. If you spoke up, he would sometimes praise and sometimes deride and always force you to compose an oration to defend your views. I came to know that most classes began with one poor boy or another rising like a politician in the assembly to deliver a quavering oration in defence of some indefensible subject.

I liked the mathematics. I came from a family of craftsmen, and I already knew how to make a triangle with a compass, how to divide it exactly in two parts, and a hundred other tricks that any draughts-man needs to know to copy figures or even just to make a nice circle on a cup.

I lacked the language to be comfortable – they were Ionians and they spoke a different dialect – but from the first, Heraclitus put me at ease. When I sat on the steps of the Temple of Artemis, I was the equal of every other boy. That made me love the lessons more than anything.

But I soon learned the language, and I drank in the ideas and words of rhetoric and philosophy the way a thirsty man drinks water. I learned to stand properly and to speak from low in the chest so that other men could hear me. I learned some tricks with words – phrases that would draw a laugh, and other phrases that were serious. I learned that the repetition of any line from Homer would make men take an argument more seriously.

We learned to sing from another teacher and to play the lyre. Calchas had played the instrument well and I was determined to emulate him. You may judge the results yourself when I play some Sappho later.

It was a game, but a great game. A complex game – as was the game of how to craft an argument.

Heraclitus was severe on the difference between disputation and assertion. You know it, young man? They teach that in Halicarnassus, do they? Hmm. Honey, it is like this. When I say that the moon is made of cheese, that is an assertion. If I say it louder, does that make it more true? If I quote Homer that the moon is made of cheese, does that make it more true? What if I threaten to beat you if you don't agree – does that make it true?

No. All mere assertion. Yes?

But, if I bring you a piece of cheese – better, if I *take you to the moon and show you it is cheese* – then I have offered proof. If I cannot prove it, perhaps I can offer theories as to why it must be cheese, offering testimonies from other men who have been to the moon, or scientific evidence based on experiment – you see? And you can offer me the same sort of evidence to prove that the moon is, in fact, not made of cheese at all.

If you laugh so hard, you will certainly spoil your looks. Hah! That was an assertion! There's no proof whatsoever that laughter hurts your looks.

Where was I? I must have been speaking of Heraclitus. Yes. He made us learn the difference, and if you rose to speak and he was displeased, that ash staff with the bronze ferrule would whistle through the air and crack you in the side or prod you in the ribs. Very conducive to learning in the young.

Weeks passed. It was a glorious time. I was learning things every day, I was exercised like a healthy young animal, I was in something like love for the first time with Penelope, and Archilogos was a fine companion in every way. We read together, ran together, fought with staves, wrestled, boxed and disputed.

Artaphernes stayed with us for all that summer and autumn while he kept watch over his tyrants and his lords. He was building half a dozen triremes to the latest design down in the harbour, and we would run all the way there to watch the ships, and then run back – twenty stades or so.

I haven't mentioned that Hipponax's household ran on the profits from his ships, not his poetry. Indeed, everyone called him 'The Poet', and we still sing his songs in this house, but he was a captain and an investor, running cargoes all the way to Phoenicia and Africa when the mood was on him, and buying and selling other men's cargoes, too. Archilogos and I went on short trips – once across the water to Mytilene, a pretty town on Lesbos, and once to Troy to walk the mound and camp where the Greeks had camped – a perfect trip in early autumn when the sea is the friend of every man and dolphins dance by the bow of your ship. It was odd, looking across the water at the Chersonese – where Miltiades held sway. If I swam the Hellespont, I'd have been able to get home. Later, we went on longer voyages – to Syracuse and the Spartan colony at Taras in southern Italy. But we went far south, along the coast of Africa – not along the Greek coast, where I would have been close to home.

I didn't want to go home. Home had Mater and poverty and death. I was in Ephesus with lovely people, a friend, a teacher and a woman. How deaf I must have been to the wing-beats of the furies!

Later we made the run to Lesbos many times. Hipponax owned property in Eresus, where Sappho came from, and we would beach our ship there under the great rock, or inside the mole that the old people built before the siege of Troy, and Hipponax would climb to the citadel and pay his respects to Sappho's daughter, who was very old, but still kept her school. Briseis had gone to that school for three years, and had all Sappho's nine books by heart.

They had a warehouse in Methymna, too, another city of Lesbos and a rival to Eresus and Mytilene. Lesbos is the richest of the islands, honey. We have a house in Eresus, though you've never been there.

I fell in love with the sea. Archilogos did, too. He knew that some-day he would be a captain – in war and peace – and he stood with the helmsman, learning the ropes, and so did I. We made these trips in the first year, and then there were others. It was part of our studies, and never the worst part, either. But I will return to the sea. Where horses merely annoyed me, the sea charmed, terrified, roused me – like a man's first sight of a woman taking off her clothes for *him*. I never lost that arousal. Still have it.

Hah – I've made you blush.

In the evenings, when we were at home in Ephesus, I would finish my work, put Archi to bed – he was Archi to his friends and to his companion – grab a quick *opson* in the kitchens and go out into the night air to explore. I had adventures – such adventures, lass. Oh, it makes me smile. One night a pair of mercenaries sat and told me stories, because they knew me from the shrine at Plataea, and they promised to take news of my plight home. That night I dreamed of ravens, and after that I really began to think of leaving, and of home. Until they came – well, it wasn't real.

Another time I was nearly kidnapped and sold, but I put my stick in the bastard's groin and ran like hell.

Most nights, though, I went out of Master's door and just down our cobbled street to the Fountain of Pollio, where I would meet my Penelope. I call her mine, but she was never *quite* mine, although we were as far around the rim of love's cup as to kiss.

I remember the night that Hippias came to our house, because Penelope and I had been sent together to the market earlier in the day – she to buy coloured yarn for tapestry, and me to watch that she wasn't molested. My name, Doru, had started to have some meaning in the slave quarters. I could make most men eat my fist if I had to, but I was no bloody tyrant. In any case, Penelope and I had a good afternoon. I was able to show off my knowledge of the agora, and she showed off her practicality in bargaining. Then we agreed to meet that night. Something in the touch of her fingers – oh, I couldn't wait.

Hippias, the former tyrant of Athens, was coming for dinner with Artaphernes. It was an odd arrangement, because Master and Mistress didn't attend – in fact, they were at the temple, sacrificing. I think that they were away on purpose, so that they could avoid Hippias. Archilogos ended up playing the host, despite his youth, and I waited on tables. This must have been towards the end of the summer, because Darkar and I were now allies. I did his bidding without hesitation, and he didn't question my expenses. Darkar knew that Artaphernes liked me, so he had me pouring wine as the Ganymedes. Laugh if you like, thugater. I was a good slave.

Hippias tried to fondle me from the first time my hip was close enough to touch. It was odd, because I had grown past the stage when Spartans liked their boys – smooth. I had hair, and muscles. At any rate, Hippias couldn't keep his hands off me, and so I served him from farther and farther away, and bless them, the other slaves got in his way as well. Slaves in a well-run house will protect each other – up to a point.

If his hands were eager for me, his voice gave nothing away. He harangued poor Artaphernes ceaselessly, from the first libation to the last skewer of deer meat, on how he needed to storm Athens to lance the boil that would otherwise fester.

Let me just say that Hippias was, in fact, correct. Don't be blinded by his enmity, girl. He was a wise man.

'Athens must have her government changed,' he argued.

Artaphernes shook his head. 'Athens is so far west that she could never be part of my province,' he said. 'Some other man would be satrap of the west. And then – Athens is part of another world, another continent, perhaps. Am I to conquer the world to restore you, Hippias?'

Hippias drank wine. His eye had gone from me to Kylix, a smaller boy who carried water and was now serving him. Kylix slipped away from his fingertips with graceful experience, and I passed between them, helping Kylix as he helped me.

'Young Archilogos, all your slaves are beautiful!' he said, and raised his cup.

Archilogos tried to be polite. 'Thank you,' he said into his cup.

Hippias ignored him anyway. 'Artaphernes, if you refuse me, I'll be forced to go to the Great King. This is not a distant threat. I have friends in Athens. Aristagoras will speak before the assembly and they will give him ships. This war is coming. Athens will drive it if you do not. You will not do your duty to the king if you do not launch a preemptive attack on Athens!'

*Assertion*, I thought. I disliked Hippias because he was a pudgy, ugly man with greasy fingers who wanted to fondle me. Yech! But he was correct, of course. Artaphernes was an honourable man who didn't want a war. But he was, in this case, wrong.

'War will hurt trade, and every man in this city will pay – aye, and in your city and in Miletus. And the cost of a war with Athens – a real war, not just a raid – could force taxes that would drive men to open rebellion – especially if men like Aristagoras and Miltiades bribe their way into men's hearts.' Artaphernes took a skewer of meat from the stand beside his couch and ate carefully, fastidiously, like a cat. 'We do not want a war like that. Why don't you take care of it for me, my friend? If you have so many friends in Athens, why not take a few ships and restore yourself? I could lend you the money from tax revenue. Would a thousand darics of gold finance your restoration?'

Hippias grew red in the face. 'I don't need a thousand darics,' he spluttered. 'I need an army, and the power of your name. And you know that. You mock me!'

'You are a friend of the Great King. I never mock the king, nor his friends. If you feel that you must go to Great Darius and speak this way, be my guest. But I have neither the ships nor the soldiers to storm Athens for you. Nor is it my duty.' Artaphernes stretched on his couch.

Hippias left soon after, when he found that none of his advances, political or sexual, were going to lead anywhere.

When he was gone, Archilogos lay on his couch and chatted with his hero. I served both of them.

Archi had no head for wine and I was already pouring pure water into his cup. 'Why do you even entertain a man like that?' he asked the satrap.

Artaphernes shrugged. 'He is a powerful man. If he goes to Darius, I will not look well.'

Archi shook his head. 'He is a petty prince from a foreign power. Surely he can be ignored?'

'He provides me with excellent intelligence,' Artaphernes said. 'And in his way he is wise.' He drank, and then said, 'Even though he plays both sides like a treacherous Greek.'

That last was not his happiest statement. 'He is on the other side?' Archi asked. 'Can't you have him arrested?'

Artaphernes laughed. 'You are young and idealistic. Ruling a Greek is like riding a wild horse. Like herding cats. Every lordling in these waters is his own master and has his own "side". I have many roles – I am the oppressive foreign master, I am the ally of convenience, I am the source of gold and patronage, I am the lord who serves the Great King. I slip from mask to mask like one of your actors – never was an image more apt, Archilogos. Because I need to be many men to keep all you Greeks loyal to my master.'

He looked at us. I think he was speaking to himself. Suddenly he smiled and shook his head. 'I am dull company,' he said.

'No!' Archi protested. This was a dream, having his hero all to himself.

'Does Hippias plot against you?' I asked. This was daring, from a slave, but there were just the three of us, and he had spoken to me before.

He looked at me and nodded approvingly. 'Archilogos, your slave has a head on his shoulders, and when you are an officer of the Great King, this one will make a good steward.' He nodded to me. 'He plots against me only to win me over,' he said. 'It is not a Persian way of behaving. Indeed, it still mystifies me.' He smiled at Archi. 'This is why I ask your mother and father so many questions, young man. Because they can explain this behaviour to me. Hippias bribes the tyrants of the islands to revolt – so that there will be a war. He will then be at my side for the war, hoping that Athens comes in with the tyrants. Then he will use me to reconquer Athens. Does that sound possible?'

I smiled. 'Oh yes. Brilliant!' I clapped my hands. Hippias may have been a lecherous fat man, but he could think like Heracles, if that was his plan.

Artaphernes shook his head. 'I need to go back to Persepolis, where men kill each other over women and ill-chosen words, but never, ever lie.' He frowned at me. 'You understand this way of planning, then?'

I grinned. 'I do, lord.'

'Women?' Archi asked, breaking in. 'Persians kill each other over women?'

'Adultery is our national sport,' Artaphernes said, his voice heavy with some adult emotion that neither Archi nor I could interpret, and we glanced at each other. He had had too much to drink. 'Every Persian gentleman covets his friend's wife. It is like a disease, or the curse of the gods.' He looked at his cup and I moved to fill it, but he covered it. 'I grow maudlin. Let us forget that last exchange, young friends. Never speak ill of your homeland when among strangers.'

'We are not strangers, I hope!' Archi said.

'I have drunk too much. You see? I offend my host. I am off to bed.' The Mede got to his feet without his usual grace and headed off under the portico. I went and helped him into bed. He mumbled things that I ignored, because when you are a slave, people say the most amazing things. Then I went to deal with Archi, who had no head for wine and was puking in a basin.

At last, when Archi was on his couch with a rug over him, I went to find Penelope.

It was rare for us to have a scheduled tryst, and I was afire. I barely did my duty in clearing the andron of the refuse of a dinner party and I took only a cupful of stew from the kitchen and drank no wine. I needn't have hurried.

The Fountain of Pollio was old then. It has since been restored, but at that time it was the meeting place of slumming aristocrats and slaves. The roof of the fountain had fallen in and been replaced with wood, and the carpenter had done a poor job. Doubtless a slave. The Ephesians used slaves for everything and had few free craftsmen.

There were seats – benches, really – all along the outer edge of the round building, but they were rickety and only the strongest had a secure place to sit. Yet it was cool and pleasant to sit at night, and the view was spectacular, out over the river and down the bay all the way to the sea. The smoke of ten thousand cooking fires rose with the incense of the temples, and the pinpoints of ten thousand household lights coloured the landscape at our feet like the gold embroidery on a rich man's purple cloak. I could look at Ephesus by night for hours.

Which was as well, because Penelope was late. I knew that she might not come at all. We were, after all, slaves. I have probably forgotten all the truly dull and onerous days, honey, but don't forget as I tell this story that we were property, like a pot or a sandal, and our master and mistress could, without the least ill will, ruin our plans, our hopes, even our dreams. I knew that Penelope might be working or commanded to sleep in her lady's bed.

It was past full dark when she came, and she surprised me, coming up behind me where I dozed and cupping her hands over my eyes. Of course I grabbed her hands, and of course she squealed, and one thing was leading very pleasantly to another – and don't, by Aphrodite's lovely ankles, imagine we were alone. There were probably twenty courting couples in that dim room, and more outside leaning against the wall, and then there were men playing polis – that's our Greek game of cities, played with black and white counters – and women actually using the fountain. Quite a crowd. When you are a slave, honey, there's no privacy. And no secrets.

At any rate, I'd got myself a solid seat and soon I had Penelope across my lap and one hand well placed under her chiton, and she was searching the inside of my mouth with her tongue – I shouldn't tell you these things, honey, but you'll know Aphrodite well enough yourself, soon, whether I tell you or not – and kissing her was like war, like hunting. My heart pounded and my head was full of her – and then she was off my lap and across the room.

'What are you doing here?' she said, her voice more full of anger than fear.

I had no idea what she had seen, but I was on my feet, ready to attack or defend. The fountain was not a safe place, exactly. There were some bad men in the shadows.

I saw the slim figure vanish even as Penelope called after him – a boy wrapped in a chlamys.

'I'll run him down,' I said. I was instantly jealous.

'No!' my faithless lover protested, but I was off.

The chlamys was an expensive garment, striped with purple, and the wearer had long legs.

I ran the rich boy down in twenty steps, tripped him and landed on top of him with all my weight on his hips. Then I pulled the chlamys away from his head. My heart was beating, and I was ready to kill. Even then, honey, I was a killer. I had already done it often enough that killing was like kissing an old flame. I knew the dance, and my fingers were going for the finish – eyeballs.

This was no rival, and my murderous fingers stilled.

She was a rich girl. She had pearls in her hair, and her face, even in pain, was flawless, a word poets use too often. She was probably fourteen, her hair was black and her lips red, and in the light of the house lanterns, her skin was as smooth as marble. She had muscles like an athlete and high eyebrows.

I was off her as fast as I'd taken her down.

Penelope appeared and stood between us. 'You fool,' she hissed, and I had no idea which of us she was speaking to.

'I had to see where you went every night, Pen!' the girl said. 'Ares, you broke my hip, you barbarian!' She looked at Penelope. 'You have a lover!'

Penelope looked at me a moment. I'd unpinned one side of her chiton the better to reach her breasts, and it was hard for her to deny what we'd been doing. She shrugged.

'What's it to you, rich girl?' I asked.

She looked at me and her eyes twinkled. It hurts me to say this, but next to her, Penelope looked like a slave girl. Like a mortal next to a goddess. A few thousand darics, a few hundred *medimnoi* of grain and a dozen slaves at your command give you poise, confidence, perfect skin and lustrous hair that no slave girl can match. Look at yourself, girl. Now look at Blondie – your Thracian. She's handsome. But she's invisible next to you. See?

Exactly. So when this rich girl twinkled her eyes at me, I reacted. And she smiled. 'I own her,' the rich girl said. She shrugged. 'I suspect that you are the famous Spear-Boy, Doru of the barbarous west. Yes?' She laughed. 'My brother's companion making love to my companion. Oh, I will have such fun!' She clapped her hands together.

And that's how I met Briseis. Yes – you know that name. She's as much a part of this story as Miltiades or Artaphernes.

I bowed. 'I apologize for hurting you, mistress.'

She raised an eyebrow. 'What will you do for me if I don't report you, boy?' She called me pais, like a small boy who runs errands. She meant to cut me, and she succeeded.

'Nothing, kore,' I returned. A kore was a little girl of good family.

'Doru ...' Penelope cautioned.

'Nothing. Report us to Darkar. Better yet, to your parents.' I smiled. 'I will be punished for hurting you.' I shrugged. But I knew a few things – I was not a new slave. I knew that allowing someone to blackmail you was deadly. Masters loved to play this game – get someone else's slave in your debt and then use them as a spy. Oh, yes. Darkar was on top of all those tricks – he was steward and spymaster, too. He knew how to put oil on bread, I can tell you.

She looked at me for a long time. 'Really?' she said. 'Very well.'

'Don't forget to explain what you were doing outside the house after dark, naked under a chlamys.' That was the free man in me, unable to shut up. Somehow, she was like my sister. And I knew what I'd say to my sister if she tried to blackmail me. Which, come to think of it, she had done, a hundred times.

She whirled. 'You wouldn't dare!' she shot at me.

I shrugged. 'Despoina, I am a slave, and slaves are notorious for protecting themselves. And you are naked under that chlamys.'

She turned red – blushed so hard that you could see it under the fretful light of a house lamp.

She pursed her lips and got up – carefully clutching her boy's cloak around her figure – and ran back into her father's house by the slaves' door.

Penelope paused only long enough to push two fingers rather painfully into the spot where my hip's muscles stopped. 'You idiot!' she hissed. 'She meant to scare you. For fun. Why did you have to challenge her?'

I thought that I had behaved like a hero. On the other hand, I also realized that I had forgotten Penelope's existence for three minutes.

I went inside, shaking my head. I didn't lose any sleep worrying about Briseis.

Morning presented me with new troubles.

I was summoned with Archi to face Hipponax as soon as Archi had breakfasted.

Briseis was standing behind her father, dressed in an embroidered Ionic chiton of linen and a pair of golden slippers.

'My daughter says that your companion was caught last night kissing her companion,' Hipponax said. His eyes were on his son, not on me.

Archi shrugged, as young men will do – a reaction that always infuriates a parent, I can tell you. 'He kissed Penelope?' Archi asked, looking at me. 'Why?' Then he grinned. 'Or rather – why not?'

Hipponax had a javelin on the table, a light spear with a shaft of cornel wood. He slapped it on the table. It made a noise like the whip of a muleteer. I jumped. Archi blanched.

Briseis smiled.

Only then did Hipponax look at me. 'Well?' he asked me.

'Yes, lord,' I said. 'I kissed her.'

Hipponax glanced back at his daughter, and then at me. 'I do not encourage flirtation among my people, young man. But I am angered by your casual use of my andron as a place to debauch my daughter's companion.'

I flicked my eyes to that lying little fox, Briseis. So I had kissed her companion in the andron, had I?

But when my eyes met hers, a curious spark passed.

Eyes can pass many messages. And faces give so much away, honey. Especially young faces.

Even as her father spoke, she realized, I think, that her prank was going to cost me. And that her dare – she was daring me to tell her father where the incident had happened – was foolish. No slave would accept punishment under such circumstances. And who knows what she had thought inside that goddess-like head. That I would protect her because I was a foolish boy?

All this in one heartbeat. With a plea not to betray her, now that she had lied and put me in danger.

'I am disappointed in you, boy. You have a good life here. This sort of behaviour is emblematic of arrogance. I must punish it harshly, so that you will understand. Do you have anything to say for yourself?'

I let it hang here for ten heartbeats. I was calm, and I already knew what I would do. So I flicked my eyes over her – and she flinched.

Archi spoke up. 'If he was half as drunk as I, Pater, it is scarcely his fault. He had to spend the evening avoiding the unsubtle grasping of Hippias of Athens.' Bless Archi, he stood up for me like a man.

Hipponax glanced at his son and then at me. 'Is this true?' he asked.

'Yes, lord,' I said. 'I did it. I meant no arrogance, lord. I broke nothing and only one hip of mine ever touched a couch. I was drunk, and I will take my punishment.'

Hipponax raised an eyebrow, and there was humour in it for a moment. 'Well said, boy. Ten lashes instead of twenty. Let it be done now, before your mistress is up. Darkar!' he called, and the steward came forward with a pair of porters.

They took me into the courtyard. They already knew what had passed, and what had really happened. Darkar tied my wrists to the flogging pole *hard* and poked me in the side. 'You are a fool, and you deserve all twenty blows,' he said. 'You are playing a dangerous game, *slave*. She will do this to you again, now that she knows she has the power.'

I took the ten blows with gritted teeth. They weren't kisses. The whole weight of the javelin haft on my buttocks, ten times. By the tenth, it took all my strength not to call out. It hurts that much.

Better your arse than your feet, though.

I cried a little afterwards, but in the amphora cellar where no one could see me. Darkar took me there. He wasn't a bad man. He left me until I was done sobbing, and then gave me a bowl of cold water and my chiton. 'You are a fool,' he told me.

Oh, aye. I *was* a fool.

Those ten blows had a profound effect, because they reminded me that I was a slave. It is one thing to offer to accept punishment to protect a beautiful woman – and that was my intention, very heroic – but it is another thing to take the blows. Humiliating and painful, and the humiliation had only just begun, because it was two weeks before I was healed, and because Archi told every one of his friends and Heraclitus exactly what I had done and how I had been punished. He began by being indignant on my behalf and ended being pleased to have such an adult story to tell of his slave, and that had an effect on our relationship. I was a slave.

Penelope avoided me. One evening I found her in the water stores and we kissed. I thought that all was well, but she never came to the fountain. I couldn't figure her out – kissing me like a *hetaira*, and then pretending she didn't know me when she passed me in the market.

And neither Master nor Mistress allowed us out together any more.

There were other girls. There was a red-haired Thracian girl who was happy to play at the fountain, and I never even knew what house she came from. Sometimes she would come wrapped in a *peplos* like a matron, but with nothing underneath, and that was fascinating, too. But when I played with her, I thought of Briseis. Briseis's face made other women ugly. Her colours made other women dull. Her figure—

This is a disease that I still have, honey. Hah! The little archer put his shaft deep in me. I doubt that I'd even want the shaft to be drawn, that's how bad I am!

But time passed, and there were other pursuits. Archi began to practise at the gymnasium. He was fast and strong for his age, and we sparred constantly – every day, I think. We had oak swords that hurt like blazes when we swung them too hard, and we had shields – a round aspis for him and a big Boeotian shield for me, like an egg shape with two round cut-outs. It was a joke to Master – he knew I was from Boeotia and the shield was the only Boeotian thing he'd ever heard of.

We threw spears, shot bows and carved each other up with wooden swords. At the gymnasium he was paired against other boys his own age, and I watched. Slaves were not welcome to compete in the gymnasium. Another reminder.

But in the Temple of Artemis slaves *were* welcome to compete. By the time a year had passed, I had begun to understand Heraclitus's theory of the logos – and to share his suspicion that most men are fools. I could never understand why the other boys were so slow to understand his principles, so slow to learn the rules of rational argument, and so utterly, painfully slow in learning the fundamentals of geometry.

Hmm. What a pleasure I must have been to have around.

Diomedes was one of the young men of Ephesus. He was a year older than Archi, so just about my age, and one day he'd had enough of being called a dolt by Heraclitus. After class, when we were all pushing down the steps, he jostled me.

I stepped closer.

He laughed. 'What are you going to do, slave? Hit me?' He slapped me with his hand open. 'Slave. Go suck Archi's dick, there's a good slave. Is his mouth good for you, Archi dear? Is that why Heraclitus loves the boy so much?'

I shook with rage.

Archi laughed. 'You're a bad loser, Diomedes. And if you had fewer pimples, I imagine you could arrange to suck a few dicks yourself, instead of talking about it.' Archi had that knack – as his sister had – of biting worse than he was bitten.

Diomedes lunged at Archi and I tripped him. He fell down the steps in a tangle of chlamys and limbs, and was hurt. He screamed with pain and his slave, a silent boy named Arete, had to carry him home.

Archi laughed and we went home. But two days later, a big man with a beard asked after me at the fountain. One of the older slaves sent him to me, where I was holding court for the younger slaves. By that time I was quite the young cock among the little ones. No man can be a slave all the time.

The big man came up out of the dark with a companion of his own size, and I knew they were trouble.

'Doru? Slave of Archilogos?' the big man asked.

'Who wants to know?' I asked.

He went for me. He had some training and he had a palm's width of reach on me, and his companion was already brushing the smaller boys out of his way to get behind me.

'Get Darkar!' I shouted at Kylix. He ran for the house and I took a punch. I got away from most of it, but the part I took staggered me, and the second blow caught my forehead.

I ducked and ran into the fountain house, but they were on me, and the slaves inside were as much an impediment to me as they were to the two thugs. One had a leather strap, and he kept hitting me with it. It stung, but it was a weapon for terrifying a cringing slave, not a weapon for hurting a warrior.

I took the strap across my kidneys and got my hand on one of the bad planks in the seats and ripped it free.

Now, mortal combat is an interesting experience, honey. I don't think I ever planned to get that plank. I ran inside the fountain house from instinct and terror. And only terror got that plank off its supports. Amazing what you can do when terror aids your muscles. But once it was in my hands, my daimon entered me, and I went from terror to attack in the blink of an eye.

I ripped it clear and hit one of the thugs right in the side of the head and he went down. His head made an ugly sound hitting the stone floor, too. Music to my ears, and the killer was loose.

The other man grunted and hit me, a light, glancing blow on my arm muscles, but perhaps the twentieth blow I had taken. He was wearing me down.

I feinted and swung my unhandy club, but he was under it and he got an elbow in my gut. I stamped a foot on his instep and we were down in the muck that lay over the stones. I hit my elbow so badly going down that my left arm was numb, then he got my head under his arm and hit me two or three times, hard enough to break my nose – again – and the next shot almost put me out.

But I was a killer, not a victim. I grabbed his balls and tried to rip them off and he screamed. He thought that he had me, with that headlock. I got his balls and I dug my thumb in while I ripped, and he screamed like a woman in childbirth.

He lay writhing on the floor and I knelt on his back, got my hand under his head and snapped his neck.

Then I went back to the one whose head I'd hit, and I snapped his neck, too.

I swore I'd tell you the truth, honey. I'm a killer. When the daimon comes on me, I kill. And remember the lesson – that dead men tell no tales.

Then Darkar came.

'Demeter, boy!' the steward said. He held me at arm's length because I tried to hurt him. I'm like that when the spirit of Heracles comes on me. 'Ares, boy! You've killed this one!'

I was losing the daimon of combat, and I shook my head and my nose hurt. 'He was hurting me,' I said.

Kylix poured water over my head. 'You killed them both,' he said, and there was awe in his voice.

Darkar looked at the shambles. He looked for some time and then he shook his head. 'I'm sorry, boy,' he said. 'I have to tell Master. This is more than I can cover.'

I don't know how long it was after my meeting with Briseis in the dark, but it must have been six months. We'd just had a trip to Lesbos and I was well-liked, for a slave. Hipponax didn't view me as a troublemaker. But this time, it was dark, I was covered in blood and Master was standing over me in his own courtyard.

'Men attacked him,' Darkar said. 'He sent Kylix for me.'

Hipponax loomed over me and his cool hands, which smelled of beeswax, touched my cheek. 'Gods – get him a doctor.' Darkar was silent. 'What is it, Darkar?'

'He killed them,' Darkar said. 'Both of them. Free men, I think. Their bodies are in the fountain house.'

Hipponax knelt beside me. 'They attacked you, boy?'

I nodded. I could barely breathe. I had a broken nose and at least two broken ribs, too.

Hipponax rose. 'Take him to the Temple of Asclepius, then. And dispose of the dead men. Pay the other slaves for their silence. I take it these are not men of property?'

Darkar spat. 'Scum, lord. Thugs.'

Archi came at a run. He looked at me and he took my hand. 'Artemis! Doru – what happened?'

I was silent, but Archi figured it out. 'Diomedes!' he said.

Hipponax ignored his son and turned to his steward. 'The fountain is now off-limits to our people. Dispose of the bodies. You may use a cart and a mule.'

'Thank you, lord,' I said.

Hipponax ignored me. To his son, he said, 'Diomedes will soon be a son of this house. Are you accusing him of attacking your *slave*?'

Archi shrugged – which, as I have mentioned, is not the way to placate a parent. You might take note of that yourself, thugater. My mind whirled. *Son of this house?* That meant that Diomedes was to marry Briseis.

I vomited on the flagstones.

After that, I was in debt to every slave in the house. It took a conspiracy of the whole neighbourhood to keep me safe. Yes – slaves are never friends. Or perhaps I should say that desperate slaves are never friends. Happy, prosperous slaves in a good house have the time and safety to be friends – selfish, backbiting friends, but friends nonetheless. But they hate the masters in their own way. Someone might have blabbed, if anyone had made it worth their while, but those two men – slave or free – they were scum. No one came looking for them.

I began to live with fear. In fact, I began to think like a slave – really think like a slave. I began to be very careful about what I said. I began to swallow insults. Those two killings taught me another lesson – and I was lucky to get off so cheaply. A week in the temple, and a year of carrying water and emptying chamber pots and fetching yarn and running errands – and minding my words. And a twinge in my chest when the rain is coming, every time – those broken ribs are still with me, honey.

A month later I was back at my lessons. Diomedes caught me on the steps. 'Your nose looks bad,' he said. 'How *could* that have happened?'

I didn't even meet his eye. I consoled myself that I had killed his thugs. I told myself that I would have my revenge.

But I crawled like a slave and didn't meet his eyes.

And that hurt more than the beating.


Heraclitus understood something of what had passed. He became more careful of his praise for me and at the same time more acerbic in his dealings with Diomedes. I kept my head down until one day, as we rose to leave the steps, I found his bronze-shot staff resting against my sternum.

'Stay,' he said. He nodded to Archi. 'You, too.'

When the other boys were gone, he looked around. 'What's going on?' he asked.

We were both silent, as young men ever are in the face of authority.

His staff pointed at my nose. 'Who did that?'

I shrugged.

Heraclitus nodded. 'Strife makes change, and change is the way of the logos,' he said. A statement I'd heard a hundred times, actually, except there and then, I think that I understood.

'Change is not always good,' I said, rubbing my nose.

'Change merely *is*,' the philosopher said. 'Why are you so good at geometry, boy?'

I bowed my head at his praise. 'My father was a bronze-smith,' I said. 'We use a compass, a straight edge and a scribe to lay out our work. I knew how to make a right-angled triangle before I came here.' I shrugged. 'Any potter or leather-worker could do as well, I expect.'

He shook his head. 'Somehow I doubt it. So – you know how to work bronze?'

I nodded. 'I'm no master,' I said. 'But I could make a cup.'

He shrugged. 'Hmm,' he said. 'I am more interested in the properties of fire than in having a cup made.'

I have to say that at some point I had learned that, far from being the penniless beggar he seemed, Heraclitus had been offered the tyranny of the city and his father and brother were lords. He was a very rich man.

He went on, 'Fire hardens and softens, isn't that true, bronze-smith?'

I nodded. 'Fire and water to anneal make bronze soft,' I said, 'but iron hard.'

He nodded. 'So with all strife and all change,' he said. 'Strife is the fire, the very heart of the logos. Some men are made free, and others are made slaves.'

'I am a slave,' I said bitterly.

Archi turned and looked at me. 'I never treat you as a slave,' he said.

What could I say? He treated me as an object every day, but I knew that he treated me better than other slaves and a hundred times better than men like Hippias treated their slaves.

But Heraclitus was looking out to sea, or into the heart of the logos, or nowhere. 'Most men are slaves,' he said. 'Slaves to fear, slaves to greed, slaves to the walls of their cities or the possession of a lover. Most men seek to ignore the truth, and the truth is that every-thing is in flux and there is no constant except change.' He looked at me. 'It is ironic, is it not, that you understand my words, and you are free inside your head, while standing here as a chattel, property of this other boy who cannot fathom what we are talking about?'

Archilogos frowned. 'I'm not as stupid as you claim,' he said hotly.

Heraclitus shrugged. 'What is the logos?' he asked, and Archi shook his head.

'Change?' he asked. He looked at me.

Heraclitus swatted him. 'Best be going home.'

I thought that I understood his message. 'You think that I should not give up hope,' I said.

Now the master looked mystified. 'What have I to do with hope?' he asked, but he had a twinkle in his eye.

Another winter passed. I could calculate inside my head without using my fingers and I could draw a man with charcoal. I could put my spear into a target ten horse-lengths distant, no more than a finger's width from the instructor's cane pointing where he wanted to see the throw. And I was growing to be the swordsman I wanted to be. I was strong. After all, I was getting the exercise of a rich man, and for nothing. Every day I could lift a larger weight stone. I could raise it behind my head and over my chest, I could lift my body off the floor of the temple with my hands alone. I was tall, and taller every day, and my chest began to grow broad. I was *strong*.

Archi grew, too. He grew as quickly as I did, or perhaps faster. Suddenly he was as tall and as wide, and when we wrestled, we could hurt each other, and we no longer dared to use oak swords to fight, because we could break bones. Instead, we fought as the ephebes fought, a spear's length apart, as if dancing, so that each blow was parried without sword and shield ever coming together.

Archilogos loved competition and he never liked to lose, so he began to apply himself to his studies, and he could suddenly do the geometry I could do and he could solve sums in his head, too.

I hated being a slave but, all the same, it was a good time. Adolescents are good at these divisions, and indeed, Heraclitus was full of such pairs of strife-riven opposites. So – at Ephesus, I was a slave, but in many ways, I was freer than I ever was again. I was poor and had nothing but my coins in the jar in the garden – although they were beginning to pile up. And yet, in just the way Heraclitus described, I was rich beyond imagining, with a young, strong body and an agile mind and the company of others like me. What young man – or woman – wants more?

Yes. So it was. And so another year passed, and we worked and played. I thought less and less of Briseis, although every time I saw her – and that was seldom – my heart beat as if I was in a fight. Diomedes came to our house to woo her. Hipponax took care that I should be on errands when this happened, not because he knew – or would have tolerated – my hidden passion, but because he suspected who had sent the thugs.

Although I still pursued Penelope, I understood that she had chosen to put space between us. I had other lovers – girls who were easier, freer, and never as much fun.

And then came the events that broke the pot that held us, and smashed the futures we had imagined in our ignorance. Strife came, and with it, change.

# 9

It was spring. I remember that well, because the end of the world began with a day of roses and jasmine and sun and beauty.

I was seventeen by my reckoning, and when I walked through the agora, women watched me. Don't laugh, thugater. I was once one of those.

And men watched me as well. What cared I? If I had been free, men would have put my name on pots. Even as a slave, I was *kalos kagathos*. I was beautiful and smart and strong.

Oh, the arrogance of youth.

Archi and I were boxing in the garden, Euthalia watching us from her couch, and Hipponax lay next to her, stroking her as she watched us fight.

We'd been at it for enough time for the water-clock to run out and be refilled. We were covered in sweat and euphoric with the daimon of it. And then Briseis came.

She seldom entered the centre of the house. As an unmarried virgin, she kept very much to the women's quarters. But that was the week that Hipponax had put his seal to her wedding contract with Diomedes, and she was gathering her trousseau and acting like an adult. So she was allowed out.

She looked like a goddess. I say that too often – but she was flawless. I know now that she must have done it on purpose, but she was arrayed in linen and wool worth the value of my father's farm and the smithy, too. The smell of mint and jasmine came off her, as light as a feather on the air.

I caught all of this in the same glance that showed me Penelope at her heels and earned me a blow to my upper chest. Archi wasn't distracted by his sister – far from it. He bore down. His blows came thick and fast.

But he had not had Calchas. And he had never killed. Later, he became a great warrior, a name that was spoken throughout Hellas, but when I was seventeen, he was never my match.

So I took a few blows and then my right shot out, a stop-attack into his flurry, straight through his guard on to the point of his chin, and he staggered.

Briseis clapped mockingly. 'Oh, Archi, show me that again!' she called.

He held up a hand to me and I bowed. Then he picked up a pitcher of cold water, drank half and tossed the rest over his sister and all her finery.

She screamed and her right fist shot out, as fast as mine, and she clipped his head with her blow.

Yet, for all that, they loved each other, and suddenly they were laughing – he naked, and she with the purple dye leaking off a garment that had cost more than I imagined my father made in his best year. Now ruined.

How rich they were.

She stripped the two garments over her head – Ionians don't worry about the nudity of women the way westerners do – and took a simple linen shift from Penelope, who blushed when she took it off and gave it to her mistress and ran for something to wear herself.

No one in the garden was looking at me, so I drank in the beauty of Briseis's body – her high, pointed breasts and the lush growth of black hair between her legs. I tore my eyes away and glanced around – Hipponax was spluttering wine at his daughter's behaviour, and Archi was staring after Penelope with the same lust with which I was watching his sister.

And Euthalia was watching me, her face set in cool appraisal. I flinched and dropped my eyes. There were rumours in the slave quarters that Euthalia was anything but a loyal wife – and that Hipponax cared little. But no one had suggested that her games extended to slaves. I was old enough, however, to know what that cool appraisal meant in an older woman – Cook looked at me just the same way, whether she meant to slap my hand for stealing bread or to get me in her bed.

My theory is that women who have borne a child learn the same lesson men learn when they face the enemy on the battlefield, and that after that, they look at you with the same look. That's my theory.

Learn what, you ask?

I'm old, and my cup is empty. Don't read into that, honey – just pour some wine. Learn the lesson yourself.

Penelope came back, decently covered, and Briseis stayed, enjoying the trouble she had caused. 'When is Diomedes coming?' she asked for the fourth time. Their betrothal having been signed, they would shortly have a ceremony at her hearth and then a party. She was an old woman of fifteen and wanted to get on with life.

Hipponax made a face. 'Girl, we have enough on our plates without you going womb-mad to your betrothal party!'

Euthalia slapped her husband lightly. 'We have a small problem, Briseis,' she said. 'Artaphernes has chosen to honour us with a visit. In fact, he has summoned many of the leaders of Ionia – great men, and famous names – to meet here in our city and have a synod.'

She didn't mention that Diomedes' father was a member of the other faction – the independence faction. And thus not a man to be delighted to find Artaphernes at his son's betrothal party. Only their mercantile links kept them friends. The betrothal had been planned since Briseis was born.

All this went by in the beat of a heart. Briseis shrugged. 'My betrothal is more important than the bickering of old men,' she said with a toss of her head.

Her mother shook her head. 'No, my dear. Your betrothal can happen whenever we ordain it. These men gather to prevent a war. You have no idea what war is, dear. None of you do.'

She seldom spoke seriously, but when she did, we listened. But inside, I thought, *I have seen war.*

'I am from Lesbos, and throughout my youth, the men of Mytilene made war on my city. Farms burned and women raped and families sold as slaves – good families. If Athens storms this city, Briseis, you will be sold in the market to a soldier. Do you understand?'

Briseis couldn't have been more shocked if her mother had hit her. 'Athens is a town of barbarians,' she spat. 'You and Pater both say so!'

'Barbarians with a fleet and an army,' Hipponax said. 'Listen, dear. Let us have the conference and then we'll have the party. You will only have to wait a month.'

Briseis flicked her eyes around the garden and she found me, and blushed. Then she sat in the chair that Dorcus, one of the house slaves, brought for her, and she leaned out over the table to take her father's wine cup, exposing her bare side and causing my whole body to twitch. All quite intentional.

'Very well, Pater,' she said calmly. This was so far from her parent's expected reaction that her father was literally open-mouthed with astonishment.

'The good of Ionia is more important than my wedding,' she said sweetly.

If we had been on a stage, the audience would have seen the furies gathering.

Artaphernes came with a whole regiment of cavalry, Lydians and Persians in separate squadrons, the Lydians armed with lances and the Persians with bows and spears. In the agora, men complained that he had brought all the soldiers to overawe them, and the soldiers were arrogant, thrusting out their chests, pushing men and flirting with women in every square in the town.

I watched them curiously. They were very different from the hoplites of Boeotia. For one thing, they were the most aggressive woman-hunters I'd ever seen, especially the Persians, and if there was a boy-lover among them, I never met him. Second, they were lazy. Not at their soldier-work – when I visited their camps, I saw swordplay and archery of a high calibre. But if they were not drilling or shooting, they did nothing but swear, fight and fuck – sorry, dear.

In my day, in the west, we had no 'professional' soldiers, except the Spartan nobles, and even the Spartans occupied themselves with ceaseless athletics and hunting. I'd never seen full-time soldiers who sat in wine shops, drinking, spitting and grabbing girls.

They were tough. They were rich, too. The average Persian cavalryman had a groom for his horse and a slave for his kit. He had his own tent and perhaps another felt shelter for his slaves and his gear. Every one of them had bronze and silver cups, water pitchers, plates – I'd never seen a soldier with so much *stuff*.

And they had women in their camps. Some were wives and some were prostitutes, and many seemed to fall in some mysterious (only to me) gap between the two defined roles. They worked hard, too – harder than the men, washing, cooking, sewing and minding children.

A Persian cavalry regiment was like a travelling town where all the citizens were lords. I liked them quite a bit. They liked me, too. Most of them had never seen a western Greek. They were contemptuous of Ionians, as poor warriors, but they'd heard that we Boeotians were fighters, and I told my war stories to the four men I liked best – a pair of brothers and their two friends, all from the same small town near Persepolis. They *were* lords, or they called themselves noblemen, and you might well ask why they talked to Greek slaves.

I was in camp on an errand to Artaphernes, carrying a herald's staff for my master. Artaphernes had a tent in camp and a lavish establishment, and he was sometimes there and sometimes at our house, for reasons that were beyond me. When he was in camp, I was the herald, mostly because he liked me and I could get to him faster than other messengers.

I was picking up a little Persian – camp Persian, hardly what anyone speaks at court. But I was there every day or two, and the delivery of a message to a satrap of Persia is *never* a simple or quick task, especially if there is an answer. One time I remember cooling my heels all day only to discover that the satrap was already *at our house*.

At any rate, one day my four Persians were on duty outside the satrap's tent-palace, and after I showed them my staff, I entertained them by pretending it was a sword and doing my exercises, since I was missing lessons by running errands. And Darius – in those days, it seemed that all Persians were called Darius – called out and asked my name.

'I'm Doru,' I said, 'companion to Archilogos, son of Hipponax.' I shrugged.

'You have the wrist of a real swordsman,' Darius said. He took my herald's staff, a pair of solid bronze rods, and hefted it. 'I'd be hard put to do my cuts with this. Cyrus, try your sword arm on this toy.' He tossed my staff to his brother, who caught it.

They were as alike as statues in a temple portico – skin the colour of old wood, jet-black hair and clear brown eyes, handsome as gods.

Cyrus whirled my staff through some exercises – not my exercises, so I watched with fascination. He tossed it to me. 'Let's see you do that, boy!' he said.

So I did. I copied his moves, interested in the differences, and all four Persians applauded, and after that we were all friends. They were easy men to like, and we fenced sometimes. They never used shields, which made them very different men to face. Cyrus also taught me a trick that has saved my life fifty times – how to kill a man with his own shield. Have you seen it?

Here – you, scribe. Take that shield off the wall – I won't eat you – and put it on your arm. So you *do* know how to hold a shield – good for you. My opinion of you just went up. Now face off against me – damn this hip. Pretend you have a sword. Now watch, honey.

Just like that, and I've broken his arm and killed him. Sorry, lad. You can get up now. Useful trick, eh? All I do is grab the rim of the shield and rotate it. There's no man born, no matter how strong, who can hold the centre of a wheel while I rotate the rim. Yes? This is based on a mathematical principle that I could explain if I was given enough wine, but for the moment, it suffices that it is true. And see how our pen-pusher's arm is in the *porpax* – that bronze strap across his upper forearm? So he can't escape his shield once I start to rotate the rim – and I break his arm.

If he was a killer, he might gut me with his blade while I break his arm. If he isn't – and few men are killers, thank the gods – then I push his now helpless arm and shield rim into his face, smash his nose and he's dead. See? Cyrus taught me that, bless him.

They were free-giving, hard-drinking men, and I grew to love them in two weeks. They seemed more *alive* than other men. More *real*. They fought duels all the time, cutting other Persians over fancied or real slights, over a misspoken word or a cold shoulder. They were dangerous dogs, and they bit hard.

My status as a slave meant nothing to them, of course. To them, all Greeks were their slaves. Which rankled, but they were so far above me that I couldn't be offended at their attitude to the Ionians – an attitude I shared.

At any rate, the summer passed with lessons and struggles. I was seeing an Aethiopian girl from a house as lavish as ours, the Lekthantae, hereditary priests and priestesses of Artemis, one of the noblest and richest families of the city. Salwe was tall and thin and dark like night, and while we never loved each other, she had a sharp mind and a vicious tongue and we entertained each other, in and out of bed. I loved going out to the Persian camp. I loved working through the ever more complex problems of geometry that Heraclitus gave me. I would sit in the fountain house – after Master lifted the ban – and sing on my lyre, and Salwe would sing with me, her voice capable of curious harmony that she said her people in Africa always sang. It was a good summer.

The tyrants of Ionia were gathering in the houses of the upper town, and so we had dinner with Hippias again, and dinner with

Anaximenes of Miletus, who had replaced the traitor Aristagoras as tyrant of Miletus. Aristagoras was reputed to have spoken that summer to the assembly of Athens, just as Hippias predicted, and to have been granted a fleet of Athenian ships to come and make war on the Great King in the name of the 'rebellion'.

There was no rebellion. All the leaders of Ionia were in and out of our house, and the great cities – Miletus, Ephesus, Mytilene – were, if not solid in loyalty to the Great King, at least uninterested in revolt. Some men wanted war, but most of them were penniless exiles.

It was odd, but as a slave, I probably knew more about what was happening than the satrap. I knew that on the dockside, where young men gathered when the ships came in from all over the Ionian, men spoke of Aristagoras as a hero and of Athens as a liberator. Gentlemen and rowers, seamen, small merchants – they were all fired by the *idea* of independence. But the nobles and the rich in the upper town were insulated from this talk, just as they were insulated from the gossip of their slaves.

As the number of incidents between the Persian soldiers and the townspeople – and the sailors – mounted, Artaphernes was forced to confront the reality that there were people in Ephesus – many people – who viewed any Persian as a foe. And his soldiers didn't help. Darius and Cyrus thought nothing more comical than to separate a pretty Greek girl from her Ionian boyfriend – by a mixture of force and persuasion that, let's be honest, young women enjoy. Some young women. At any rate, multiply their efforts by a hundred, and there wasn't a Greek virgin left in the lower town to marry her behorned and already cuckolded man, and that is the fastest way to violence.

The Persians were fastidious. They didn't rape and they didn't pick on slaves, the way Greek soldiers will. So the slaves didn't mind them. But the Greeks – the smallholders of the lower town – killed a few in ambushes, and then the swords were out all over town, and Artaphernes' troubles began in earnest.

It wore him out. I saw him every day and ran messages for Mistress to him, offering him a remedy for headache or sometimes just carrying a verse or a flower. I liked running errands for my mistress, because she was kind to me, gave me money and it was an excuse to be in the women's wing. She favoured me, and she must have said something, because suddenly, after a year of forced parting, Penelope warmed to me again, and we were allowed to go out together on errands to the agora and to be together in private.

This is what I mean, my honey, when I say that masters have effects on their slaves that they never intend. I don't think Hipponax ever intended that I never see Penelope again, nor, I think, did Mistress understand how far Penelope and I might go – or perhaps she knew exactly what was happening. In fact, even as I tell this, I wonder if she sought to end another liaison – one whose discovery hurt me more than anything.

Anyway, it was on one of our errands together that I contributed unwittingly to the problems of the town. I was in the agora with Penelope – hand in hand – when a man clouted me in the head and sent me tumbling into the muck beneath the tanners' stalls. Penelope screamed. Once again, there were two attackers, but this time I was badly hurt. If my attackers hadn't been fools, I'd have died. One started kicking me and the other grabbed Penelope. In a crowded agora, that was a foolish move. She had a healthy scream and she bit him hard. Unlike a free-born girl, slave girls know *just* how to deal with attack. But I didn't see any of it, because my initial attacker had put his foot into my guts and I puked. He grabbed my hair – and then I was covered in blood.

Cyrus killed both my attackers. It was the will of the gods that Cyrus and Pharnakes, his particular friend, were in the market, looking for trouble, and I provided it. They killed my assailants with the joy with which men do such things.

But because there was a Greek lying on the ground and a screaming woman, many others in the agora jumped to the wrong conclusions. As I began to return to my senses, an ugly crowd was forming and Penelope was still screaming. She'd never seen a man's intestines before. Not her fault.

I got to my feet and had the sense to offer my hand to Cyrus, and he had the sense to take it, mud and blood and all. Then I embraced Penelope, and she let me lead her away.

'Best come with me, lord,' I said to Cyrus, and he and Pharnakes did as I suggested, like good soldiers. I led them up the hill and the crowd followed us for a few streets, but soon enough we got free.

After that I was much more careful when I was out of the house. Diomedes wanted me dead. I had forgotten him. The very best revenge. His betrothal had been put off all summer, and I suppose he thought to take it out on me. I told Hipponax before he went off to Byzantium on a short cruise, and he told me that he would see to it.

Cyrus told me that it was I who had saved his life, by leading them out of the agora, and not the other way around, and he treated me with courtesy and gave me more lessons. As the summer passed, my Persian got better, and by the time Hipponax returned from his ship, no one else had tried to kill me.

The 'conference' went on and on. The tyrants were not willing to raise men for Artaphernes or to give the assurances he wanted. Nor were they awed by his soldiers. Most of them were islanders, and they had a hard time imagining the Great King's cavalry coming to their shores.

Oft-times, when the guards admitted me to the satrap's presence, I would find him sitting with his head in his hands, staring at his work table. That's how bad the summer had grown, towards the end. Not that he was ever less than courteous to me, and he always paid me a compliment and gave me a tip. Even when he became my mortal foe, I never forgot his basic goodness. Artaphernes was a *man*. Some men are noble by nature, honey. He was one.

Heraclitus once told us that the value of a man could be measured in the worth of his enemies. Well, if that's true, I was doing well.

One day in late summer, I brought Artaphernes an invitation from my mistress for dinner. We walked back together – he usually rode, but this time he left his escort in camp, and all he had was my four friends in a loose knot about him. Twice he stopped to speak to common people with petitions. He was that kind of man.

I waited on him at table, and Archi, who was suddenly tall and handsome, shared his couch and they talked together like old friends while Euthalia plied them both with fine food and too much wine. Kylix was mixing the wine as thin as he dared, but still all three were drunk in fairly short order. My four friends were in the kitchen with Cook and Darkar waiting on them. They were lords, but they were simple soldiers, and they weren't offended. We were having a fine evening. I went back and forth from kitchen to andron, and sometimes I'd carry a joke from the high to the low, or even back.

Late in the meal, Hipponax came in. He'd taken a new ship to sea that morning to try her, and he was back early and none too happy with what he'd just seen.

'There was a riot in the lower town,' he said.

This was old news to me, and shows how little they knew, really.

'Two of your men dead and five lower-class people – but citizens, damn it!' Hipponax shook his head. 'Artaphernes, you *must* send those soldiers away before you create the very climate you seek to avoid.'

Artaphernes sat up on his couch. 'No man tells me what I must do,' he said quietly, 'except the Great King whose servant I am.'

Hipponax smiled. 'It's like that, is it? Very well, be the satrap, lord. But those soldiers are doing more harm than good.' He wasn't drunk, thank the gods, or we might have had trouble.

Artaphernes shook himself. 'Bah, I'm drunk,' he admitted. 'I need to get out of this cesspool. Before I do something I'll regret.' His frustration showed. And something about Hipponax's arrival set him off. He frowned. 'This stinking cesspool.'

Hipponax refused to take offence. 'I've never heard sacred Ephesus described as a stinking cesspool before,' he said. 'I must say that it won't make it as a poetical contribution.'

His wife laughed. She brought wine to the satrap with her own hands. I could smell her perfume from my station – heady, musky stuff. 'Perhaps I will smell less like a cesspool, lord,' she purred.

'You are the only thing worth having in this town,' Artaphernes said.

Hipponax's eyes met mine. I bowed and fetched two slaves to help me move a kline for him, and we set him up with a wine cup and some food. Darkar came up from the kitchen and caught my eye. I slipped out.

'You have this under control?' he asked.

I shook my head. 'There's something here I don't get,' I admitted. 'The satrap is angry and he's taking it out on Master.'

Darkar looked at me with something very like pity. 'I will take your place. You go and wait on your young master only, and get him to bed as quickly as you can convince him – or just feed him wine.'

'What of Cyrus and the others in the kitchen?' I asked.

He shook his head. 'They're no trouble. Off to your duty, now.'

So I tried to put wine into Archi. I needn't have bothered. He had a head for wine by then, and he could probably have gone bowl for bowl with his father, but suddenly he smiled at me and shook his head, pushing away his bowl. 'I'm for bed,' he said.

Darkar shot me a glance, but it was none of my doing. I escorted my master to bed, but he was impatient with me, and after a few attempts at conversation I was dismissed.

I went back to the kitchen to visit my friends. I was off duty, unless

Cook or Darkar, the two senior slaves, chose to order me about. In fact, as I waited on the Persians while I chatted to them, we were all at our ease. I served them wine and they laughed and joked and flirted with Penelope when she came through – I assumed on an errand for Briseis, bored in the women's wing and not invited to the party. I'd seldom seen Penelope in the kitchen. She didn't linger.

After an hour, Darkar leaned in and shot me a look. I drank off the wine I'd poured and followed him into the hall. He looked flustered and somehow apologetic. 'Master is going back to his ship,' he said. 'I need you to be a porter.'

Well, that's the life of a slave. It wasn't my job, but by this time all our porters were asleep or drunk. It was a feast day, I think – I can't even remember where they all were. So I went to the portico and hoisted Master's bags and followed him through the dark town.

He didn't say a word.

The Pole Star was high by the time we made his ship. He exchanged a few terse words with his boatkeeper and walked along the waterside. Then he whirled on me.

'I'll be damned if I'm to be thrown out of my own house,' he said, as if I had ordained this strange fate.

I fell back a step.

'Oh – sorry, lad. Not your fault. Come on!' He started back up the hill.

It was a hard walk, but we were healthy men, and anything I had on him in youth was balanced by the weight of his sea bags. At the portico, he put a hand on my shoulder. 'Here's a daric,' he said – a fortune. A gold daric? Then, suddenly, I knew that something was wrong. Masters don't give slaves a daric for carrying their bags. Not on purpose, anyway. 'Go somewhere, Doru. Go – go and check on Archilogos.'

Whatever was happening, he wanted me gone.

I bowed, took the coin and walked into the house, heading into the men's quarters. I walked across the hallway that separated the servants and slaves from the family, and something – automatic obedience, I suppose – caused me to walk into Archi's room instead of going straight to my bed.

He had lamps lit, and he was riding Penelope. She saw me instantly, over his back, his buttocks pinned between her thighs, her mouth slightly open. She wasn't unwilling, to say the least.

He didn't see me.

I flattened against the wall, my heart beating as if a horse race was crossing my chest. Let me say it – I had never ridden the girl myself. She had been very careful with me, and I got a blow to the ear if my fingers strayed.

But I didn't see red, either. I've said it before – when you are a slave, you know that you don't have control of some things. Such as your body. If Archi had ever had a mind to have me, I'd have had no choice. He took Penelope, instead. And I'm no hypocrite – I'd been with a girl or two that summer. Penelope owed me nothing.

I walked around the corner, then stopped and took some deep breaths.

I don't know how long I stood there. Longer than I realized, because suddenly she was there, a shawl over her, slipping along the wall of the portico towards the women's side. I knew her movements. I followed her and called her name. She looked back and ran.

I ran after her. I ran right into the women's quarters.

Then everything began to happen in slow motion. I was running like a fool and suddenly she stopped. In the light of a single hall lamp, I saw that there was a man in the hall, and that Penelope had run into him full tilt. He had a sword.

Penelope screamed.

But I knew him immediately. It was Master. With a sword. In my state, I took it in without understanding – somehow I thought he was there to punish me for entering the women's quarters.

Penelope must have recognized him, because she was silent after that first scream.

And then Artaphernes stepped out of the room behind me – Mistress's room – and I understood.

'You've always told me that you never lie,' Master said to Artaphernes.

He had the sword loosely in his hand. He was no swordsman. And he was calm – murderously calm, I think. He had already dismissed Penelope and me as superfluous to the scene. Penelope backed away from him and into my arms. I put a hand over her mouth.

Artaphernes was naked, and it was no secret what he'd been doing. 'I do not lie,' he said. He was afraid, but covering it well.

'Why did you have to fuck my wife?' Hipponax asked.

Artaphernes met Hipponax's eyes. He shrugged. 'I love her,' he said. 'And if you kill me, Ionia will burn.'

Hipponax laughed grimly, and I knew what he intended. 'Let her burn, then,' he said.

I had spent the last heartbeats with my hand over Penelope's mouth, and now I pushed her, hard, into Hipponax. Remember, I'd walked with him – I knew he was sober. But it was a risk that he would spit her. Perhaps I did blame her for her little ride. She'd looked well pleased under Archi's cock, damn her.

At any rate, she was not spitted on Master's sword. He lifted the blade to keep her safe, and I stepped in and stripped it from his hands. And then fell to the ground, as if I too had stumbled.

All three of us went down in a tangle.

Artaphernes was no fool. He ran.

Everything might yet have been well – or well enough – but Pharnakes came into the corridor with his three friends at his heels. They had blades in their hands, and as soon as they had their satrap clear, they charged us. Who knows what they thought.

I had the sword. I got to my feet and stopped their rush with a parry and then Pharnakes and I exchanged a flurry – four or five cuts and parries. That's a lot in real combat. A man can only take so much, and then he falls back. The tension is too high. We both backed a step, and Cyrus said, 'It's the slave boy. Hold hard, brother!' in Persian.

I didn't have the daimon in me yet – I hadn't been injured.

'Our lord is safe,' Darius said. 'Let's get out of here!'

Pharnakes shook his head. 'We should kill the husband.'

'This isn't Persia, you fool!' Cyrus said. 'Greeks don't care! And murder is not what our lord needs right now.'

'Come and try,' I said in Persian. Aye, I'm a fool.

Pharnakes shot me a look – such a look. Even in torchlight, I knew that look. But Cyrus laughed. 'Quite the bark, for a pup,' he said.

All that was in Persian.

And then they were gone.

Pharnakes was right, though. They should have killed the husband. Because that night, Ephesus changed sides, and the Ionian Revolt began, in a corridor in the women's quarters. The Long War. And like the Trojan War, it started over a woman.

# Part III

## *Freedom*

It is hard to fight with anger, for what it wants it buys at the cost of the soul.

Heraclitus, fr. 85

# 10

You bring more of these handsome boys into my hall every day, thugater. Is the tale so good? Or the opposite – so dull that you need supporters to get you through it? You are not the first young woman I have known, honey. Don't let the power of your sex go to your head, or you'll be one of those ambitious harridans who haunt our tragedies.

Don't give your love to every comer, either, or you'll be a priestess of Aphrodite and no wife. Hah! I'm a crude old man. Do as you will, thugater of my old age. It is the irony of my life that you grow up to look like Briseis. What fury, what fate, put those looks in your mother's womb? Will we have games to settle your suitors? Perhaps I can meet them in single combat, one at a time, until one of them bests me. Even at my age, I think you would be a maiden for some time.

You blush. Ah – honey, when you blush, you most resemble my Briseis. But when she blushed, she was dangerous.

You might think otherwise, but my status in the house didn't change at all, that day. In the morning, Master called me to him. He embraced me and thanked me. He never asked me what I was doing in the women's quarters.

That was all, until the next blow fell.

That was all, but in every other way, our lives changed. Because Master barred the house to the satrap. And Artaphernes' peace conference collapsed in an evening, because every house in the city was closed against him.

Your eyes shine, honey. Do you understand, indeed? Let me explain. Artaphernes was a guest, and a guest-friend. Persians and Greeks are not so different, and when a man, or a woman, becomes a frequent visitor, he and the household he visits swear oaths to the gods to support oikia.

Adultery is the ultimate betrayal of the guest oath. Pshaw – happens all the time. Don't think I haven't seen it. Men are men and women are women. But Artaphernes was a fool to risk a war on getting his dick wet – hah, I *am* a crude old man. Pour me some wine.

Hipponax did a rare thing. He told the city what had happened. That was the only punishment he inflicted on his wife – he branded her faithless in the assembly. From then on, Artaphernes was a breaker of the guest oath. No citizen would receive him.

He tried for two days to make amends, and he offered various reparations. Hipponax ignored his messenger and finally sent me with a herald's wand to tell Artaphernes that the next messenger would be killed. Indeed, there were armed men in every square of the city. Archi was being fitted for his panoply – the full hoplite armour – even as I went on my errand.

Those were bad days in the household. Mistress didn't leave her rooms. Penelope wouldn't speak to me. I admit that I called her a whore. Perhaps not my best course of action. And Archi – I couldn't fathom whether he knew he had wronged me or not.

At that age – the age you are now, honey – it is often hard enough to know which way the wind blows. Eh? And any betrayal is magnified by the heat of your blood, tenfold. Yes – you know whereof I speak.

So my head was spinning when I went to the Persian camp. I was worried that Darius would spit me on sight – I had dared to cross blades with them. I was worried that my harsh message would result in my own execution. I was angry that my brave deed – and it was brave, honey, facing four of the Great King's men in a dark corridor – had received no reward but curt thanks, because I loved my master and wanted his approval with all the passion of the young who want to be loved. I was desolate that Penelope was Archi's, even though I knew inside my head that she had never really been mine.

I ran up to the Persian camp, wearing only the green chlamys of a herald and a pair of 'Boeotian' boots. I'd never seen anything like them in Boeotia, but in Ionia they were called Boeotian. They were magnificent. They made me feel taller. I thought that, if I was going to die, I should look good.

The gate guards sent me straight to the satrap's tent with an escort. The escort halted before the tent-palace and while their officer fetched the palace guards, one of the soldiers whispered, 'Cyrus wants to see you.'

'I am at his service as soon as I have seen the satrap,' I said. 'If I am alive,' I added. A keen sense of drama is essential to the young.

Artaphernes was writing. I couldn't read Persian then. I waited as his stylus scratched the wax. There was an army of scribes with him, some Persians, mostly Greek slaves.

Finally he looked up. He smiled grimly when he saw me.

'I had hoped Hipponax would send you,' he said.

I stood straighter.

'You saved my life.' Sweet words to hear from the satrap of Lydia.

'I did, lord. It is true.' I grinned in sudden relief.

He leaned forward. 'Name your reward.'

'Free me,' I said. 'Free me, and I will hold the deed well done.'

Abruptly he sat back and shook his head. 'I have tried to buy you for three days, and now Hipponax sends you to my camp. What am I to think? That you are a guest? A gift?'

The satrap had tried to buy me? That explained much that had passed in the last three days. But I was an honest young man, mostly. 'He tests you, lord.'

Artaphernes nodded. 'Yes. I must be getting to know the Greeks. I, too, see it as a test. I must send you back, or break my master's law and help cause the war I came to prevent. Name something else.'

I shrugged. The only thing I wanted was my freedom. I had rich clothes and money. But some god whispered to me. Perhaps, like Heracles my ancestor, Athena came and whispered in my ear. 'You owe me a life, then, lord,' I said.

Artaphernes sat on his stool, playing with his personal signet ring. He looked me over carefully, as if he was indeed going to purchase me. 'If you are ever free, you will be quite the young man,' he said. He took his ring from his finger. 'Here. A life for a life. If you are ever free, come and return this to me, and I will make you great, or at least start you on that road.'

See it? I still wear it. It is a beautiful ring, the very best of its kind, carved by the old people from carnelian and set in that red, red gold from the highlands. See the image of Heracles? The oldest I have ever seen.

I fell to my knees and accepted his ring. 'I have a message,' I said.

'Speak, herald.' This was official business, and now I was a herald before a king.

'The assembly of Ephesus decrees that your next messenger will be executed in the agora.' I held my bronze wand over my head in the official pose of a herald.

I waited.

A look of pain passed over his features. He looked older. He looked like a man who had taken a wound.

'Very well,' he said. 'Go with the gods, Doru.'

'Thank you, lord,' I said, and walked out of his tent. Slaves do not offer blessings to masters.

The four Persians were waiting for me – Cyrus, Darius, Pharnakes and silent, dour Arynam, who was always, I thought, a little drunk.

I was hesitant about approaching them, but Pharnakes came and embraced me – me, a foreign slave. And even Arynam, who had never been my friend like Darius or Cyrus, came and clasped hands as if I was a peer.

'Cyrus was right about you,' he said. 'You saved our lord's life. You are a *man*.'

Well – that was good to hear.

They all embraced me, and pressed me with gifts.

'Come with us,' Cyrus said. 'You'll be free as soon as we cross the river. You can ride – I'll see to it that the Lydians take you as a trooper.'

I was tempted. Honey, I'd like to say that I was a Greek, and they were Medes, and I wasn't going anywhere with their army – but when you are a slave, freedom is the prize for which you will trade anything. To be free, and a soldier?

But I knew that Artaphernes wouldn't allow it. He wanted any scrap of credit with Hipponax, and sending me back offered him the hope of reconciliation, or so he thought.

And so I found myself running back down the road to Ephesus. I had no message except my own return, which marked the subtlety of the satrap very well, I thought. I did have a leather bag full of gifts from the Persians.

I came home to a silent house. I stopped in the courtyard, amazed by the silence, and my first thought was that Hipponax had murdered his family. Men do that, when they catch their wives in adultery.

But they had merely gone – all of them, slaves and free – to the Temple of Artemis. The priestess had asked that all the people gather.

I ran up the steps with a dozen other latecomers to find the whole of the people crammed like ants inside the temple precinct. Teams of priests and priestesses were going through the crowd, with purifying smoke and water, cleansing us.

No one said, right out, that Euthalia had made us all unclean by having a Persian between her legs. But she was there, standing with Hipponax in a dark mantle, and she was surrounded by the smoke of a dozen braziers. When the ceremony was over, she smiled.

I still wonder at that smile. What did she mean by it? Had she meant all along to be caught?

At any rate, I saw Heraclitus and he motioned to me. It was odd to see him in public, without my young master nearby, but I approached, still in my herald's cloak.

'The satrap received you?' he asked.

'Yes, teacher,' I said.

He nodded. 'You have seen war, I think?'

I inclined my head. 'I have served as a hoplite,' I said.

Heraclitus looked around. 'Your master is about to go to a different school from mine, lad. A harsher school, where the punishment for failure is death. Will you take an oath to protect him?'

Heraclitus had no idea what my young master had done to me – no idea, I suspect, what had transpired on that night, except that he would have known that Mistress had been with the Persian. Or perhaps he knew everything. Young men told him all their secrets. In any case, he didn't order me to swear.

'I want to be *free!*' I said. I was suddenly bitter. I had done great things for these people, and I was still a slave. Perhaps I'm a slow learner, but for the first time I began to consider that the greater my services were, the more valuable I made myself.

Heraclitus looked into the purification smoke. 'Do you believe that I can read the logos?' he asked me.

I nodded. I would have nodded if he had asked me if I thought he was Zeus come to earth.

He smiled. 'Doru, if you swear this oath and abide by it, you will be free.'

I frowned. 'Death is a form of freedom,' I said.

'Yes …' he said. 'Listen, lad. War is not the only thing that faces you and Archi. This will be a testing time. Stay and help him pass the test. It will help you, too. Will you swear?'

I sighed. I had been toying with running – to the docks. It must have shown. I thought that perhaps I could work an oar to Athens, or find Miltiades in Thrace. But it was a dream, and besides – besides, just at that moment, I caught sight of Briseis. An eddy of smoke revealed her, talking to her betrothed, my enemy Diomedes.

'Yes,' I said, 'I will swear.'

'Good man.'

We swore together. He was a priest of Artemis, holding one of the hereditary roles. He led me into the inner sanctum and showed me the statues and gave me a branch from the sacred tree – just a pair of leaves, but a sign to show my master where I had been.

Then I went home.

Home was not normal. Days had passed and all our rhythms had changed. Mistress never left her room. Master drank. Archi took no exercise and that night he pulled me close and burst into tears.

'Why has Mater done this to us?' he asked me through his tears. 'No one will speak to me!'

It was true. I had seen it in action. Archi was effectively in exile in his own city. None of his classmates would meet his eye, and no one invited him to a symposium or a ramble or even a troll through the stews.

'It will pass,' I said. I thought of Heraclitus. 'Listen, master. Our teacher made me swear an oath to support you. These will be tough times. I'm here.'

Archi was holding me tight, and suddenly he sobbed. 'I betrayed you as surely as Mater betrayed Pater!' he said. 'I knew she was yours. I wanted her. Oh, Doru, forgive me!'

I sat on his couch and held him. I did *not* want to forgive him. In fact, now that he'd confessed that he knew what he was doing, I wanted to knock his head off. But Penelope's face had not been the face of a slave being taken against her will. I had some experience with women by then. Women can pretend many things, but few of them pretend when they think no one can see them. All this went through my mind.

'Penelope is a slave, but she is her own woman. She wanted you, not me. Why not?' I said bitterly. 'I am just a slave.'

Pitying ourselves, we wept. Foolish boys! We were about to learn what tears are really for. But when our eyes were dry, we were better friends. And the next day, Archi called Penelope to him while I was in his room. He did it without warning. And when she came, he shrugged and left the room.

She looked like a trapped animal – like a doe run down by dogs on the flanks of Cithaeron. Her eyes followed Archi as he walked out of the door, and that gave her away. She really liked him. Perhaps she loved him, or just saw him as a chance for liberty.

'I'm sorry I almost got you killed,' I said. I was stiff and formal. 'I understand that you prefer my master. I won't bother you again.'

She turned her head away. Then she looked back. 'You aren't even really a slave,' she said. 'You're like a man who plays at being a slave. You will die for it, and I will weep for you, but I won't be your lover. Archi is kind, and I think he'll free me when I'm pregnant.'

None of that made much sense to me – although it does now. I said she was smart. She saw things I didn't see, for all my reading and training. So I shrugged, and she bowed her head and left the room without speaking. We should have embraced, but we were too young to forgive and forget.

I was still standing there when I heard a scream from the courtyard. I ran. I thought we were being attacked. Remember that apart from my life as a house slave and companion, I was already a man of violence, and that Diomedes seemed to have a bottomless purse when it came to sending men after me.

When I reached the courtyard, Hipponax was standing stony-faced, staring at a man dressed in the same green chlamys I'd worn a few days previously. Briseis was screaming, her face contorted, all her beauty gone. Penelope was trying to drag her away.

The herald backed out of the gate.

Penelope looked terrified. Briseis's face was the face of a fury, deep lines carved across her smooth brows as she wailed with screams of pain. Her father glanced at her and turned away. Poor man. He had nothing to offer her. Gods send that I never be in his place.

Archi tried to hold her and she began to fight him, and she landed a blow – a foul blow. She was a good fighter, that girl. Down he went, and then she spat like a wild cat and raked her nails across Penelope's chest – I thought they were her nails – and blood flowed.

She screamed again.

I thought she was having a fit. I took her down. I wasn't her brother, and much as I thought I was in love with her, she was a danger to everyone in the yard. I swept her feet and held her arms and put her down on the ground hard enough to drive all the breath from her. She had the strength of a goddess but no *palaestra* skills, and on her way to the ground I rolled her in the end of her own peplos to pin her arms. She ripped her left arm free and her nails drew blood from my cheek and neck.

But when she wrenched her head back with superhuman strength, a hand shot out and smacked her across the face – once and then again.

'Silence, girl!' her mother said.

I had not seen Euthalia in days. She was neatly dressed in sombre colours, and she did not look as if her life had ended.

Briseis sat back on her haunches and the daimon left her. I saw it leave her eyes. It takes one to know one. But then the bitterness exploded.

'It's your fault, you faithless bitch!' she said to her mother. 'He called me a whore! Diomedes called me a whore! In public! Now I'll die barren. He's broken the marriage contract.' She didn't cry. Crying would have been better than her imperious self-pity. 'If you hadn't been so busy riding the Persian's cock-bird, I might be a matron.'

Euthalia's hand shot out and snapped her daughter's head back again. 'Be civil or take the consequences,' she said.

'I can't even blame him!' Briseis cried, and for the first time her voice cracked and she began to sob instead of scream. 'My mother's a whore! I'll be a whore too! I should kill myself!'

Penelope was cowering. She had a bad scratch across her breast and her Doric chiton was filling with blood. She was sitting on a step crying. I saw now that Briseis had a pin in her hand. She had ripped Penelope with it, and me too, I realized.

Euthalia reached into her bosom and her right hand came out with a knife in it. 'Here,' she said. 'Get on with it.'

This was the family that I had so envied when I joined them.

Briseis picked up the knife and ran her thumb across it like a man getting ready for sacrifice. Then she stepped towards her mother, and I felt that her intentions were plain.

I stepped in on her and raised my left hand as Cyrus had taught me. She tracked the hand with the knife and not the body, and I caught her wrist and disarmed her. She got the pin into my chest, but the gold bent and I only took a finger's breadth. It was cold in my chest, and the pain made me want to kill her.

Just for a moment, the pain and the urge to kill balanced against the knowledge that this was *Briseis*. She saw the daimon come into my eyes and her own widened. As I have said, it takes one to know one. But those eyes saved her, and I took control of my body with my left hand closed around her throat.

Her mother was shaken. Close up, I could see that her hair was not dressed and she was not herself. But she would not relent. 'Take the knife and finish it,' she mocked. 'You think your life is ruined, little princess? Perhaps it is time a dose of reality came into your life. You despised Diomedes when you had him. You are *acting*. There is a world bigger than that inside your head. *Wake up.*'

Archi stepped in between them. I still had Briseis, and she had dropped her gold pin of her own volition.

'Take her to her room,' he said. He nodded to me. Suddenly, we were allies. I obeyed, lifting Briseis and carrying her. Penelope came after us. She was holding her side. She got ahead of me and led the way, which was as well, as I had no idea where Briseis's room was.

Briseis put her arms around my neck and let me carry her without struggle. She smelled of jasmine and mint. It was hard to imagine, while carrying her, that she had just intended to kill her mother with a knife.

We pushed though a curtain of glass beads into a room painted in scenes of gods and goddesses – fine work. Archi's room was plain white, with a border of Hera's eyes painted around the cornice. Briseis's room had all the gods done as vignettes. Hera stood with mighty Zeus – a loving couple, painted as her mother and father. Her brother was Apollo with a lyre, and she was Artemis with a bow. Penelope was Aphrodite, and Darkar was a mighty Pluton. Diomedes was painted as a young and rather ambiguous Ares, and then I saw that I, too, was in the pantheon, as Heracles, a club on my shoulder and a lion skin draped over me. I didn't know the rest of the figures, but it was good work. Excellent work. The figure of Aphrodite-Penelope was unfinished, and the paints were there along one wall. The room smelled of marble dust and ox-blood.

Despite everything – adultery, betrayal, drama – I stopped and looked at the paintings on the wall. I took in the paint pots and the smell.

'Your work?' I asked Penelope, amazed.

'Hers,' Penelope said. 'I need a bandage,' she said, and fled.

I laid Briseis on her bed. She was crying. I knew that sound. That was despair. The sound new slaves make when they are taken. The sound you make when your life is taken away from you.

I actually pitied her. So I put a hand on her back.

'It will get better,' I said.

She rolled over, and her eyes held anger, not sorrow. 'Kill him for me!' she said. 'Kill Diomedes!'

You have no idea what it is like to be alone with Briseis. I didn't slap her or run from the room.

But neither did I agree. 'I cannot kill him for you, despoina,' I said. I remember smiling. 'But I could hurt him for you.'

She brightened immediately. 'You could?' she asked. 'Really hurt him?'

She reached out and took my hand, and a flame licked me from my palm to my groin and up to my head.

'If I hurt him, will you stop this foolishness of hating your mother?' I asked. 'Diomedes is a piece or horse shit. You lost nothing in losing him. Your mother did you a favour.'

Her eyes widened. 'I had never thought of that,' she said. Her hand was still stroking mine. 'I know Archi hates him. And he tried to hurt you, didn't he? He bragged of it to me. And Penelope said you were too tough to be hurt by a thug.' She smiled at me.

Oh, the flattery of a beautiful woman. Let's look at this as adults, thugater. She never wanted Diomedes, but she was dutiful enough – she certainly wanted to be an adult, and she liked the attention. But being jilted was turning out to be *better*. More drama.

Who wants to play the dutiful wife when you can be Medea?

And I played into her hands – all reasonable, knowing and male. Zeus Soter, honey, she played me like a *kithara*.

I pulled my hand out of hers and left the room. Then I went to find Archi.

He was making love to Penelope.

I found Darkar instead. 'See to Briseis,' I said. And then I understood. 'You knew Archi was doing Penelope!' I said.

He nodded. And shrugged.

I shrugged back. 'Thanks for trying to keep it from me, anyway,' I said. 'I suppose. But I know.'

Darkar looked at me for a moment. 'Come into my office,' he said. And when I was in, he closed the door. His office was a tiny room under the cellar stairs where he did the household accounts.

'You seem to know everything.' He paused. 'Listen, boy. You have a level head. If we aren't careful, this household will fall apart. And if it does – if Master kills Mistress, if Briseis kills herself – we will all be sold. Understand me? It is not just our duty to keep them all apart until things get better – it's for our own skins, too.'

'Ares!' I said. 'Is it that bad?'

'I drugged Master's wine the night – the night it happened. And every night since.' Darkar had hollows under his eyes. 'He's going to kill her.'

'We should give him something else to think about,' I said. 'Like war with Persia.'

Darkar shook his head. 'I thought that would happen, but it's worse, not better.'

I shrugged. I was seventeen, and I didn't want to be responsible for the happiness of a household. 'I have a task to do,' I said.

Darkar nodded. 'Can I count on you?' he asked.

'I swore an oath to Artemis to support them,' I said.

He smiled. 'Good man. Go on your errand. What did she tell you to do?'

'She told me to kill Diomedes,' I said.

He stroked his beard. 'You can't kill him.'

'But I can hurt him,' I said.

'His father would have you killed,' he said.

'Not if Archi comes with me,' I said. 'I'm waiting for him to finish consoling Penelope.'

Darkar was a hard man. His eyes glinted in the lamplight. 'That would help the household,' he said. 'People will know we are still standing. I approve.' He looked at me. 'You could still end up dead, though.'

I laughed. Even then, I had begun to feel the power. I was not going to die in some night squabble in Ephesus.

An hour later, Archi was done with Penelope, and I walked in on them with a clean chiton for her and clothes for him.

It may have been the most courageous moment of my life. It was hard to meet her eyes – she was naked, entwined breast to breast with him, and all but purring. She had wept and been comforted. And they smelled of sex.

'Master, I need you now.' I tossed clothes and a towel at Penelope. 'I am sorry to intrude.' I raised a hand – something a slave never does – and silenced my master. 'I have consulted with Darkar. We need to strike Diomedes. We need to show the city that we are not dead as a household. He insulted your sister. He might have broken the match in a dignified manner, but he *called her a whore*. Let's punish him.'

Archi met my eye and smiled. Bless him, he understood immediately. 'This is for my sister?' he said.

'For all of us,' I said. 'For your mother, too.'

Penelope looked at us. 'You are a *slave!*' she said. 'You cannot punish a free man!'

I ignored her.

Archi nodded. 'Let's get him. How do you propose we do it?'

'He'll be in the agora or the gymnasium bragging – shaming her and excusing himself. You know him – you know what he'll do. On and on, to everyone he meets. We take Kylix as a spy. He'll watch the fucker. We follow him when he leaves for his dinner, catch him in a street and beat the shit out of him.' Pardon my language, honey – that's how men speak when they are ready for violence.

Archi pulled a chiton over his head and I pinned it for him. Penelope was wiping herself with the towel. I watched her. She turned her back and blushed.

Archi took his new sword from a peg on the wall. I shook my head. In those days, I assumed that every man had the same daimon I had. 'We aren't going to kill him, master,' I said.

'He has thugs,' Archi said. Of course, I'd been going back and forth to the Persian camp for weeks. I'd missed a change. Diomedes' father, Agasides, had hired him a pair of Thracians as guards. In fact, like most of the gentlemen of the city, he was hiring bodyguards to increase his fighting strength if Persia came, but Diomedes flaunted his pair of Thracians everywhere.

I rubbed my chin. 'We can't just kill his thugs?' I asked. 'Your father—'

Archi shook this off. 'You have the right of it, Doru. We need to strike back. Just killing his thugs might be enough. But we have to get them, or they'll keep us off him. Right?'

Youth has its own logic. It isn't like the logic of the assembly or even the phalanx. Archi was angry, and Penelope had made him brave – and she was right there, bolstering his desire to be strong. In youth logic, we had to put those men down.

Poor bastards. A pair of Thracian slaves with clubs. It was three hours later, and Diomedes was heading home. He'd bragged so long and so loud about the insult he'd given us that we'd heard him in the agora, ranting like an orator. Kylix tracked him for us, and we were waiting when he turned off the broad Avenue of the Artemision and cut up the hill through an alley that ran between the looming walls of rich men's yards.

Diomedes saw me first. I was lounging against a wall, cleaning my nails with a knife that Cyrus had given me in my bag of gifts.

'Look who it is,' he said. 'The cock-licker! Get him, boys!'

Sometimes, the gods are kind. And hubris is the worst of sins. Diomedes had, in a single day, spurned a guest-friendship, broken a solemn vow and bragged of it in the public places.

The two Thracians were big men, and tattooed like warriors, although slavers often tattoo a peasant to get a better price.

They split up and came at me quickly, no nonsense, one on either side. I backed past the gatehouse of the next house and then turned and attacked, going for the Thracian on the left. The thug on the right tried to take me in the flank and Archi emerged from the shadow of the gatehouse and gutted him.

It was Archi's first kill, and it took him out of the fight. He just stood there, blood dripping from his blade, as the man writhed and screamed from the thrust into his kidneys.

The other man swung his club, and I backed away a step as they taught in Persia and Greece both, and then I swayed in and cut his wrist with the knife, and he dropped the club, but I was still moving – right foot past left foot, down cut – and suddenly he was sitting in the street with his guts around him.

I don't think they had earned their tattoos. I fought Thracians later – real Thracians – and they were, and are, scary bastards who will swing at you when their lungs are full of blood.

Diomedes turned to run, but Kylix tripped him. Before he could get to his feet, I was on him.

Archi was recovering, although he was white as Athenian leather. 'I killed him!' he said. And then, 'I killed him!'

'If you so much as touch me, my father will have you ripped apart by dogs!' Diomedes said. 'Don't touch me – I might be polluted by a family of prostitutes!'

He was a fool. We really should have killed him.

I grabbed his nose between my thumb and forefinger and broke it with a vicious twist. I'd seen a slave do it to another slave in the pits. 'Bring your dogs,' I said.

Archi kicked him in the groin while he writhed in the muck, his nose pouring blood. He kicked him quite a few times. In fact, it was then I discovered that my master wasn't any nicer than I was.

We beat him pretty badly. I'll save you the details. Except that when we were finished, we took a jar of Briseis's paint and tied him to a pillar in the portico of Aphrodite and painted 'I suck dicks for free' on his back while he wept. Why the portico of Aphrodite? That's where men sold their bodies in Ephesus. The boys cleared out while we did our work. They knew a revenge beating when they saw one.

We sneaked back into the house by the slaves' entrance. We thought, I think, that if we weren't caught coming in, Hipponax would swear to our innocence. Or some such adolescent foolishness.

The whole house was dark – it was late. Dinner had been served, and we'd no doubt been missed – so much for our so-called plan. And we were both covered in mud and blood and worse.

I got Archi past the kitchen, where Darkar was talking in a low voice, and to his room. 'I'll get you water,' I said.

'Bathhouse,' he said. 'I need to wash my soul.' But then he smiled. It wasn't a boy's smile, or a nice smile. But it was a brother's smile, not a master's. 'You need to be clean. If you're caught, they'll kill you. Me? I can take the weight.'

Frankly, I agreed. 'I'll bathe first, then,' I said. I slipped out of the door and down the hall into the kitchen. Cook was leaning on the counter, talking to Darkar.

Darkar understood everything as soon as he saw me. 'Burn it,' he said, pointing at my chlamys. I dropped it in the kitchen fire and Cook piled wood on top, squandering shavings and bark prepared for fire-starting to make the blood-sodden thing burn. All my extra work and helpfulness and popularity had come to this – Darkar and Cook conspiring to keep me alive.

'I need a bath, and then Archi needs one,' I said.

Darkar squinted at my use of the young master's name.

'He says it's death if I'm caught, but mere annoyance for him. So I bathe first.' I pulled my chiton over my head – a work chiton of raw wool, and no loss to anyone. Kylix was in the kitchen by then, and I handed it to him. 'Go and give this to the ragman,' I said. 'Better yet, just throw it on his pile.'

Darkar nodded.

'Bath is hot,' Cook put in. 'You got the bastard?' This is the ultimate sign of a good house – the slaves are loyal to the master's revenge. Like the *Odyssey*.

I told them where he was. 'They won't find him until morning,' I said. 'Maybe some Spartan visitor will come and bugger him!' That got a nervous laugh.

The kitchen was filling up with slaves. I hadn't told Kylix not to spill to his friends – he was already spreading the whole tale. He told it to the slaves at the fountain when he took the cloak to the ragman's pile, too. That's the world of slaves. Word gets around.

We hadn't considered that.

Darkar shut them up and pushed me out of the door. 'You what?' he asked as he pushed me towards the bathhouse. '*You what?*'

'I told you,' I said.

Darkar was alone with me in total darkness. The bath was like that – no windows. He smacked me, hard, in the head. 'I thought you'd have the master beat him. Not you, *boy*.'

'Ouch!' Lo, the mighty warrior. The steward hurt me more than the Thracians had.

'You will be killed. Do I have to remind you that you are a slave? You scout for him, you take a blow for him, but you do not strike a free man!' Darkar slapped me again, this time at random, because he couldn't see any better than I could. Then, after a pause in the dark, 'I think you'll have to run or die.'

With that, he left me to the bath.

It was a big oak tub, the kind where men crush the grapes at harvest time when they don't have stone basins. It leaked slowly, but it held enough water for two to bathe together. Archi and I had shared it many times but, covered in blood, a man doesn't really want to touch anything much. Different from a feast-day bath.

There was pumice and oil, and I worked hard. I knew I had blood under my nails and in my hair. Even then – even as a slave – I had long hair.

I was washing my hair when the door opened. The bath was in a low shed and that door let a little light in from the kitchen windows, so I saw Penelope's robe fall to the floor. Then she was in the bath with me and water sloshed over the sides and on to the floor.

If you imagine that I was going to take this moment to protest about her faithlessness while her naked skin was under my hand, you don't know what it is to be young. I put my mouth on hers before she could speak, and she laughed into my mouth – not something she had done before. Perhaps I should have cared that she was unfaithful to my master – and now, I think, my friend – Archi.

Instead, I half stood and half sat with her astride me, and we kissed and kissed, her breasts against my chest and the hot water up to our hair. Her kisses were clumsy at first, and then warmer and deeper. My hands roved her and then she planted herself on me – her choice, and perhaps I had a qualm, or a suspicion that this was wrong, because I remember that I hadn't pushed into her.

It makes me smile, though. Hah! The gods are often kind, and Aphrodite chose to send me to Tartarus with a glimpse of heaven. When we were finished, we kissed, and kissed, and kissed.

Darkar called my name from the back door. Penelope slipped out of the tub, picked up her robe and vanished – not a difficult trick in the dark. I was sore and happy and suddenly clear-headed, and I had the taste of cloves in my mouth. I got over the side of the tub and thought that on a normal night there'd be trouble from Cook for making such a mess of the bathhouse. Then I grabbed the olive oil, doused myself and strigiled as fast as I could.

I went through the kitchen as clean as a newborn. Darkar tried to slow me down, but I passed him and went into the hall.

Penelope was crying in Archi's arms. Archi was still covered in blood and crap, and so was Penelope.

And her hair wasn't wet.

A chill went through me like a rainy wind in winter blowing across my soul. In my nose, I discovered the scent of mint and jasmine. The hair began to stand up on the back of my neck.

Archi let go of Penelope. 'You look worse, not better.'

Penelope looked at me. 'You'll both be killed,' she said.

Oh, Aphrodite. Oh, Mistress of Animals. Who had I just been with in the bath?

'I am afraid,' I admitted to Archi. I just didn't tell him why. 'You must go and bathe.'

'Stay where you are,' Hipponax said from behind me.

I assume that Darkar told him. We were young and stupid. We had not thought through the consequences. And the game of revenge has no rules.

Hipponax looked at his son. Archilogos met his eyes. They were the same height, by then. 'What have you done?' he asked.

Archi shrugged – I've mentioned what I think of this as a gesture from child to parent, eh?

'What have you done?' he shouted.

166

Archi smiled. 'What needed doing,' he said. 'Diomedes called my sister a whore and we made him one.'

Well, not precisely, but it made a good line.

And then Hipponax surprised me. I should have known – he was always a good man and a poet. He understood rage and lust and the human and the divine. He stood back from the doorway, so that Darkar could enter.

'You must go away,' he said. 'Tonight. Now. I will have a ship manned.'

Then there was a flurry of packing and crying. Archi took his panoply and his sea bag, and I took mine. He went for a bath, and Hipponax took me aside.

'Heraclitus tells me you swore an oath to protect my son,' he said.

I nodded. I raised my eyes to his.

'Here is your freedom. I expect you to keep that oath. As does Heraclitus. Until the end of the war. You stand by him. But as a free man, Diomedes will have to try you, at least. I wrote out your manumission for yesterday. A friend will witness it in the morning – as if it had been done yesterday.' He shook his head. 'I should have freed you for what you did with the Persian,' he said. 'Is all my family cursed?'

I stood silent, awed by his generosity, and conscious of what I had just done in the bath. The furies were laughing. And sharpening their nails.

But I was *free*.

It was worse when Archi went to say goodbye to his sister. Worse because she wept, real tears without anger. She loved her brother better than the rest of us, I think.

And worse because her hair was wet.

She looked at me several times, and her look was one of calm triumph. She was *beautiful*.

Thugater, I have never doubted the presence of the gods. In that moment – in that look from that damp-haired girl – the long, dark shaft and the barbed point of the arrow that comes from Aphrodite's bow went through me, and the pain was never sweeter. Even when Hipponax announced to the whole oikia that I had been freed – even when all the slaves crowded around me, and Penelope took my hand and gave it a tentative squeeze, all I could see were her eyes, that glance. I see it still.

I'm an old fool. Forget me. Imagine what it was like for poor Penelope, honey. Her free lover was leaving her. Her chance of freedom was walking away. And Archi said nothing. I think Hipponax might have freed her, had Archi asked. But he didn't. He wasn't bad, my master. Just a self-centred ephebe who thought he'd just made himself a hero.

The Pole Star was high, and the oarsmen, grumpy and drunken, had been roused from their brothels to their oars, but by luck, the trade trireme *Thetis* was supposed to leave the north beach with the sun anyway, bound for Lesbos with a cargo of Cyprian copper and some finished armour for the gentlemen of Methymna. We walked down through the town in the first light and boarded, Kylix carrying our gear. For all we knew, Diomedes was still tied to his pillar. I wondered if by putting him there, I had made sacrifice to Aphrodite, so that she granted me – Briseis.

As the sea wind blew my hair, I let myself think that I had kissed Briseis in the bath, and – what word suffices? Did I 'possess' her? Never. If anyone was the owner, it was she. Did I 'take' her? No. Men's words for sex are often foolish, you'll find, honey. Briseis was more like a goddess than a woman.

And then, as the good salt wind blew over me and the rain squalls danced to the north, towards where Miltiades might be rising from his bed, it suddenly struck me.

I was free.

Archi was next to me at the bow-rail, over the box where marines might ride in a fight. Today it was full of bull hides for aspides. Every item between our benches had to do with war. The world was going to war, and I was free.

'I'm free!' I said.

Archi punched me in the back. 'You are,' he said. 'Will you – leave me at Methymna?'

It is odd, looking back across the years at that boy – oh, aye, I'd have put my fist in a man's face for calling me a boy then, but I was, and my actions shout it. But in that moment, I knew that I was free – and I had no idea who I was or what I wanted.

No, that's not right, either. What I wanted was Briseis. Hah. More wine. That's all I wanted, and all I could keep in front of my eyes. And then there was the little matter of my oath to Artemis. To defend Hipponax and Archilogos. For all that home – Plataea

– had begun to seem sweeter, the sudden, heady unwatered wine of freedom washed that dream away.

I shook my head. I couldn't tell Archi that I loved his sister. 'No,' I said. 'I promised your father I'd watch you for a while.'

Archi smiled. 'Well, that's not so bad, I guess,' he said, but his smile said it was anything but bad.

I bent and started to look at the armour we were carrying. The breastplates were bronze and they were unfinished, but they had fancy decoration worked in, the waist and closure left undone so that the final fitting could be made by a local smith. I shook my head.

'Mediocre work,' I said. 'I want better. I want a panoply. I assume we're going to fight the Persians!'

Archi grinned. We embraced.

It sounded like fun. We were young.

# II

I've already said that I think Lesbos is the prettiest island in Ionia, and I still think Methymna is the handsomest town in Hellas. I always swore that if Plataea sent me into exile, I'd go and be a citizen in Methymna.

She's no Ephesus. Methymna sits high above the sea, yet the sea is at her doorstep. Methymna is where Achilles landed and took the first Briseis as his war bride. The beach is black and the town rises to a high citadel on the acropolis that has foundation stones laid by the old people – or giants. The town itself climbs the hills and sits below the fortress where the lord lives. That fortress is the only reason the men of Methymna are not serfs of Mytilene. It is almost impregnable. Indeed, only Achilles has ever taken it.

We beached on the black gravel and kissed the first good ground. The beach was full of hulls – twenty, stretching along to the east, each black ship with its own fire and two hundred men, so that the beach itself was like a city.

I went to a shrine to Aphrodite and said a prayer that Briseis would not quicken. Archi found the customers who had ordered his goods and began putting things ashore. It was early afternoon before we had the benches clear. We sold every hide we brought and every ingot of copper that hadn't been ordered. I saw that Archi had kept a full ingot back.

I raised an eyebrow and pointed.

'Your armour,' he said. 'You can pay an armourer and have your metal, too.'

I clasped his hand. 'Thanks,' I said. I couldn't think of a jibe worth giving. Then we climbed into the town, up the steep streets, some with more steps than a temple, and explored, leaving flowers at the shrines. Later we went back to the beach to meet the other shipowners.

The men on the beach were Athenian. When they learned we were from Ephesus, one of their helmsmen came up to us and joined us where we'd started a fire to feed our rowers. Heraklides was a short, powerful man with sandy blond hair and a no-nonsense manner. He looked at our helmsman and spoke to him, and our man sent him to Archi. They clasped hands and Archi had me fetch a cup of wine. Slavery doesn't just fall away from you.

By the time I'd returned, they'd exchanged all the formulas of guest-friendship. Captains were always careful that way. When you meet a man on a beach, you want to be sure of him.

I handed them both wine, and then defiantly poured my own. Archi smiled.

'Doru, this is Heraklides of Athens, senior helmsman of Aristides or Athens. He commands three ships.' Archi was excited.

'Arimnestos of Plataea,' I said. 'Son of Technes.'

'Technes the war-captain of Plataea?' the older man asked. His clasp tightened. 'Aye, you have the look, lad. Every man who stood his ground against the fucking Euboeans knows your father.'

I wept. On the spot, without preamble, as if I'd been struck. I was free, and on the first beach I landed as a free man, I met men who knew my home and honoured my father. Heracles was with me – even in the name of our new friend.

'I was there,' I said, perhaps more coldly than was warranted. 'I saw him fall.' Suddenly I was chilled on the beach. And afraid, as if it was all happening again.

Archi looked at me as if he'd never seen me before.

'You were there?' Heraklides asked. He wasn't exactly suspicious, but he gave me a queer look. 'He died. There was a fight over his body. Aye,' he said, peering at me. 'I remember you. You took a blow, eh? We sent you home in a wagon. My uncle, Miltiades, said you were to get special treatment. We sent you home with your cousin. Cimon? Simon?'

'Simonalkes?' I said, and a terrible suspicion came to me. 'I fell at the bridge when they tried to strip Pater's armour,' I said. 'When I awoke, I was a slave in a pit.'

That took him aback. He looked at Archi. Archi shook his head. 'I've never even heard this story,' he said. 'We just freed him, the day before yesterday.' He looked at me. 'Why didn't you tell me?'

I drank some wine. I knew Pater was dead – but there is knowing and knowing.

Heraklides shrugged. 'Aye, I too was a slave for a year when pirates took my ship. What's to tell? Masters don't give a rat's shit, eh?' He nodded at me. 'Thing is, you're free now. Miltiades will want to know. He was – an admirer of your father, eh?'

'I've met Lord Miltiades,' I said. But I had to sit. My knees grew weak, and down I sat on the sand, unmanned.

It's all very well to say I never mourned Pater. In a way, that's all crap. Cold bastard that he was, he was my *father*. And the next thought that came unbidden – unworthy – was that the farm was mine, and the forge. Mine, not anyone else's.

I needed to get my arse home and see what was what. Because if they'd sent me home with Cousin Simonalkes – why, then, what if the bastard had sold me into slavery himself? That thought came to me from a dark fog, as if the furies were signalling my duty through a cloud of raven feathers. What if he was sitting on my farm, eating my barley?

I stood up so quickly that I bumped my head against Archi's chin where he'd leaned down to comfort me.

I think I'd have gone for home that very night – that hour – if I could have walked. Or – and the gods were there – if there hadn't been war. But war was all around me, and Ares was king and lord of events.

I took to Heraklides very quickly. Most men who've been slaves never admit to it – you flinch every time I mention it, honey. He had it worse than me – pirates and a lot of ill treatment – but it never broke him, and you'll get to know him as the story goes on. He was a few years older than me, but young to be a helmsman already, and getting a name as one of the best. He wasn't really any relation of Miltiades at all, but his father's brother had died in the family service and that made them like family – Athenians are like that.

The Athenians were on their way to Miletus, because Aristagoras had convinced them that the town was ready to revolt. That evening, over roast pig, I met Aristagoras for the first time. A few weeks ago we'd called him the traitor of the Ionians – running off to Athens, revolting against the King of Kings – and now I was standing behind him on a beach of black sand and toasting the success of the war.

He was not the leader I would have chosen. He was handsome enough, and he pretended to be a solid man, a leader of men, bluff and honest, but there was something hollow about him. I saw it that night on the beach – even with everything at the high tide of success, he looked like a stoat peering around for a bolthole.

He promised them all the moon. Greeks can be fools when they hear a good dream, and Ionian independence was like that. What did Ionians need with independence? They were hardly 'oppressed' by the Medes and the Persians. The taxes laid by the King of Kings were nothing – *nothing* next to the taxes that the Delian League lays on them now, honey.

More wine.

You'd have thought that Persians had come to Methymna and raped every virgin. The men on the beach were ready for war. They had their own ships, and they'd already met with their tyrant and held an assembly. Methymna manned only three ships, but they were all joining the Athenians, and so were the eight ships from Mytilene. And you knew, back then, that if the men of Methymna and Mytilene were on the same side, something was in the wind.

But what really excited the Athenians was that Ephesus – mighty Ephesus – had sent the satrap packing.

'We could have this war over in a month,' the Athenian leader said.

He too was no Miltiades. In fact, at the ripe old age of seventeen, I looked at the Athenians – good men, every one – and the rest and thought that we were forming a mighty fleet, but we didn't have a man as good as Hipponax – or Artaphernes or Cyrus, for that matter – to lead.

Even a seventeen-year-old is right from time to time.

I never did get that panoply made, and that ingot of copper sat in our hull as ballast – well, you'll hear soon enough – until she went to the bottom. None of the smiths in Methymna were armour-makers. They made good things – their bowls are still famous – but none had ever shaped the eyeholes on a Corinthian. I did buy an aspis, though – not a great one, but a decent one.

We took on a cargo of men – men of Methymna. We took the hoplites who hadn't made the grade to go on the town's three ships. Archi counted as a lord of the town – he was a property owner there, and his mother's people were citizens, so they treated us as relatives.

A trireme can take about ten marines – more if you don't plan to do a lot of rowing, fewer if you plan to stay at sea for days and days. When you fit a fleet, you pick and choose your marines, at least in Ionia – it's different in Athens, as I may have cause to explain later, if I live to tell that part. Even little Methymna had three hundred hoplites. Her ships rowed away with thirty of them. We took another ten and left good men on the beach. Then we cruised south, weathered the long point by the hot springs and beached at Mytilene. We picked up ships there and drank wine. It was more like a party than a war.

The next night we were on Chios. I had rowed all day and felt like a god. The rowers were all paid men, but one was sick with a flux and I wasn't proud. I was free.

Heraklides approved and offered me a place on his ship.

'Hard to be a free man with your former master,' he said. He made a motion that suggested that he assumed we were lovers. No, I won't show you!

I laughed. 'I swore an oath,' I said. One thing all Greeks respect, from Sparta to Thebes and all the way to Miletus, is an oath.

'Will Miltiades join us?' I asked.

He rubbed his beard. 'Heh,' he said. 'Good question. Miltiades is fighting his own war in the Chersonese. You might say he's been fighting the Persians for five years.'

'In Ephesus, Heraklides, we called him a bandit,' I said.

Heraklides grinned. 'Aye. Well, one man's pirate is another man's freedom-fighter, right enough.' He laughed. 'And you can drop the formality and call me Herk. Everyone does.'

That gave me something to think about. Miltiades was a soldier – a real soldier. And he wasn't coming. And Herk's friendship was worth something.

The next night, we were on another Chian beach. The Chians had a lot of ships, and a lot of men, and they were powerful and had never been conquered. They were going to have seventy or eighty hulls to put in the water. The Athenians were delighted, and decided to wait. The local lord, Pelagius, declared a day of games on the beach, and offered prizes. Really good prizes, so that even Archi wanted them. There was a full panoply for the winner. Spectacular stuff – a scale shirt, the smith's nightmare, six months to make. The aspis was fair, nothing spectacular, but with a worked bronze face to it, and the helmet was fine, although not as good as the shirt and nothing on my father's work.

There was a race in armour – just becoming the fashion, then – as well as a fight with swords, wrestling and javelin-throwing.

I was a free man, and Archi encouraged me, so we walked down the beach to where Lord Pelagius had his ship pulled in by the stern. We wrote our names on potsherds while his steward watched us, and the lord himself came up – an old man, as old as I am now, but sound.

'Now, there's a pair of handsome boys, that the gods love to watch compete. You'll race?' he asked Archi. Archi had the best body of anyone our age. He had surpassed me in size by a finger's breadth, and his muscles had a sharp edge that mine never had.

We both blushed at such praise. 'We'll enter all the contests,' Archi said.

The old nobleman smiled but he shook his head. 'Not the sword-play, lads. That's for men.'

Archi nodded, but that was my best event, I thought in my youthful arrogance. I spluttered.

'Fancy yourself a swordsman, do you?' the old man asked. He peered at me. 'Well, you look old enough to take a cut. If there's a place left, I'll put you in. But we don't fight past the first cut, and if you die, or kill a man, it's your fault. We expect careful men, not wild boys.'

I blushed again, and nodded. 'I've trained since I was ten, lord,' I said.

He looked at me again. 'Really?' he said, and smiled. 'That might be worth seeing.'

Archi put an elbow in my ribs as we turned away. 'Trained since you were ten? The gods will curse you for a liar, my friend. Even though you are the best sword I know.'

Archi was a typical master. He'd never asked where I came from or what I'd done. Never. I loved him like a second older brother – but he never knew me well.

We walked back along the beach, and I was pleased to see men looking at us and, I think, taking our measure. Games are good. Competition is good. That's how men measure themselves and others.

The games were still a few days away, though. So I walked around the promontory to exercise alone. I had a sword of my own, although nothing like what I wanted. It was short and heavy, a meat cleaver. I wanted a longer thrusting blade, because that's what I'd learned with, but Ares had not seen fit to help me.

When I'd worked up a healthy sweat and swum it off in the ocean, I walked back. Slaves cooked for us, and that made me think, every time I took bread from a boy, that I was lucky – and free. Honey, once you're a slave, you never forget it.

Anyway, Heraklides came and sat with me.

'How many ships does Athens have?' I asked my new friend.

'Mmm,' he said. 'A hundred?' he answered, before spotting a pretty Chian girl up the beach. I let him go.

Athens had a hundred ships, and Miltiades alone, or with his father, had another twenty. Then there were other Athenian noble families with ten or fifteen ships of their own.

Athens was half-committed to the Ionians. Not even half. They sent a tithe of their strength. I had spent enough evenings listening to Artaphernes to believe him when he said that the weight of Persia would crush the Greeks like so many lice between his fingers. He always said this in sadness, never in boastfulness.

I looked at our fleet, and it seemed very great to me. We filled the beach at Chios, and by the time the levy came in and all the Chian nobles and traders brought their warships, we had a hundred hulls – I counted them myself.

That night, while men sang Ionian songs around the fires and chased Chian girls up the sand, I sat on my new aspis with Archi.

'I think Athens is using us,' I said.

Archi laughed. 'Stop being a slave!' he said, which made me angry. 'These men have great souls. I have talked to a dozen of the Athenian captains, and they are gentlemen. Why, one or two of them are rich enough to be Ephesians!'

I shook my head, stung by his slave comment and sure that he was wrong. 'Athenians are the most grasping bastards in the world,' I said. I had watched the slow seduction of Plataea – I had been there as Miltiades brought the men of Plataea to his way of thinking. I could imagine him doing the same from island to island across the Aegean.

Archi sat back, took a long drink of wine from a skin and laughed. 'We're going to go home heroes,' he said.

'Has it occurred to you that we're going home just weeks after we left? Diomedes won't be over his injuries yet. His father will be panting for revenge. Niobe's children will be nothing on us, Archi!' I was growing louder and angrier because his good humour and cheerfulness were like the feathers on a heron's back, and my words rolled off him.

Archi laughed. 'I understand that you are a good companion, warning me of dangers ahead. But I'm the hero – I won't be worried. You can whisper good advice in my ear and I'll use my spear to cut my way to glory.'

He looked very much the hero on that beach, by firelight. He'd been homesick for the first few days, but he loved the sea life, camping on beaches and drinking wine by the fire every night.

'Soon we'll be home,' he said, watching a pair of Chian girls run by, their oiled hair swinging and their linen chitons plastered to their bodies. One looked back over her shoulder. She knew just how to play the game. Archi shot me a look. Then he rose to his feet and chased her.

Her companion flicked me a glance and then came nearer. She was younger and seemed too shy for her business.

'Not interested,' I said gruffly.

She stood there. I drank wine and saw in my mind's eye the Persian fleet crushing us against the coast. I must have been the only seventeen-year-old on that beach who wasn't chasing a girl.

I'm a killer, and I lie sometimes, and my stories go on and on – but I have never been called inhospitable. So, when a hundred heartbeats had passed and she squatted by our fire and began to play with the embers, I poured my bronze cup full of wine and handed it to her. She was sitting on her haunches, a very unladylike posture. I'd never even seen a slave do it.

'Careful,' I said. 'No water.' I sat back on my shield, curious about the Chian girls. 'Are you a *porne*?'

She spat my wine in the sand, put down my cup and jumped up. 'No,' she said. 'And fuck you.'

'Sorry,' I said. I stood up. 'Stay and drink the wine. I thought that you and your sister were prostitutes.'

'That's an apology?' she asked. 'Some alien stranger calling me a prostitute?' But she squatted down again and picked up the cup. 'I'd slap you, but your wine's too good.'

I sat back down. 'There's bread, olive oil and fish.' I waved around the fire. We were messy, and our baskets were spread over three or four oxhides of beach. Men only learn from long campaigns to be tidy when they camp, and we were as raw as an ingot of copper.

She wandered from basket to basket, picking a dinner. It was getting dark, but I could see that her chiton showed the signs of hundreds of washings, with that patina of old dirt and hard work that a garment gets when it is worn and worn. I remembered my own chiton at home, in Plataea.

She wasn't beautiful, she wasn't exactly pretty, but her legs were long and muscular and the angle of her hip pushed against her chiton. Her face was too pointy and her eyes were a little too close together, but she was quick-witted and bold without being rude – a good thing in a woman.

'If I told my brother you thought I was a prostitute, he'd kill you,' she said. 'We're fishermen. My father and my brother will pull oars for Lord Pelagius.' She smiled, under her hair, which was long, black and heavily oiled. 'He's big.' She rolled some of our fish in bread, poured a little oil on top and went back to her odd squat by the fire, eating her meal with satisfaction. She licked her fingers when she was done.

I thought that she was like a cat – a kitten, actually. Lesbos and Chios are full of cats – hungry ones.

'So,' I said, curious, but seeking to avoid offence, 'what are you doing, wandering among men, *galay*?' *Galay* is the local word for a cat, or a ferret, and I used it with affection – she was like a ferret – a pretty ferret.

'You're a westerner, aren't you? You keep your women in houses and screw each other, right?' She laughed. She was *maybe* fourteen. Everything from the motion of her hips to her language made Penelope, the slave, look like a lady of quality. Anyway, I remember how she laughed, as if she pitied me. 'Chian girls have their own lives, at least until some man fills us with a baby.' She shrugged. 'I've killed a deer!' she said, with a childlike change of topic.

I laughed and leaned back. 'Me, too.'

She stuck out her tongue at me. We both laughed, and that was the end of the coldness.

An hour later she was sitting with her back against me. It was a chill evening, and I had put my cloak around her. I told her stories of hunting on Cithaeron, and about my sister, and Pater, until I cried a little. She was kind and said nothing. She told me about riding her father's boat in a storm, and I told her about the storm we'd ridden up by Troy, and then we talked of the gods and we sang some hymns together.

People passed us constantly – don't imagine we were alone on that beach. While we were singing, Heraklides came to the fire with a girl called Olympias, the grandest name for the broadest-hipped peasant in all Hellas, but she and the girl in front of me were from the same village and they chatted in their rapid Ionian that I could just barely follow.

Herk was older than me, but he was a good companion. He drank some wine and made jokes – good jokes – and then we were all silent together. Oh, honey, I remember that evening as one of pure happiness, the happiness of good fellowship. It raised my mood, so that I didn't feel so doomed. Which was wrong, of course. I'd have been better to be wary and afraid, but really – and I ask you, sir, to agree with me – if we worry all our lives, when will we drink wine and enjoy ourselves? Eh?

Exactly. Hours passed. We sang again, and now I noticed that the girl leaning against me – I still didn't know her name, although I knew her sister's and her father's and how old she was when her first blood came and which goddess she followed – I noticed that she had a beautiful voice. I had heard the choir at the Ephesian Temple of Artemis, mind you – I knew a good voice when I heard one.

I was just pondering how a village girl got such a voice when a trio of big men came to our fire.

'That's my sister, lad,' the biggest said. He said it with a smile that robbed his words of malice. He was too damned big to have to worry about any man on that beach.

I had come to my full growth, minus a finger's width or so, and I was not a small man, but this Chian stood a head bigger and a hand's span broader.

'Stephanos!' my girl said, and she leaped up, taking my spare chlamys with her, and embraced her brother.

I got up, too, in the complex welter of thoughts that affects a man when he's confronted by the brother of a girl that he has *not* debauched. I didn't want to seem afraid, but he was big. He didn't seem angry, but I'd seen men like him launch a blow without a sign of it crossing their faces. He had that look.

'I'm called Doru,' I said. 'Your sister's my guest-friend. Sit at the fire and drink some wine, if it pleases you.'

Pretty good, eh? You know, honey, sometimes we make up these speeches later to sound better to bards like your friend, but I'd had the right amount of wine that night – enough to loosen my tongue and not enough to clog it up, eh?

Stephanos grinned. 'Guest-friend, eh?' he said. He laughed. 'You must be a gentleman, sir. No Chian fisherman would ever have a "guest friend".'

He grunted when he tasted the wine. 'Good stuff. Sorry, lord. I guess you are a gent and I'm making an ass of myself.'

No one had ever called me lord in all my life. 'Stephanos, I was born a farmer in far-off Boeotia and I've been a slave for years. Just freed. No lords here, unless my master Archi comes back.'

Then he slapped my back and laughed – he laughed quite a bit, a deep, throaty laugh that made everyone else want to laugh, too. Ares, he was big! And he introduced his two friends – oar friends, the men who sat below him in his spot in his lord's ship. I don't remember their names. I know where they died, and I'll tell that part when I get to it. But they were good men, and good companions, and I'm sorry I've forgotten them. Here's a sip of wine to their shades.

I hate it when I forget names, honey. The names are all we have, and all that ever gets remembered. Now I'm a lord, and while I live, every son of a bitch in the Chersonese will fear me and know my name. But when I die – who will remember me? Who will know the name of Arimnestos?

By the ravens of Apollo, pay me no attention. Fucking maudlin old man. Too much wine. What was I saying? Aye, it was a good evening. The night I met Stephanos.

We ended up all curled together around the fire. Archi never came back that night, but there were a dozen or so of us, and one of the local girls ran off and came back with a bundle of straw – she'd been selling it all day, she said – and we lay on the straw like chicks in a nest and slept, woke and talked, and slept. Melaina was her name, I learned from hearing Stephanos chide her for sleeping next to me.

'You'll wake up with his dick in your arse,' he said, and laughed. That's what passed for a sense of humour, on Chios. They thought we all loved boys. Or pretended to think that.

I woke with the dawn. Melaina's hair smelled like fish. She snuggled her hips against me and whispered that I was not allowed to move. But I had to get up and I was embarrassed by the, mmm, projection I had grown, but she just laughed, not even awake, and told me that if I had to piss, I should piss for her, too, so she could go on sleeping.

Only when I was well away from our fire, pissing in the sand, did I realize that the games were to start in a matter of hours – perhaps less, as games always began with the sun – and I had been awake most of night. I blessed Lord Apollo that good company had kept me from drinking a foolish amount.

I went back to the fire and warmed up while I built it up. All the slaves were asleep. Then I oiled myself. Archi was nowhere to be seen. I was pretty sure Stephanos had mentioned wrestling, so I woke him.

'Are you in the games?' I asked.

'Mother fuck!' he said, or words to that effect, and rolled out of his cloak. 'You are a good man,' he said. 'Can you spare some oil? I can't run home and get back in time – the foot race is first.'

So I oiled him, and we went up the beach together. In those days, men didn't compete naked, like fools. We wore loincloths, and I had to give him my spare. Then we ran. He had long legs but no training.

We got to the crowd just in time to catch the second heat of the two-stade race. I won – not easily, but I had his measure from the run up the beach and all the other competitors were local boys who were no match for him.

You run the foot race, honey – and you, sir? Good. Easier to tell this to people who know how games go. But in those days it was all informal. The lord had put up cairns, and we started by one, turned at the other and elbows flew in the turns. If I wanted to beat a man as big as Stephanos, I needed to be well clear of him at the turn, eh? Heh, heh. Otherwise I would have kissed the sand.

Then we watched another heat, this time mostly gentlemen – hoplites, especially Athenians. They were all trained men, and they didn't even trouble to jostle each other. It was like watching a different sport. And most of them ran naked, which I found – imposing. And odd.

A final heat of local gentry, and a big youth won by knocking most of his competitors flat. Stephanos stood by my shoulder watching. As first and second in our heat, we'd be running in the final. He pointed at the winner. 'Cleisthenes,' he said. 'He's a right bastard.'

'I can tell,' I said.

Kylix came up then, and Archi. Archi shook his head. 'My own damned fault,' he said. 'Hard to be a hero in the night and morning too,' he quoted from Heraclitus, who was full of such sayings for the young.

'Archilogos, this is my new friend Stephanos,' I said, with Ephesian formality. They eyed each other as potential rivals, and I was annoyed that they couldn't be friends – but neither saw in the other what I saw in both, and they stood apart.

I sent Kylix back for my armour. I looked at Archi, but he shook his head. 'You have to be the hero today, Doru,' he said. 'The only muscles I have that are hard are in my head and my dick.'

That got a laugh from all the men. Indeed, Archi was not alone, and half the men there – more than half – were showing signs of a good night of feasting. I heard later that the man they called 'Kalos', the beautiful, the best of the Athenian athletes, was hung-over from the beginning to the end.

So we lined up in the sand for the two-stade final. I was next to the big Chian lordling, with Stephanos on my other side. Luck of the draw.

I'd watched the lordling in his first race, and I knew I'd get an elbow in the ribs off the starting line. So when Lord Pelagius dropped his arm, I shot off from a low crouch just as the trainers in Ephesus taught, bless them. Then I cut diagonally across the field.

The tall, pretty Athenian, Kalos, was on the inside and I let him lead me. From the first, we were alone. There was a roar behind me, and some shouting, but I just kept pounding up the beach, and the naked Athenian was a stride ahead.

Damn, he was fast. And he was better trained, I'd say. Hangover or not, he was the better man. And he wasn't running full out, either. He was saving himself, measuring me.

I decided on my tactics well before the turn. As we closed on the cairn, I poured it on, everything I had, and I passed him in one burst before he was on to my tactic. I was ahead of him at the cairn by a stride and I angled sharply *across* him so that he had to lose a stride or risk crashing into the cairn – not the most genteel manoeuvre. Illegal, in the Olympian Games. But that's youth. And then I hammered my feet on the sand, my trick done, and all there was left was to run the stade back.

There's a point in the race where it is no longer muscle and training. It's all in your head, eh? I was ahead. He would put everything into catching me, but my burst of speed must have made him wonder. And I thought – fuck it, if I can burst like that, I can run like that all the way home, if I have the guts.

So I did.

I might have been the depth of an aspis ahead of him when I crossed the line. But by Ares, I took him, and after he vomited in the sand, he came and wrapped his arms around me. 'Good run,' he said.

I grinned – I knew he was the better man. And I liked him for his good humour.

In those days, all the games counted and there was no resting. So while I was still breathing hard, Kylix brought my armour for the next race, the *hoplitodromos*.

That's a laugh. My armour was an old leather *spolas* that I bought on the beach from a mercenary, recut by a leatherworker to fit me. I had an outdated Boeotian shield that Hipponax had bought and a pair of greaves. Without them, I wouldn't have been allowed to compete in the race. On Chios, they carried an aspis and wore greaves, that was all. In Plataea, we ran in full panoply. So I snapped on my greaves, which fitted well enough, and lined up.

Lord Pelagius played no favourites, although by the time I had my armour on, I knew that the big lordling was his grandson. He could have made me run in the first heat, but he didn't, and he ran the pulls – the removal of names from a pot – fairly. He was, in fact, a good lord and a fair judge – a rarer bird than you might think, friends.

Cleisthenes and Stephanos hadn't finished the two-stade final, as they'd ended up fighting on the sand. Stephanos said that the big aristocrat tripped him, and the lordling claimed the same. But they were still in the contest. They ran in the third heat – I think the judges felt that they hadn't squandered the energy that Kalos and I had used up in the run. We ran together in the fourth heat, with another pair of Athenians and one of the Lesbian hoplites from our own ship. He ran well, too. He and Kalos and I led our pack, and Kalos was well ahead until the cairn and then he dropped back, his wine head stealing his chance for glory while the Lesbian nipped me for the victory. Epaphroditos was his name, and he couldn't believe he'd won. I worked to be as gracious as the Athenian boy had been with me. It wasn't easy. I hate to lose.

But I was still in the finals. They took place right away, and I was tired. There was quite a bit of jostling on the line, and I thought, Ares, there are four events to go, and I made the finals. I don't need to win. All I need is to finish.

The lordling was in the race, but he wasn't next to me, thank the gods. To start with, I ran easily, without any attempt at real speed. I was the last man off the line, except for another Chian who Cleisthenes tripped as we started. That boy was vicious.

I ran at a good lope to the cairn, and made the turn, still last, but in touch with the pack. *Everyone* was tired. It was my first games, and I had no idea how a real athlete hoards his strength. I knew my body, but I knew nothing of how to read the others.

We were halfway to the finish – the hoplitodromos is two stades, and good men sprint the whole way – when I realized that I had plenty of strength left in my legs and I had just passed one of the Athenians. So I grinned and put my helmeted head down and ran. I didn't bother to look around, or back – until there was a blow to my shield and I realized I was running alongside Cleisthenes.

We were running shield to shield, and the Lesbian was a stride ahead, the horsehair on his helmet within easy reach. Cleisthenes punched at my shield again and grinned. He was a mean bastard.

Me, too.

I put my shield rim into his hips and he screamed and fell, and then it was just me and the Lesbian with fifty strides to go. We ran our guts out. He was faster.

I hugged him anyway. He had a great heart, that man. There aren't many men who can say they beat me, but Epaphroditos was so *happy* that I couldn't be angry.

'This is the best day of my life!' he said.

Then Cleisthenes came up and swung his shield at my head.

There was no warning, but a year of ducking Diomedes' thugs had finally had its effect, and Stephanos shouted, and I ducked. The shield missed. Men rushed to pull us apart.

'When we wrestle, I'll dislocate your shoulder,' he shouted. 'And break your pelvis. By mistake!' Every man on the beach heard him.

People like him have always raised the daimon in me. I said *nothing*, but I let him look me in the eye, and he didn't like what he saw.

Then the lord was there. He slapped his grandson, and he ordered the big man to apologize to me. Cleisthenes refused.

Now that I had the attention of the whole beach, I leaned in towards Cleisthenes. 'I've been a slave half my life,' I said, so that every man heard me, 'and my manners are better than yours. What does that make you?' The daimon spoke. Had it been me, it would have been young man's bravado, but when the daimon had me, I was as calm as a summer sea. My words fell like harp notes in a quiet hall, and he flushed.

The next contest was wrestling, although as the Chians practised it, it was more like *pankration*, since everything was legal – blows, tripping, punches, everything but eye-gouging and grabbing the testicles.

I drew an early opponent – but by the will of the gods, I drew a beardless Athenian boy who was in his first contest, as I was. We grinned at each other, and grappled, and I had his measure by so much that I could give him a throw. In fact, I dragged it out, because I was *resting*. And I made him look good. His father was there, and he slapped my back at the end and said I was kind.

The boy grinned at me.

Then I went to my second bout, against a big-arsed oarsman from Lesbos. He was tall and untrained and I was smaller and well-trained. There are men out there who'll tell you that size doesn't matter in combat, and what they are full of, honey, smells bad. Eh? Big men have all the advantages. I'm not big, but you can see that I have long arms – like an ape, an Aegyptian once told me – and those arms have saved my life a hundred times.

I've put a hundred big men down in the dirt, but they always scare me and I always thank the gods when I walk away from a contest with one.

This one saved me by being afraid of me. I could see it – I was a man who'd won the stadion and come in second in the run in armour and my muscles gleamed in the sun, and he flinched. I still had to wear him out, and it sucked the energy out of me. My ankles hurt where my second-hand greaves had bit them during the run, and those little things start to add up when it's high noon on a hot beach in the third competition of the day.

I played him, and he put me down once, and his morale improved, but by then I had him tired and the next time he came in at me I broke his nose with my fist, and then I had him.

I got him a cloth for his nose, and on the way back I met Melaina, who was pouring water over her brother. She kissed me. 'You go and win now,' she said. 'Then I can tell all the girls I slept with a great athlete.' She giggled.

Stephanos frowned.

'You all right?' I asked.

'I drew that bastard Cleisthenes,' Stephanos said. His sister didn't worry him, I could tell.

'You can take him,' I said.

Melaina spat in the sand. 'His father's our lord,' she said. There was quite a lot of information in that short sentence.

I stepped close to Stephanos. 'You know how to break a finger?' I asked.

Of course he didn't. Only trainers and professionals know tricks like that. I smiled to think that I could have been the best wrestler on Chios. So I bent close and told Stephanos how to break a man's finger in the grapple.

He looked at me, and I think he was shocked.

I shrugged.

'You're a bastard!' he said.

'He's going to knee you in the balls,' I said. 'I'd wager a gold daric on it.'

'Aye,' Stephanos said.

'Get his hands at the first engagement, go for a leg sweep and go down with him. Break his finger in the tangle and apologize a lot after you're declared the winner. And it is absolutely legal.' I shrugged.

Stephanos nodded. 'I can take him.'

'Not wheezing from a groin kick,' I said.

And then I was called for my third bout. It was another big man – bigger than the last. In fact, I remember him as being bigger than Heracles, but that can't be true. But my good fortune was that he'd pulled a muscle in his groin in his last bout, and I took him. I took him so fast that he apologized afterwards. I told him that I thought he was probably the better man, and he liked that, and we clasped hands.

Stephanos broke Cleisthenes' hand. If we'd all been lucky, he'd have broken the lordling's right hand. But he broke the bastard's left, and he apologized, and Lord Pelagius himself said it was an accident.

So it was me and Stephanos in the final. We were already breathing hard, and Archi strigiled me – as if he was my slave, he said, and I loved him for it – and put fresh oil on me. Melaina proclaimed that this was the best bout – because she liked both the contestants and was sure to be pleased – and Lord Pelagius looked at her fondly and then told the circle of men and women to keep quiet. It's odd – at Olympia and Delphi, they forbid matrons to watch men compete, but allow maidens. In Ionia, women had their own foot races and they *all* watched.

Stephanos came at me with a grin, and tried to break my left hand at our first engagement, the bastard.

I didn't fight back the same way. My blood wasn't up, and I knew he had to pull an oar. I'm not always a bad man. So I punched him, even when we were grappling, and I got his shoulders down for a count and had a fall.

The second fall, he roared like a bull and came in at me, going for a throw. I stayed away, avoiding his hands, and just barely kept him from pinning me against the crowd. But by my third retreat the crowd was hissing at my apparent cowardice – especially as I was up by a fall – and like a foolish boy I let the crowd noise sway me. I saw my opening. Went over the attack, and found myself face down in the sand.

Then I was angry – angry at myself – and I tried to stand toe to toe with him. I got a leg behind him and I went for a throw and missed – we all miss sometimes, honey – and he got hold of me and then I was grappling a bigger man. He got me, although we put on a long grapple and a good contest and we were both covered in sand and sweat, and when we rose, Stephanos looked at me with a certain wariness.

Down two throws to one, I was a sober fighter. I was bone weary, but still unhurt.

Stephanos made a mistake, or was unlucky. Seconds into the fourth round, as I circled him, he crossed his legs – a foolish thing to do, and something even Chians must have trained against. I was on him in a flash and he was down, and although he was strong I got my legs around his hips and I had a control hold on one arm. I knew I had him – and after some long minutes of struggle and some grunting, he knew it too.

They applauded us like heroes after that round. We looked good. And I had him. He'd squandered energy trying to match my hold with sheer strength, and now he was beaten.

So I stepped in to finish it, grappled him and got dropped on my head for my pains.

Never believe all those stupid country-yokel stories. That Chian played me like the city boy I had become. He let me think him exhausted. He let me believe it with everything from posture to his weary 'you've got me beaten' smile as we stretched our arms out and started the last engagement. I don't think I ever made that mistake again.

I came to with fifty men around me, and Stephanos all but weeping on my chest. He'd dropped me just wrong – but thank the gods, he hadn't snapped my neck, although it hurt like blazes, a line of cold that was worse than fiery pain running up my spine.

Heraklides was there, too. He had a reputation as a healer, and he had my spine under his palms. 'Can you move, lad?' he asked me.

'Yes,' I said, and swore. Ares, I hurt! My fingertips hurt. But I was on my feet, swaying, but up.

They gave me a lot of applause and some back-slaps, and somebody, one of the Athenians probably, groped me. So much for heroism.

'Sorry, mate,' Stephanos said.

I laughed, and we clasped hands. 'Last time I teach you anything,' I said.

He grinned. 'I like to wrestle,' he said.

Then we had a break before the next event – until the sun was past a certain point in the sky, no water-clocks on a beach on Chios. I slept, and when I awoke, Stephanos came and massaged me himself.

'I can't throw a javelin, and I've never touched a sword,' he said. 'So you're my man to win. You're ahead, you know.'

I lay like a corpse under his hands. He knew how to get his thumbs deep in the muscle. He said his father taught him. Melaina had the trick too – she came and did my lower legs and feet, bless her.

When they were finished, I felt like quitting once and for all. And I felt like sex. Melaina suddenly appealed to me – the touch of her hands – hard to explain.

Instead, I got up and took javelins from Archi. I didn't even have my own – they were back in Ephesus. Archi slapped my back. 'You're in first place, you dog!' he said. 'That'll teach me to drink too hard.'

Not just sour grapes. Archi and I were always a dead match, except as swordsmen. If I was winning, he'd have been with me – except that the luck had been going my way in every encounter. It takes luck to be a winner. I've seen the best man trip on a stone or lose his footing in a match. Read the chariot race in the *Iliad*, honey – that's the way of it. The best man does *not* always win.

Or maybe it is the will of the gods, as some men say. Or the logos seeking change, so that one man does not dominate others, or to effect some other change.

I was never a great man with a javelin. I've killed my share of men with spears, thrown and pushed, as they say, but that's because the daimon in me doesn't lose its skills in the press of bronze. In a contest, I can't throw as well as other men, and that's a fact.

But that day I threw the best spears of my life. My first throw did it – which god stood at my shoulder I don't know, but I smelled jasmine and mint and I swear that it was Athena putting her hand under mine and lifting my spear. Other men matched my throw, and Cleisthenes beat it, the bastard. I threw twice more, and never came within a stride of my first throw.

I placed seventh. Cleisthenes won. But I placed in the top eight, and by the Chian rules I had won or placed in every contest, and no other man had done that. Cleisthenes argued that he had, but his grandfather overruled him, saying that he had failed to finish the two-stade run.

I had won. I couldn't believe it.

I think my slavery really ended there, on that beach, just before the sun started to swoop for the sparkling blue sea. I wasn't just free – I was a man who could win a contest with hundreds of other free men.

We Greeks love a contest, and we love a winner. They mobbed me, and I was kissed a little more than I liked and patted a little too much, but I didn't care. They put a crown of olive leaves in my hair.

And then Lord Pelagius took me aside.

'Listen, lad,' he said. 'You're the winner – clear winner. No judge even needs to count.'

'There was a goddess at my shoulder, sir,' I said.

He nodded. 'What a very proper thing to say! Who was your father?'

'Technes of Green Plataea, lord.' I bowed.

'I gather you were a slave?'

'I was taken,' I said. 'The family that had me – freed me.'

He nodded again. 'A fine story. Damned fine. The way good people should act.' He was an old aristocrat, and he had the best notions of how his class ought to behave. A few of them do.

The rest are rapists and tax-takers with pretty names and better armour.

At any rate, he put his arm around my shoulders. 'Listen, lad. You asked to fight with the sword. You're welcome to do it – we can all see you're a trained man. But after winning today, no one – and I mean no one – will think you're a shirker if you want to step aside.'

But, ignoring the hubris of it, and the sound of wings I might have heard, I shook my head. 'I want to fight, lord.'

He smiled. 'Well,' he said, 'I can't give you your prize yet. So go and armour up.' He meant that all the prizes were given at sunset.

So I put on my old leather spolas, not a tenth as glorious – or protecting – as the scale shirt I was so soon to own. I put my aspis on my arm and my crude, cheap and cheerful helmet on my head, picked up my meat-cleaver sword and went down to the lists.

In those days, we took wands – willow or linden, usually – and planted them at the four corners of the lists, and then we fought to the first cut. Men died from time to time, but most men were careful, and few fought all out in the lists.

Calchas had told me about such fighting, back on Cithaeron by the shrine of the hero, and I had thought that it sounded like the Trojan War. Here I was, five years later, standing by a row of black ships on a beach with a blade in my hand and the weight of my bronze helmet pressing down on my nose. While I listened to the judges caution us against using our full strength, my heart sang inside me – freedom and victory in games are a heady mix, like wine and poppy juice. The stars were out, although the sun hadn't set. There were only eight of us to fight – which, had I thought of it, might have made me wonder about our army.

Yet I tell this badly. I wanted to talk to the past. I wanted to tell the boy in the olive grove, and the slave boy in the pit, that there was this at the end of the road – that someday I'd stand on the sand, a hero.

Who knows? Heraclitus says that time is a river, and you only dip your toe once. But maybe you can skip a stone, too. I only know that the boy in the olive grove and the boy in the slave pit made it to be the victor on the beach.

You don't understand. Perhaps just as well. And just as well that the victor on the beach didn't know what was to come, either.

Count no man happy until he is dead.

We paired off, and I was up against a Chian. We exchanged names, but I've forgotten his. I was too inexperienced to be afraid, and too eager to show my skill.

We circled for a while. No man with steel in his hand lurches into a fight without feeling his opponent. It's like foreplay with a beautiful woman. Well, it's not, actually. But there are a few things in common, and I like making your friend blush. Young lady, if you turn that colour every time I mention sex, we'll be good friends. What's your name? Ligeia? How fitting.

At any rate, we circled, and then we started to make jabs at each other's shields. It is hard to hit a man who has an aspis, when all you have is a short sword. The only targets are his thighs, his ankles and his sword arm. In a contest, his head is out of the question. Bad form. Which is funny, because in a real combat, that's what you go for.

I became bored with circling and tapping shields. I shuffled forward, shield foot first, and then I cut at his shield, stepped in hard with my back foot and cut back – the 'Harmodius blow' they call it in Athens – and caught him just above the greave. A nice cut and no real harm.

I think I made him happy – he was out with honour.

Men are fools. Combat is not for honour. I hadn't learned that lesson yet, but I almost knew it, and I was annoyed with him, that he'd wasted my time and energy.

I was the first to finish, and I watched the others fight. Cleisthenes had his broken hand inside his aspis, and he was hammering his opponent, an older Athenian who was angered and afraid of Cleisthenes' bullying, hammering attacks that were well beyond the spirit of the contest. Cleisthenes was swinging as hard as he could, chopping his opponent's shield with his heavy sword, a curved *kopis* or *falcata*, depending where you're from, a weapon like an axe with a sword blade attached.

Another Athenian effortlessly dispatched his man after a long shuffle in a circle. I saw him do it. He faked a cut to the man's head and tagged his thigh under the rim of his shield – perfect coordination, perfect control. He was one of their noblemen. He was fast and elegant and had better armour than anyone else, including bronze on his thighs and upper arms.

It was good that I saw him, because he was my next opponent. The light was starting to go, and we fought between two bonfires. He smiled at me – he had an Attic helmet with spring-loaded cheekpieces, and as soon as I saw it, I knew my father had made it. I held up my hand to him.

'My father made that, sir,' I said, pointing at the helmet.

He took it off. 'You're a son of Technes, the smith of Plataea who fell in Euboea?' he asked.

'I am, sir.' I bowed.

He returned my bow, although he was a child of the gods, the son of the greatest family in Athens. 'I am Aristides,' he said, 'of the Antiochae.'

I nodded. 'I am Arimnestos of the Corvaxae,' I said, 'of green Plataea where Leitos has his shrine.'

He grinned. He liked that I could play the game. Then he put his helmet back on and I pulled mine down, and we faced off.

The Chians cheered us, because we were both foreigners. Aristides was probably the best-known man in the fleet, while I had just won the athletics, and that made it a good-natured match with lots of cheering. I could hear Melaina's clear soprano and her brother's bass.

And then they all went away, and I was alone on the sand with a deadly opponent. He moved the way a woman dances, and I admired him even as I tracked his motion.

As far as I was concerned, he was beautiful, but he put too much energy into it. That is, he looked wonderful – and he was good, very good, a true killer. But he also played to the crowd.

He had not, on the other hand, run several stades and wrestled.

Early on, he came at me with his kill shot. All swordsmen have one – a simple combination they have mastered, that can get the fight over in a hurry. Listen – if you live past a man's kill shot, it's a whole different fight. But most men go down, in sport or play or on a blood-spattered deck. Calchas taught me that, and every swordfighter in Ephesus said the same.

I didn't buy the feint to my head and my shield caught his blow to my thigh, then I cut back at his arm and my blade *ticked* against his arm guard.

He nodded at me as we drew apart – acknowledgement that I'd hit him. Then we circled for a long, long time, until the crowd was silent. I wasn't going after him. He was better than me. And he wasn't in a hurry. And, frankly, I knew he was the best man I'd ever faced – better than Cyrus or Pharnakes, even.

Twice, we went in. The first time, he came forward gracefully – and fooled me, his swaying approach a trick as he darted to the right and his blade shot out in a cut to my right hip, of all unlikely targets.

I parried the blow on my blade and hammered my aspis into his. I cleared my weapon and tried to reach under his shield, but he didn't allow it, and we were kneeling in the sand, shield to shield, pushing. The crowd roared but the judges separated us.

The second time, I saw him stumble. It was dark now; the fires gave unsteady light and the helmets didn't help. But before my attack was even fully developed, he had his feet under him. He cut low and then high, and our blades rang together, and we *both* punched with our shields, leaning our shoulders into the push, and our blades licked out and we both rolled left and broke apart. The ocean cold of his blade had passed across my sword arm and my blade had *ticked* against his thigh armour.

I raised my blade for a halt. 'He touched me,' I said. I can be an honourable man.

But his blade had been flat on, and Athena was by me, and when the judges looked, there was no blood.

Stephanos gave me a drink of wine while the judges looked at my opponent. Archi pointed at him.

'Back of his knees, brother,' he said. He'd never called me brother before, and it was the warmest praise of the day.

'Cleisthenes hurt his last man,' Stephanos said. 'He'll face the winner here but his grandfather is mad as fury. The man he cut is bad.'

Cleisthenes came and started to catcall. He was a rude fuck, and while other men cheered, he jeered. My blood started to rise.

I decided to go for the Athenian's knee. Archi was dead right – when you're in the fight you don't always see. He was a tall man and the back of his knee was the best unarmoured target on him.

He went for his kill shot again. I think he felt that he hadn't got it off perfectly the first time. But as soon as he started, I knew the combination. I knelt, ignoring the head feint, and snapped my wrist in a long cut against the back of his left knee while his sword *cracked* on to my shield and bounced up on to my helmet – I'd knelt too low. The blow was hard – not as well pulled as his first, and I fell sideways with a bump on my scalp where my helmet turned the blow but not all of it.

He gave me a hand up and apologized.

I pointed my heavy blade at the black line of blood running down the back of his greaves.

'By Athena!' he said. 'Well cut, Plataean.'

Men cheered, but Cleisthenes jeered again, calling us pansies. And then he insisted on fighting, right there.

'I want this,' he said. 'Unless you're afraid.' And closer up, 'I'm going to hurt you.'

His grandfather tried to stop it. But the other judges said there was enough light, and I was an arse, and simply insisted I'd fight.

'You're a fucking slave,' he said, and he grinned. 'I own you already. Slaves always fear men like me – real men. Do you feel the fear, boy?'

The thing I hated was that of course I *did* feel the fear. I did fear men like him – big, brutal men who wanted to inflict pain. And my fear made me hate him, and the daimon came.

Suddenly I was as cool as if I had bathed in the sea.

When we came together, I already knew how I would fight, and what I would do. The daimon was in me, and I give no quarter then. And truly, I have done shameful things, but this was hardly one of them. He was an evil bastard, and he earned his way to Tartarus all the way.

But I regret – some of it.

As soon as his grandfather gave the word, he came at me, his sword high, and smashed it into my shield.

He cut at the top, his tactic simple. He would cut the bronze band that held the rim in five or ten strokes, and then start chopping the shield until he broke my arm or cut my shield arm. It was a brutal technique, and he was a brutal man.

I ducked and dodged. I wanted him contemptuous and hurried.

He was *easy*.

He laughed and spat and chased me, landing a blow or two on the shield face. He finally stopped.

'Fucking coward, stand and fight!' he yelled.

I laughed. 'Come and catch me, arse cunt.'

Some men heard me. Others didn't. He heard me, and he should have paused to consider that if I had the breath to insult him, I wasn't afraid. But he was a fool.

But his grandfather had heard *him* and threw down his staff. 'Stop!' he roared.

He picked up his staff and prodded his grandson in the stomach. 'Boys talk like that,' he said. 'Men respect their opponents. One more jibe and I will throw you from the lists.'

Cleisthenes didn't even pretend to obey. He did not fear the gods, and they knew him for what he was.

Before Lord Pelagius gave the word, he came at me again, and he almost caught me, because, in fact, he cheated. His sword hammered my shield and we were shield to shield. The sword went back and he cut at my head. His blow clipped the rim of my shield and then my helmet, and it *hurt*.

'I'm going to kill you,' he crowed.

I could tell you that the pain of his blow made me do what I did, but I promised not to lie much when I told these tales. I knew from the moment we crossed swords. I always meant to kill him. Honey, I'm a killer. A little more wine. Your friend is blushing.

I danced away and he came after me, sure that he had me. And I let him come. He came in to hammer my shield, and I cut his sword hand off his arm as easy as making your friend blush.

See, he'd over-extended a little more with each cut, trying to get the biggest part of his blade into my shield rim. I just led him by the nose until I had his arm where I wanted it. And I could have simply given him a cut to remember.

He fell to his knees. He couldn't get the shield off his shield arm and he couldn't get a hand on his wrist to staunch the blood, and it was pumping out, almost like a neck wound.

If he'd had a friend in that circle, perhaps that man would have stepped up and stopped the blood. Or maybe not. What's a man worth with no right hand, like a criminal?

His grandfather stepped forward – and then paused.

That was the awful part. His own grandfather let him bleed out. And the other men in the circle – a conspiracy of two hundred.

He was gone quickly, but his eyes went to mine near the end, and suddenly he wasn't a bad man, a rapist, a tax-taker, a bully. He was a deer under my spear, and he didn't understand the darkness that was coming, or why it had to come to him. And in his eyes I saw the reflection of that god who comes to every man and every woman, and I also saw myself – the killer.

I didn't look away. I held his eye until he fell forward and everything was gone.

But as his soul left his body, I think something of me went with it.

I killed him because I didn't like him.

And when my eyes met Aristides', I could see that other men knew it as well as I did.

I won't go on and on about this, friends, but before I killed Cleisthenes, I was one man. Briefly, I was a victor, a man men admired. That might have been my life, however brief.

But the fates, the gods and my own daimon said otherwise. And when Cleisthenes fell face forward into the sand black with his own blood, I was another man. Some men admired me.

But aside from a few, the rest feared me.

# 12

I was wearing my new armour the next morning as we began to load the ships. Armour is a silly thing to wear for work, but by the gods it was good to look like a nobleman, and I was young and arrogant. My shoulder still hurt from the pounding of my shield against it in the fight and the race.

I noted that men were careful how they spoke to me.

Stephanos was closer, if anything. He wasn't afraid of me, and he was overjoyed that Cleisthenes was dead. In fact, I earned his friendship with that blow. And when I was maudlin that first night, Melaina told me stories of Cleisthenes and the local girls until I felt like a public benefactor.

I felt like less of a benefactor as the ships were loaded. There I stood, sparkling in a scale corslet worth a farm, a good helmet and a fine aspis. Other men were loading the ships – we had no discipline, and so every ship loaded at its own speed – and we were so late leaving the beach that we saw Lord Pelagius and the women of his household with the body, building a pyre. And the older woman, whose tears seemed pulled from her as you'd pull the guts from a dead boar, she must have been his mother.

Only then did I find fully what it is to be a killer of men. When you kill, you take a man's life. You *take* it. He can never have it back. When the darkness comes to his eyes and he clutches his guts, he is *done*. And you don't rob just him but his parents and his family, his sisters and brothers, his wife and children, his lovers, his debtors, his master and his slave – all robbed.

Cleisthenes was a bad man, I have no doubt, but all his people were on that beach, and it was like a scene in a play in Athens – not that they came at me like furies, just that they were all there: his horses and hounds, his women, his slaves, his son. All there in one place, for me to see.

I killed him because I didn't like him. Let's not lie. So – I stood there, coming to terms with the consequences. Most killers are dull men. I truly think they never see the funeral pyre. They never think. I walked down the beach, and every one of them saw me, and they looked at me as if I was some kind of beast.

I think too much. So I drink. Here – you. Blush for me and make me happy. There – ahh! My world is brighter for your presence, lady.

I never promised you a happy story.

We landed in Ephesus and all the lords of the fleet met with the lords of the city, but I stayed on our ship. I was afraid of being taken. Afraid of being a slave again. Afraid of what I'd done with Briseis. Afraid that she had already forgotten me.

And I dreamed of Cleisthenes and his funeral pyre. I still do. He's the only one. I've killed enough men to make a phalanx, and he's the only one who haunts me.

Archi was distant when he went ashore, but he came straight back to the ship with word that Diomedes' father had sent his son to a farm in the country to recover, and *nothing* had been said.

Typical. The things you most fear never come to pass. Diomedes and his father might seek revenge, but they had not gone to law.

I left the ship and entered the house as a free man, wearing armour. I felt odd – everything was odd. Food tasted wrong, and I longed to go and eat in the kitchen, but I didn't, just as I wanted one of the slaves to tell me how bold I looked in my magnificent shirt of scale armour, but none of them even met my eye.

Not even Penelope, who threw her arms around Archi when we returned and didn't even look at me.

Briseis looked at me, an enigmatic half-smile at the corner of her mouth. I found that I couldn't really breathe. I felt as if I'd been gone ten years, and I found that I'd forgotten what she looked like. She stood in the courtyard to welcome us because her mother never left her room any more and Briseis was, in effect, the lady of the house.

'Well,' she said. That was all.

I didn't see her again for days. I took baths and thought guiltily of our love-making – if that's what it was. And I found that I thought of Melaina – which seemed like treason, except that she was more my speed, if you take my meaning. I wondered why I hadn't even tried to kiss her.

Archi went to the conferences, and met with men like Aristides and Aristagoras, plotting a campaign against the Medes for the freedom of Ionia.

I found myself a lonely man in a city that had been my playground. I couldn't exactly go and sit by the Fountain of Pollio, could I?

I met my Thracian girl in the back alley, almost by accident, and tried to get her to go for a walk with me, but she ran. That hurt.

So after two days of failing to be the returning hero, I went up the hill to the Temple of Artemis. And there I found boys sitting in front of Heraclitus. I wasn't a boy, but I sat at his feet.

He nodded to me. He was laying out the rules of triangles. There were three new boys. I had been gone just two months, and even that world had changed. But I listened, and my mind went down the paths of numbers and figures in the sand, instead of death and war and sex, and I took a little healing, as I always have from the wise.

When he was done with the other boys, he came and sat next to me.

'What you did to Diomedes was cruel,' he said.

'The logos speaks through strife,' I said, quoting him.

'Don't give me that shit,' he said. His gaze met mine and ground mine down like stone against iron. 'You hurt that boy.'

I shrugged. 'He had it coming.'

Heraclitus sat and leaned on his staff. I can't remember another time that he sat with me. Finally he looked at me. 'I have so many things I want to say to you. You can all but see the logos – and yet you are so far from true understanding, aren't you? You understand me when I talk, and yet you can hurt a boy like that – for a child's reasons.'

I blinked tears. I had been blinking tears since he sat with me. Hah! I feel them in my eyes even now. No one else had cared, except Stephanos and Archi. He sat there, and listened.

'I did it because he broke his engagement with Briseis,' I said. 'He hurt her. I did the right thing!'

Heraclitus's eyes rested on me, and you could almost see the sparks as his gaze ground away at mine.

Finally, I hung my head. 'No, I did not.'

'No,' he said. 'Tell the truth, at least to yourself. I knew the truth as soon as I heard that the boy had been hurt. You hurt him. Cruelly. Is that who you are? A man who hurts for his own satisfaction?'

I couldn't meet his eyes. And I began to weep. I sat on the steps and told him the tale of Cleisthenes. He shuddered when I cut off the hand. But he smiled when I told him, through my own tears, of the funeral pyre.

'It is the pity of the world that we must come to wisdom through fire,' he said. 'Why can no man learn wisdom from another?'

I couldn't answer him. Perhaps no one can. After a while he went on, 'You have discovered one of the secrets of the world of men.'

'What's that?' I asked. Those boys – most of them knew me – were wondering why the teacher was sitting with me, and why I was pouring tears the way a mended pot leaks water.

'The secret is that men are easy to kill. That if you are brave and have a steady hand and a cold heart, you can have whatever you desire.' He looked away. 'This city is about to go to war with Persia, and then it will learn a lesson that I think you already know. War is the king and father of all, my son. Some men it makes lords, and others it makes slaves. Do you understand?'

'No,' I said.

'Ah!' he said, and laughed – at himself. 'The strife I preach – some men master it without knowing why, and use it for themselves, without a thought to consequence. War makes them lords and kings. But they are not good men. The killer lies in every man – closer to the surface in some than others, I think. I saw the killer in your eyes when first your master led you up the steps.' He nodded. 'If you would master the killer in you, you must accept that you are not truly free. You must submit to the mastery of the laws of men and gods.'

'Men fight wars!' I protested.

'And men return from them, confused as to what the laws of men and gods ask of them.' He looked at a raptor, climbing in the distance over the mountains. 'That bird can kill twenty times a day and never be the agent of evil – merely change. But men are not animals. What they mate and what they kill becomes who they are.' He looked at me. 'You are a warrior. You must find yourself a path that keeps you among men and not among animals. Avoid the confusion. Law is better than chaos.'

It doesn't sound like a helpful speech, although I think I can re-member every word. And yes, that line about strife and war – he said it all the time, and it's in his book. Don't think I was the first to hear it, either. But it stuck.

Listen, all of you. There are men and women – you're old enough to know – who discover what their nether parts are for and go mad with it. It is the same with killing. Turns out that killing is easy. Inflicting pain is easy. Cleisthenes learned that. And when I gave him the other half of the lesson, he never got to benefit from it. Perhaps if he'd had a teacher like my teacher . . .

For weeks the ships came up the river and dropped soldiers – Greeks – on our shores, and we gathered a mighty army. At least, we thought it was an army. Aristagoras promised us an easy fight. He said that the Persians had short spears and no shields and that their riches were there for us to take.

It is the dark comedy of men that every Ionian knew that he was full of shit. Many of them had faced Persians – or run from them – and they knew how good they were. And yet this disease, this mania, swept them as if the deadly archer had shot them with arrows of inflammation and disease – failure to fear the Persians.

There's a name for this disease in all the tragedies. We call it hubris, and all men and all women are subject to it.

So they debated and planned. No one drilled, though, and no one appointed a commander, although all but the Athenians took orders, or at least suggestions, from Aristagoras. He went to dinner at the house. I wasn't excluded, but I wasn't comfortable attending formal dinners. Oh, my manners were up to it – I had learned the manners of aristocrats. But to lie on a couch and be served by Kylix?

I went and ate in taverns by the water. Which proved to be a good choice, because I found Epaphroditos in one and Stephanos in another, and learned to play knucklebones like an islander. Stephanos's victory as a wrestler had promoted him off the oar bench and into the ranks of his lord's retinue, and now he was a hoplite. He and Epaphroditos and I had the games in common, and that was enough. And when we found Heraklides, we were four, which is a good number for men.

Four weeks of dicing in taverns and drinking cheap wine, exercising in the gymnasium – all the allied soldiers were welcome there, and no one knew me – and four weeks of sitting at Heraclitus's feet. Indeed, I took my friends to hear him speak. They were pleased but mystified, and all three agreed that he was a great man, but they never went with me again.

Heraklides spoke for the other two. He was in the agora, fingering a plain bronze camp knife. The vendor was a slave for the smith who made it. It was mediocre work.

'I'll pay you in obols what you ask in owls,' Heraklides said to the slave. I had just asked him to come with me a second time to hear Heraclitus. 'By the gods, man – three obols, then!'

He turned to me with a grin. 'Yon philosopher is a little above the likes of me, Doru. I could see he was a great man – it was a pleasure to hear him. But I scarcely understood a word he said.' He whirled back on the slave. 'Four obols – take it or leave it.'

Heraclitus sat with me every day after the other boys walked away, and we talked about laws – laws of men and laws of gods. You've heard it all from your tutors, I'm sure. Aye, I'll have his head if you haven't heard it, honey! That most laws are men's laws for men's reasons. In Sparta, every man takes a boy as a lover, and in Chios, it is death for a man to lie with a boy. These are the laws of men.

But the gods hate hypocrisy and hubris, as any history that is true will show. And murder – and incest. These are the laws of the gods. And there are laws we can only guess at – laws of hospitality, for example. They seem like god-given laws, but when we meet men who have different guest-laws, we have to wonder.

Bah – I talk too much. I should have been a philosopher, as the priest of Hephaestus said.

And then there was Briseis.

I can't remember how long I had been in that house before I saw her again. I was in her father's room, with her father's permission – he was formal and polite to me, but a little cold – reading his scrolls. He had the words of Pythagoras and some of Heraclitus and Anaxagoras, too. And I was reading them. I was also helping him and Darkar do sums. I would have carried water to the well at this point, I was so bored and felt so under-used. Archi didn't want me when he went to the daily conference, and so I seemed to have no duties at all except to match him in the gymnasium, at the palaestra and on the track.

I was reading, as I say, when Briseis came in. She smiled at me – quite a happy smile – and took a scroll from my basket.

'Have you read Thales?' she asked. 'For all that he sounds like a soothsayer, he seems the wisest of the lot. Or perhaps he just hated women less.'

'Heraclitus doesn't hate women,' I answered hotly.

'Oh!' she said, and her eyes flashed. 'Wonderful! I'll ask him to accept me as a student straight away.'

I had to smile. I raised my hand the way a swordsman does at practice, when he acknowledges a hit. 'Well struck,' I said.

'I was happy at Sappho's school,' she said. 'I wish I could go back, but I'm too old.' Old at sixteen.

Her father glared at us. 'I'm working,' he growled.

'May we read in the garden?' Briseis asked sweetly, and he kissed her hand – absently – his eyes on his work.

We picked up the scroll baskets and walked into the garden together.

'Why don't you read to me?' she said. There was very little question to it.

And that was that. I read to her every day. We read Thales' book on nature – really just an accumulation of his sayings. We read our way through Pythagoras, and laughed over what we didn't understand, and Briseis asked questions and I taught her what I knew of the geometry, which was not inconsiderable, and I took her questions to Heraclitus, and he answered them. He was contemptuous of women as a sex, but friendly to them as individuals, which Briseis said was a vast improvement on the reverse.

If I thought that I loved her when I was a slave, that was merely the lust for the unattainable. Every boy loves someone unattainable, and no few attain the one they want anyway, to their own confusion. But when we sat together, day after day, then I saw her another way.

I am an intelligent man. All my life, my wits have cut other men like my sword.

She was my better. I saw it with the geometry. In three weeks, she had everything I could teach. By the gods, if I could have taught her to smith, she'd have made a Corinthian helmet in three weeks! Once her mind bit into a thing, she would never let it go, like a boar with his tusks in his prey.

Have you ever seen an eagle kill close to you? She turns, and you catch your breath, and she hits her prey, and if you are close, you can see the blood – a brief red cloud, a mist of blood – and your heart stops with the beauty of it, even as you think that this is an animal killing another animal. Why is it so beautiful?

And so with the mind of Briseis.

After two weeks, she leaned close while I showed her a bronze *pyxis* I had made for her – we had a small forge – and she leaned close and ran a finger down my jaw.

'Come to my room tonight,' she said.

I leaned back, her touch like a burn on my jaw. 'If I'm caught—' I said, and like a coward, my eyes darted around for the slaves.

She shrugged. 'I wasn't caught. Or am I braver than you, my hero?'

She said nothing more – nothing. Not a glance did she give me, nor a touch of her hand.

I went to her room wondering with every heart-pounding step if I had, in fact, created the whole thing in my head. Had she really asked me? Really?

I stopped in the hall outside her room, although there was no cover there. I took a breath and my knees were weak and I shuddered. I had done none of these things before I killed Cleisthenes. Every man is brave for some things and a coward for others. I stood there for a long time, and I'll tell you in honesty that I could feel the shit at the base of my intestines, I was so afraid.

Aphrodite, not Ares, is the deadliest on Olympus.

Then I made myself push through her curtain.

She laughed when her skin was against mine. 'You weren't this cold in the bath,' she said.

'I thought that you were Penelope!' I said with foolish honesty.

There are women who might be offended by that sort of revelation. Briseis bit my ear, rolled off the couch and lit a lamp from her fire jar.

'Aphrodite!' I said. Probably squeaked.

She got on top of me. 'I want you to see me,' she said. 'So that next time you won't mistake me for my maid.'

When we were done – and the moment we were done, she laughed and bounced to her feet – I asked, 'Why?' I reached out and touched her flank. 'Why did you come to me? In the bath?'

She laughed, and her eyes flashed in the lamplight. 'I decided that you should have what Diomedes gave away,' she said. 'Promise me that if you ever have the chance, you'll kill him for me?'

I shrugged. Later, I swore.

I'm a man, not a god.

★

I took to spending my days in the little forge shed in the work yard. It was a tiny shop with one small bench, and Hipponax only had it so that his pots could be mended without being taken to market, but Darkar once told me that they had had a slave who had some skill with iron.

I made instruments at first – a compass for Briseis, and then a ruler marked out in *daktyloi*. I made a fine compass for Heraclitus, as well. It was simple work, but good. Briseis was pleased by her geometry tools, as she called them, and Heraclitus was delighted, embracing me. I think that he had no use for such things, as he once told me that he could see the logos and all its shapes in his head. But the long bronze dividers were comfortable in the hand, and excellent for showing a student, and their points were sharp and probably used to prick a generation of dullards, which gives me some satisfaction.

When I had my eye back, I bought some scrap bronze and poured myself a plate, pouring directly on to a piece of slate. Then I forged the pour into a sheet, which made me feel better. Making sheet is long work, and finicky. I did an adequate job, although my heart told me that I stopped planishing too early.

Oh, lass, you'll never be a bronze-smith's daughter! Planishing – endless tiny hammer strokes to smooth the forge-work. When you change something's shape, you use the curved surface of the big hammers, pulling the metal or pushing it, this way and that. But that leaves big, lumpy marks. See this cauldron? Look at these marks. See? But a good smith, a master, never lets an item out of his shop with these divots. He uses ever-smaller hammers, working the surface a blow at a time, until it is one continuous surface – like my helmet. See?

Making sheet is about getting the surface to a single thickness and a flat shape, two things that seem like enemies when you are new to the process. More than you wanted to know, eh? But something had changed since I killed Cleisthenes, and I wanted to go back, I think – back to a world where I could do good work.

I had begun to have dreams about home. I had the first in Briseis's bed, the first night I went to her. I dreamed that ravens came and stripped my armour from me, and took me to their nest.

I dreamed of ravens, and their green nest of willows, night after night, until I realized that the ravens were Apollo's, and the green nest was Plataea – was home. And then, for the first time in years, I was homesick. I began to dream more fully, about the farm on the hill, and about the tomb of the hero on the slopes of Cithaeron, and about hunting with Calchas.

The dreams were powerful but they could never compete with the reality of Briseis. Or the coming war. I told myself that it was time to go home – soon.

Anyway, I tell this story awry. I gambled on the waterfront and made love to Briseis; I listened to Heraclitus and read philosophy in the garden; I worked and played on the palaestra and in the gymnasium with Archi. It sounds like a good life. In fact, it was a bad time, but I could not tell you why, except that I could feel the doom over me.

When I had my bronze sheet forged, I cut some scrap from the edges and began to work them, chasing figures into them as practice. I did olives and circles and leaves and laurels, and then I tried a stag, but my stag became a raven early in the process. I made six or seven ravens, until I had done one well.

I remember that raven, because while I admired my work, Darkar came in and asked me to wait on Archi at dinner. That was the third time that Hipponax hosted Aristagoras. This time Briseis was the hostess, with most of the great men of the army as guests. The house was busy, and in those days, it was perfectly acceptable for a free man to wait on his lord, and I did it willingly enough.

I should have refused.

First, Aristides was confused to find me at his elbow. He smiled at me. I had to look at him for a long time to see the cool swordsman – my toughest opponent from the beach. 'So,' he gave his slight smile, 'you have come to take your place among the captains?'

I grinned, and walked off to pour wine for Archi, and then I caught the Athenian's look, and it was one of anger. None of the men at the party knew how to talk to me – was I a cup-bearer or a champion? It made them uneasy. Which, in turn, made me uneasy.

Then there was Briseis. She moved among them, dressed in a Doric chiton of pure new linen, shining white, and transparent, and they watched her the way dogs watch the slave with the food.

I had to watch the interplay among the captains, and I didn't like it. Aristides was not the chief of the Athenians – that was Melanthius, an older man, and an astute politician, but not, I think, much of a fighter. Melanthius shared a couch with Aristagoras and they drank together like friends, but I could see that Aristides thought little of either of them. Aristagoras was belligerent and fawning by turns, a depressing sight. Diomedes' father, Agasides, was there and Briseis treated him as if he were made of dung, which he reciprocated. And yet, Hipponax supported him as the war leader of the Ephesians.

There was a captain named Eualcidas from Eretria in Euboea, a famous athlete who had been praised by Simonides the poet, and another Eretrian, Dikaios, who made clear that he loathed all the Athenians more than he hated the Persians. I stared at them, for every one must have been at the fight by the bridge where my father died and I was made a slave.

The Eretrians had come with five ships because of their ancient alliance with the men of Miletus, of which Aristagoras was once again ruler, although he disdained the title of tyrant now that he had returned to them, and claimed that he would liberate all the Greeks of Asia and give them democracies.

The Milesians and Eretrians had sailed up the river together, fifty ships or more, and landed their men in the precinct of Koressos. Aristagoras was now the accepted commander of the war, and the whole purpose of the war had changed, because all the Greek cities had declared. Now it was the Trojan War. Now all the Greeks were going to make war on Persia. They planned to seize Sardis, expel the satrap Artaphernes and then perhaps march on Persepolis. And that night was the first I had heard of any of these things.

None of them noticed me, but they bickered among themselves aplenty, thugater. If I had been half the veteran I thought myself, I'd have smelled the trouble the way Aristides did.

Aristides watched them with contempt, and Archi worried and fidgeted. Hipponax watched them looking at his daughter, and Briseis rode the wave of their lust like a skilled helmsman.

It was not a pretty party, and I should not have been there. They drank, and quarrelled, and each of them thought he was Agamemnon or Achilles. On the sixth bowl of wine, Dikaios the Eretrian raised the cup.

'Your daughter moves like a dancer – can her lips do what flute girls do?' he asked.

Men hooted – and then fell silent. Hipponax rose from his kline and he looked ready to kill.

'Leave my house,' he said.

Dikaios laughed. 'You dress her like a whore and put her at a party, and then you're offended when I speak what every man thinks? You easterners are soft, and your women are whores.' He drank the wine.

The cup rang like a gong when it hit the floor, and his head hit only a moment later. It rang hollow, like a gourd. He was out.

I had put him in that condition, and now I lifted him – I was strong, then – and carried him to the courtyard, then threw him into the street, in the dung. Oh, it is easy to make enemies!

Darkar stopped me from going back to the party. So I went to my bed, and later I went to Briseis, and she embraced me with a vigour that frightened me.

'I loved how you hurt him,' she said. 'What do flute girls do?'

I explained, with some blushes, what they do. She laughed. 'Not enough in it for me,' she said. 'What pleasure does the girl get?' and we laughed together.

The next morning, I ran six stades with Archi and he beat all of us. We threw javelins and fought with spears. After we had clashed shields and bruised each other for an hour, Agasides came and ordered us down to the beach. Heralds were crying in the agora and on the steps of all the temples, and the whole army was assembling for the first time.

The beach was a vision of Chaos. We stood together in a mob, perhaps seven thousand men, and Aristagoras placed his contingents in the phalanx. He put the Athenians on the right of the line, in the place of honour. The Ephesians were in the centre, towards the left.

When Agasides had his place in the battle line, he chose men for the front rank. He chose Hipponax, but he did not choose me or Archi. Few men of Ephesus knew me, and despite my excellent armour and my victory in games, the Ephesians didn't see me as a citizen (which I was not). Agasides, of course, knew me – as one of the men who had injured his son, and as a former slave.

So Archilogos and I were placed together – in the fifth rank. We were, without a doubt, the two best athletes in the city, and probably the best men-at-arms, but Ephesus had known three generations of peace, and Agasides placed men according to his likes and dislikes and with no eye towards the phalanx as a fighting machine. Hipponax had fought pirates several times, and despite his reputation as a soft poet, was a good choice. But all the other front-rankers were Agasides' drinking companions, business partners and political allies.

We were one of the last contingents to form, and we looked bad. Other contingent commanders came and stared at us while we grumbled and switched places endlessly. A man would make his claim to the front rank – always couched in political terms – and Agasides would stand indecisively, balancing one interest against another.

When, at last, we were in our places, Aristagoras came and addressed us, and for all his faults he had lungs of brass. We were told that the army would march up-country to Sardis over the passes in the mountains, and that all the hoplites and their slaves should assemble in two days, after the feast of Heracles – that is the feast that they celebrate in Ephesus, nothing like our Boeotian feasts. Two days, and we would march.

It was the first time most men had heard that we'd be marching up-country, and there was much grumbling.

I talked to the men around me and realized that none of them had ever stood in a shield wall or fought with bronze or iron. They were like a pack of virgins going to do the work of flute girls. I was a mere seventeen, but I had seen three pitched battles and I had killed.

Archi took me aside after the muster. 'You've got to stop talking so much,' he said. 'You'll take the spirit out of us! Sometimes I regret that you are free. You cannot speak to the first men of the city as if they were simpletons.'

I shrugged. 'Archi, they are fools, and men are going to die. I have fought in a phalanx. None of these men have. I should be in the front rank.'

Aristides had his helmet perched on his brow. He was leaning on his spears, listening to us, and then he came over. He glanced at Agasides and spat. 'You were there when your father stopped the Spartans?' he asked.

I nodded. 'I was there,' I said. I didn't mention that I had been a psilos throwing rocks.

He nodded. 'You should be in command, then. These children,' and he nodded to Archi, 'will die like sacrificed goats if we face the Medes.'

Archi blushed. 'I will stand my ground,' he said.

Aristides shrugged. 'You'll die alone then,' he said.

I went back to the house and spent hours putting a pair of ravens over the nasal of my helmet. I softened the worked metal by annealing it, and then I had to cut my punches shorter to use them from inside the bowl of the helmet, but the work came along nicely enough. Sitting on a low stool at the anvil, tapping away at my work, alone in the shed, I was safe from the anger that had followed me from the muster.

I had started putting a band of olive leaves at the brow when the light from the doorway was cut off.

'I'm working!' I called without turning my head.

'So I see,' Heraclitus said. He came in, and I stood hurriedly.

'Stay where you are. I thought I would find you here.' He looked around, examined my practice pieces. 'You seem infatuated with ravens,' he said with a smile.

'My family calls itself the "Corvaxae",' I said. 'The Crows.'

'Ah! And why is that?' he asked.

I told him the story of the ravens and the Daidala, and then I told him about my sister's black hair, and how my father had always put the raven on his work.

Philosopher that he was, he wanted to see the metal worked, so I punched an olive leaf from inside the helmet and then made the work finer and neater by working it from the outside. I showed him how the work made the bronze harder.

He watched me anneal the back of the crown, and he reminded me of old Empedocles, the priest of Hephaestus, when he commented on the bronze tube that I used to raise the heat of the forge fire.

'I have seen the fire and the metal together before,' he said. 'I suppose that I already knew that fire softens and work hardens.' He smiled. Then he frowned. 'With iron, fire hardens.'

I shook my head. 'You are the wisest man I know, but no smith! Fire softens iron. To make it hard, you quench it in vinegar when it is hot.'

'It is fire that is the agent,' he said. 'The agent of change is always fire.'

I could hardly argue with that.

He looked at the new leaves around the brow of the helmet. 'You won the olive wreath at the games at Chios?' he asked.

I smiled with pride. 'Yes,' I answered. 'Now I will wear them for ever.'

He turned my work this way and that, and I explained planishing to smooth and harden the metal. And then I showed him how I melted the bronze and poured it on slate. He played with the bronze tube, just as Empedocles had, and blew through it, making the fire leap, and he laughed with joy.

'All things are an equal exchange with fire, and fire for all things,' he said. 'Look at how you use the charcoal to make the fire, and the fire melts the bronze. You merely trade the charcoal for the heat, the way men at the docks change gold for a cargo.'

I nodded, because that made sense to me.

'So it is with anger and with war,' he said. 'Anger is to men what fire is to your forge. And if we eradicate that anger, much might follow.'

I shrugged.

He took me by the shoulder. 'You are full of anger,' he said. 'Anger gives strength, but it comes at the price of soul. Do you know what I am saying?'

I said yes – like a boy. In fact, I heard him, but had no idea what he was saying – that is, how his words were meant for me. He had come down from the temple just to say those words, but I was young and foolish.

I embraced him, and he left me, and then I finished my work.

That night I went to sleep early, intending to rise and go to Briseis, but I was tired and I slept through the night. Then the next day we had an assembly of arms, and we drilled – raising and lowering our shields, and forming to the left, so that we marched up the beach and formed a front on the Athenians from a column into a deep line.

Aristides said it was horrible. I had no idea. This kind of drill was outside my limited experience of war.

In the afternoon, I read Thales to Briseis. She smiled at me. 'I was lonely last night,' she said, and I started, because she said it in front of Penelope.

So that night I went through the bead curtain into her room. We made love, and it was good. And then we began to talk of my going up-country.

I wanted her to tell me that she loved me, and that she would miss me. But she was merely playful, and when I searched for an endearment, she grabbed my manhood and kissed me until I lay with her again.

I am making all of you blush. But the blushing time is over, and the hard part has come.

We were lying together on her kline after that second time. She lay on top of me, the weight of her – not much of a weight, I'll allow – pressing down on my hips. She was idly licking the bruise on my shoulder when I heard heavy footfalls in the hallway. I had time to roll her off me.

The beads parted and Hipponax burst into the room.

He had a sword.

Behind him was Darkar, and behind both of them was Archi with Penelope in tow, her eyes wide with terror.

Hipponax raised the sword. He hesitated – unsure, I think, which of us to kill first.

I took the sword from him as easily as you would take a spoon from a child. Then I stood between him and his daughter.

Oh, the furies must have been laughing.

What hurt most was the look of pain on Archi's face.

Hipponax was weeping. He hit me with his fist, ignoring that I had a sword – that's how angry he was.

I flung the sword away rather than kill him with it. And he hit me again. I fell.

When he turned on Briseis, she had the sword. She looked at me – with contempt.

'Stop this,' Briseis said. She was sixteen, and yet her voice stopped all the war in the room.

'You *whore!*' her brother cried. He sounded as if he was in physical pain.

'How could you—' her father started. He sobbed. 'What is the curse of the women of my house?'

Briseis stood there, naked, the sword in her fist. She held it steady, and when her father approached her, she pricked his chest with the point. 'No closer,' she said. 'My virginity was never yours to barter.'

'What?' Hipponax asked. 'Drop the sword!'

She shook her head. 'Go to bed. We will talk about this in the day.'

Hipponax took a shuddering breath and exploded. 'You faithless bitch!' he roared. 'And I allowed your brother – and this piece of offal – to beat Diomedes! He was right! I will flog you in the streets – I will sell you to a brothel. I will sacrifice you—'

She pricked him with the point. 'No,' she said.

She looked at Archi. 'Take Pater to bed,' she said.

Archi was shaking. He flicked a glance at me. 'He must die,' Archi said.

So much for friendship.

She looked at me. 'Why?' she asked. 'He is not anybody, and he will never tell.'

Her words cut me as if the blade she held pricked my flesh.

So much for love.

She laughed. 'You are all fools. This body is mine. I will use it as I wish. If I wish to take my pleasure with a man or a dog, so be it. I learned that from Mater, and from Diomedes, and you two fools will need to learn the lesson. Men will not be my masters. By Artemis the virgin, and by Aphrodite, I will be the master and not the slave.'

They stepped back.

'You will die a lonely old bitch,' her father said.

Briseis laughed. 'Pater, you are dear to me, but you are a fool. I will die the queen of Lydia. Aristagoras has agreed to marry me.' She laughed.

Something in me died. 'What?' I spat. It was good, then, that I had no weapon in my hand.

Briseis smiled at me – the smile matrons give to simple children in the agora. 'You thought I was going to marry you, because you have a fine suit of armour?' She pointed the sword at her father and brother. 'As soon as Sardis falls, I am to wed him.'

She turned to me and smiled. 'You have served your turn, Doru. Take your armour and go from this house. I don't think you should come back. Pater might hurt you. And you love him.' She said the last as if it made me the greatest fool in the world.

But I obeyed her, and my world filled with darkness. I went to my bed with Darkar at my heels. He spoke, and I have no idea what he said. I took the wool bag with my armour, and I took my sword and my spears. I rolled my heavy cloak and my sleeping pad inside my aspis.

Darkar was still talking at me when I got to the gate.

Archi was there.

'How could you?' he asked.

'I love her,' I said. He had a naked blade in his hand, and I drew my blade. 'Loved her,' I spat.

'Never come back,' he said. We faced each other with blades in our hands.

I found Aristides on the beach in the morning.

'Will you take me as a hoplite?' I asked him, straight away.

He looked around. 'Tell me why,' he said. 'You served with Archilogos of this city, last I heard.'

'I serve him no longer,' I said.

Aristides nodded. 'More fool he.' He smiled. 'Will you stand in the seventh rank?'

The lowest place. An eighth-ranker was a file-closer – a form of officer. But a seventh-ranker was a man either too young or too small to fight.

'I'm better than that,' I said, with all the anger gathered in the last few hours.

Aristides was only a couple of years older than me, but he had a way about him, and he gave me his famous half-smile. 'I know that you can kill,' he said. 'I don't know you otherwise. Seventh rank, or stay on the beach.'

So when we marched on Sardis, I marched with the Athenians, the wings of betrayal beating about my head, the furies at my back and all of Persia before me.

In the seventh rank.

# 13

As it turned out, I had Herk as my file-leader. Of course, as helmsman, he was an officer – I was unused to taking orders, which may
seem a foolish comment from a former slave, but it was true. Still,
I did well enough, and the men in my file were all veterans, at least
of some raids and a siege or two, and I had plenty to learn about
camping and eating and keeping clean. I was amazed at how much
time the Athenians spent on their gear – polishing and cleaning with
pumice and tallow and scraps of tow, every spare moment.

Agios was my file-closer in the eighth rank. He was a well-known
man, and at sea he was a helmsman – far too important to serve
in the front rank and get killed, or so I understood. He and Herk
were peers, and good friends. Later, they were my friends, but on
the march to Sardis, Agios had few good words for me. Even as I
was amazed at how hard the Athenians worked on their gear, so
Agios was disgusted with how careless I was with mine. It was there
– marching to Sardis – that I learned how much of the business of
war was in maintenance.

My mood was black – so black that I have no memory of march-
ing upriver to Sardis. We crossed the mountains through the pass, I
assume, but I don't remember it. I had to carry my own gear because
I had no slave. I don't remember anything of that, either, although
I must have sweated like a pig and been the laughing stock of the
Athenian taxeis.

I had a hard time with Briseis in my head. I hated her, and yet,
even then, I knew that I was lying to myself. I didn't hate her. *I understood her.* But I also knew that my life had been smashed – again
– as thoroughly as my enslavement had smashed it.

I was locked inside the prison of my head for the whole march.
It rained and I was wet and at the top of the pass it was cold. I

know that my friends talked to me – Stephanos and Epaphroditos and Heraklides, because they all referred to it later. But I remember nothing but a waking nightmare of the loss of Hipponax and Archi – and Briseis.

Hipponax and Archi were in the same army I was in – there were only eight or nine thousand of us, all in, and I saw both of them every day, at a distance. They must have known that I was with the army, marching just a stade or two from them. I *do* remember wanting to go to them, every day – a yearning to face them, to receive blows or embraces. I think I believed that they would commiserate with me. Now, I shake my head.

We were fifteen days marching on Sardis, and despite our long delay at Ephesus, we caught the city unawares. Which will give you an idea of how badly prepared the Medes were for us. I think that Artaphernes never really believed that men he had counted as friends and guest-friends – men like Aristagoras and Hipponax – would actually march on him. And so great was the name of Darius, King of Kings, that no man had ever dared to strike at him. Amongst the Ionians, they talked openly of conquering Persia. Amongst the Athenians, they laughed and talked about increasing their trade with Ionia. No man so much as mentioned Persia. I remember that, too.

At any rate, the Persians were unprepared.

When we came down the pass, the scouts told us that the gates of the great city – one of the richest in Asia – were open.

We lost all order. The whole army broke into a mass of sprinting soldiers racing for the gates. At least, that's how it seemed to me, and I was close to the front. Aristides roared like a bull to make us stand our ground, and we ignored him and raced for the nearest gates.

I followed Herk. He was fast, but nothing like me, and I loped easily, keeping pace. The rest of our file fell behind – Herk wasn't the fastest, but he had stamina. Other men caught us, and a few passed us, but the upshot was that a dozen of us came to the Ephesus Gate of Sardis, just around the hour men leave the agora, and the gates were open.

Even as we ran up, the Lydian gate-guards finally decided that they were in peril and began to close the great wooden doors – or perhaps they closed them every day in late afternoon.

Herk threw himself at the nearest door and men joined him. I flashed through the narrowing gap and my spear caught a Lydian and killed him, and the other guards broke and fled and the gates were ours, and I was the first man in the city.

Then I saw men behave as animals, and men treated as animals, and it was amidst the slaughter that I awoke from my nightmares of the loss of Hipponax and family and Briseis. I found myself in the wreckage of the agora, watching a trio of Eretrians raping a girl while others looted the stalls in an orgy of destruction, like animals let loose from cages. Oh, you haven't seen what men are until you see them let loose inside a city.

I did nothing to stop it. It was happening all about me. And my sword was red, and blood dripped down my hand.

The storming of a city is the grimmest of man's acts, and the one most likely to draw the wrath of the gods. Sardis was defenceless, and the men and women of the city had never resisted us, or done us any hurt greater than taking some of our money in their trades. But we butchered them like lambs.

Some fools set fire to the Temple of Cybele, and that sacrilege was repaid a hundredfold later. But worse was to come.

The initial assault took the city, but we had no officers and no enemy to fight, so we all became looters and rapists, roving criminal bands. The men of the town gathered, first to fight the temple fire and then to resist us, and as the flames spread, they were driven towards the central agora.

Because we had no leadership and no order, we didn't storm the citadel. I was no better than the rest – I assumed that the city had fallen. I stood in the agora, watching the city burn, refusing to rape and contemptuous of the looters, and I watched the other side of the market fill with men – panicked men, I assumed.

And then Artaphernes was there. His armour glittered in the fires, and he led the Lydians of the town and his own picked men of the citadel straight at us, and the Greeks were scattered the way sheep are scattered by wolves.

I saw Artaphernes coming. Greeks ran past me and some were already casting aside their shields. That's how bad we were. We must have outnumbered the Lydians three or four to one, and they scattered us.

When the attack came, Herk was stripping a gold-seller's stall like a professional sea wolf, which he was. 'Fuck,' he said. 'I knew this was too easy.'

He began to blow on his sea whistle, and I fell in next to him.

He had his shield and I had mine, and other men who were not utterly in the grip of chaos and panic joined us, and in a few moments we were a hundred men. I noted that the man on my right was the athlete from Eretria, Eualcidas, whose friend I had thrown from the symposium. War makes strange shield-fellows. Agios was close on me, standing behind Herk.

The Lydians stopped short of us.

That was their mistake, because as soon as the other Greeks saw the Lydians halt, they turned and became men. So it is in any fight.

Aristides was there, then. He ran across the front rank and praised us for standing, a few quick words, and more men joined us, Chians, mostly. Our shield wall covered the agora, and we were four or five men deep – not a proper phalanx, but a deep line of mixed men.

Then the Lydians came at us. They weren't big men, or well armoured, except Artaphernes' bodyguard in the centre, where I was. And the fates laughed, because the man coming at me in the fire-lit afternoon light was Cyrus, with his three friends around him. They halted ten paces from us, to see if we would give way, but we had Aristides to give us some wood in our backbones, and we shuffled but held.

Artaphernes' men began to shoot at us with powerful bows at close range. Eualcidas on my right took an arrow through his shield into his shield arm – that's how strong their bows were close up. I saw that Heraklides slanted his, and I did the same, and then, under cover of my shield, I got the shaft out of Eualcidas's arm and two other Eretrians dragged him to the rear. The next man to stand beside me got Cyrus's arrow in his ankle – I saw the shot – and then Aristides exposed himself to the fire and ran along the front, ordering us to kneel behind our shields, and we did. He was magnificent. He was only a couple of years older than me, and I wanted to *be* him.

So I indulged in some bravado of my own. I called Cyrus's name until he saw me, and I stood up and took off my helmet. Arrows rattled on my shield, and one pinked my naked thigh above my greaves, scraping along the muscle without penetrating.

'Cyrus!' I roared.

He raised his axe over his head and waved it at me. 'You fool!' he called, and laughed. The Greeks around me wondered aloud how I knew a Persian, one of the elite, and I laughed.

And then their line stopped shooting and charged us.

Artaphernes led his men from the front. Never believe all that crap about the Medes whipping their men forward – that's the slaves they sometimes use as living shields. The real Persians and Medes – like Cyrus and Artaphernes – are like lions, eager for a fight all the time.

They only had ten paces to come at us. I had a stranger behind me and another on my right, but I had Heraklides on my left. I looked back at the man behind me. He seemed steady. When the Medes charged, I stood crouched, shield on shoulder, and as they came up I punched out with my first spear and caught Cyrus in the leg, my spear in his calf, and down he went. Pharnakes was right with him, and he had a heavy axe, which he put in the face of my shield as I threw my second spear into the second rank, where an unshielded man took it in the gut – a Persian – and went down. I pushed my shield in Pharnakes' face, axe and all, and the man behind me stabbed him while I got my sword out from under my arm.

And Heraklides yelled, 'Back! Back up! Back, you dogs!'

I raised my shield and backed a pace. Our line was shattered. Lydians were butchering the men who ran.

I got back in the line – I'd pushed forward into the Medes – but they weren't fighting my partner or me. They were flowing around us, left and right, towards easier pickings, as men do when the mêlée becomes chaotic. I got my shield under the front edge of Heraklides', and the man who had been at my back now stepped up to fit in next to me – it was all going to shit – and then he was gone, an axe in his head, and his brains showered me.

I grabbed a spear and fought with it until it broke. We could hear Aristides and we followed his voice – back and back and back, and the enemy seldom fought us, because we kept together. There were men behind us, Agios and two others, and I never knew them, but they stayed with us, and more than once a spear from over my shoulder kept me alive, until the four of us made it to an alley entrance where the Athenian captain had another little knot of men. He had waited for us. I never forgot that, either. It probably only took us a minute to reach him, but he might have been as safe as a house for that minute, and he stood and waited.

Well, Heraklides was his helmsman, of course.

We got to the alley, and then we ran.

We ran all the way to our ships, eh? Well, not quite. We ran back across the bridges and made a better stand, and Artaphernes took a light wound as his advance was stopped. I fought there, and I was in the front rank, and I probably put a man or two down, but it was desperate stuff, no ranks or files, and the Ionians were a pack of fools with no order. Mostly, I was trying to keep Heraklides on my left and my shield with his. I don't know who hit Artaphernes, but that man saved our army. Because their attack petered out at the bridges, and we managed to withdraw to Tmolus across the Hermus River, and there was no pursuit.

Half of the army had never been in the fight at all, and they wanted to storm the city again. Those of us who had fought were angry, and those who had run magnified the number and ferocity of the enemy, and many angry words were said.

I was sitting, bleeding from a few wounds and breathing like the bellows for a forge, when a man came up. He was an Eretrian and he had a scorpion on his aspis, and he looked like a hard man.

He came straight up to me.

'You are the Plataean?' he asked.

I was sitting on my shield, so he couldn't quite see the device. I nodded. 'Doru,' I said.

He nodded. 'You saved my father – he's telling everyone how you covered him against the arrows and drew the one from his shoulder.' He offered me his hand. I took it. 'I'm Parmenides.'

I clasped his hand, and he offered more praise. I shook my head. But later, he came back with his father, and they brought a full skin of wine, which I shared with my mess. Then Stephanos came from the Aeolians – the men of Chios and the coast of Asia opposite – and sat with my mess group. He was a sixth-ranker, and proud just to wear the panoply. For him, it was an enormous promotion – as great as my step from slave to free man. The Aeolians take noble blood much more seriously than Atticans or Boeotians.

When Stephanos went back to his own mess, I lay down, my head spinning from the wine. Heraklides lay down beside me, and we missed the part where Aristides accused the Milesians of cowardice.

I've done poor Aristides an injustice if I've failed to make him sound like a prig. He was always right, and some men hated him for it. He never lied and seldom even shaded the truth. Indeed, among the Athenians, some men mocked him as a man who saw only black and white, not the colours of the rainbow.

But Melanthius had taken a wound in the agora of Sardis, and Aristides was in command of the Athenians now, and he took this very seriously. We loved him, for all his priggish ways. He *was* better than other men. He just couldn't keep his mouth shut.

A failing I understand, honey.

Anyway, the Milesians had, indeed, hung back from the city. Aristides apparently told them that their cowardice had cost us the city. Aristagoras, as their chief, resented the remark, and the army's factional nature increased to near open enmity.

The next day, my body ached, I was filthy, with blood under my nails and matted in my hair, and there wasn't enough water, because we were too far from the banks of the river and the Persians would shoot any man who went down the bank for a helmet of water – filthy water, in any case. Later in the day, parched, angry and dirty, we stumbled back to the pass, and we heard that the Lydians were rising behind us – that the men of all Caria were marching to the aid of their satrap. In those days, the Carians were called the 'Men of Bronze' because they wore so much armour, and they were deadly. Later in the Long War, they were our allies. But not that week.

We washed at the springs of the Hermus, and we filled our canteens and drank our fill and were braver. But we were no longer an army, we were an angry mob. The Athenians did nothing to hide their contempt for all the Ionians as soldiers. The Ionians returned their contempt with angry rejection, and it was muttered that the Athenians were sacrificing the Ionians for their own ends.

Which was true, of course.

Aristides grew angrier and angrier, his pale skin constantly flushed, and he walked along in silence, his slave trotting to keep up.

I stood around, watching Aristides, watching the army disintegrate, and I understood why soldiers were deserting. We were doomed, and the rush of bad omens that surrounded us, including a live hare dropped on a sacrificing priest by an eagle, only confirmed what every man knew. In addition, men who had murdered and raped in the city knew that they had brought their own doom upon them, and they were sullen, guilty or merely dejected.

The Athenians did not suffer from these problems. Heraklides gave me a heavy necklace of gold and lapis that he had snatched from the stall in the agora. 'You only saved my life ten times,' he said. 'And I saved my loot. I got the whole bag behind my shield.' He laughed, showing his snaggle teeth. He was only six years older than me, but he seemed like the old man of the sea himself. I put the necklace on, drank wine from my canteen and marched with the Athenians, who were still a disciplined band. We had come over the pass as the advance guard, and we were going home as the rearguard, with the Eretrians just ahead.

'At home, they're our worst enemies,' Heraklides grunted at me. 'But you know that, eh? You were in the fight at the bridge?'

'I was,' I said.

'They held us a long time there,' Heraklides said. 'Good fighters. Glad to have them, out here.'

Aristides came up to us. 'You can go into the front rank in place of Melodites,' he said without preamble. He didn't smile, but I did. He had his helmet on the back of his head – all the Athenians did, because they marched ready to fight at all times, as did the Eretrians.

I grinned like a fool. 'Thanks, lord,' I said.

He looked grim. 'Don't thank me. When we face the Medes again, you'll be the first to face them.'

I shrugged. 'I was in the front rank in the marketplace,' I said. 'Let's not stand around and let them shoot us, next time.'

He walked off, and I thought that he hadn't heard me, or, more likely, had chosen to ignore me. I was young – very young to be in the front rank.

I took the dead man's place and was a file-leader, and the other men of my file thought well enough of me to help me make a plume-holder and a plume to mark my new rank.

I no longer thought of Briseis. I was in the grip of Ares.

When Aristides saw me with my horsehair plume, he came up and slapped my shoulder. He didn't say anything, but it was one of the proudest moments of my life.

From the top of the pass we could see the river in the distance, and the Ephesians cheered as if we'd been gone a month and marched a thousand stades. We were the last ones down the pass, and we knew from the scouts that there were Lydians and Carians right behind us.

Aristides wanted to hold the pass, and we halted at the narrowest part of the down slope. He picked his ground brilliantly – a gentle curve in the pass, so that the longest bowshot was about one hundred paces, and the sides of the pass as steep as walls on either side. We made camp, a cold, cheerless camp with no water. Aristides sent me as a runner to Aristagoras. I was to ask him to send relays of slaves with water for us.

'Tell him we'll hold the pass a day,' he said, 'to give the Milesians time to recover.'

But Aristagoras had no nobility and he was more interested in scoring points than in beating Persia. The pompous fuck! He laughed at the message. 'Tell your chief,' he said, 'that we will do *nothing* for the convenience of Athens.' He said the words loudly, so that all his Milesians heard him and joined his laugh.

I ran the message back. No man had so much as offered me a canteen.

I ran straight to Aristides. He was sitting on a rock, and I crouched at his feet and pulled my chlamys around me against the chill air and tried to spit. My mouth was so dry that my tongue wouldn't move. So I just shook my head.

Mutely, Aristides took his canteen over his head and handed it to me. I drank a mouthful and bowed. 'Thanks,' I said.

He looked away. 'They said no?' he asked.

'They said no. Aristagoras said that he would do nothing for the convenience of Athens.' I shrugged.

While I spoke, Eualcidas came up. He pulled off his helmet – he wore a great, winged Cretan helmet – and he was grey with fatigue. His arm hurt him, but famous men can't show pain.

'You planning to hold the pass?' he asked. He was ten years older than Aristides and, although he commanded many fewer men, he was a much more famous warrior. He looked up the pass, where we could see a handful of Lydian slingers prowling around. 'You bastards stood by us in the city,' he said, and spat, by way of explanation.

Aristides shrugged. 'I asked them to send us water. Aristagoras refused.'

'And you're surprised? You called them cowardly fools, lad.' Eualcidas laughed. 'Which they are! But they'll never forgive you.' He looked around. 'Fucking Ionians, eh?' He smiled at me. 'You're a handsome man. And thanks for my life. Not many men can say they saved Eualcidas!'

I blushed, and he laughed. He winked at Aristides. 'You *do* have some handsome men. Listen – we'll stand here with you. Better than trying to face the Medes down on the plains. Any day now they'll get their cavalry together – then we'll be doomed. Better fight them up here.'

Aristides shook his head. 'We can't camp here without water.'

Eualcidas shrugged. He had a boyish grin. He was a hard man to dislike. 'That's why we have slaves,' he said. 'Send them down the pass. Tell them to bring wine, too. If I'm going to die tomorrow, I think I want a feast.' He turned away with a salute and put his hand on my hip. 'A feast,' he said into my eyes.

Hah! I've made you blush again. Listen, honey. He was a famous athlete and a man who had grown up at a trading station on Crete. All Cretans are boy-lovers – it's their way. It is in their laws. Superb soldiers and athletes. Not much for the crafts. Not always the smartest. Oh, he was beautiful – the most famous warrior in our army. What he wanted was obvious.

So we sent all our slaves down the hill for water, and the Medes pushed some skirmishers around the pass. A handful of our men with a few dozen slaves chased them off with rocks and spears, and we settled to our cold rocks.

I remember that night because my body hurt. It's something that the bards never talk about, eh? The bruises you take in a fight – gods, the bruises you take in the gymnasium! Split knuckles, broken fingers, a rib bruised here, the black burn on your shoulder where your shield rim rides your shoulder bone, the cuts on your legs – Ares knows the toll. It is worst for the men in the front rank, and I had stood my ground in the agora of Sardis and now, three days later, I *still* hurt. My wound was slight, but it ached when I rolled on it, and I was lying on the ground – on sand and gravel. And we had few fires, because we were high in the pass and there were no trees.

The word was, we were going to die. I was too inexperienced to do anything about such talk.

Eualcidas came out of the dark with Aristides and Heraklides and a Euboean I did not know. My file was not asleep – we were huddled together in the dark, whispering, afraid of the morrow and trying not to show it, as soldiers always do.

Aristides had a little bronze lantern and he put it on the ground, and I swear that bit of light did more for our morale than all his talk.

Aristides was a serious man, and he spoke seriously. He explained that we were going to do a deed of arms, that men would never forget our actions to save the rest of the Greeks, and then he explained that as long as we held our ground, we were safe.

He was a good man, and my file was better just seeing his face and hearing his voice.

Eualcidas waited until he was finished and then he smiled his infectious smile. 'We'll kill us a load of Medes tomorrow,' he said. 'And then we'll slip away tomorrow night while they get ready for a big assault.' He looked around in the dim lamplight. 'I've faced the Medes before, boys. Thing to remember is that they all wear gold, so when we push forward over their dead, our back-rankers need to get their rings and brooches. And then everyone shares together.'

That's how you inspire troops. Dying for all of Greece may appeal to a handful of noble young men, but everyone likes the sound of a gold ring.

We were the junior file, just left of the centre of the Athenians, and we must have been the last group they needed to visit. Aristides slapped a back or two, gave my hand a squeeze and walked off into the darkness. He left his lamp – at the time, I thought that it was a tribute to how rich the man was, that a bronze lantern with a fancy bronze oil lamp inside could just be abandoned on a rock. I remember picking it up and looking at it carefully. Pater never made anything like it. It wasn't good work – I could do better – but the construction was crisp.

Eualcidas hadn't left. He was watching me look at the lamp.

I was young. I felt that his gaze held some censure, and I put the lamp down and shrugged. 'My father was a bronze-smith,' I said.

He nodded and lay back, stretching his legs. 'You're not Athenian. I can tell.'

I shook my head. I have to put in here that I was the only non-citizen among the Athenians, and they never held it against me, because while I had been a slave, the friendship between Plataea and Athens had hardened into something like love – or maybe it was forged in those three battles and somehow they'd managed not to fuck it up. But some of the older men would actually touch me for luck, because Plataea had brought Athens luck, or so they said.

So I shrugged. 'I'm from Plataea,' I said. 'But I've been a slave for a few years.'

He laughed easily, and the muscles in his throat were strong and golden like bronze. It was, for me, like talking to Achilles – he was that famous. 'How did a man like you end up a slave?' he asked.

'I didn't end up a slave,' I retorted. 'I ended up in the front rank yesterday.'

He nodded, smiled and said nothing, a talent few men possess.

'Your people enslaved me,' I said.

He frowned. 'I've been a war-leader for five years,' he said. 'I've never marched on Plataea. You came to us, once, with the Athenians. You beat us like a drum!' He laughed.

That got me. I had heard it elsewhere, of course, but always from men who might have had the story wrong.

'I was there,' he continued. 'Right opposite your Plataeans. I have a scorpion on my shield. Were you in the phalanx? You must have been young.'

I nodded, and there were suddenly tears in my eyes. 'My brother died fighting the Spartans,' I said, 'and I took his place in his armour.'

'He was brave?' Eualcidas asked.

'He was. And he died facing a Spartan, man to man.' I was weeping and the Euboean rolled over and put an arm around me. He didn't say anything. After a while he rolled back to where he'd been.

I was better. I hadn't really let myself think about it – my brother's death, and my father's, and now, in the dark with a battle looming, I was filled with a bitter, angry grief for both. They were in the ground and I was still here. It's an odd thing, honey – one I've seen often – that soldiers rarely mourn a comrade when he falls. Sometimes it takes years.

'My father fell fighting your phalanx,' I said quietly. 'I was behind him, and I stood over his body for a little.' I stopped, because it was a bitter memory – how I had been too weak to stand my ground, and how the rain of bronze and iron had beaten me to my knees and knocked me down.

I told it just like that. 'When I awoke, I was a slave,' I finished.

Eualcidas shook his head, and his teeth gleamed in the dark. 'You need to go to Delphi,' he said. 'You are god-touched, and you have been betrayed. No man of Euboea sold you as a slave. We ran. I ran,' he said, and he smiled that boy's smile. 'If you live long enough, you'll run, too. The day comes, and the moment, and life is sweet.'

I found that I was holding his hand. He had hard calluses on his palm.

I felt better. 'I don't think there's shame in running when everyone runs,' I said. I'm not sure that's really what I thought, but he was a great man, and suddenly he was looking for my comfort.

He smiled, and it wasn't his boy's smile. It was a very old smile indeed. 'Wait until you run,' he said. He shrugged. 'You're a good young man. I like you, but I have a feeling you won't come and share my blanket.'

I shook my head. 'Sorry, lord,' I said. I was, to be honest, tempted. He was *kind*. He was a killer of men, but something in him was basically good. And just sitting with him taught me – I don't know what, but maybe that what I was becoming could be greater than the sum of the corpses I left.

In many ways, Aristides and Miltiades were better men. They built to last, and they did things for their city that will live for ever. Aristides was a noble man in every way, and his mind went deep. And Miltiades was the best soldier I've ever known, except maybe his son.

But Eualcidas was a hero, a man from the age of gold. Almost like a god.

He kissed me. 'Let's be heroes tomorrow,' he said. And went off among the rocks, back to his own men.

They tried us in the dawn, but we were cold, surly and awake, and the shower of thrown spears bounced off our shields and we chased them down the pass without trouble. My part of the line wasn't even engaged.

The slaves brought us some dried meat and some cheese, and I ate what I could get down and drank my share of water. My canteen was still full, and I kept it and my leather bag on under my shield, while most of the Athenians sent all their gear away with their slaves.

Late in the morning, I saw men on horseback round the bend and come forward, and I saw that it was Artaphernes, his right arm in a sling. We were standing in our ranks, and he rode quite close, but had the sense to stay a spear's cast away from us. Then he shook his head, made a quip to one of his aides and rode away.

It was perhaps an hour before they made their effort. We were bored, and nervous, and Aristides and Eualcidas kept walking along our front and talking – which made the boys nervous. You – the writer with the wax tablet – if you ever lead men to war, let me tell you something not to do. Don't have long conferences with your subordinates. Got that?

What an old bastard I am. My pardon, sir – you are a guest in my house. Have some more wine. And send some to me – talking of battle is thirsty work.

Do you know that most of what men say about war is a tissue of lies? All the girls know it – women get a distrust of male bragging in their mother's milk, eh? Hah, you aren't blushing now, my pretty.

No – what I say is true. When the spears go down and the shields smack together, who in Tartarus remembers what happens? It all goes by in a blur of panic and desperation, and you are always one sword thrust from the dark, until you stand there breathing like the accordion bellows in my father's shop and someone tells you it is over.

What soldiers remember is the time before, and sometimes the time after. At the fight in the pass, I remember Cleon – my second-ranker – had to piss four times, even though he hadn't had enough water for two days. And Herk's best spear's head was loose, and he kept making it rattle in irritation – not that we could hear it, but the vibration annoyed him, and he kept at it the way a man will pick at a sore.

Heraklides – in the front rank on the right – had the finest horsehair plume of any men among the Athenians. He removed it, combed it out and remounted it, which was a nice way of showing his contempt for the Medes, and did a lot for the rest of us.

Then Eualcidas threw one of his spears. He didn't run or hop – he just stepped forward and threw with all his might, and, Ares, he was a hero. I had time to say something while it was in the air – I said, *will you look at that?*, or something equally inane while it cleft the heavens.

It struck point first, and then he ran along the front. 'Unless you bastards think you can out-throw me,' he said, 'no one throws a spear until the Medes are closer than that. No waste!'

We cheered him.

And then the Medes came.


They knew their business. They *poured* around the corner of the pass – the bodyguard itself and then more Persians, their high hats and scale armour obvious, less than half a stade away. They halted and formed their front in a matter of instants, much faster than any of us had anticipated.

The first flight of arrows hit while we were still watching them in admiration. We were mostly veterans, and all our shields were off our insteps, up on our arms and held high. I doubt a man died in that first flight, but a few men took an arrow in the instep. Cleon had one ring his helmet and it dazed him, and all of us had shields *moved* by the weight of the arrows. Two arrows punched through the thin bronze on the face of my aspis, and the heavier one went right through the rim.

And that was just one volley.

The second volley came in and the third was in the air, and already men were losing their nerve. After the second volley there were screams, and I can't remember the next five or six, except that it was as if a big man was throwing stones at my shield. I took a graze along the outside of my left thigh and another arrow hit my left greave so hard that I almost fell – but the bronze held despite the mediocre work.

I turned and looked because Cleon's shield wasn't pressed against my back. He wasn't far away – an arm's length – but he was also looking back.

'Close up and get your fucking shields up!' I yelled, and then the next pair of volleys hit. More screams. Now we had men down, and other men pressing back.

Heedless of the arrows, Eualcidas ran across the front of the phalanx. 'Ten men to run with me!' he shouted.

I had no idea what they had planned, but if Eualcidas was leading it, I was going.

'Front rank!' I shouted at Cleon. I stepped out as the next arrow storm hit.

Aristides was no coward. He stepped right out from his place as the strategos. 'As soon as you rush them, we'll march!' he shouted.

Oddly, ten paces in front of the phalanx, only one arrow hit my shield. The Persians were lofting their arrows.

Now I understood what we were doing. And how suicidal it was.

Most of the men who stepped up were Euboeans. I think there were eight of them, and Eualcidas wasn't waiting for more.

'First man into the Medes will live for ever!' he said.

And we ran.

We ran as if we were running in the hoplitodromos, the race in armour. We ran right at their line – three hundred Persians, a front rank of spearmen with big shields, scalloped like Boeotian shields, and then eight more ranks of men with heavy bows and short swords. Cyrus would be there, and Pharnakes, if I hadn't put him down, and all the others I knew.

I thought all that in one step, as my sandal crunched the gravel.

I had about two hundred more strides to run, or die.

We must have surprised them, and we surprised them again by being so fast. We were *fast*. When I think of that run, I remember what it was to be young – to be so stupid that I would dare to cross a field of Persian arrows alone, and to be so strong that it seemed a reasonable risk.

We set the Medes a quandary – shoot the runners, or shoot the phalanx? The phalanx came in behind us, and they were not slow. They began to sing the Paean, and it wasn't the best I've ever heard, but it was loud in the narrow confines of the pass.

Then you have to understand the Persian way. The front rank, as I say, is spearmen – sometimes the second rank as well. So all the archers have to shoot *over* the first two ranks, and that means that they lose the ability to pick off individual men. Master archers – the officers – decide how they will shoot. It is hard for them to detail a few men to shoot one target while the rest shoot another.

Not that I knew any of this. I just ran, and the only sound I could hear was my feet on the gravel. It was like running for a prize.

I ran fifty paces – perhaps more – before they began to shoot at me. It wasn't the storm from before, either – it was a steady impact of single shafts against my shield. Something stung my foot, and then I felt a blow like the kick of a mule against my shin, but again the greave held and still I ran forward.

And then the world cleared for me. It is hard to describe, really. I was running and then, as if my eyes had been closed, I was running like a god. I felt as if I *was* a god. I had been running with my aspis held in front, and high, which made me blind to everything but the ground under my feet. Now I let my shield go down a fraction, and I ran looking at the Medes.

And they were close.

I have so much to say about this that I will only bore you, thugater. Except that something changed, and it was as if I could see, having been blind. I could see that I was going to live. I could see that I was about to be a hero. Athena granted me this, I think, or my ancestor Heracles.

Twenty paces from their shield wall, I decided not to slow down.

It is worth saying that when men run at a shield wall, they slow as they close in the last three or four paces. They have to, or they risk being spitted in the knee or thigh by a cool hand. And most men correctly dread the moment when they crash into the enemy's shield. You are vulnerable, then. You could fall.

I didn't even slow. I lengthened my stride like a runner finishing a race, as if a garland or a crown of laurel waited for me.

An arrow rang off the front of my helmet so hard that I almost lost my balance. And then I smashed into their wall, and all the sight and sound and smell of it hit me at once.

I killed men.

No man killed me.

I didn't know it at the time, but I was one of just two men to reach their wall. But we did reach it, and I was told afterwards that we knocked holes in their shield wall like a big iron awl punching bronze.

The phalanx was close behind us, and no arrows were falling on them. They roared, although I didn't hear it. I was in a world no bigger than the blood-soaked ground beneath my sandals and the limits of my helmet. I remember that blows fell on that helmet like Pater's hammer on his anvil, and more blows glanced off the scales on my back and slashed my outer thighs and my right arm, but I refused to stop. I remember that. I remember deciding that I would go all the way through them and see what happened then. I pushed and stomped and killed, and I have no memory of fighting the spearmen, but only of killing archers, hacking their faces and their bows and pushing forward, always forward, and the pain of the blows on my back and my helmet, and then, faster than I tell it, I was through. I was against the rock face of the pass, and I turned. Both my spears were gone – the gods know where – and I drew my sword, put my back to the rock and cut at every Persian who came forward.

They were brave. A dozen of them, rear-rankers, inexperienced men, pressed at me. They had neither shields nor spears, and they were not much, hand to hand, and they pressed me clumsily, and despite the ringing in my head, I killed them. Not all of them. Just enough to make the rest pause and doubt themselves.

Then there was pressure, the kind of pressure you get in a nightmare, and I was crushed against big rock, and the aspis pushed into my neck and thighs, and I cried out from the pain of it.

And then men were screaming my name, and it was over.

Eualcidas was the first to embrace me. He pushed his helmet back on his brow and he was shaking from head to foot and had an arrow clean through his helmet.

'By Ares,' he said. 'I knew you were beautiful!'

And in those five minutes, in the time that the water-clocks give a man to speak his mind in the assembly, I was no longer a man.

I became a hero.

Most of the other eight men who ran with us were dead or badly wounded. Only Eualcidas and I had made the enemy line. And we had hurt the Medes badly, killing fifteen and downing another twenty. We had captives.

I was so dazed that I was sick. I threw up on the rocks, and Heraklides held my hair. Then we went back down the pass to where we had started. The slaves buried our dead and we waited in the sun. I drank the water men gave me, and then I drained the water and wine in my canteen.

Eualcidas came by. 'If they come back, will you do it again?' he asked.

I grinned. 'Of course,' I said.

It was like madness, or the smell of fine wine, or that moment when a woman lets her peplos fall but before you can touch her.

You want to know what makes Achilles different from the other men among the noble Achaeans? Homer must have known some killers of men. He knew us. Because any man – any good man, and the world is full of them – can stand his ground one fine day. He sets his mind – or he is angry, or simply young. And he will stand his ground and kill, fighting his fears and his enemies together. We honour those men.

But the killers *come alive* when there is nothing left but that fear and the rush of spirit, when all of your life falls away and you *are* the edge of your sword and the point of your spear. The killers will fight every day, not one fine day. Eualcidas was serious. He knew we might have to run into the arrow storm again – and now that he had my measure, he wanted me to run with him.

And of course, I wanted to go.

No, that doesn't mean I wasn't afraid. I was terrified. But I had to feel that terror again – and again.

But they didn't come back, and an hour after dark, we marched away into the torch-lit darkness, down the rest of the pass and on to the plain.

# 14

Artaphernes followed us on to the plains, but now he had Lydian cavalry and some Medes, and they harried our retreat. We had bought Aristagoras a day, only for him to squander it like the fool he was. And so, just two days later, while my wounds were still unhealed and the aches from the fight at the pass were at their height, he forced us to battle.

Aristagoras arrayed us. He hated the Athenians by then, and he was visibly afraid – a traitor in a losing rebellion. Eualcidas didn't hide his contempt, and Aristagoras retaliated like any petty tyrant, by putting us on the left and questioning our courage. He put his Milesians on the right, opposite the Medes, and he put the Ephesians in the centre with the Chians and the Lesbians. He set the lines in full view of Artaphernes. The satrap responded by moving his best infantry – Carians, who later joined the rebellion – against us. Unlike Aristagoras, Artaphernes never believed his own propaganda. He knew that the Athenians and the Euboeans were the most dangerous.

Aristagoras set our lines in the late afternoon of the second day after the fight in the pass. We stood in our places until the shadows were long, and then we walked back to our fires and ate. I didn't have a slave, but Cleon's slave, a surly Italian boy, made me stew and took my coppers with carefully hidden delight.

Eualcidas and I sat together after we ate. Most men thought us lovers. Perhaps, if things had gone otherwise, we might have been lovers, because he was Patroclus in every way that mattered, and perhaps I was Achilles. At any rate, we sat and talked, and other men came and sat with us – not just Athenians or Euboeans, either. Epaphroditos came with some men of Lesbos, and there were Chians and even Milesians around that fire. We drank wine and Eualcidas's singer – he had a rhapsode – gave us a thousand lines of the *Iliad*. His son sang another poem, and Stephanos came, clasped my hand and drank wine with me.

Men treated me differently. I liked it. I liked being *lord*. I was a hero, and other heroes accepted me as such. We lay on sheepskins and listened to the *Iliad* and drank wine, and life was good.

Here's a truth for you, thugater. War is sweet, when you are one of the heroes.

Late in the evening, Archilogos turned up. He stood in the fire-light until I saw him. I rose and went to embrace him, but he held his hand between us.

'We are not friends,' he said.

I remember nodding. I understood then, perhaps for the first time, that it was not possible for us to be friends and for him to retain his place in the world.

'I heard that you had the name of a hero,' he said. 'That you slew ten Medes in combat.'

I nodded.

He smiled, but only for a moment. 'Damn it, Doru! Why did you fuck my sister? We could have been brothers! My father loves you!' I reached out again, but he turned his head away.

'Pater intends to prosecute you in the courts,' he said. 'Aristagoras pretends he does not know what happened, but he has suggested that we revoke or deny your manumission and have you taken as an escaped slave. Neither Pater nor I will accept this.' He crossed his arms. 'Why?' he asked me, and suddenly he was angry. He had come to talk – but I had ruined his life, or so he reckoned it.

I knew that a shrug might start a fight. 'I don't know,' I said care-fully.

'Was it because of Penelope?' he asked, his face towards the new moon.

I tried to reach him. 'The – the first time, I thought that she *was* Penelope.'

That made him turn. 'I didn't even know that you and Penelope were – anything,' he said.

'Yes you did. You just forgot – because you were the master and I the slave,' I said. Then I shrugged. 'Penelope liked you better. And like all of us, she wanted her freedom.'

'She's pregnant,' he admitted. 'I'll free her. And see to it she has employment. Mater will take her to weave.'

'She'll like that,' I said.

'My fucking sister will marry Aristagoras. Oh, he's a worm,' Archi spat.

'She – plans. She makes plans and then carries them out.' I decided that anything I said would make things worse. We were having a conversation, but it was a fragile thing, like a spiderweb in a flood.

'Why does she want to marry him?' Archi asked.

I paused again. Perhaps it was three days with Eualcidas, but I wanted to watch my words carefully. 'Part of her believes she deserves no better,' I said. 'Part of her wants a man she can *control*.'

'Which were you?' he asked. He was angry now. I had not given the right answer.

'Both,' I admitted.

He took a deep breath. 'If we win tomorrow ...' he said, and my hopes rose. Because despite all my talking to your fine people about heroism, what I really wanted back was my family – that house in Ephesus, and daily lessons with Heraclitus.

'Yes?' I asked.

'Run,' he said. 'Run far. And don't let Aristagoras catch you.' He threw his chlamys over his shoulder. 'I wish I'd been there – in the pass.'

'Me, too.' That's all I could say. It was true. I knew my former master. He, too, had it in his soul. He would have run all the way into the Medes, or died trying.

He walked away.

I let him go.

I still think about it. I've changed that conversation a thousand thousand times, said better things, chased him and wrestled him to the ground.

That's not what happened, though.

Maybe, if I had, a great deal of pain might have been averted.

I never promised you a happy story, thugater.

In the morning, we formed early. I was in the front rank now, and for the first time I could see the whole army. The Athenians were on a slight hill, with the remnants of an old town under our feet. I rested my shield on the edge of an old wall buried in the ground. This had been a village with a tiny acropolis a thousand years ago, I could see. Then I looked south along our lines, and I could see what a worthless army we were.

No two contingents would form together, except the hereditary enemies from Athens and Euboea. The rest of them were in little regiments, and their lines weren't even level. Aristagoras had put his Milesians slightly in front, to show us all how brave they were, and every time another contingent tried to match shields with them, he'd shuffle a few paces forward.

Aristides put us up on our little hill. He placed Eualcidas and his men on our right. They had a talk, and then Aristides came over and pointed behind us. 'If the army breaks,' he said, 'we go north. We can go all night and reach the estuary in the morning, and let the Medes catch the locals.' He shrugged.

Heraklides pointed at the Lydian cavalry who were coming up on Artaphernes' left – so they'd come at us. 'Why don't we just leave now?' he asked.

Aristides shook his head. 'Because no man will say that the Athenians ran first.'

Behind me, Cleon spat. 'I'll die knowing that I gave my life so that my city had a good reputation with the fucking Ionians,' he said. 'They already hate us. Let them do the dying.'

These sentiments were widely echoed, but Aristides ignored them, and we stood our ground while the Carians came and formed against us.

They glittered. Not for nothing did the Medes call them the men of bronze. They had more armour than any men I'd ever seen, and every man in the front rank had a bronze corslet and greaves, and most had thigh pieces and armlets and some had cuffs of bronze and even bronze foot armour that covered their sandals. Their shields were faced in bronze, and they were *big men*. I've always hated fighting men who were bigger than me.

Artaphernes rode up and down his line, and they cheered him, even though he was the foreign overlord. He had more Ionian Greeks in his army than we had in ours, I'd wager.

Aristagoras didn't give a speech. We stood around all morning and then, just before midday, the Milesians sang their Paean and went forward.

The rest of the rebels went forward, too, but they did it by fits and starts, and the left hung back. Aristides didn't seem in a hurry to leave our hill.

The Lydian cavalry rode forward at a brisk trot, determined to flank our phalanx and rip us apart. I watched the cavalry and I feared them. Greeks don't have much cavalry, and we aren't always good at standing against it.

But Aristides had done his job, and over on the flank of our hill there were orchards and vineyards – small, but walled – and all our slaves and *skeuophoroi* were inside those walls. They ripped into the flanks of the cavalry with slings and javelins, and the Lydians didn't stay to fight. They turned and rode off. I've always thought that the fatal flaw with cavalry is the ease with which they ride away.

Then the Carians came forward. From my ripe old age, I now suspect they had intended to hit us while the cavalry chewed our flanks to ruin, but as with most plans that require men to cooperate on a battlefield, they screwed it up, so that the men of Caria came forward alone.

Aristides came and said a few things. They sounded good, and we cheered him, but all I could see was that wall of bronze coming at us, and how *big* the Carians were. I didn't feel like a hero at all – I kept waiting for that wonderful feeling to come, and *it wouldn't come*.

'When they reach the foot of the slope,' Aristides said, finally, 'we will sing, and go forward into them.'

I could see that this surprised the men around me, and that meant it would surprise the Carians. We had a nice secure hilltop, and they had to climb to us in the sun.

'Fuck,' Cleon said behind me. 'Look at that.'

We all stopped watching Aristides and looked south instead. We had a superb view of the battlefield, so we were able to watch as the Milesians broke and ran.

They had never even reached the Persian lines.

Aristides stared at them with disgust.

The Carians would have done better to give us a few minutes. We'd have marched away. The battle was over. Our strategos was already running.

Instead, they did as they'd been ordered and came forward.

'We beat them, and then we get out of here,' Aristides said. Then he gave orders for something we'd practised but never actually done in combat. 'Rear-half files!' he cried. 'Close to the front! March!'

We formed a dense wall – what Spartans call the *synaspismos*, where we put shield on shield. But we were only half as deep – only four men instead of eight.

As soon as we formed close, we raised our voices and sang, and we moved down the hill.

In many ways, this was my first fight in a phalanx. Oh, I know – it was my fourth or fifth, but in all the others I'd been at the back, and the fighting had broken up quickly, or I'd been alone, as in the fight at the pass.

This time, both sides fought like lions.

When you are in the front rank, there's an instant just before the lines close when a skilful man can hurt his opponent with a spear thrust. Once the lines come together, there's no fine spear-fighting – you just thrust as fast and hard as you can until the shaft breaks, and then you draw your sword.

I had two spears – most of us had a pair, balanced for throwing, with long leather thongs. When we were five paces apart, I stepped forward with my left foot in time to the Paean and threw my first spear. Most of us did, and two hundred heavy spears crashed into the Carians as their spears came right back at us. If the pounding of the Medes' arrows had been like the fall of hail on my shield, the jar of a Carian spear was like being hit with a log.

I had my second spear in my hand in the last three paces. I remember being pleased at how well I threw and changed hands, and I stepped forward, planted my foot and thrust overhand, diagonally right.

We crashed into their front and they stopped us dead. And we stopped them.

My spear went in under the Carian's helmet and he went down.

I let the spear go. I was locked up against a big man and his spear was over my right shoulder, trying to kill Cleon. Ares, that press was close! We were doubled up, and we had the hill behind us. They had armour and size.

No one gave a foot.

I got my sword from under my arm and I thrust under my shield, because the crush was too close for a cut. The point glanced off his thigh armour and I thrust again and again, and finally – gods, it seemed to take for ever – I got the blade around his out-thrust leg and cut his sinews and he went down.

I raised my sword up over my head in the single breath before his file-mate slammed his shield into mine. I cut at his helmet and scored, shearing off part of his crest and slamming the helmet against his cheek. He stumbled and I pushed into his shield – and he fell, tripping over his mate, and quicker than thought my sword went left and right at waist level or a little below. I cut at their buttocks and the backs of their legs – back-cut, fore-cut – and then the third-ranker got past the tangle into me, and I hammered my sword into his helmet. He had no crest and his helmet rang and I hit him again. He dropped his spear to get at his sword and Cleon put his spear right into the *tau* of his faceplate – a magnificent thrust.

I knew my job – and now I felt the power. I *roared* and pushed past the dying man, slammed the fourth-ranker with my shield and back-cut at the third-ranker without even looking at him, so that my sword broke on his helmet, but he went down, probably unconscious.

Cleon thrust over my shoulder and I took his spear. He let go and I started fighting with it, and he must have got another from the men behind him, because when that spear broke he gave me another.

They were pushing away from me now, the fourth- and fifth-rankers in the Carian host. None of them wanted to face me and I began to hurt them, sniping against their thighs and necks with accurate spear thrusts. A killer like me is most dangerous when no one will face him. Never give a man *time* to plan his hits, or he'll reap a whole rank.

I didn't kill them. I just made them bleed and they fell. No one is brave with the red flowing from an open vein.

Beside me, Aristides and Heraklides and all the files on either side of mine pushed forward into the hole I was cutting, and they pushed.

And then, as suddenly as the storm of bronze had begun, it was over. The pressure on my chest faded and then it was gone. The dust rose and I punched my borrowed spear at a man as he turned away, knocking him sprawling without killing him. As I stepped over him, he tried to roll and get his shield up, but I put my spear point into the unguarded spot at the top of his back and it grated on his spine and he thrashed like a gaffed fish, dead already and alive enough to know it.

Cleon grabbed one of the wings on my scale shirt that covered my shoulders and tugged.

'Let's go!' he said.

The whole Athenian phalanx was turning away into the dust. The Carians were running, and we were running, too – unbroken, but we knew what was coming.

I wanted to run every fucking Carian down and kill them. They were just men, under all that bronze, and now that the power was on me I wanted to punish them for making me afraid.

That's how men feel when the enemy breaks – for a little while, they all become killers, and many husbands and fathers die before they regain their wits and realize that the enemy is running and they can sit down and revel in victory.

Men are fools.

Cleon was not a fool, and he'd held my back like a champion in story and probably saved my life. So when he turned uphill, I followed him and we moved fast, up through the dust and over the hilltop, and then down the other side, heading north.

I stopped at the top and looked south. Even through the rising swirls of battle haze, I could see that the whole Greek army was in flight. In the centre, where Artaphernes stood with his bodyguard against the Ephesians, the great Eagle of Persia shone like the sun and the Ephesians ran like frightened children.

I looked back over my shoulder and saw the Lydian cavalry moving forward.

I called a warning to Aristides and got back in my place. We trotted along together, down the old acropolis and out on to the plain, then around a farm pond.

Aristides shouted and we turned. There was a moment of confusion and then our shields locked – and the cavalry turned away, throwing spears.

Six times we turned and stood our ground. The last time, I'd had enough, and as they turned to run, I broke from the front of the phalanx and ran after them. They were contemptuous of us and the dust was high, and I caught my man before he'd even begun to ride away. My spear killed his horse, and then I put my point in his eyes as he lay under the animal. Other horsemen began to turn to come back, and that was their error. Aristides charged them, the whole Athenian phalanx changing directions like a school of fish, from prey to predator in a heartbeat. The Lydians wrestled to control their horses and we must have killed fifteen or twenty of them before they broke away.

The first Lydian I killed had gold on his sword strap, and Cleon helped me pull it over his head. Then I saw the sword, and it was a fine weapon – a long leaf-blade, thin near the hand and wide and sharp near the point. See – there it is on the wall. Take her down – that's my raven's talon. Her blade snapped on me later and I got her a new one. Same scabbard – long story there, she took some time to come back to me once, like an angry wife.

Touch that blade, honey. Fifty men's lives fell across that edge. Aye, maybe more. That Lydian had a good sword and a good horse and later I heard that he was a good man – a friend of Heraclitus, more's the pity, but Ares put him under my hand and I took him. He thought we were beaten and he and his mates died on our spears.

And then we got back in our ranks and scampered off.

We went ten stades at something like a run, and then we stopped. It was mid-afternoon, and the sun was still high. We drank water – we'd run clear and we were safe enough.

The Euboeans were weeping.

Eualcidas had fallen, and they had left his body.

I never heard how it happened. He must have gone down in the first moments of the fight against the Carians, because that's when mistakes happen. And when we turned to run, no one was quite sure he'd been hit. The Euboeans took more casualties than we did, and perhaps all the men around him died, too.

But the shame of leaving his body to be spoiled was more than could be borne.

Aristides, for all his nobility, couldn't understand what they were talking about. We'd lost two dozen men in the fight, and we were leaving them so that we could run for our ships. To Aristides, base as that was, abandoning the corpses was the price of saving his command, and he was never a man to put his own honour above the saving of his men – which is why we loved him.

But the Euboeans began to shout, and they were weeping, as I said.

'Will the Medes accept a truce to bury the dead?' Heraklides asked.

Aristides shook his head. 'We're rebels against the Great King,' he said. 'Artaphernes won't accept a herald from us.'

Men started to look at me. I don't know who started it – but soon a dozen heads were turned my way, and I knew what was expected. It's the most unfair part of high reputation – once you choose to be a hero, you have no choice in the matter.

I reslung my new sword until I liked the way it hung, and hefted my borrowed spear. 'I'll go and fetch him, then,' I said. 'Shall I?'

I could see it all cross Aristides' face. I wasn't a citizen – I didn't count against his numbers. My loss was – acceptable. And yet, he was a truly noble man.

He came over to me. He kept his voice low. 'We all saw you,' he said. He meant, we all saw you shatter the Carians. His eyes rested on mine. 'Say the word, and I will forbid your going.' He meant, if I wanted out, he'd provide me with an excuse. That, my fine young friends, is nobility.

Damn, he was a good man. A man who understood men like me. And remember, he stood in the front rank five or six times – not because he loved it, but because it was his duty. He was brave. Because he didn't love it. Oh, no.

But I shook my head. 'I'll go,' I said. 'Give me two slaves to carry the body.'

Cleon volunteered his Italian, and the Euboeans pushed forward their hero's Cretan boy. He was weeping.

I took a deep breath, searching for the power of combat and finding nothing. I didn't even want to walk to the ships, much less turn and go back ten stades. I had no plan and no idea what I was up against.

But I knew my role already – Eualcidas had taught me. So I shrugged as if it was nothing. 'I'll meet you at the ships,' I said, trying to sound reassuring, grand and noble.

I had taken three paces when Aristides caught me and embraced me. Our breastplates grated together, his bronze *thorax* and my scales. And then Herk came up.

'Go straight to the river,' he said.

'How?' I asked. I wasn't really listening – I was trying to get my head around what I'd just said I would do.

He pushed an arm out and pointed down the long slope to the distant river. 'I'll set my rowers moving as soon as I get to the beach,' he said quickly. 'Go south with the body. I'll come to you. I swear it by the gods.'

Suddenly, it didn't seem so bad. It was still stupid and impossible – but Herk was going to come and rescue me. 'You're a fine man,' I said. 'No matter what I say about you when your back is turned.'

He laughed – we all laughed, the way heroes are supposed to laugh. And then I turned to the slaves. 'Let's go,' I said.

And we were off.


The first thing I did was to tell the slaves that they were free as soon as we got that body to the ships. That changed their demeanour. Desperate mission, impossible odds – but if freedom was the reward, they were game. Heh – I was a slave, thugater. I know the rules.

We walked forward. I wasn't in a hurry – in as much as I had a plan, my plan was to lie low until dark and then go for the corpse. We made it back to the farm pond, and there were Lydian slaves burying the men we'd killed. We went around a thicket, well to the north of the corpses, and then we stopped in a copse of olive trees and had something to eat and drank some of the wine and water that the three of us carried – which, to be honest, was a fair amount. By now, I was afraid – afraid to turn around and quit, and afraid to go down to the battlefield.

The two slaves – Idomeneus and Lekthes – were not afraid. Idomeneus had been Eualcidas's bed-warmer, a beautiful boy with kohl on his eyelashes, but the muscles in his arms were like ropes, and he had wept for his master until the kohl ran down his face. He looked like a fury, or a mourner at a funeral.

Lekthes was a different kind of boy, short and squat and just growing into heavy muscle, with a thick neck and a pug nose. He was brave enough to give me lip when I told him to polish my armour, so I had some faith in him.

I was a famous warrior, and a hero. They believed in me, and I could see it in them, which made me braver. Sad, but true. I drank in their admiration, and when I'd had enough food and enough wine, we walked down into the darkening fields where vultures already ripped at the corpses.

The little acropolis was easy to find, and the Carians hadn't disturbed the bodies. They lay where they had fallen.

And then the task began. I'd expected – Hades, I don't know what I expected, but I think I'd wanted to fight fifty Persians and take the body by force. Instead, the three of us moved from ruined body to ruined body, turning each over to look at the man.

Don't ever go on a darkening battlefield.

Most of the bodies were already stripped. Imagine – we were forty stades from Ephesus, no one had come to bury the dead, but human greed was enough that every peasant in the area was hurrying to the battlefield to strip finger rings. Only the gold was gone – most men were still in armour, although here and there a good helmet was missing.

After we combed the hill once, I realized that I was looking for a bareheaded man. The human vultures would have stripped his high-winged helmet.

My hands were foul with old blood and ordure – most men soil themselves in death, and many spear wounds open a man's entrails anyway. I stopped to throw up, drank some wine and held my hands away from my face because they stank. And then I went back up the hill. This time, I tried to think like a philosopher. I found my own place on the battlefield, and then I reasoned where Eualcidas should have been, at the right-most point of his line. And then I walked down the hill, *being* Eualcidas in the half-dark.

I found him just as Idomeneus whistled. I had left the Cretan boy at the hill crest because he was weeping and because I'd decided that we needed a lookout. His whistle froze me, my hand on Eualcidas's shoulder. He was dead, with a clean stab through his throat-boll that had almost decapitated him.

Lekthe was a tough bastard, and he was right by me. 'Cavalry,' he said.

I glanced down at them. They were behind us, half a stade away. 'Strip him and put him on a stretcher,' I said. 'Use his cloak and some spears.'

He nodded.

I picked up a pair of spears – they were everywhere – and went uphill until I reached the Cretan kid. 'Go and help Lekthe,' I said.

'You – found him?' he asked.

I pushed him down the hill. Then I crouched by a rock – or perhaps the foundation stone of the old temple – and watched the Lydians. They weren't interested in me.

From the height of the hill, I could see a hundred other parties gathering wounded, and my hopes rose immediately. There were wounded men all over the field, of course. Why hadn't I thought of that?

In fact, the worst mistake I'd made was to come armoured and armed. Because the winners, as soon as the fighting ends, shed their kit and go and find their friends. Of course they do.

But I was not abandoning my arms. So I went down the hill and rooted among the dead men until I found one with his *himation* strapped inside his shield to pad his shoulder – older men do it – and I used the cloak to cover me. By then the slaves had the body on a couple of spears. I used one of my spears as a walking staff and discarded the other, and I made Lekthe carry my aspis on his back while Idomeneus carried his master's shield – a scorpion – on his own back.

243

And then, like a funereal procession, we walked down off the old acropolis and into the valley, heading for the river. I felt clever, brave and more than a little godlike.

Heh. The gods can smell hubris a stade away.

Any of you young people ever been on a corpse field? Eh?

I'll take that as a no.

It is not quiet. We say 'as quiet as the grave', and it may be that once the soul has flown out of the mouth and gone down with the other shades, the grave is quiet, but a battlefield is a noisy place. The animals come to feast, the crows and ravens fight over the tastiest morsels, and men scream their last pain or defiance to the gods, until they cannot scream, and then they cough and pant and rattle.

Once dark falls, it is the worst place you can imagine.

May the gods preserve you from ever having to visit one in the dark or pass your last hours there, although I always expected it for myself. It unmans me just to think of it. Better a clean death in the heat of battle, so that the soul goes burning with the pure fire of strife to the logos, than the foul death amidst the carrion-eaters.

And women and children who have to go searching among the corpses for a father, a lover, a brother, a husband – by Hades, that is a cursed way to see a man for the last time, with the ravens picking at his eyes.

We walked down from the hill that the Athenians and Eretrians had held, and darkness fell as we made our way among the corpses. I didn't know it, but it wasn't so bad there, because the worst of the kills happen after one side runs – and we didn't run, and neither did the Carians, so there were not as many dead as there might have been.

It was down in the valley that the corpses became thick, and they were all Greek. Hades, but they were thick, honey. The darkness hid the worst of it, except for the sounds, but I still had to stop and retch when I saw a dog rooting inside the chest cavity of a man and his eyes seemed to move. The slaves saw and dropped the body. When I had finished retching I put my spear in the man's throat to make sure.

I think the slaves wanted to run away.

I didn't blame them, but I wiped the spear and then myself. 'If you won't carry him to the ships, I'll run you down and add you to the pile of bodies,' I said.

Neither of them met my eye. They picked up the spear-poles and we started off again, stumbling and cursing.

There were pinpoints of light in the dark, most of them in a clump to the west. We made to skirt around them, and ran into our first patrol.

I had assumed that the battlefield was empty except for scavengers and mourners, but of course the Persians, who organized everything in their lives, had patrols to keep the scavengers from the corpses of their own slain until the sun should rise again. I heard them in time, and the three of us lay flat. There was some moonlight, just enough to make the whole scene hazy and hard to see, like a foul dream. I lay there, the pale circle of my face hidden in my cloak, and listened.

All I could hear was a dying man at my side grunting. He tried to grab my elbow.

'Please?' he managed. The poor bastard had lain there for six hours or more. No water. I could smell his guts.

I elbowed him. Now I could hear footsteps.

'He-eh? He-eh?' the dying man said. And little grunts and mewls, like those a toddler makes.

'Camel-fuckers!' a Persian voice said. They were *close*. 'Come to loot our dead, the cowards. Effeminate boy-fuckers! I hate the Greeks. Run from a battle and come back to steal from the dead!'

The man ranted on and on, as men do after battles. I didn't know his voice.

'Shush, brother,' another voice said. 'Shush. Ahriman walks the dark. No man should curse here.'

'Heh-eh,' the dying man cried. He gave a convulsive jerk.

'What was that?' the first Persian said.

'Men take a long time to die. Come, brother. Keep walking. If I stop, I will have to start getting water for these poor bastards.' The second Persian sounded familiar. Was he someone I knew?

It didn't matter, because even Cyrus and Pharnakes would kill me if they took me, or so I thought.

'Boy-fuckers,' the man who was angry spat, and they walked off. I heard him stumble on a corpse, and he fell. 'Ah!' he cried. 'I am foul with the juices of his body.' His voice shook. 'I am unclean!'

The second Persian spent half the night reassuring him. He was a good man, that one. While he talked to his frightened brother, he emptied his canteen into two wounded men, and then he started killing them. I heard him, and though it sounds foul, I knew that he was no murdering fury, but a bringer of peace.

'Eh-eh-eh . . .' said the dying man at my elbow.

I looked at him, and he was younger than me – and *kalos*, even at the point of death, with big, beautiful eyes that wanted to know how his world had turned to shit. His skin, where it was not smeared with sweat and puke, was smooth and lovely. He was somebody's son.

I drew my short dagger, really my eating knife, from under my scale shirt where I keep it, and I put my lips by his ear.

'Say goodnight,' I said. I tried to sound like Pater when he put me to bed. 'Say goodnight, laddy.'

'G'night,' he managed. Like a child, the poor bastard. *Go to Elysium with the thought of home*, I prayed, and put the point of my eating knife into his brain.

Give me some fucking wine.

Oh, war is glorious, thugater.

I dream of him. I never saw his face in the dark, you see. He could have been anyone. Any one of hundreds of men I've put down myself. Battlefields, sieges, duels, ship fights – all leave that wastage of dead and near dead, and every one of them was a *man*, with all of a man's life, before the iron or the bronze ripped the shade from him.

It's funny. I have killed so many men, but that one comes back to me in the dark, and then I drink more and try to forget.

Here, fill it.

The Persians lingered and lingered, but at last the older one got his brother to walk away into the dark, and I picked myself up, found the two slaves and we headed west to avoid more Persian patrols.

West brought the sound of mourning. Here the Persians and the Lydians had reaped the Ionians like weeds at the edge of a field, cutting them down from behind as they fled. Now local women were out looking for their men, and fathers and children, with torches. The Persians didn't disturb them, and they thought we were more of the same – which we were, or close enough.

As the moon climbed, we could see the curved line of corpses like sea-wrack on a beach, and men and women desperately turning them, pushing torches down to look into a face. Grim work.

I knew Heraclitus by his voice. He was talking to a boy and the boy was weeping by his side. I couldn't help myself. I walked up to him in the dark and he raised his torch.

'Doru!' he said. 'You live!'

I threw my arms around him. I wept. I was no different from the younger Persian – I was unmanned by my reaction to the fight and then to the battlefield.

He let me cry for as long as my heart beat a hundred times – no longer. 'You are searching for him too?' he asked.

'I – I came for Eualcidas. Of Euboea.' My voice shook. 'Searching for who?'

Heraclitus nodded. He had a torch and it made his face look like a statue's. His eyes were pools of darkness. 'Hipponax fell here, trying to keep the line from breaking,' he said.

'Ah.' I choked. I remember that suddenly I couldn't breathe. The weeping boy was Kylix, the slave. 'Is Briseis here?' I asked.

'Don't be a fool,' Heraclitus said. 'News won't even be in the city yet.' More softly, he asked, 'Will you help me find him?'

'Put the body down and rest,' I said to the slaves. 'These are friends.'

Lekthes came and touched my arm to get my attention. He pointed to the river, which was clear, just a stade away in the moonlight. 'We are close, master,' he said.

He didn't want to risk his soon-to-be-accomplished freedom, he meant.

'Stow it,' I growled. I came back to Heraclitus. 'You fought?' I asked. I had a hard time picturing him in the phalanx.

'Do I look like a slave?' he asked. 'Of course I fought.' He reached out and touched my sword. 'This is a bitter night for me, Doru. And for you – I know.' His eyes were shadowed, but I knew he was looking over my shoulder. 'Help me find him,' he said quickly.

'Of course, master,' I said.

I found him in a matter of moments. I knew his bronze-studded sandals. I had put them on his feet often enough.

I sobbed to see that alone of the men at that part of the line, he lay with his face to the foe and he had a great wound in his side where a spear had gone in under his armpit where his rank-mate should have protected him. A Mede lay by his head, and Hipponax's spear point was stuck in the man's ribs.

I assumed that Hipponax was dead, but that was not his fate, or mine. I touched him to roll him over and be sure, and he flinched and then screamed.

That scream was the worst sound I had ever heard.

It happens sometimes, that a man will go down on the field – a blow to the head or a sudden cut, and the shock of it puts him under. But later he awakens to the awful truth – that he is almost a corpse, lying amidst pain, waiting to die.

That was Hipponax's fate. He had a second wound, a cut that had gone right into his leather thorax, so that his guts glistened in the torchlight and lay hidden under his body, and when he moved, the pain must have been incredible. But worse than the pain – I've seen it – is the realization.

When you see your guts in a pile, you know you are dead.

He screamed and screamed.

Have I not said that I loved him? If not, I'm a fool. He was more my father than Pater – with his humour and his slow anger, his sense of justice and his poetry. He was a great man. Even when I was a slave and he ordered me beaten – even when he threatened me with a sword – I loved him. I hated to leave him, and I knew that if I had not been exiled from his side, he wouldn't be screaming away the last heartbeats of his mortality amidst the ravens.

I got down in the bloody mud and put his head in my lap.

He screamed.

What could I do? I tried to stroke his face, but his eyes said everything. The unfairness and the pain. Remember that he never wanted war with the Great King. And yet he had fallen with his face to the foe and his spear in a Persian's guts, while worse men ran.

Have I mentioned the glories of war, thugater? Fill it to the top, and don't bother with water. All the way. *All the way.* When I give an order I expect it to be obeyed.

That's better.

Where was I?

Oh, I'm not even to the bad part yet.

I told you how he screamed. You have heard women in childbirth – that's pain. Add to that despair – which most women, thank the gods, don't need to fear in childbirth – and that was his scream.

He'd been out, so his voice was fresh and strong.

After ten screams, I couldn't think.

After twenty screams, I stopped trying to talk to him.

248

Who knows how many times he screamed.

Finally, I put my knife under his chin. I hugged him close, and I kissed him between screams, and then I pushed it up under his jaw and into his brain.

Heraclitus had told me once that this was the kindest stroke. I've done it often enough, and I know that it ends the screams the fastest. Cut a man's throat and he has to bleed out.

I don't know how long I sat there. Long enough to fill my lap with his blood.

'You – killed him,' Archi said. His voice was surprisingly calm. I had no idea how long he had been standing there.

Heraclitus had his hand on my shoulder. 'You are a brave man,' he said to me.

'You killed him,' Archi said again. Now there was a lilt to his words.

'Archilogos.' Heraclitus stepped between us. 'We must take his body and go.'

Kylix came, still crying. He began to strip the armour from his dead master's body. Another of the house slaves was there – Dion, the water boy. No doubt he had come as Hipponax's skeuophoros. Together they rolled the corpse off my lap and stripped him. Idomeneus helped without being asked.

'*You* killed him,' Archi said, after the body was rolled roughly in a himation and laid across spears.

Heraclitus struck him – a sharp blow with his hand open. 'Don't be a fool, boy.' He turned to me. 'Your eyes are younger and sharper than mine. Can you lead the way?'

'YOU KILLED HIM!' Archi roared, and came at me. His sword was in his hand, and he cut at my head.

I drew and parried in one motion, and our swords rang together with the unmistakable sound of steel on steel.

It was dark, and the footing was bad. The only thing that kept him alive was that I wasn't fighting back. He made wild, savage sweeps at me and I parried them, and my new sword took the whole weight of his wide cuts and the blade held, notching his blade again and again.

He hacked at me and I parried, and Heraclitus finally tripped him with a spear and then rapped him on the head with the spear-butt.

But it was too late for us. Even as Archi slumped to the ground, half-stunned, the hoof-beats that I had half-heard while I blocked his savagery came closer, and suddenly we were surrounded by torches and Persian voices. They surrounded us efficiently, despite the bodies on the ground. Most of them had spears, and there were more than ten.

I knew Cyrus immediately, even mounted in the dark. He was giving orders.

'Hail, Lord Cyrus,' I shouted.

He pushed his horse forward past his companions and raised a torch. 'Doru? Why are you here – oh! Of course. You were looking for your master.' Cyrus slid from the horse's back. 'This is Hipponax – a fine man.'

'That's one of yours,' I said, pointing my sword at the dead Mede.

Cyrus held the torch back over his head so that he could see the ground.

'Darius,' he said. 'He didn't muster after the battle.'

More hoof-beats.

'Sheathe that sword or you are a dead man,' Cyrus said at my side.

I looked at him. I felt – perhaps I felt a hint of what Hipponax felt, awakening to pain and the knowledge that there was nothing to come but death. They would enslave me. No one on earth would pay a ransom for me, and I would not be a slave again.

So I smiled, or my face made an imitation of a smile. 'I think I'm a dead man anyway,' I said.

'Why?' Artaphernes asked from the dark. I knew his voice, too. 'Put up that sword.'

Heraclitus took my arm and stripped the sword from my hand as if I was a child. I had forgotten that he was at my side.

'Damn you,' I spat.

Artaphernes was on a white horse. He rode between the two close-wrapped corpses, Hipponax and Eualcidas. The wind was picking up, and the torches were snapping like angry dogs.

Oh, he owed me a life. But only a born nobleman expects the world to work like that – like an epic poem. A slave expects the instant revocation of every favour, every promise.

But Artaphernes was a different sort of man. He gestured to me. 'You,' he said. 'You are a rebel?'

Cyrus spoke up, and he was never a better friend to me than in that hour. 'Master, they came to retrieve the body of Hipponax, your guest-friend in Ephesus.'

It was obvious in the torchlight that I was wearing a scale shirt. 'You were in arms today, boy?' the satrap asked.

'Yes, lord,' I said.

He nodded. 'I have already declared an amnesty for all those taken in arms,' he said. 'No man will be sold into slavery or executed if he returns to his allegiance. I will punish only those who came from over the sea to attack my lands. The Athenians and their allies.'

I shrugged. 'I served with the Athenians,' I said. 'And you won't find another one to punish. They broke your Carians and then marched off to their ships.'

'Are you a complete fool?' Cyrus hissed in my ear.

'But you were born in the west. I remember you telling me so.' The satrap shrugged. 'Go home, boy. Tell them in the west that the Great King is merciful.'

He was going to let me go. I took the ring – his ring – off my hand and held it up to him. 'You repay my favour,' I said.

He shook his head. 'Gentlemen never repay,' he said. 'They exchange. Keep the ring. Go with your gods. Who is that other man?'

I knew he didn't mean the slaves. 'Heraclitus the philosopher,' I said.

Artaphernes dismounted. 'I have long wanted to meet you,' he said.

Heraclitus shrugged. 'You have the advantage of me, lord.'

'You were in arms today?' the satrap asked. He ignored the insult.

'Aye, lord,' Heraclitus said.

'Do you accept my amnesty?' Artaphernes asked.

Heraclitus bowed his head. 'I do not, lord.'

'Your name carries much weight,' the satrap said. 'Will you not speak to your fellow citizens?'

Heraclitus shook his head. 'No,' he said. 'No words of mine could sway the wind that blows now, lord. War, not reason, is master here. Too many men are dead.'

'Can we not stop before more die?' Artaphernes asked. 'There is nothing for you Greeks to fight for. We do not enslave you – you do that to yourselves. This freedom is a word – just a word. A Greek tyrant takes more from a city than one of the Great King's satraps ever would.'

Heraclitus grunted. He raised his face, and his tears showed in the firelight. 'The logos is but words,' he said. 'But words can take on the breath of life. Freedom is a word that breathes. Ask any man who has been a slave. Is it not so, Doru?'

'Indeed, master,' I said.

'Every man is slave to another,' Artaphernes said.

'No,' Heraclitus said. 'Your ancestors knew better.'

Artaphernes let anger master him. 'You have been held up to me as a wise man,' he said. 'As long as I have come here, men have told me of the wisdom of Heraclitus. Yet here I stand, surrounded by the stinking corpses of your friends. I offer to preserve your city, and you prate to me of freedom. If my men storm Ephesus, who among you will be *free*? Have you ever seen a city stormed?'

Heraclitus shrugged. 'My wisdom is nothing,' he said. 'But I am wise enough to know that war is a spirit that can never be put back in a wine jar once released – like the spirits of strife in Pandora's box. War is the king and master of all strife. This war will not end until everything it touches has been changed – some men will be made lords, and others will be made slaves. And when the world is broken and remade, then we can make peace.'

Artaphernes took a deep breath. 'Do you prophesy?' he asked.

'When the god is on me. Sometimes I see the future in the logos. But the future does not always come to pass.'

'Listen to my prophecy then, wise man. I will come in two days with fire and sword, and I predict that submission would be the wisest course.' Artaphernes remounted his horse. 'I desire to show mercy. Please allow me to do so.'

Heraclitus shook his head. 'Every woman whose husband lies here will demand vengeance,' he said.

'And their vengeance will be to spread their legs for my soldiers?' Artaphernes sighed. 'There is no Greek army in the world that can stand against the Great King. Go – use your head, philosopher.'

Heraclitus was wise enough to bow, instead of saying what came to his lips.

Cyrus came over to me. 'You are a fool,' he said. 'Ten times over. Why do I like you?' He embraced me. 'Do you need money?' he asked, with typical Persian generosity.

I shook my head. 'No,' I said. 'I have my loot from Sardis,' I added, with the foolishness of youth.

'Don't let me find you at the end of my spear,' he said. 'Walk in the light,' he called as he mounted, and then he followed his lord and they rode away into the darkness.

And just like that, the enemy left us with our dead.

The enemy. Let me tell you, friends – I never hated Artaphernes, not when he was ten times deadlier to me than he was that night. He was a *man*. Hah! It is fashionable to hate the Medes now. Well, many are better than any Greek you'll find, and most of the men who tell you what they did at Plataea or Mycale are full of shit. Persians are men who never lie, who are loyal to their friends and love their wives and children.

Aristagoras, now. I hated him.

We walked down to the river together. We had no choice, because Heraclitus and I had to carry Archi, who was unconscious – so deeply gone that I had begun to fear that the teacher had hit him too hard.

We only carried him a stade, but it gave me a taste of what the slaves had endured all evening.

When we got to the water's edge, I realized that I had no plan past that point. As I stood there, my hand in the small of my back like an old man, panting from the exertion, I wondered where Herk could be and what I would do if he didn't come.

Heraclitus sat in the grass, catching his breath. He was not young, and he had stood his ground in the phalanx – or the mob, to be honest – and then helped carry the bodies. Now he was done. Too tired to move, or even be wise.

I left them in the false dawn, cold and desperate, and walked the riverbank a stade to the south and then back again.

Herk appeared just as the first streak of orange came to the sky. Every Persian must have seen his ship in the river, but no man stirred to challenge the triakonter.

I got my party aboard and fell heavily on to the helmsman's bench.

Herk was full of apologies. 'My ship wouldn't go far enough up-river. We had to row to Ephesus and take this pig of a vessel from the docks,' he said. 'Who are they?'

I shook my head. 'Men of Ephesus,' I said.

We took them downstream. I slept fitfully, and then the sun was scorching my face and I felt as if I had drunk wine all night. We took the boat to the beach below the city, where some jabbering fool insisted that we had stolen his ship until he saw the philosopher, and then he was silent.

That man aside, it was a silent city. The army was sprawled in exhaustion just upstream. A few panicked fools had made it home, however, and the city held its breath, waiting to find out how bad it might be.

We brought Hipponax home, and his son. I hired a pair of public slaves to carry Archi, and as we climbed up the town, my sense that this was an evil dream was heightened by the routine around me – men were rising to transact business, and slaves waited by the wells and fountains to fetch water.

At every little square, women came and asked us for news of their husbands, and I protested that I had served with the Athenians, and Heraclitus didn't speak. I think he knew, or had an idea, and even his courage was insufficient to meet the needs of telling a hundred wives that they were widows.

We didn't go quickly. The sun was high by the time we made the upper town and the steps to the Temple of Artemis gleamed white, like a stairway to Olympus. I began to think that Heraclitus would take me aside, awaken Archi and we would go and have lessons, and when I came back down the white steps, I would be a happy man, and Hipponax would meet me in the courtyard and ask me to fetch him a cup of wine. Time plays tricks like that – Heraclitus used to speak to us often of how, with age, a wise man begins to doubt the reality of what we imagine is time. It seems so possible that Hipponax, dead, is in the same place as Hipponax, alive and laughing.

Heraclitus used to tell us that time is a river, and that every time you dip your toe, the water it meets with is different – but that all the water that ever flowed over your toe is still there, all around you.

And then we came home.

Euthalia met us in the courtyard, and she knew who was wrapped in the himation. She took charge of his body and her face was set and hard.

Archi had been conscious for half an hour by then. But every time he raised his head he retched. I offered him water, but he turned his head away from me.

Doubt the gods if you like, thugater, but never doubt the furies. I had sworn to protect Archi, and to protect Hipponax. But it was my knife that took his life, and that polluted me, and they took my friendship – almost my brother – as their price. Fair? There's no such thing, honey.

Nothing is fair.

Penelope came and she and Dion took Archi away.

I stood in the courtyard, waiting for Briseis.

She didn't come.

After a while, I left with Heraclitus. He offered to take me to his home, but I shrugged him off and went down the hill to where Aristides was camped, and I rejoined the Athenians.

The next morning I went back to the house, and Darkar met me in the portico.

'You are not welcome here,' he said. 'Go away.'

'How is Archi?' I asked.

'He will live. You *killed* Master? My curse on you.' Darkar slammed the gate on me.

The following day, as the Persian army came down the river and prepared a siege, I tried the house from the back, the slave gate. And I found Kylix. He embraced me.

'I told Darkar,' he said. 'I told him you did what you did from love, not hate.' He kissed me.

'Will you take a message to Briseis?' I asked him. He had always worshipped me.

He shook his head. 'She's gone!' he said. 'She is to marry the Milesian lord – Aristagoras. She has gone to his brother's house.'

'She will come back for the funeral,' I said.

Kylix shook his head. 'I doubt it. The things she said to her mother – Aphrodite, they hate each other.'

I had scribed some words on a piece of bronze. 'Give this to her if she comes.'

Kylix nodded and I gave him a coin. Worship is one thing – service another.

I walked back down the hill.

That was the day that Eualcidas had his funeral games. We were a beaten army, but he was a great hero, a man who had triumphed at Olympia and stood firm on fifty battlefields. I felt sick and low, and I won only the race in armour. There was no *hoplomachia*, no fighting in armour. Stephanos won the wrestling, and Epaphroditos won overall and carried away the prize – a magnificent feathered helmet. Then we all drank until we couldn't stand, and we set fire to his corpse, and the two slaves were formally freed.

Epaphroditos stood by the fire with his arm around Idomeneus and tears streaming down his face. 'May I end as he did,' he said.

Stephanos shook his head. 'I'll take home and hearth, lord.'

I thought of the battlefield. 'He went fast, and in the fullness of his strength,' I said. I nodded. I was drunk.

Herk laughed and held out his hand for the wine. 'Don't camp on the wineskin, lad. When it's your turn – and you're one of them, I know that look – you'll think your time was too short. Me – I'm with the Chian boy. Home and bed, and all my relatives gathered around, arguing over the pile of silver I'm leaving.'

Cleon looked at the fire. 'I just want to *get* home,' he said.

I stood there, and loved all of them, but the one I wanted with me was Archi. And that door was still locked.


Every man in the army knew me now, but I was not a captain or even an officer. So when they had their great conference, I did not go. Aristides went to speak for Athens, and he took Heraklides and Agios and another file-leader. Too many of the other leading men were wounded or dead.

They came back so filled with anger that it showed as they walked towards us on the road.

Aristides ordered the ships loaded. Then he summoned me. 'We're leaving,' he said. 'You served with me and you served well, but you are not one of mine. Yet I don't think I can leave you here. Aristagoras knows your name – what have you done that he hates you so much?'

I shook my head. 'It is a private matter,' I said. Had sex with his bride? But how would the fool ever learn that?

'Why are we leaving, lord?' I asked.

Aristides raised an eyebrow. Even in democratic Athens, men like Aristides are not used to being questioned by peasants from Plataea. 'Apparently, we abandoned the men of Miletus on the battlefield,' he said.

'Ares!' I said.

'Aristagoras is one of those men who not only lie to others but to themselves,' he said. And shrugged. 'I am not sorry to leave. Will you go to Athens?'

I took a deep breath. 'I think I'll go home, lord. To Plataea. Unless you would take me in service? As a hoplite?'

Aristides laughed. 'You are a foreigner. Listen, lad. Here you see me as a warlord with a retinue – but once I go home and lay my shield on the altar, I'm done – I'm just another farmer. I don't keep warriors. We're not Cretans – we're Athenians.'

Herk spoke up for me. 'We could find him work, lord,' he said.

Aristides shook his head. 'He's a killer, not a worker. No offence, lad. I would have you at my back in any fight. But I don't see you as a farm worker.'

I nodded. 'It's true.' I had to laugh. 'I could find a bronze-smith. Finish my training.'

Aristides looked interested. But Agios shook his head. 'You said that you knew Miltiades.'

I nodded.

Heraklides narrowed his eyes. 'I could take him. I have half a cargo for Byzantium, and I can get copper at Cyprus or Crete.'

Aristides shook his head. 'Herk, you'll make a profit off your own death.'

They both looked at me, and I was warmed by how much they both sought to do right by me. 'Lord, I think that it is time that I went home. I will not go to Miltiades,' I said.

'I will write you a letter,' Aristides said.

'Come with me anyway,' Herk said. 'I'll end up in Piraeus soon enough if Poseidon sends a good voyage – you'll make a few coins with me, and be the richer for it this winter at home.'

I was still afraid of going home. There's no easier way to put it. A few weeks with Herk seemed delightful – a respite. 'Yes,' I said. 'But I have sworn an oath, and I must see to getting my release.'

'We'll be off with the evening breeze,' Herk said. 'If you have goodbyes, say them.'

I ran up the hill.

I ran all the way to the gate, and then I knocked, and Darkar opened it, and I pushed past him into the house, until I found Archi. He had a bandage around his head.

'Get out of my house,' he said.

I had had time to think, and I spoke words I had considered. 'I am leaving,' I said. 'Aristagoras has cast the Athenians out of the army – the fool. I'll go with them.'

'Go!' he spat.

'But I swore to support you,' I said. 'And you need to get your family into ships—'

'Support me? The way you supported my father? And my sister? You are the fucking curse of this family!' He rose to his feet and then sank back, still woozy from his blow to the head.

'You have to get out of here!' I shouted at him. 'Pack the slaves and go! When Artaphernes takes the city—'

'I don't need any words from you!' he screamed.

'Have you freed Penelope yet?' I said, and he froze. 'Free her. You owe her. By Ares, Archi, get your head out of your arse.' I stood over him.

Darkar came back with two big slaves. I looked at them, touched my sword and they backed away.

'Go!' Archi said.

'Diomedes has not given up on revenge,' I said. I didn't know it – it came to me from the gods. 'Your father is gone and Briseis's idiot husband intends to hold the city against Artaphernes.'

'Scuttle off, cockroach,' he said. 'We will hold the city.'

I took a breath and let it out. 'I would stay, if you wanted,' I said. All my plans for careful speaking were gone, and I could only beg.

'So you can kill me?' he said. 'Or would you rather fuck me? Whichever way you choose to wreck me? Did you hate us so much? Did we treat you so badly? By Zeus, you must have lain awake plotting how to bring us down. Did you bring Artaphernes into the house, too?' Spittle was coming from his mouth. 'The next time I see you, I will kill you.'

I shook my head. 'I will not fight you,' I said.

'The better for me, then,' he said grimly. 'But your oath didn't protect my father and it will not protect me. Run far, Plataean.'

So much for friendship.

At the door, Kylix pressed a slip of papyrus – a single leaf – into my hand. Written in her hand, it said only 'stay away'.

So much for love.

When we sailed, the men of Chios and Miletus gathered on the beach to mock us as cowards.

There is no fairness, honey.

I thought that I was sailing away towards home – I hoped I was. But when we sailed out of doomed Ephesus, I was leaving home, and I wept.

# Part IV

## *Scattering the Leaves*

The wind scatters the leaves on the ground, but the live timber burgeons with leaves again in the season of spring returning. So one generation will grow while another dies.

Homer, Iliad 6.147

# 15

I never saw Byzantium that trip. The storm hit us four days out of Cyprus with a hull full of copper. We ran before it, because we were crossing the deep blue between Cyprus and Crete and we had nowhere to land and we didn't dare show the low sides of our trireme to the wind.

It hadn't been a good trip. We'd had weather out of Ephesus, weather all the way to Cyprus, weather while we collected copper and weather while we rowed – all rowing, no sailing – to Crete.

Men looked at me. I was the foreigner, and the gods of the sea were angry. Well they might. I was an oath-breaker, fleeing from my oath to Hipponax, and the sea had no love for me.

I took turns with Herk at the steering oars. We'd been trained well, Archi and I, when we made the runs up to the Euxine and across the wine-dark sea to Italy. I could handle a ship, even a long killer like Herk's light trireme. I marvelled at the Athenian build style. They really were pirates – the hulls were thin as papyrus, and the ship itself was narrower and lighter, and the rowers were packed even closer than rowers in Ephesian ships – free men every one, with a sword and a couple of javelins, the richer men with a spolas or a thorax.

South and east of Crete, the weather seemed to abate and we made a good landfall, and the first night that we slept on a beach, every man kissed the sand. I speak no blasphemy when I say that the furies must have had a lot of law-breaking and oath-breaking to pursue. Perhaps some other bastard took up their attention.

Cretans aren't like other Greeks. The men of Crete are war-worshippers, and they have aristocrats and serfs – most of the farmers are not free men at all, but something like slaves. Only the aristocrats fight, and some of them still use chariots. I didn't think much of their primitive agriculture. It is a curse of youth that you cannot keep your mouth shut and so, on our third night in the 'great hall' of the local lord, Sarpedon of Aenis, I found myself arguing with local men about how best to grow wheat and barley. I used an unfortunate phrase in the heat of my anger at the fool's intransigence – we don't call them Cretans for nothing – and this fool called me out, demanding blood.

'You must be joking?' I asked. I'd had some wine.

He slapped me like a woman. 'Coward,' he said. 'Woman.'

Idomeneus came and told me that I had to fight or be ashamed. I laughed. I wasn't ashamed and I had little interest in fighting. But the lord glowered and the other men hooted at my apparent coward-ice.

His name was Goras, and I killed him. He was a good fighter, but half drunk and no match for me. The only danger was from the dark-ness and the drink – I vowed never to fight under such conditions again. His first blows were wild and thus dangerous, but I set my feet and put my spear into his throat and down he went, and the hall fell silent. Herk shook his head. He gathered me with his other men, paid an indemnity and took us away. In the morning we sailed, heading west along the south coast of Crete.

'That cost me the whole value of my trading there,' he said to me in the morning. 'Can't you keep that sword in its sheath?'

I wasn't surly. In those days, killing often brought me a black cloud – I would sit alone and mope. But I heard his words, and they were just words.

We had good weather as we coasted Crete, and we sold our Athenian olive oil and beautiful red-figured and black-figured vases at enormous profit in the market of Hierapytna, and the mood of the crew improved. But not for long.

Herk took me aside after we were invited to the lord's hall. 'Could you refrain from killing anyone until our business here is done?' he asked.

I nodded. 'Silent as the grave.'

But of course, I wasn't.

In truth, there's little I could have done about it. Word of my fight up the coast had made it here. And word of the Ionian Revolt was everywhere, and men behaved like men – like warriors. As they had taken no part, they had to belittle those who had. As we had lost, we were to be humbled.

I have watched this pattern play out too many times. More wine, here.

We were in the lord's hall, and Herk had sent Idomeneus to watch over me. I was quiet, listening and not talking, striving to be the sort of man – well, the sort of man that Eualcidas had been, silent and cheerful. Grown men always tell you that this is the way of excellence, but they neglect to tell you that it is easier to be silent and dignified and cheerful when you are forty and have won ten battles. It's like getting women – much easier when you are too old to enjoy them.

Hah, I'm a foul old man. Too true.

I listened to them demean the Ephesians and the Athenians, and I said nothing. I said nothing when they laughed at Aristides' youth. But I suspect my attempts at dignity weren't much better than stubborn glowering. I was easy meat. Finally, an older man, a leader, came over to where I stood, and he grinned.

I grinned back – glad that someone, at least, was interested in being my friend.

'I heard that you killed a man down the coast,' he said. 'But I have to assume you stabbed him in the back. I mean – look at you. No intestines. No reply to the insults we heap on you. Or are you some sort of woman?' He laughed, showing all his teeth.

I sputtered. This is where heroes are supposed to make a good speech, but I was taken by surprise and I failed. Blood rushed to my head and when Idomeneus tried to hold my arm, I punched him in the mouth. Then I turned.

'You want to die?' I asked. I don't remember what else I said – just that.

He laughed. And threw a punch, a fast punch, right through my defences, and knocked me flat, dislocated my jaw.

I lay there in a rage of pain, and he laughed again.

'This is their great killer?' he asked his friends. When I got to my feet, he didn't even take a stance. He feinted, and then I was on my back again, and my right temple felt as if his knuckle had gone through it.

They all laughed – all except the Athenians. They didn't laugh – but they did nothing to help. My friends – the men I'd fought beside – they weren't all on Herk's ship. And Herk himself shifted uneasily, but he stayed put.

Not cowardice. Just being practical men of business.

I got to my feet slowly. I wasn't thinking too well. And I was filled – suffused – with the purest spirit of Ares. Ares, the hateful god. I was glowing with hate. I felt *betrayed*.

I was young.

My tormentor came forward again and I stumbled towards him, and he laughed. They all laughed. That's what I remember best – the laughter.

The rage and the hate were all through me, and with them came a plan, and I followed my plan.

I let him chase me around the hall. I fell over benches. I accepted the humiliation, backing, always backing – running, even. Oh, yes. I was the coward he thought me, step by step, and men roared with laughter to see my antics.

Except Herk. He knew me, and his eyes grew big, and when I was close to him he yelled something at me, pleading.

Then my head cleared. Two heavy blows to the head do not leave you with much, in a fight. But if you are used to taking blows – and I was – you can get your own back, if you stay alive and keep your blood pumping. I'd run around the hall for five minutes by then, and I'd taken blows – to my abdomen, but it was thick with muscle, and to my thighs, where the other tormentors rained their fists on me as I hopped past.

When my head was clear, I jumped a bench and a kline in one bound and stood in the open space in the middle of all the men. He came at me, and he was still laughing.

He threw his punch, and I caught his fist in the air and broke his arm. The sound of his arm breaking was like a limb snapping from a good, old olive tree.

Then I broke his neck.

And they all stopped laughing. I said nothing. I watched them lie on their couches frozen in the act of fondling their boys.

Now they had the rage and I was calm. I watched the rage flow out of me and into them. He'd been someone they liked – someone they fancied. Now he was meat.

They were warriors. They had elaborate codes of honour, and they did not rush me like a pack.

Herk shook his head and all the Athenians gathered together. Knives began to appear around the hall, and swords.

I let my eyes rove over the Cretans, looking for a leader. I'd like to say I was like a ravening wolf, or a lion who had just killed a bull – but I was shaken by the killing. I had broken his arm – had I always meant to break his neck, too?

*Yes.*

'He attacked me,' I said to the room. 'And insulted me. How would you have me respond?'

Herk touched my shoulder and I flinched, not from fear, but because I was tense, waiting for them to rush me.

'Come,' he said. 'Before they kill you.'

They let us walk away. I still wonder about it – I didn't see fear in them, only rage – the same engulfing redness I had felt.

We were not welcome after that. No mess – the Cretans live in messes of warriors, like the Spartans – no mess would have us to dinner, and no man would trade with us. My fellow oarsmen looked at me with fear and I heard them whisper behind my naked back as we rowed the long ship west along the south coast of Crete. That was a black time.

We rowed along the coast and the next night we camped on a beach. I tried to sleep by myself, but instead I sat awake, watching the stars. Then Herk came, and Cleon, the man who had held my back when we sacked Sardis.

They shuffled, and I shuffled. Hard to explain how men who can fight and kill in the phalanx can't tackle, oh, many things, like talking to a friend who's doing wrong, or getting a girl you really like to look at you. So many ways to be a coward. So we sat a while, looking at the stars.

'I can't keep you aboard,' Herk said, suddenly.

There it was. We'd all known what he had to say. I had hoped for something different, but I knew – I knew from the heavy silence. Nor had I forgiven them – for letting me down. Nor had they forgiven themselves – so they held it against me. See? Nothing is simple.

So I watched the stars a while longer. But my rage mostly died with the man whose neck I broke, so after a longer pause than anyone wanted, I said, 'I know.' I shrugged, I think. But I was bitter, and young.

'Tomorrow we will come to Gortyn,' Herk said. 'The richest kingdom on Crete. The king is always hiring mercenaries. I'll do my best for you – I promise. By Hermes, lord of trades. But you – my friend, you are under a curse, and it burns black over your head, a sign for every man who can *see*. And your curse *kills*. The men – they should love you. You are a hero. Instead, they're afraid of you. And so am I. I can't risk taking you across the blue water to Piraeus. Someone will put a knife in you, and feed you to Poseidon. One storm – that's all it would take. They'd gut you.'

I nodded. 'I just want to go home!' I said suddenly.

Herk looked away.

Cleon put an arm around my shoulders. I've never forgotten that. Cleon stood by me. Later, I stood by him, and if you keep listening, you'll hear. But he said, 'Herk is right. And you can get a ship to Piraeus – in the spring. Stay here a while. Make some money. Go to a priest – find out what you've done. Purify yourself.' The arm tightened. 'Stop killing.'

Aye, I think I wept.


Herk was as good as his word, too. Better.

Gortyn sits in the mountains above the sea – a strong place, if not a beautiful one, and it rests on the bones of an older castle, and that rests on stones placed by giants and titans – the past is all around you, at Gortyn, so that when you stand in their Temple of Poseidon Earth-Shaker, you can look down through a hole in the floor at the stones placed by the gods, a thousand lives of men ago or more.

The port town is called Levin. The lord of Gortyn owns all the towns on that stretch of coast, and nowhere have I been in a place where the divide between low and high was so deep. As deep as the sea – as high as the grey-white mountains that rise from them.

Herk sold me, in effect, bragging about my fighting skills and my learning to the king and his leading warriors in the king's mess. The king had a palace but he spent no time there – instead, he lived with nine other rich aristocrats in a fine marble building on the street that ended with the ancient Temple of Poseidon. The building was new-built, but in the fashion of an old-style *megaron*. The ten men had their couches arrayed around the hearth, and there were more slaves than you could shake a stick at.

I stood silently while Herk talked me up.

'He's a killer,' one of the aristocrats said. 'He killed Laenis down at Hierapytna – that's what we hear. What happened? You – lad, tell it yourself?'

I shook my head. 'Men mocked me,' I said. 'Mocked my friends, mocked the men I stood with in battle. I became angry.'

The king's name was Achilles. He was old enough that his hair was mostly grey – all grey on his chest and back, although he had muscles on his chest like a statue. He nodded.

'My son needs to learn from a killer. But not if the killer can't control himself.' He got up. 'Let us hunt a boar tomorrow, gentlemen.'

They all nodded. Hunting is an excellent way to take a man's measure, and they were going to take mine.

I remember that I slept badly – not from worry, but from shame. Or rather, fear. Was I mad? Had the war god taken my wits?

Tired and red-eyed, I walked out of the guest megaron as the sun rose, found a spring on the hillside and washed. For the first time in many days – perhaps longer – I prayed. I prayed to Heracles my ancestor, and to Athena, because she was the enemy of Ares and I wanted no more from Ares. Then I walked down the hill to where forty or fifty men were gathered with spears. Naked. On Crete, men always hunt naked. The highest fashion is to have a perfect body. And having put in the work to have one, no one wanted to cover that work with cloth.

I got my spears and stood with them. The king emerged from his mess with his officers, and they shook hands with or embraced most of the men there, and then the dog-handlers came, and we were off – up the hillside, past my spring.

The day went on and on, the sun rising hotter and hotter on us. The dogs flushed two pigs – and both evaded us, so that the men began to talk of nets. But the king would have nothing to do with them. I heard one voice, shriller and angrier, demanding nets, and I could see the resemblance. This was his son. He had enough spots to be a fawn.

The third pig that the hounds eventually flushed for us was a little bigger than a dog and not very dangerous. But she was smart enough to keep the dogs off her and fast enough to make us run to keep up, and before long, I was the only man still pacing the front coursers. Those men were all in top shape, but I'd been at war – and at an oar – all summer, and I was half their age. I ran up the mountain and I began to catch the dogs. It was so steep that I knew that if I stumbled I'd have to stop and climb – but for the moment, momentum and pride kept me going, and I could see the pig.

I had no idea about the etiquette of Cretan hunting and no desire to annoy the king. In any case, Lord Achilles had bandy legs and a broad chest and ran slowly, but he was strong as an ox and had the open friendliness that only big men seem to have. Despite his ugly body, men liked him. He was a powerful lord. And he was next behind me on the mountain – the others were way behind us. Slow he might have been – but he wasn't to be stopped. And there I was, love-sick and fury-hounded, sprinting along beside the lead hound, wondering what Artemis would have me do.

The pig lost her nerve when she saw a stand of oak. We were well up the mountain and the ground was rough with stone. The oaks were scrubby things, nothing like the trees of Cithaeron, but I knew what she meant to do. I put on a burst of speed and threw one of my heavy spears – missing the pig, but turning her away from the trees and back towards the hunters.

She lacked the experience of hunting to know what to do. She turned and I stooped, picked up a jagged rock and threw it just beyond her. She turned again and the pack closed in on her.

Achilles came up with his officers and their lovers and there were ten spears in the pig within a few heartbeats. I got my spear wet in her blood out of habit. In some circles, a hunter who does not wet his spear is a coward, or not a man – different hunters have different habits.

Old Achilles – he seemed old to me, although he was ten years younger than I am today – took me by the shoulder. 'Well done. You are a man of courtesy – like a warrior of the old times.'

Achilles' eldest son – I had pegged him correctly – was introduced. He was just a year or two younger than me, a lout named Nearchos, all pimples and straggly black hair and youthful anger. He glowered at me and then turned away, affecting boredom.

'My son is a rude fool. Nearchos! This foreigner is a *man*. He has killed in duels and in war. Look at him! No need to run a little pig down and kill it when he could share the kill with the rest of us – he doesn't need that little glory for himself, see?' Achilles squeezed my shoulder. 'He needs a man to take him in hand and show him the path.' He winked at me.

Nearchos looked at me from under his eyelashes and then blushed and turned his back, more like a maiden at the well than was quite right.

As we walked back to the hall, Idomeneus took my spears. 'They want you to be his – well, his lover. His *erastes*. To teach him the ways of the world.' Idomeneus batted his eyelashes at me.

I rolled my eyes. Boys will be boys, and what happens after a hunt is not for a maiden's ears, but I've never understood the peculiar mating of boys and men that some practise, and even if I did appreciate such stuff, Nearchos's face would not have launched a single scow, where Helen's launched a thousand ships.

On the other hand, I was flattered to be treated as a hero in a foreign land. Back at the hall, the pig grew in size with every retelling, and my act of generosity was magnified to near legendary status.

Herk took me aside. 'They love you,' he said. 'I thought they might. Will you stay?'

'Do I have a choice?' I asked.

Herk shrugged. 'Don't be a prick. I'm doing my best for you.' And he was.

I shrugged. Nearchos was leaning against a pillar, whittling a stick with a pretty knife and looking at me when he thought I couldn't see him.

'I could live here for a season.' I shrugged again. 'But sooner or later, they're going to know that my father was a bronze-smith. Not a noble.'

Herk tried to hide a smile as he saw how it was with Nearchos, and he turned his back on the boy. 'Lord Achilles is as rich a man as Miltiades and he's asked me twice if you might be interested in staying on as his boy's war tutor. And to fight in his war band, of course.' The big Athenian sighed. 'It's a soft life here. But you already have a name. What's waiting for you at home? A farm? Farming is for fools. Stay here, and be rich. And when you leave here, *everyone* will think of you as an aristocrat. Crete is the most aristocratic place in Hellas. What in Tartarus does *home* have, by comparison?'

'I'll let them know who I am,' I said, with a little too much youthful emphasis. 'All right. I'll stay.'

'And Cleon's right – see a priest.' My friend raised an eyebrow. 'Before the furies come for you.'

I looked at Nearchos. Then I looked back at Herk.

'You don't have to lie with him,' he said. 'Be unattainable. But teach him. You have a great deal to teach. You have a brain, lad – remember that sophist you took us all to see?'

'Heraclitus?' I asked.

'That's it. You have a formal education. You can teach.' He pointed his chin at Lord Achilles, who was laughing with his leading men. 'I'll negotiate your price, if you like. And I can set it high – ten times what Miltiades would pay for a spearman.'

'Very well,' I said. And the knucklebones were cast. I was not going home.

*

Both Idomeneus and Lekthes chose to stay with me as my 'men'. Old Herk wrote them into the contract like the wily Athenian he was, and so we all had bed and board and wages from Lord Achilles, and they became my sworn men in the Cretan way. Idomeneus was all for it – he was a peasant from down the coast and he understood the system better than I. In three weeks he'd gone from bed-warmer to warrior. He began to grow proud.

I had few friends on the ship, as I've said, but Cleon was one. We embraced, and I promised to visit him in Athens. He laughed. 'I live in a house smaller than a grain-byre,' he said. 'But I'd love to see you. By Zeus and Hermes and all the gods, it is good to be going home, and here's my hand and a prayer that I see you framed by my doors!'

Good man. Listen, honey – the Poet talks about heroes, but there's never enough about the Cleons – good men who love their wives and their children but still stand their place in the battle line. He *hated* war. But he did it.

Then, richer and lighter, Heraklides and Cleon and their ship sailed away, and left me and my little entourage with the lords of Crete. And Cleon's eagerness to be *home* rang in my ears.

In fact, Idomeneus, the scared boy of the battlefield, Eualcidas's catamite, became my confidant and adviser. He knew the local words, he knew the laws and he understood the complex relations between lord and lord – so much more complicated than life in Boeotia, or so it seemed to me then. Now I understand that every man's customs seem natural to him and alien to a foreigner.

When I discovered that Idomeneus and Lekthes were to fight in the line with me, I bought them simple arms and armour – good stuff from a local smith of god-sent talent called Hephaestion, a fitting name for a smith. They had simple leather corslets and good bronze helmets in the local style, and it was my fancy to have us all carry Boeotian shields, to mark us as different.

You hardly ever see a Boeotian any more. Take mine down, thugater. Try that on your arm, young man. You see? The porpax runs the opposite way from what you might expect, eh? Long and narrow – and the cut-outs in the side are not for putting your spear through! Older men on Crete told me that those holes are for wearing the shield on your back in chariot combat – the holes make it easier on your back and elbows, or so I'm told.

I think it's just because that's the way a bull's hide cuts. Those old

Cretan noblemen never made a shield, and I've made quite a few.

But you can see that it is lighter than an aspis. Not as safe – thinner. And a man with a Boeotian shield has to be aggressive in his blocks – no messing around. You can stand behind an aspis and take blows, but with a Boeotian you have to get that forward edge out and in your opponent's face.

Anyway, that was my whim. I was flattered by the attention of all these Cretan aristocrats, and the word of my killing the warrior Goras on the east coast had come to Gortyn.

I trained the two of them and Nearchos together. Nearchos had already received years of training, or what the Cretans called training, meaning that he was in top shape and could recite the *Iliad*. So we ran, and we hunted, and I began by teaching them the Pyrrhiche – the Boeotian war dance in armour that shows a man how to move his body, flex his hips, thrust low and high, and drills a group of men to move in unison. I drafted an old flute player from the hall and in two weeks they were able to do the dance. Men came and watched and laughed.

Lord Achilles watched one afternoon. Nearchos was surly, because he hated performing in front of people. I knew him a little by then and liked him a little better. There was a noble young man buried beneath the angst and the boyhood and the burning desire.

When we had completed the dance ten times, and all three of my students were stumbling with fatigue, Lord Achilles got up and nodded. 'You give them grace. But how is it different from our dances?'

I had seen their dances. In Gortyn, when the ephebes dance, they dance with weapons and armour, but it is all show – postures meant to show a man's muscles, to stretch him and prove the soundness of his legs. On Crete, they use the dances to pick the fittest – by which they mean the most beautiful.

It's the same dance in Plataea, and yet utterly different. We dance for war, and our dance has all the feints, all the attacks, all the shield parries – and the first figure is the hardest, where men learn to rotate from one rank to another. On Crete, they never rotate ranks – the front-rank dancers are the most beautiful. I don't know what they do when they get tired in combat.

'If we are all trained the same way,' I said, 'we will all move together in combat.' I shrugged, I think. 'And he needs something different. This is different.'

Then I remembered something that Calchas had said. 'And men

are scared in combat,' I added. 'If they learn to block and thrust by rote, over and over, then they can do it even when terror and panic pull at their guts.'

Old Achilles had been in a fight or two. He nodded. 'How many fights have you seen?' he asked.

I thought for a minute. 'Four field battles. Ten duels.' That was an exaggeration, but not by much. 'A skirmish or two,' I added with modesty that was, in fact, the exact truth. *And some beatings and a murder*, I thought. I was just eighteen, and I'd seen more violence than any of the men in the lord's hall.

After that day, there was less laughter when we danced, and other men came and asked to join in. They came self-consciously, with servants carrying their armour. I accepted them all, and I moved the dancing to the broad field with a rose garden behind it. The scent of roses coloured everything that summer, for me. We danced, and then I put a heavy paling in the ground with the help of some slaves and I taught my students to use their swords and spears on the paling, cutting at it, lunging at it, developing the fine control of the weapon that allows you to put your spear into a man's throat or between his eyes, to feel how much thrust it takes to kill and how much is too little.

Winter came and we trained in the hall, we ran in a pack across the hills and we hunted deer. News came that Ephesus had fallen. According to a Cyprian merchant, when the Persian siege mound was even with the walls, Aristagoras filled his ships and sailed away, leaving the Ephesians to their fate. And the Ephesians had surrendered on terms.

I cried. I should have been there. I was wasting my life in a backwater, far from the woman I loved. It was a good life but dull, and I was beginning to get tired of avoiding Nearchos. I wasn't home, I wasn't with Briseis and I wasn't – anyone.

The next spring, when the plants were in bud and all women were becoming equally attractive to me, I was saved by Heraklides, who arrived with a cargo and told me that Aristagoras was raising men and ships throughout Ionia to liberate Cyprus.

'And his wife?' I asked.

'Medea come to life.' Herk rolled his eyes. 'He is a fool to marry a girl so young, and so intelligent. If only she was the strategos.' He laughed and I went back to dreaming of my lost love.

In the autumn, as the wheat was coming in, Aristagoras came to Crete. He came with five ships and he toured the lords, asking for support – and receiving it. Cyprus was rich and the Cretans longed to have a piece of Cyprus. They had not been to war for many years, and every young man clamoured to go.

The wheat was in jars by the time Aristagoras made his way to us at Gortyn. He lorded it over us, wearing a purple cloak and flaunting his wealth, and they followed him as men will follow a Siren. I avoided him at first – a difficult trick in the close confines of a hall – but soon enough I saw that he didn't know me from any other Cretan, and then I listened to his words and attended his dinners.

He was a hollow man, his vanity unchanged by failure at Sardis and Ephesus, and I listened with the blood pounding at my temples as he described how the Athenians had broken and run in the great battle near Ephesus, leaving the Ionians to struggle on alone. Men in the hall looked at me. I wanted no part of this man, but my own reputation would suffer if I allowed him to denigrate the Athenians. Finally, I stood up.

'You lie,' I said.

Silence fell over the hall, and Aristagoras turned, his face composed and regal. 'I lie?' he asked in the voice of a councillor or an advocate in the courts.

'You lie,' I said. 'I was at Sardis, when the Milesians hung back and stayed out of the town. I fought in the agora with the Persians, and then I stood my ground at Ephesus when we stopped the Carians cold and sent them back to their sisters. The centre broke first. I know, because when I looked out over the battle, the centre was already gone – and I was still standing my ground.'

Aristagoras looked around. 'Who is this man, that he is allowed to speak in your hall?' he asked Achilles.

'He is my son's war tutor,' Lord Achilles said. He crossed his arms. 'He is young and full of fire – but he has the right to speak here.'

Aristagoras shrugged. 'I say that the Athenians were the first to break.'

I smiled. 'I say you lie. And there are other men here who were at the battle, Aristagoras. Perhaps you should watch your words. Cretans are not as ignorant as you seem to think.'

But Aristagoras was not to be tripped up by a man as young as I. Instead, he smiled at me, rose from his couch and crossed the hall. 'Young man, you know how it is in battle. Neither you nor I could see anything beyond the eye-slits of our helmets. Men tell me that the Athenians were the first to flee. Myself, I was fighting.'

I was old enough to know that loud assertions would only lose me the argument. But my temper was up. 'I was in the front rank,' I said, 'and I was done fighting when the Carians ran. When I had killed three of them, my spear in their necks.' I looked around the hall. 'Any man who says that the Athenians or the Eretrians were the first to run – lies. And can meet my sword.' That was the Cretan way, as I had discovered my first night on Crete, against Goras.

Aristagoras took my hand. 'We should be friends – our argument causes the Persians to laugh at us.' His words were sweet – but his eyes were full of hate. I had interrupted his performance. What a petty tyrant he was. Even now, my hate for him makes my hands shake.

'How's Briseis?' I asked.

It must have been in my voice. He froze, his hand clasped in mine, his other hand on my elbow, and both of his hands tightened. Oh, she's a bad girl, I thought. My smile must have been too knowing.

'No man speaks of my wife in public,' he hissed. Men around us looked at him curiously. His mask of benevolence was slipping.

'Really?' I asked. 'Let go of my arm, my lord. Before I kill you.' There – it was said, right out in public. He didn't know me from before, the fool. My hand was on my fighting knife – we didn't wear swords in the hall, but hung them on pegs, as the poet says.

Oh, the hate in his eyes. 'You – you were Aristides' butt-boy,' he said in a gentle voice, as the recognition dawned. And then his expression changed, as he felt the prick of my dagger against the inside of his thigh, hidden from the other men in the hall.

'Send my regards to Briseis,' I said. In one push of the dagger, I could make her a widow.

And then she'd marry another nobleman. That was the way of the world, lass.

Aristagoras looked at me in disbelief. He was a coward in his soul, for all his posturing, and I could see the collapse in his eyes. He let go of my elbow and stepped back. I bowed slightly and dropped my blade on the couch behind me so other men would not see what had passed, and Aristagoras backed away quickly.

But Achilles liked him, or liked his ideas, or was simply too greedy to see the foolishness of what was proposed, and he promised three ships for the campaign against Cyprus, to be launched the next autumn.

Aristagoras sailed away. Then the war preparations started in earnest.

Men flocked to my teaching, and soon I was teaching my way of war in the agora, and I found that I was saying Calchas's words and Heraclitus's words together, as if they were one philosophy. And perhaps they are, at that. We danced, and we cut and thrust at billets of wood, and at each other.

The need for men – armoured men – drove Hephaestion the smith to distraction, and I began to spend more time with him. I was no smith, but I could make sheet out of an ingot, and none of his apprentices could.

In the agora, or at his shop, I spent a lot of time in the town. And the town was full of dangers.

The dangers all had to do with sex. Will I shock you, thugater? I wanted someone to share my bed, and Nearchos wanted to share my bed, but the two were in opposition. We were a balanced duality, as the Pythagoreans say. If I had taken a slave girl, Nearchos would have pouted for weeks – indeed, his father might have disowned me. Nearchos and his father had assumed that I would take Nearchos as a lover when he reached some level of heroic achievement that existed in their imaginations.

In fact, I was coming to like the boy, and by my second spring with them, he was my equal in most things. I had no idea whether he would stand in the battle line, but he was fast and strong and he could use his spear point to chip out his name in a billet of wood – a neat trick.

A year and more, I had lived like a Pythagorean, taking no lovers. To be honest, for a long time I had no interest, at least in part because I wanted no woman but Briseis. By the second spring in Crete, however, my body was becoming too much for me. The spring dances were all around me, the older men took younger men hunting, and I was alone.

I went to the smithy to hide from my lust, and hammered bronze into sheet with Hephaestion, who enjoyed my company but was not inclined to empty flattery. Far from it. He was the teacher I never had, at metal-forming, critical and derisive when I deserved it, full of praise when I did well. His only son was long dead, fallen in one of their local cattle-raid wars, serving his lord. Hephaestion taught me many things about forming bronze, and yet he was not the smith my father was. That is one of the mysteries of learning and teaching, I suppose.

I'll take this moment, while this pretty girl serves me wine, to say that good times, like the time I spent with Hephaestion, are never as memorable as bad times. It is odd, and sad, that I cannot make a story out of Hephaestion, because in a way I loved him the best of all the men I knew on Crete. He was gentle, strong, kind, garrulous and grumpy. He might strike a slave in anger, but he apologized later. And he was never above learning from me, either, when I could remember my father's techniques, for instance. I would have gone mad without him.

The other warriors thought it odd that I played with bronze, but they feared me, so there was no talk that I heard – and they needed armour. Swinging the hammers made me stronger too, and kept me from trouble. I practised arms until I was exhausted, and then I swung a hammer until I was exhausted all over again. That was life.

And then, as I said, the second spring came, and all my careful reserves began to melt away as the sap rose in the trees and the first flowers bloomed. Persephone was returning to the earth.

I wanted a girl. All girls were beginning to look equally beautiful to me, young or old, fat or thin, and yet I knew that to tumble a slave in the lord's hall would have instant consequences.

Women know things, too. Well might you toss your head, you hussy – I'm sure that women know what men want as soon as their hips get broad. All the women in the hall knew me for what I was – a man who liked women. And that fascinated them, because their men made a fashion of disdaining women at every turn. The lord had three daughters and all of them made Nearchos look handsome, but they all tossed their heads at me just like that – blush as much as you like, young gentlewoman, I love your blushes. My thugater should bring you every day!

But there were other girls. Down by the beach there was a town – not big enough to be a city, even such a city as Plataea, but Gortyn had two or three thousand free people, and a substantial number of pretty girls.

Hephaestion's shop was at the top of the town, in the no-man's-land between the lord's hall and the merchants. I would work at his forge and girls would come to watch me, stripped to my waist, the famous warrior getting his hands dirty.

It was the day before the Thesmophoria, which has a different name in Crete. All the girls were getting ready – on Crete, it is a woman's holiday, and all the unmarried girls dress like priestesses in their best linen chitons, so that when the sun is behind them, no man need doubt a line of their bodies. They put sashes around their waists and flowers in their hair, and the girls who came to the forge were waiting for disc brooches that the smith and I had spent the morning making. Now we were polishing with the slaves – just to get the job done.

One girl was bolder than the others, fifteen and pretty with the flush of maidenhood and spring, and she brushed her fingers against mine when I gave her a brooch. Next to Briseis she was probably as plain as a daisy next to a rose, but she had a slim waist and high breasts and I wanted to have her on the dusty floor of the forge. Our eyes spent a great deal of time together.

Hephaestion laughed when she was gone. 'Troas's daughter, and no better than she ought to be. They're fisherfolk. You want her?'

I blushed – I do blush, lass – and hung my head.

Hephaestion laughed. 'Are you hag-ridden, boy?'

I shrugged. Up in the hall, I was a young lord, a warrior. Down in the forge, I was a boy. And I acted like one.

'Does Nearchos know?' Hephaestion asked.

'No,' I said. And then, 'I don't lie with Nearchos.'

Hephaestion reacted as if I'd slapped him. 'You don't?' he asked. 'He must be bitter.'

I shook my head. 'He thinks he is unworthy.' I shrugged.

Hephaestion laughed. 'You are a failure as a Cretan,' he said. 'But you're a good smith and you serve Hephaestus like a dutiful son.' We polished for a while, our rags full of powdered pumice and oil. The slaves and apprentices were silent, terrified to have their master working such menial duties.

'I think perhaps while we make the helmets, you should stay here at the forge,' Hephaestion said. 'You, pais, go and get me wine. And wine for Lord Arimnestos.' He only called me lord to mock me.

While we drank watered wine – wonderful stuff, the wine of Crete, red as the blood of a bull – he nodded at me. 'You sleep here. Until the Chalkeia. We'll dedicate all the helmets as our sacrifice – as our sacrifice of labour. And then you can go back to the hall. Lord Achilles will understand why I need you.'

We've never had a Chalkeia here, thugater. We should. I'm a sworn devotee of the smith god, and I can say the prayers. Why have we never had one? In any case, it is a smith's holiday, and the smith has to dedicate work and pay the value of his labour as a tithe – and the smith god judges the quality of the work. In Athens – even in little Plataea – there's a procession of all the smiths, iron and bronze and even the finer metals, all together, with images of the god and of Dionysus bringing him back to Olympia after Zeus cast him out. There's a lot of drinking. We should institute it. Send for my secretary.

I'm not dead, yet, eh?

I had no idea why old Hephaestion suddenly wanted me staying in his house – the walk to the hall was only a matter of half a stade. But he was my master, as much as the lord was. Everything in that town was dedicated to preparing the lord and his men for the expedition to Cyprus, and we were two months from the date of launch. Women wove new sails of heavy linen from Aegypt. The tanner made leather armour as fast as he butchered oxen. The two sandal-makers worked by lamplight and, down by the slips, twenty fishermen and their boys worked all day to build a third trireme in the Phoenician style.

Young men are all fools.

I sent Lekthes up to the hall for my bedding, and he came back with Idomeneus. They made me a bed where the smith directed – not even in his house, but in his summer work shed, a pleasant enough building, but only closed on three sides. The two of them swept it clean and brought a big couch from the house and made it up.

Idomeneus took a cup of wine with me. Lekthes had a girl up at the hall – he was a warrior now, not really a servant, and he was considering marriage. But Idomeneus's tastes ran in other directions, and he was in no hurry to leave the forge.

'Nearchos asked after you,' he said. His eyes sparkled and he wore half a smile. 'He burns for you, master.'

I shrugged. 'I'm not your master.'

Idomeneus stretched out on a bench. 'You call Hephaestion master,' he said.

I shrugged. 'He is a master smith.'

'You are a master warrior. And you made me a free man.' Idomeneus nodded. 'I have a way out of your tangle, lord.'

I ran my fingers through my beard. 'Tangle?' I asked.

He laughed. 'You've run off down here to avoid Nearchos. And lord, he thinks – you must know – that when the ships sail, you and he will be lovers. Why shouldn't he think this? Even his father says it.'

I shook my head. Cretans. What can I say? And all of you tittering. Laugh all you like – this was my youth.

'So – I have found a thread that you can follow out of our labyrinth.' He poured more wine straight from the amphora.

'Am I Theseus or the Minotaur?' I laughed. 'And who does that make you?' We both laughed together.

'I am prettier than any of Nearchos's sisters,' he said, and we both guffawed until Hephaestion came and put his head under the eaves.

'Is this the Dionysia?' he asked. 'By the smith god, I didn't expect a symposium your first night under my roof!' But seeing my wine, he sat, poured himself a cup unmixed and leaned in. 'Tell me the joke?'

Idomeneus was fond of the smith – more than fond, I think. 'I am solving my lord's dilemma,' he said.

Hephaestion winked. 'Bed the boy yourself and pretend to be Arimnestos?' he said.

Idomeneus blushed. Then we started listing things that Nearchos might notice, and we drank a great deal more, and Hephaestion went to bed drunk.

'I never heard your idea,' I said.

Idomeneus was drunk, and he put his arms around me. 'I love you,' he said.

'Yes,' I said. 'Go to bed!'

'Ish – is that an invitation?' he asked with heavy innuendo, and then he grinned. 'Lisshen, master. Tell the boy that he'sh a warrior now – too noble to be your lover. Tell him you free him to have a lover of his own.' Idomeneus burped, which rather spoiled his performance.

'Hmm,' I said, or something equally useless. I was drunk myself.

But the next morning, pounding metal with a heavy head – not something I recommend to any of you – the idea seemed better and better.

I drank water and worked, trying to sweat the wine out of my head. Which was for the best, because in early afternoon, a long line of dancing women came up the hill from the town, heading for the mountain. Troas's daughter was at the head of one of the files of dancers, and she led her laughing girls in a full rehearsal around the yard of the smithy.

I had a pair of roses that Idomeneus had plucked, at my direction, from the garden behind the hall, and I'd woven them with bronze wire so that they would sit with the laurel in her hair.

Hephaestion had a mirror, and I showed her what she looked like in the golden light of the bronze surface.

'Oooh!' she said, patting the flowers gently. 'I wish I was prettier, though.'

'You are beautiful, Gaiana!' I said. Or words to that effect.

She laughed. I kissed her, and she did not kiss like a virgin. She laughed into my mouth like Briseis.

And then I knew why the smith had given me the shed. I grabbed her hand, but she pulled away and straightened her chiton. She grinned. 'Too fast for me, lord,' she said.

I had a horn comb, and I combed her hair a little. She leaned back against me and we kissed again, then she stood up. 'No one expects the girls down from the mountain until dawn,' she said. Outside the shop, the other girls were calling for her.

'I will be in the shed,' I said, and ran a finger around one of her nipples, and she smacked me – playfully, but hard.

'Don't go to sleep,' she said, before darting out of my arms and out of the door.

And I didn't. Nor did Gaiana.

That's another happy time in my memory. She came to me every night and I worked all day in the smithy. Her father came on the third day and Hephaestion introduced me.

'He's smitten with your daughter,' Hephaestion said.

'You don't look like the kind of man who marries a fisherman's daughter,' Troas said. He had a scraggly beard and the hands of a man who dragged nets all day, with enormous shoulders.

'Marries?' I asked, and I suspect, thugater, that my voice cracked.

Troas laughed. 'If I tell the priests you took her maidenhead, you'll owe me her bride price.'

I felt foolish. We were bartering. Before you think ill of the man, remember that the lords of the town might take his daughter for nothing, and he would have the care of any resulting children. That's Crete. Democracy has a great deal to recommend it, honey.

Mind you, daughters were usually safe from lords on Crete. Hah!

'What is her bride price?' I asked. In truth, he scared me more than a Persian battle line.

'Ten silver owls,' he said.

I almost laughed my relief. Hephaestion interrupted me.

'Ten? For a girl who has lain with any man who will have her?'
He spat.

Troas flushed. I think he was hurt. 'I thought we were friends?'

Hephaestion glared at him. 'When you come to buy a bronze
knife, what do you tell me? That it is a beautiful item, that the blade
is as sharp as obsidian, that it feels perfect in your hand? No! You tell
me that it is too small, dull, ugly – anything to lower the price. Why
is your daughter different from my knife?'

I served them both wine, and Hephaestion, pretending to be my
father, arranged the bride price at six owls.

It was odd, but I knew I would be sailing away with the fleet, and
I knew in my heart that I wouldn't come back. So out of something
– it was hardly love – I said that I would marry her.

Troas looked as if he had been axed. 'No, lord,' he said.

Well, there you go. He had a son-in-law lined up. Not some useless sword-swinger who would vanish in the summer, but a strong
young man with a broad back for hauling nets.

Beware, when you think too much of yourself. I realized in an
ugly moment that Troas didn't think much of me. He wanted six
silver owls so that his daughter and her boy could have a good start
– his own boat, probably.

I was born a peasant, lass – never let yourself believe that peasants
have a simpler life.

I went up to the hall, still wearing my leather apron. I opened the
cedar box where I kept my goods – my embroidered cloak, my good
linen chiton, the gold and lapis necklace from Sardis, and my pay.

I took twelve silver owls from the hoard – a little under a third of
my coins, and turned away to find Nearchos gazing at me from the
other side of the hall.

I smiled at him. I couldn't help it.

He came across to me, dressed in a scarlet chiton with matching
sandals. His pimples were gone and his chest had filled out and his
hair was long and oiled.

'You are an odd man, Arimnestos,' he said, and we embraced.

'Walk with me,' I said.

He looked around and his face was red. I sighed and prayed to
Aphrodite.

I caught the eye of Idomeneus, and he winked.

So we walked out into the garden, and then up the mountain, and the gossip of the older warriors followed us like a living thing.

'I'm not taking you for an afternoon of love,' I said, as soon as we were out of earshot of the other men.

He flushed. 'I didn't expect as much,' he said – but he had hoped it.

'I want you to look at yourself,' I said. Like many a teacher and father before me, I dare say.

But he looked away, expecting censure.

'Do you listen to me when I tell you what Heraclitus said? Do you understand anything of the logos, and of change?' I asked.

He shrugged, the angry young man I'd met more than a year before.

'I am not a Cretan lord, Nearchos. I am a peasant from Boeotia, and I have made my name with my spear.' I took his shoulders and he looked at me then, because this was not the speech he expected.

'You are a lord's son,' I said. 'And now you are a man, not a boy. You are waiting – all of you are waiting – for me to take you as a lover.' I shrugged. 'That would be wrong. I admire you – but you are a man, now. A man chooses his own lovers.'

He stood, suddenly. 'But I want *you*!'

Suddenly I realized that this boy deserved the truth and not some story, some manipulation from Idomeneus. He was an honourable boy, with his whole life before him.

'I am not available,' I said primly. There – the truth.

'I am not worthy yet,' he said.

'Don't be foolish,' I said. 'Customs are different. I am from Plataea. In Plataea, we frown on relations between men.' Well, not exactly. But close enough.

That made him smile. 'My sisters said the same to me,' he said, smiling because it was so silly – to him.

'I am taking a girl in the town as a lover,' I said. 'I will not bring her to the hall. I do not seek to embarrass you. And if you require it, I will leave.'

He shook his head. 'A *girl*?' he asked. 'You are the oddest man. You spend your spare time pounding bronze and reading scrolls, and now you make love to women. It is – unmanly!' He spat the last word.

'I will leave, then,' I said. There – I'd told the truth. I felt better for it. Idomeneus's way might have worked, but the deception would have required too much effort. And I think that Heraclitus would not have approved.

He took my hand. 'No,' he said. 'No, I am being stupid. I love you.'

I embraced him. 'We will fight side by side,' I said. 'Better than sex. Now – go and take a lover. And be kind to him. Or her.'

'A girl?' he asked. He laughed. 'We might set a fashion. I was with a girl once – they're soft.' He laughed again.

'You can get used to it,' I said.

On the way down the hill, I considered that Idomeneus and Nearchos both loved me, and said so, while neither Penelope nor Briseis nor Gaiana ever said they loved me. Perhaps it is because none of my three women ever stood with me in the battle line. Hah – that would be a phalanx. And not a coward among them.

At any rate, after that day, Nearchos and I were friends, and a little more. I lived in the smith's shed until the festival, and afterwards, too. We made fine helmets, and good armour, that turned Persian arrows and kept men alive. At the Chalkeia I made myself known to the priest with signs, and was raised from the first to the second degree because my sacrifices were found worthy.

I was happy. Too bad it doesn't take long to tell. I am honest – too honest, and look at her blush when I say Gaiana and I made love every night – every night – ten times, if we wanted. Oh, youth is wasted on the young, honey. But you might ask – what of home? Didn't I want to go home?

Didn't I want to avenge my father, live on my farm? Or kill Aristagoras and take Briseis for my own? See? You do want to know. Well, children, this isn't the *Iliad*. If I had a fate, I didn't know it. And when you are eighteen, or perhaps nineteen, and men treat you like a hero, when your hands make beautiful things, when every night has a soft mouth and your couch is warm with love . . .

No one who is that happy gives a crap about fate, or furies. I was happy. I didn't give my father, my farm or Briseis any more than a passing thought. And of the three, Briseis would have won out.

For two months, I was happy. Two months of making love while the rain fell on the roof of the shed, and making beautiful things all day with the power of my arms and shoulders – dancing the military dances, drilling with weapons, wearing armour.

★

A week before we were due to sail, Lord Achilles paraded us in the agora, and we made a fine sight. There were men lacking swords and men lacking greaves, but every man had a thorax of bronze or leather, a good helmet, spears and a knife. Every man – even the rowers. Six hundred men. Sixty of us – the lord's retainers and relatives – had full panoply. On land, we would be the front rank, and at sea we would fight as marines.

Nearchos had the new ship, of course. He was the lord's son. And I, of course, was to be his helmsman.

We celebrated with a night of drinking, and we poured wine over the ram of the new ship and I called her *Thetis*. Then we spent a week practising at sea. Our fisherfolk could row, and our officers were decent enough, but I needed that week, and more. I was not really a helmsman and I made mistakes every day, getting the *Thetis* off the beach and back on, stern-first. But I was smart enough to go for help, and I found it with Troas, who was rowing in our upper bank and wearing one of my helmets. I brought him aft as 'assistant' helmsman. He had his own fishing boat, and he knew the sea far, far better than I.

Never be too proud to get help, honey bee. And he did help. After all, I'd paid him double his price, and I'd given Gaiana good gifts – I'd made her a mirror, and I'd made her two pairs of bronze oar-pins, guessing that her eventual husband would want them.

The last day was hard for Nearchos and the other local men. Me, I was anxious to get away. I could feel the draw of the world. It was as if I had been asleep and now I was waking up again.

Gaiana came to me one last time at the shed. I had presents laid out for her on the bed – a length of good Aegyptian linen and a necklace of silver with black beads. She cried a little.

'I'm pregnant,' she said.

I smiled, because I was a man of the world and I had expected this. 'How do you know?' I asked.

She smiled – no wild talk. 'Girls know,' she said. 'I could just be late,' she admitted.

'Best marry your fisher-boy, then,' I said.

She looked confused.

'Don't you have a boy to marry?' I asked.

'How do you know?' she blurted out. And then she met my eyes. 'I like him.' Defiantly. And then, hesitantly, 'I like you, too.'

'I won't be coming back,' I said, more harshly than I meant. 'I offered to marry you and your father turned me down. He knows I won't come back.' I shrugged. I was growing to like the purity of telling the truth. Sometimes it was very hard – sometimes I still lied just to make things easier – but simple truths seemed to make things, well, simple. 'Is your boy on my ship?'

She shook her head. 'He wants to go, but Pater won't let him.'

Pater – Troas – sounded smarter and smarter.

I gave her my gifts and we made love. It should have been gentle and tragic, but it wasn't. Gaiana never had tragedy in her. She laughed in my mouth, and she laughed when our fingers last touched.

'What shall I call your boy?' she asked. 'If he's yours?'

'Hipponax,' I said.

# 16

The Battle of Amathus was my first sea-fight.

We sailed and rowed the long way around Crete, because Lord Achilles, who hadn't been to war in ten years, was still a canny old bird and he had a head on his shoulders. So we rowed away towards Italy, and the rowers cursed.

Lord Achilles knew what he was about. We spent two weeks going around the island, and by the time we put our bows to the deep blue east of Crete, our muscles were hard as rock and our rowing was excellent. Our helmsmen – even me – could handle our ships. We could sprint and we could cruise and we could back-water.

I have said that Nearchos commanded the *Thetis*. In fact, I commanded it, while teaching him to command, while Troas taught me to be a seaman. Laugh if you like.

Lord Achilles commanded the *Poseidon* and his brother Ajax, a long-limbed nobleman I had only met twice, commanded *Triton*. We didn't practise formations much, although we did take turns rowing in the middle of a three-ship line, so that we could get used to the length of another ship's oars.

We made the rendezvous off Cyprus just a week late, and found the Council of Ionia in full assembly on the beach of Amathus.

I stayed at Nearchos's shoulder. We spent a week listening to Aristagoras talk. Other men talked, too. The leader of the Cyprian rebels was Onesilus, king of Salamis. That's Salamis on Cyprus, honey – your friend from Halicarnassus knows it, don't you, lad? Technically, Onesilus had summoned all of us, and he was the leader of the fight on Cyprus. He and his men were laying siege to Amathus, a Cyprian city that had remained fiercely loyal to the Great King while the rest of the island had thrown off the yoke a year earlier.

Here, boy – fill this with wine. I need to talk about the Ionian rebellion, and that is thirsty talk!

It was the curse of the gods on the Ionians that they were doomed to listen to Aristagoras and his promises. From one end of Ionia to the other, the army of Artaphernes and the navy of his Phoenician allies, the greatest seamen in the world, defeated the Ionians every time they stood to fight. At Byzantium and in the Troad, at Ephesus, in a dozen ship duels, the Ionians had been worsted every time.

And yet the rebellion spread.

It was against all sense, and against all reason, but despite Artaphernes' fairness and Aristagoras's arrogance and failure, the rebellion grew with every defeat. The Carians, who had stood against us at Sardis and at Ephesus, were with us now. Cyprus was in revolt and all the Greek cities of Asia were in the Ionian Council, as they called themselves. Aristagoras was their leader and strategos.

We needed a victory. There really were no more cities to join in, unless Athens or Sparta chose to join. And neither seemed disposed to fight.

Aristagoras argued that we needed just one victory to convince both Athens and Sparta to join us. I doubted him. I had seen Aristides' face when he boarded his ship, and I suspected that nothing short of a Persian fleet in the Piraeus would get him to fight again alongside the Ionians. But I was a mere helmsman and no one asked my opinion.

I had a week to get to know that fleet, and I counted two hundred and twelve ships on the beach. There were ships from Lesbos and ships from Chios, Miletus and Samos, and even exiled ships from the cities already retaken.

Such as Archilogos of Ephesus. There he was, ablaze in magnificent panoply of blue and gold, looking like a god. I felt the tug of our friendship and my oath. But I stayed away from him.

I also heard that Briseis was on Lesbos, and that she had borne no children to her husband. I learned this from Epaphroditos, after many an embrace. He had his own ship now. And he and Nearchos became friends in an hour.

It flattered my vanity that so many men remembered me. We had games on the beach and I won the hoplitodromos, although I didn't win any of the other events until the duels on the last day, and that was too easy. Ionians don't really like to fight in the duels. The Cretans did, though – so I found myself exchanging cuts with the very men I had trained, and Nearchos and I fought in the last bout, for the prize.

He thought that he knew me.

I gave him a nice scratch on his forearm as a reminder that he didn't.

We laughed about it afterwards, and Lord Achilles came and took my hand. 'You are too good a man to hold in Crete,' he said. 'You could have your own ship with any lord here.'

Indeed, several men had offered me ships – Epaphroditos first among them.

'Yes, lord,' I said.

'I would keep you in my service until we face the Medes,' he said.

'I will stay, lord,' I said. 'After the battle, I will go.'

'Thank you. You are a fine young man, whatever your tastes. And may I add another thing? As long as you serve with my son, you will keep him safe. Eh? All young men seek to be Achilles. My son will be a king. Do not let him off the leash. Am I clear?'

I nodded.

He looked around, then looked back at me. 'What have you done to Aristagoras?' he asked.

I shrugged. There are some things best left unspoken. 'Why?'

'He asked me if you were my man. I said yes, and he said that he would not have you killed until you left my service. So – watch your back. He hates you. It's in his eyes when he speaks of you.'

I frowned. What had someone told him?

I thought of how Briseis could be when angered. Oh, yes.

My thoughts must have been on my face, because he chuckled. 'Our fearless leader is hardly a man to fear,' Achilles said. 'But he strikes me as the womanish sort who would cut your throat in the dark or put poison in a cup. When you leave me, watch yourself.'

We left a great deal unsaid. He knew things, and I knew things. He was not altogether comfortable with the loyalty his warriors showed to me, and he was not always happy with the man I had made of his son, either. But I'm a father now and I understand him better – and he never used me ill. Here's to him.

I had a man in the host repaint my shield, which was battered from a year of weapons drill. He made the raven all but leap from the bull's hide. 'An old Boeotian,' he said. 'You don't see many of those!'

The three of us – that's me, Idomeneus and Lekthes – we probably had half the Boeotians in the whole army. But I wanted reputation and I wanted men to know me.

The Persians landed across the island, as we expected, and they marched towards us by slow, careful stages.

Their fleet, the cream of the Phoenician cities, accompanied them, and both travelled every day in battle order, daring us to fight. They approached us slowly, and any day we might have met them, if we chose.

A Persian army and a Phoenician fleet. I could hear the gods laughing.

The Cyprians were gentlemen, and they offered the Ionian allies a choice – man our ships and face the Phoenicians, or form our phalanx and face the Persians. The Persian commander was not a man I knew. Artybius, he was called, and he had a strong force of cavalry. So did the Cyprians, and they had chariots as well, which made me feel as if I was serving in the Trojan War – no one but Cyprians and Libyans use chariots any more. And yet – I had trained as a charioteer, and they made me smile. I had never seen a chariot used for anything but a parade or a wedding or local travel, or for races, and the Cyprians were good. They had over a hundred of them. Everyone seemed to be excited by the prospect of using chariots in combat – even I thought it sounded marvellous, which goes to show how little I knew of war.

Aristagoras chose to take on the fleet. I suspected that he made the choice so that it would be easier to cut and run, but I was in the minority. Most of the rest still worshipped him, and he wore his purple cloak at every meeting, as if he was the King of Kings.

After making the decision, we had three days of rough weather, and we put out every day, struggled to form our lines and suffered from the wind and waves. The Phoenicians stayed on their beaches by their camp and jeered at us. The Great King's commander was cautious – he fortified his camp and would not risk battle until his fleet was there to cover his flank.

The fourth day dawned like a proper summer day on Cyprus, the sort of golden pink dawn when you can imagine the Cyprian goddess coming across the foam to your beach. We rose, cooked our breakfasts and sang a hymn to that goddess and to Zeus, and then to all the gods, and finally we boarded our ships.

The sea was as calm as a sheet of hammered bronze, and I knew that this time we would fight. My hands shook, my stomach did flips inside my scale thorax and I drank a little too much wine.

We formed up well, though, and that counts for a great deal in a sea-fight. North and west of us, on the beaches north of the city where the Persians had their camp, we could see them forming, and their allies with them, and the Cyprians forming against them, two great phalanxes and a taxis of cavalry on either flank, with the chariots farthest from the sea.

We Cretans were untried, and our heavy Phoenician-style ships were slower than the other Ionians, so they put us in the second line. It was an insult, if you like, but the fleet was well ordered and there was a rumour that Aristagoras was receiving advice from a Samothracian navarch. Whoever he was, I thought that he knew his business. We Cretans were on the landward flank, the left of our line, so far out from the centre that my ship was second from the beach, and by the whim of the gods, Archi's ship was in the first line, just seaward and ahead of us.

I swore to myself that if I had a chance to make good my oath to his family, I would do it.

Nearchos was shaking with nerves. I hugged him, our breastplates rubbing together oddly. 'Relax, *O phile pai*. The fear falls from you with the first arrow.'

He gave me a shaky smile, and we began to row forward with our line, as did the enemy, until we could see the eyes painted on their bows as clearly as we could see our own rowers. But then, before we could come to grips, I had cause to bless all the training Achilles had done with us, because the Phoenicians tried the oldest trick in naval warfare – they backed water. They were professionals, and we were amateurs, and they assumed that if they backed far enough, we'd lose our order and they'd kill us in small groups.

And indeed, our line did begin to break up after half a dozen stades – keeping a line at sea is hard enough, and every wave and current is against you. We split our first line into three, because there was a current off the rivermouth by the city and the rowers couldn't stay in the midst of it.

But the strong current from the river split the enemy, too. And they didn't break into three even groups, as we did – again, the whim of the gods and no cleverness of man. But their beachward division was the smallest, and it seemed to be out of order – caught in some indraught near the beach by their camp, or so it appeared to me.

'Troas!' I called, and he came to my side. We were rowing lower bank only, creeping across the great bay and saving our men for ramming. I pointed at the chaos among the landward Phoenicians. And now that they were closer, I could see that they weren't Phoenicians, either – they were Greeks.

There were plenty of cities who served Artaphernes, of course.

'Tide rip,' Troas said before he even reached the command deck. 'Not much, but enough to pull them apart. They should row faster – they'd be fine.'

'Stand by me,' I said. I nodded at Lekthes. 'Take his bench.'

Lekthes was used to this, but the look he shot me was full of reproach. He'd had a year of feasting as a warrior in the great hall – he had no desire to go back to rowing. But he went.

Ahead of me, the Samian ships to the seaward of Archi suddenly dashed from the line. They were twenty strong, and they acted in concert. They went from the slow cruise all the way to the fastest attack stroke so quickly that we were watching them pull away before we were sure what they were doing.

But the other ships in our part of the first line followed them.

Nearchos looked at me blankly.

'The Samians are going for the enemy Greeks!!' I stood on the rail and bellowed to Lord Achilles. He could see it as well as I could, but in my youthful arrogance, I assumed he wouldn't know any more than his son.

He nodded.

Ahead of us, the exiled Ephesians and Lemnians followed the Samians.

Lord Achilles had his squire raise a banner of red cloth and wave it.

'Up tempo to fast cruise,' I said. I ran to the midships fighting platform, leaving my 'navarch' with the steering oars. We didn't need to stay up with the first line, or so I'd been told, but I was anxious to get forward and I wanted to go faster than Lord Achilles had ordered.

Speed changes require orders, and now I was amidships I couldn't see as well. I got Thetis to fast cruise and then ran to the bow.

The Samians were just putting their beaks into the enemy. You could hear the collisions clearly across the water.

I watched Archi's ship, but he was cut off from the first impacts by the rush of Samians, and he and the other exiles were rowing diagonally across the beach, going to seaward, north and east across the current, to try and find an opening.

Somewhere in the enemy line, some oily Phoenician made a decision and the battle changed in the twinkling of their oars. Their centre broke up like an egg under a hammer, and the bulk of the centre turned landward – into the flank of the Samians. Our very aggression would now count against us, and our vulnerable flanks would be open to the rams of the heavy Phoenician ships.

That's why you keep a second line, of course.

I ran back down the centre plank between the upper-deck benches. To the north and west, our front left, the Phoenician centre was turning south and Archi's exiles were all that stood in their way. The Milesians and Chians seemed paralysed – just as they had been at every other battle.

'We need to turn north!' I shouted across the strip of sea between our ships at Lord Achilles, ignoring his son by my side.

Either the lord didn't hear me or he chose to ignore me. If we held our course, we'd enter the winning part of the combat close to the beach, a position where even in the event of a disaster, the Cretans could beach their ships and escape. Lord Achilles was thinking like a king.

I was thinking like a nineteen-year-old with an oath to fulfil.

I turned to Nearchos. 'If those ships are crushed, we lose the battle,' I said, pointing to the north. And the gods sent me an inspiration, because ships were sprinting out of the centre to help the exiles – Lesbian ships. 'Epaphroditos is going too! We have to support him!'

Nearchos rose to the moment. 'Go!' he said. 'Let my father follow *me!*'

I was sure that I had been hired to prevent just this sort of incident.

'Troas! Take the oars!' I pushed him into the steering rig. 'Nearchos – get forward with the marines and be ready to lead the boarders.' Lord Achilles would have a fit, I knew – but I wasn't sending the boy anywhere I wasn't going myself.

Troas got between the steering oars, and we were turning even as I ordered the last increase in speed. All our decks were rowing now, and the oar masters were thumping the deck with their canes, so that the whole ship rang with the tempo.

We were turning out of the second line, heading across the bows of other Cretan lords. It was exhilarating. There is something to war at sea – the speed of a ramming ship, the brilliance of the sea, the wind, the oarsmen singing the Paean. I felt like a god come to Earth. My fear fell away, our bow swept north and then we slipped into our new course as if it was carved like a trough in the sea, and we were moving as fast as a galloping horse.

'You have it?' I asked Troas. My not-quite-father-in-law was, in effect, commanding the ship.

'Never done this before!' he said, but he laughed. Some men rise to their moment. Troas – a man who could bargain for his daughter's virtue – was ready for his, and we stooped on the Phoenicians like a hawk on doves.

I saw the first engagements in the centre. Archi got his ship turned in plenty of time and up to full speed. He had a light trireme and he turned like a cat, passing *between* the first Phoenicians he met. One ship got his oars in, but the other got oar-raked, the broken shafts of the oars ripping men's arms and the splinters flying like arrows. Men *die* when their oars are shattered.

It was a brilliant stroke, but Archi would have a professional helmsman, as good as any Phoenician – indeed, the man might be a Phoenician. He was through in five heartbeats, right through their first line.

'Follow that ship,' I said to Troas. 'At all costs. Ram what you have to.'

Troas grinned.

The faster of the two Phoenicians – the one that hadn't lost his oars – was now closing with us at a terrific rate. A sea-fight is a scary thing, friends. It starts very slowly, but once everyone decides to engage, the speed is bewildering. Two ships at full stretch come together as fast as two galloping horses. Imagine it in your head – we were ram to ram with this enemy, our ships the same weight.

I paused and turned back to Troas. '*Diekplous*?' I asked. 'Ram to ram?'

He shook his head. 'At the last minute, I'll go left,' he said. 'A little flick to port and we're into his oars.'

'I'll warn the rowers!' I said, and ran to the command platform. 'On my command – all starboard-side oars inboard!' I roared.

The oar masters all raised hands, showing me they'd heard. Otherwise, their attention was on the stroke. One missed beat here and we were all drowned men.

Over my shoulder, the enemy trireme looked as big as a citadel. And fast as a porpoise.

And I had no one to help me. When *exactly* do you order your oars in? How long *exactly* does it take ninety men to drag their oars inboard?

I stood on the balls of my feet. I flicked a glance at the enemy – and saw that there was a second ship just abaft him.

Troas had seen it too – and it was too damned late to change our minds.

'Ready to ram!' I screamed.

Forward, the marines and Nearchos would be bracing against the bow.

The rowers would be praying.

Troas was grinning like a madman.

I wanted to shit myself.

I glanced at the enemy. So close it felt as if we should already have hit – I could see the face of their marine captain, and an arrow clanked against my helmet and flicked away. Good shooting.

'Starboard side!' I yelled. Wait for another stroke. Don't give the game away.

'Oars in!' I roared, blowing my voice for a day in one great shout, trying to use the strength of my lungs to get the oars in through the ports.

*Whamm*. We hit so hard that I fell and lost my helmet. It fell between the benches and vanished below.

The starboard-side rowers had their oars in, but it didn't matter.

Both ships had settled on the same tactics and jibed the same way, so we'd hit beak to beak – the hand of the gods. Our beak – a month out of the shop – held. Theirs broke off. Their ship was filling with water and my mouth was full of blood, Ares only knew why.

'Starboard oars – out!' I screeched. My voice was gone, but the petty-officers got the message.

'Back-water! Nearchos!' He was still stunned from the impact, but he came to me. His great helmet with bronze wings was a little flattened, and he had it buckled.

'Get that thing off and take command,' I said. 'My voice is gone!'

A sailor clambered up from inside the hull and handed me my helmet. I got it on my head.

Troas was on the ball, and he got the bulk of the sinking Phoenician between us and the next enemy by backing to starboard. The second

Phoenician overshot and went past us. I looked back, and most of the right flank's second line was behind us, coming up fast.

By Poseidon, thugater, that was a fine moment. We'd *sunk a Phoenician in one pass*. Call it luck if you like. It was luck. Nike was with us and her handsomer sister Tyche, too!

And Troas, just by thinking fast and steering, got us around the wreck, our timbers creaking but our ship intact. There was water coming in – I can't imagine how hard those two ships must have hit – but the sailors were bailing and we weren't finished yet.

Archi's ship was gone into the maelstrom in the centre. There were a dozen Phoenicians coming our way.

I looked at Nearchos. 'Pick one and let's get it,' I said. My oath would have to wait. We were, in effect, alone against the Phoenician centre.

The trick to staying alive in a sea-fight is never to show the long side of your ship – the oar banks – to the enemy. If you keep your bow to their bows, there should be a limit to how much damage you can take. Despite what had just happened to the ship we'd killed.

Troas played safe and Nearchos didn't interfere. We bumped hulls with the second Phoenician ship in line, cathead to cathead, and we damaged his oars a little, but he got most of them inboard. We lost two men – one oar fouled in the port and the loose end killed the rower who should have had it in and knocked the man above him in the oar loft unconscious, and just that small error left us vulnerable, because when the rowers were ordered to put their oars back in the water on the next stroke the whole port bank faltered and we turned to port, losing way and turning across the path of another enemy.

But the gods were with us and he passed us just a spear's length astern, and then we had our stroke back and we were alive.

But our rowers were tired. I could feel it. Tension is its own fatigue, thugater – the more you are afraid, the more tired you feel. And the more tired you are, the easier it is to feel fear.

I looked around, because suddenly we were between the fights. To the north, Archilogos and Epaphroditos and their allies were engaged with the second line of the Phoenician centre. Behind us, the Cretans were overwhelming the first line by weight of numbers, and the Samians had already polished off the enemy Greeks.

Even Aristagoras could scent victory. He released the centre and left, and the Milesians and the Chians went forward.

In fact, we had won the battle. I knew it and, more important, the

Phoenician navarch knew it. His right flank declined the engagement and began to row backwards again. I never saw their signal, but all at once, enemy ships began to flee.

Not the ships around Archi, though. They were locked together with grapples and marines, spear to spear.

I pointed to the fight in the centre.

Nearchos's fears were gone. He grinned.

'Now we make you a name,' I said. Not the words Achilles paid me to say.

But we were young.

Troas put us in well. We actually rowed a little past the mêlée and turned south, taking our first Phoenician in the flank. I was in the bow, my helmet down over my eyes, arms braced against the bulkhead, when we hit, and I could see the upper-deck oarsmen and their round mouths and terrified eyes as our damaged ram broke open their long side. We'd had a full stade to turn and race at our target; the men had the heart for one more burst and we were a heavy ship.

The enemy keel snapped under our ram and the ship broke in half. It was a spectacular kill and every ship in the centre of our line saw us do it. That's how you make a reputation, honey.

We probably also killed our own ship with that impact. The bow seams probably gave way right there.

We were too wild with the daimon of combat to care. Our beak went home into another enemy lashed alongside the one we'd broken like an old toy, and we spent our remaining momentum scraping down his side and coming to a rest broadside to broadside, oar bank to oar bank.

I leaped up on our ship's side and Nearchos was beside me, Idomeneus and Lekthes at my back, and the oar benches were emptying.

I balanced on the rail and waved down on to the Phoenician's deck. 'After you, my lord!' I said.

He grinned and we all leaped.

That was a great day, and a great hour. The enemy already knew they were doomed and doomed men seldom fight well. We cleared that first ship faster than it takes to tell it, killing their sailors – all their marines were elsewhere, boarding the Lesbian ships. I cut the captain down by his helmsman and Nearchos gutted the helmsman, and then we went over the side and down into the next ship – another trireme, and now we were coming up behind the Phoenician marines as they fought shield to shield against Lesbians and Chians and Ephesian exiles.

Behind me, the Cretans were clearing the Phoenician decks, tripping from bench to bench. A Cretan ship is a fearsome thing because every bench has another warrior. We were worth five ships' worth of marines.

My spears were gone and my good sword was in my hand. I was standing on the rail of a Lesbian ship – there were twenty ships all locked together in a single mass of death – and I balanced there for three heartbeats while I looked for Archilogos.

Then I saw him, a flash of blue and gold, still on his feet, his right arm covered in blood and his aspis a flapping mass of splintered wood and collapsed bronze. Some men fight *better* when they are doomed.

And I blessed the gods that they had given me the moment to redeem my oath.

Hah! I killed like the scythe of Hades. I won't bore you with the tale – oh, you want me to bore you?

It was one of my finest days.

All the doubt left me. I cared nothing for their wives and their children and their petty lives. As fast as my arm moved, they died. If they turned, I cut them down, and if they didn't turn, I put my sword into their throats and thighs. I could have cleared a ship by myself, but I had Nearchos by my side, and his blade was as fast as mine, and Lekthe's spear flashed over my head from time to time when I was pressed, and they *died*. The four of us were the cutting edge of a living axe of Cretans, and we flowed over their decks as fast as men can clamber from bench to bench. My right arm was red to the shoulder with the blood of lesser men, dripping down my chest inside my armour, and there was the smell of copper in my nose like an offering to the god of smiths, and still I killed them.

After we cleared our second ship, I got my voice back and called 'Archilogos!', and he turned. Because if he died without me, I would never forgive myself. He had to know I was coming.

Another ship, the last before Archi's, and I was suddenly blade to blade with a giant. To make it worse, he was standing on the command platform and I was in the benches. He was an officer of some sort, because he'd gathered a dozen marines and turned them to face our rush.

I paused. He was huge, and I felt the blood and the fire in my muscles.

'Spear,' I said, reaching back, and Lekthes put his in my hand.

That's right, honey. And he eventually died a lord, and his daughters play with you. I thought you'd recognize the name – I've mentioned it a dozen times.

The giant raised his shield, ready for me to throw the spear.

Instead, I charged him. Raising the shield cost him a second, and I got a foot on the platform and my shield went against his, and before I got the other foot up, I slammed my spear point into the side of his helmet, a broad bowl with cheek pieces, riveted in the middle. Phoenicians are masters of many things, but bronze-work is not one of them.

He stumbled back. I'd rung his bell. Then he cut low at my legs, but I dipped the Boeotian and put the bronze-bound base into his sword. Then I slammed my spear into his helmet – again.

In the same place.

He stumbled back, and I roared. I remember that moment best of all, because this giant of a man was *afraid* and that fear was like the scent of blood to a shark.

He cut at my legs again, but I blocked it, stepped in and put my spear point into his helmet a third time, where the brow-ridge met the bowl, and the third time, the rivet popped and the point went under the bad weld, right through the top of his skull.

I stepped over him and a spear punched into my side. By Ares, that was pain – the scales held, but the rib broke, and I was knocked to my knees.

Never saw the blow that got me. There's a lesson there.

Nearchos got him.

I knelt there, almost dead, unable to raise my head – Ares, the pain; I hurt even thinking about it! And Lekthes and Idomeneus stepped past me, dancing the dance, and men fell back before them. They cleared the platform and I could breathe, although it wasn't good, and I got a leg under me and then another.

Then the rest of them dropped their weapons.

Cretans were flooding aboard from all directions. I'd taken Achilles' heir into the heart of the chaos and his father had come with all his warriors to save him.

Nearchos was as tall as a titan in that moment.

I managed to walk forward.

Achilles glared at me but embraced his son. I passed behind him and led my men across to Archi's trireme.

Half of Archi's rowers were dead, and all but two of his marines. He himself was covered in blood and had an arrow right through his calf, but somehow he was still standing.

I walked up the centre plank from the bow and the spear shaft in my hand had a tendril of blood that ran all the way down from the head. The Phoenician marines tried to surrender, but there was no quarter just then, and my Cretans rolled over them like a wave rolling over a child's castle on the beach, and they were gone, their blood flowing into the sea, and I was so close to Archi I could reach out and touch him.

'Archi!' I said, and pulled off my helmet.

'Get off my ship,' he said, and fainted.


We bandaged him. He was cut eleven times, I remember that. And the arrow through his calf. When he came to, he swore at me and demanded that I be executed. No one paid him any heed, but my dreams that our friendship would be restored when I saved him went the way of many dreams.

I had a couple of broken ribs and six bad cuts. My sword arm had taken a lot of abuse – desperate men cut at your arm instead of defending themselves, and die while doing it. Death robs them of force, but I'd always meant to buy vambraces and now I knew why.

I sat on the deck of an alien ship and let Lekthes bandage me. We'd taken four ships, or so Idomeneus told me – which was good, because our own had sunk. It sank empty, but sink it did, the bow opened like a slit belly.

Nearchos came and gave me some shade, along with Troas.

'My father is angry,' Nearchos said, as if it delighted him.

'I suspect he feels that I should have protected you better,' I said. I think I managed a smile.

'Pick any of the ships and it is yours,' he said. 'We can crew it from the survivors. I'm taking this one – unless you want it.'

I raised my head. 'Do I get Troas? What on earth am I to do with a ship? And how is Archilogos of Ephesus?'

Nearchos shook his head. 'You've been out a little while, friend. We lost the battle.'

That snapped me awake, blood loss or none. 'What?'

'Oh, we won the sea battle,' Nearchos said. How godlike he looked

– and not a mark on him. He shrugged. 'The Cyprians shattered like glass, and half their nobles changed sides in mid-action. Onesilus is dead. Cyprus is lost.'

'Ares,' I muttered.

'Aristagoras has ordered us to stay together and run for Lesbos.' He shrugged. 'Pater says that we'll crew you a ship and you'll go for all of us. The rest of us are going home.' He made a face.

'Your father is a great man,' I said. 'Troas, you go home. May you have a hundred grandchildren.'

He laughed. 'Never planned anything else. But I'll choose you a good crew. If you swear me an oath that you'll send them home.'

I got to my feet. I felt like crap, but there was something – some weight gone from my shoulder, and not just my scale shirt.

I'd kept my oath. I could feel it.

'I have one oath already on me,' I said. 'I'll do my best, but that's all I can promise.'

# 17

The second day out from Cyprus, and we were in the deep blue under sail, reaching north for the coast of Asia and familiar waters, and my heart was in my throat with every rise of the bow. The cuts on my arms hurt the worse for the salt air and there was a storm rising in the east. I had one trick of command – I wasn't going to show my fear to Lekthes or Idomeneus, so they assumed all was well and transmitted that confidence down the decks.

But darkness was coming. I knew that I'd fucked up – pardon me, ladies, and by Aphrodite, despoina, you blush like a maiden of twelve – I mean that I knew I'd left it until too late in the day, and I knew we weren't on a course of true north, and that meant we were still at sea when we should have been cooking. And no sight of a coast.

The rowers were sitting on their benches enjoying the rest, and no doubt planning how to retake the ship.

I called my two men and gave it to them straight. 'We're going to spend the night at sea,' I said. 'And the crew will try for us once it is too dark to see.'

Lekthes winced. Idomeneus grinned maniacally. The sea-fight had changed him. For all his limp wrists and exaggerated pretty-boy habits, he was getting to be a hard man. And he knew it and loved it.

'Let them come,' he said. 'There aren't ten men among them.'

I shook my head. 'The ten men you kill are the same ten men we need to get to Lesbos alive,' I said.

Lekthes shook his head. 'So, what then?'

'Get the Cretans up and armed. Then walk up and down confidently and see if there are any of the Greeks worth having. If you find a man you like, send him aft while there's still light.'

The two of them went forward, armed the Cretan deck crew and then began to move through the ship. I'm sure that none of you well-bred ladies has ever been on a warship, so I'll tell you how it is at sea. A trireme has three decks of rowers – they aren't really decks, but three levels of benches with a sort of crawl-space between them. It takes men time to come and go from the oar benches. There's a single walkway, the width of a man's shoulders, that runs from stem to stern the length of the ship. On an Athenian ship, there's a command platform amidships. Some of the easterners do the same and some build a little deck aft, by the helmsman. Regardless, the helmsman sits in the stern between his two oars, which in a modern ship are strapped together with bronze or iron. He's the real commander of the ship, and it is the helmsman's voice that the other officers – the deck crew – obey. Under the helmsman there's an oar master who keeps order and counts time, and a sailing master who manages the two masts and their sails – the mainmast and the boatsail mast, which is up forward in the bow. The rest of the deck crew manage the sails and bully the oarsmen and provide a reserve of labour. On a Cretan ship they also serve as extra marines. Then there are marines – usually citizen-hoplites.

Lord Achilles didn't send me with any marines. I had two dozen of his men as deck crew, and not one of them would make an officer. A more worthless group of men I'd seldom seen, and Troas had his revenge for my 'corrupting' his daughter – by the gods, I swore to have vengeance on him if I ever caught him – not one man who could be trusted between the steering oars. Nearchos may have wanted me to get the very best men, but what I got was the dregs. Men no one needed. Human waste.

The prisoners were the better men in every instance. I had at least forty Phoenicians and twice that in captured Greeks. I didn't even have a full rowing crew – I couldn't man all the lower-deck oar shafts. In good weather, it should have been enough, but there was a storm coming and Lord Achilles didn't give a ram's fart whether this ship made it through the storm or not.

Well – I'd made a small fortune from him, and I didn't mean to die at sea. And yet I remember thinking that I had, at least in part, redeemed my oath, and that meant that I was free to die, in a way. The thought relaxed me, to be honest. I was an honourable man again.

So I stayed in the steering oars, and we sailed north, or more likely north by west, and the sun sank in the sky, and the murmurs from forward grew louder.

302

A water-clock before sunset, Lekthes came forward with a black man. I'd seen the Nubian when the prisoners had been herded aboard by marines – you couldn't miss him, with his skin as black as new pitch in the smithy, ready for the forging of fine bronze.

'Lord?' Lekthes asked, coming aft. 'This one claims he was helmsman on a Phoenician trireme.' He prodded the black man, and the man looked at him with ill-concealed resentment.

'Claims, my arse, lord,' the Nubian said in Ionian Greek – better Greek than mine. 'Lord, you are too far west of north – I've been watching since the evening star rose. I know these waters.'

'That will be all, Lekthes,' I said, borrowing Aristides' manner when dismissing a man. Lekthes snapped a salute and went back to the decks.

'What's your name?' I asked.

The Nubian crossed his arms and looked forward. 'Paramanos, lord.'

'Your Greek is excellent,' I said.

He nodded. 'It ought to be – I grew up with it. My family owns ships at Naucratis, and there's more of us in Cyrene.' He looked forward again. 'And my daughters will be orphans if you don't point this ship north, lord.'

Naucratis? A Greek city in the Nile delta. They say it was founded by mercenaries serving the pharaohs at the time of the siege of Troy. And Cyrene is a colony – richer than the mother city – in Africa. What is it that your tutors teach you?

'You are a helmsman?' I asked.

'I've been navarch of a blue-water merchant,' he said.

'If you are lying, I'll kill you,' I said. 'Take the steering oars.'

I could see his fear, and smell it, but I didn't know whether he was afraid of me or simply afraid of death – the coming storm – hard to tell. I stepped off the helmsman's bench and he took the oars. 'I have the ship,' he said.

'Yes, you do,' I said.

He shook his head. 'I'm changing course. See the evening star there by the moon? That's well west of north from here.' He swung the oars, his arms taut with muscle, and the ship changed course smoothly, the wind passing from under our quarter to dead astern.

'Before the north star rises we'll be in with the coast, or you can feed me to the fishes,' he said. But his voice shook.

I didn't trust him.

At sunset, Idomeneus came aft with a trio of lanky Asian Greeks. 'All three brothers?' I guessed.

'They were taken in arms as rebels on the mainland and pressed as rowers,' Idomeneus said. 'All citizens of Phocaea in Aeolis.' He looked aft. 'We've a dozen more Aeolians. They shouldn't be prisoners to start with.'

The eldest brother fell to his knees. 'Lord, we are Ionians! We fought at Sardis! I was in the agora when you fought, lord!'

It was an easy claim to make – I had no idea who had been in the agora at Sardis, but I *had* been a slave. I knew that tone. Besides, let's be honest – I liked being called lord.

I held up my hand. 'Will you swear – to me? Now?'

All three knelt on the deck and swore. Ionians swear the way Cretans do, hands between the hands of their lords. They aren't much for democracy, like mainland Greeks. I took their oaths by Poseidon and Zeus Soter, and then I armed them and set them to choosing any other Aeolians that they knew. Herakleides was their leader, and his brothers were Nestor and Orestes, and they were good men.

I have a soft spot for men who carry the name of my ancestor.

I was just congratulating myself on having some good men when the Phoenicians decided to take the ship. They must have been desperate – as they saw the Aeolians separated out, they must have known that their chances of taking the ship were dropping by the moment.

They almost killed Lekthes in the first rush. They clubbed him with oars broken short – what a labour that must have been! They'd worked in secret below decks, of course, muffling the sound in their cloaks and rowing cushions, I suppose. I had no idea. They were brave men, desperate men, and they came in one gallant charge, up the benches, oar shafts falling like axe blows. Lekthes took one on his helmet and fell to his knees, but Idomeneus stood by him, put a spear point in one big Syrian and slammed his shield into another, shoving him over the side. They went to get around him, but I got my sword out of my scabbard, cursing myself for a fool – I had ordered my men to arm, but I was standing nearly naked, my helmet and scale shirt stowed uselessly under the helmsman's bench.

Short sword against oar shaft is not a good match. I took a blow on my shield arm and killed the man – my arm was numb.

The three Aeolians weren't armed, but they threw themselves into the fight, fists and gymnasium-trained muscles. The oldest took the oar shaft from the nerveless fingers of the man I'd hacked down. I climbed on the next bench, the rage of combat on me and all thought of leadership lost, while Idomeneus, the only fully armed man, was laying waste to the Syrians. There were two dead at his feet and a third was trying to hold in his guts while grappling Idomeneus's feet. I stepped on his throat and blocked a blow meant for Lekthes, then one of the Aeolians doubled up my opponent with a vicious blow to the man's stomach and they broke.

We hunted them through the boat, and killed them all. It isn't pretty to say it but, with a wind rising and the peril of mutiny and the blood hot, we didn't take any prisoners. Syrian Phoenicians can't hide among Greeks, and we weren't too fussy about who had carried a broken oar shaft and who hadn't.

When I came back aft, my arm still numb and my feet as red with the blood as if I'd been treading grapes in Boeotia, I found four more Phoenicians clustered around the helmsman's bench.

Their pointed beards gave them away. I raised my arm to kill them and the nearest put up his arm to protect himself.

'Stop!' the Nubian demanded. 'Stop it!' He tried to catch my arm, and I socked him in the face with my sword fist. He fell back into the steering rig and the ship yawed. His nose pumped blood but he was back on his feet.

'Stop it! Or Poseidon will take us!' he said. That got through my blood-drunk head. 'They're trying to surrender!' he said again. 'Zeus Soter, lord! These are noblemen, worth ransom. This one was my navarch. Stop it!' He was screaming at me while leaning all his weight on the oars, and I saw that while I'd been slaughtering Syrians, the wind had come up.

'Get forward,' I said to the four Phoenicians. 'Throw the bodies over the side.' I knew it was heartless, but the bastards had tried to take my ship and I suspected that these four fine noblemen were just as guilty – or *more* guilty.

After the slaughter of forty Syrians, we were down to half a compliment of rowers. The coast was nowhere in sight and the wind was shifting around. My new helmsman looked at me as if he thought I was mad.

I looked at him as if he was a traitor. 'You seem awfully friendly with the Phoenicians,' I said.

I'd broken his nose. He shook his head to clear it. 'I don't know who the fuck you are,' he said, 'with your barbaric Greek and your murderous temper, but we *all* used to be friends with the merchants of Tyre. I've traded with them all my life.'

There was something funny about a black man in an Asian chiton telling me that I was a barbarian. I laughed. 'You are a brave man,' I said.

'Fuck your mother,' he growled. 'We're all going to die anyway.' He spat over the side. 'You just killed the whole lower oar deck. We don't have the manpower to beach the ship.'

I laughed again. 'We'll stay at sea, then. Nothing to fear from a night at sea.' I laughed, and pointed at the blood running out of the oar ports. 'Poseidon has had his share of sacrifices,' I said.

His eyes said that he didn't agree.

'And the ship is rid of vermin,' I added. If I was going to play the mad captain, I'd play it to the hilt.

Even the Cretans were different in the morning. They might still be useless, but now they were terrified of me, and that made them better sailors. Paramanos got us in with the coast of Asia – the long east–west reach south of Aeolis and west of Lydia, full of pirates and dangerous rocks. But he knew that coast, and we ran west with the new storm at our backs all night, and morning showed the teeth of the mountains dead ahead.

'Unless we row south,' Paramanos said, 'we're dead men.'

I agreed, so I had all three decks rowing – well, at least the two I could man – in the grey rain, and we had the sea broadside on, pouring through the oar ports and pushing us steadily west for all the southing that we made, which was precious little.

Some time in that endless grey day, I sent the deck crew to row, and even gave orders for the handful of armed Aeolians who still stood by to serve wine to every man, strip their armour and take up an oar.

My left arm was still numb, and even in the rain I could see a bruise as black as the darkest night where the oar had hit me, but I knew that I had to row. Leadership is an odd thing – sometimes you want your men to fear you as they fear the gods, at others you need them to love you like a long-lost brother. So I settled to an upper-deck bench, and for the first time I could see how much water was swirling down in the hold below me.

My stomach clenched. We were a third full of water, and if the Phoenicians had still been manning the lower benches, they'd have been drowning.

306

I called to the Nubian and told him that we were full of water. I could see him smile at my ignorance. He was conning the ship – of course he would know just how sluggish we were. Truly, I was a piss-poor commander. I had too much to learn.

It was a Phoenician ship, and it had tackle I didn't understand. It had pumps – sliding wooden pumps that rigged to the top strakes and allowed a strong man to shoot water up and over the side, straight up from the bilges. The Nubian got them rigged and shooting water while I rowed on in a haze of pain, because now that I was active, my left arm hurt like fire with every stroke, and the whole thing seemed pointless.

Every rower harbours a secret fear in a storm – that by rowing for the safety of all, he is losing his own strength to swim, if the ship founders. I was a strong swimmer – I'd learned in Ephesus and swum every day on Crete, and now I knew that if we wrecked, I would drown, dragged under by a weak left arm and a hundred cuts and bruises.

'What'd you do?' the man below me asked out of nowhere. 'Weren't you deck crew?'

'Everyone rows,' I said, gritting my teeth.

'Trierarch's a madman, ain't he?' the man asked. 'A killer, that's what I hear.'

I laughed. 'I am the trierarch,' I said.

He twitched and almost lost the stroke, and I felt better. 'Listen, boy,' I said, using the Ionian phrase for a slave, or a man of no value. 'If we live, you owe me an apology. And if we all die, you'll have the satisfaction that I'll be as dead as you.'

That was the end of conversation with my rowers. I don't think they loved me. They thought I was insane.


Another nightfall found us still at sea. We were resting fifteen men at a time, and I was relieved eventually by another shift of reserve rowers, and I could see that if there was no less water in the bilges, at least there was no more. But I also knew that our rowers were almost finished. I knew because I was as strong as an ox, injury or no injury, and my arms were like wet rawhide.

I went aft, cold now that I wasn't rowing, and pulled my dry cloak from under the bench and put it around me.

Paramanos was still in the steering rig.

'Can you take the helm?' he asked.

'Give me cup of wine and a hundred heartbeats and I'll do my best.' I shrugged. Lekthes and Idomeneus were both rowing, and there wasn't another man on deck. 'It's a miracle we've made it this far, isn't it?' I said.

He nodded. 'I'm good,' he said. He pointed aft. 'When the rowers fade, I put the sea behind us for a few minutes.' His grey-black face had a ghost of a grin. 'Not my first storm.'

I knocked back a cup of neat wine. It flowed like warm honey through my veins, and I was alive. 'Give me the oars,' I said.

He handed them over, and the moment I took them I felt the strain. I looked to starboard, and I could see the coast passing in the fading light. The combination of wind and oar was moving us at a speed that seemed superhuman.

I thought that the Nubian would collapse – he'd been between the steering oars for twelve straight hours, dawn to dusk – but instead, he ran forward.

The oars rose and fell to the beat, but the men were barely moving them. The wind was doing the work, and it would soon bring about our ruin. I reckoned that at roughly the time the sun finally set, we'd touch the rocks. No beach at all, there at the foot of the Olympus of Asia.

I poured another cup of wine and drank it. I would die with my oath redeemed, doing my best. What more can the gods ask?

Paramanos came back aft and the grey fatigue was gone from his face. I handed him the wine cup and he drank off the rest.

'If you served out wine,' he said, 'we might get another water-clock of strong rowing. And I think we might – *might* – save the ship.'

We traded places again while he explained. I didn't think his wine would work. I thought that words would, and I ran forward to the command platform and raised my voice over the rain.

'Listen, you bastards!' I shouted into the wind. 'We'll be on a beach cooking hot food and drinking wine before the sun sets if you'll put your backs into it. What a bunch of shits we'll look in Hades if we drown a horse-length from a safe beach!'

It was my first battle speech. It worked.

They all thought that they were dead men, and the merest glimpse of hope was enough to fire them. I walked up and down the central plank, and I told them exactly what Paramanos planned. Over and over again.

'We're going to thread the needle between the Chelidon and

Korydela,' I said. 'And then we'll be in the lee of the greatest mountain in Asia – calm water and rest. Our Nubian says we can beach at Melanippian, even in the dark, with this wind, and I believe him.'

It's easy to believe, when the only other choices are extinction and black death, and they rowed with their guts and their hope of life. Sunset – not that we'd ever seen the sun – gave way to a horrible grey light and then to full night, and still we lived, and I knew that our bow was due west now. The storm was full at the stern and the motion of the ship was easier; the only rowing we needed was to keep her stern on to the wind.

But I knew that we were still in a race with time, and I got my three Aeolians and Lekthe and Idomeneus and two men they seemed to know, and we raised the boatsail. I'd seen it done by Hipponax's trained mariners – you lash the furled boatsail to the mast, then raise the mast, secure it ten times, and then you cut the lashings on the sail and it spreads itself. The Ephesians did it to show off, but Hipponax had said once that it was a life-saver in a storm.

It is one thing to lash a boatsail to its mast on an autumn day in a brisk breeze, with the warm sun burning your shoulders, surrounded by men who love you, and another to do it in driving rain with your hands so cold that you can't tell whether you have rope between your fingers or not.

We managed to tie the boatsail eight times with hemp rope, and then we found that we didn't have the strength to raise the mast. The wind caught it and hurled it over the side, and only the luck of the gods kept the pole from holing us as it went over.

But damn it, we were close to making it through the strait. I could see the cliffs rising on either side.

The rowers were finished. Even hope can't make spent muscles move an oar.

I wasn't finished. I got the spar from the mainsail and let the wind take the mainsail over the side like a hundred-handed monster – twenty silver owls of linen lost in two heartbeats, and I didn't give a damn. The spar was only three men tall, much smaller than the boatsail mast. But we carried a spare boatsail and we bent it to the spar and tied it down, and then I stripped the upper deck of rowers – the oars were in all along the deck, with only the middle men pretending to row, and we were beginning to fall off and broach. Time was running out, we had cliffs on both sides and even Paramanos was out of – of whatever drove him.

They thought I was mad. We were turning so that our long side was vulnerable to the wind – the men still rowing didn't have the coordination or the strength to keep our head to the waves, and like a ship in battle, once the long sides were to the waves, we were done.

I went from man to man in between lightning flashes, pushing rope ends into unwilling hands. I knocked a man sprawling when he was too slow to obey. He went over the side and the sea took him.

'Pull, you bastards!' I called.

Love is a fine thing. Love will take a man above himself, whether it is love for a man or a woman or a ship or a country. But fear can imitate love in most situations, and I knew they didn't love me.

'Pull or die!' I screamed, and my sword was in my hand. 'Still time to bleed!' I shouted, and I laughed. Let them think me insane.

The spar shot up like a stallion's penis. 'Lash her down! Belay her!'

*Then* they were willing. Then they believed. It was easy when we came to it – but someone had to get them over the belief that they would fail. Now every man worked with a will, and Paramanos was next to me, lashing the new stays as fast as his hands could work. Already the wind, that brutal east wind, was on the mast and the tight-wrapped boatsail, and our bow was cutting the sea. Little Idomeneus was at the helm, doing his best to get the bow headed west. Paramanos worked by my side as we tied the ropes and belayed. Ten ropes. Ten heavy cables to hold a mast smaller than the one a day-fisher carried.

Then Paramanos was gone, back to his steering oars.

We were three horse-lengths from the rocks of Chelidon, and there was no more time to worry. My sword was in my hand.

I cut the lashings in two sweeps as accurate as any sword cuts I'd ever made in combat, and the whole sail blew free of the lashings as if Poseidon's fist had struck it. I thought that the mast would snap, it bent so far, and the bronze-clad bow *plunged* into the sea, so that I thought we might dive to the bottom like a cormorant. Fear took me, but I got my arms around that mast and held on as the water drove aft. And then the bow began to rise. I felt the change under my feet even as I choked on the water in my mouth.

The bow came up, sluggish at first, and then the first stay rope gave with a crack like a thunderbolt, killing the man it hit, one of the Aeolians. He didn't even get to scream.

The new mast gave a grunt and moved the width of a man's arm – and held.

The whole ship seemed to groan and the bow rose again, clear of the sea. The waves were at our stern, and we'd put more blood into the water – the Aeolian was our last sacrifice.

I had a chance to see the cliffs of Chelidon, and I don't think that I have ever moved faster across the surface of the earth than I did in those heartbeats, as the full weight of the storm blew into our tiny sail and we raced across the sea like a mare run wild.

And then, as fast as it takes to tell it, we were through the strait. First the force of the gale diminished by half, because the cliffs were no longer funnelling the whole storm into our little sail. And then Paramanos, grinning like a titan, was turning us – oh, so gradually – to starboard.

It took us longer than we could have imagined – I think that if I'd told the men, back in the teeth of the storm, that we were still half a watch from safety, we'd all have died.

But the moment came when every man aboard knew we were *not* going to die. Hard to define, but between one breath and the next, the wind had dropped so far – broken by the weight of Asian Olympus to our north and east, now – that if we'd all slumped on our oars, we'd have floated the rest of the night and come to no harm. And in the contrary way of the human heart, that gave us strength – we were all one animal by then, and we were going to rise and fall together, no mistake.

My Cretan oar master was gone – swept over the side by the wave when the bow went down – and I beat the deck with my good spear and chanted the *Iliad* at the sea, and men laughed. It was as dark as Tartarus under the lee of the mountain, but the beach rolled on for ever, and we turned the ship in water as calm as any harbour and the stern grated on the gravel, the kiss of life, and the ship stopped, all our oars out over the side as if we were a dead water bug.

We lay in a huddle on the beach, a hundred exhausted men who didn't even try to start a fire. It was hot in the midst of the pile of men and cold and wet on the fringes, and no man slept, but no man died.

In the morning, the sun rose late over the mountain and we rose slowly, like men who have survived a hard fight – which we were. We caught some goats, sacrificed them to Poseidon and ate them half-cooked. We drank wine from the hold, poured more libations than an assembly of priests and swore that we were brothers until the sun died in the sky.

The next morning, I got them back aboard and, with the bow pointed at Lesbos, we sailed away with our toy boatsail. And as luck would have it, twenty stades up the bay, we found our own boatsail mast with the sail still lashed to it, floating with the wrack of the storm, and further downwind we found the mainsail floating below the surface like a dead creature.

'Truly, the gods love you,' Paramanos said.

I shrugged. 'I have some luck,' I said.

He nodded. I was at the steering oars, and he was drinking fresh water from a little horn cup, a Phoenician habit. 'I've never seen that trick with the boatsail before,' he said. It was a peace offering, if I wanted it. He was a better sailor than I and he'd taken command when he had to, and he expected me to resent it.

He had me wrong. I waited until he'd finished his water, then I put my arms around his neck. 'You fucking saved *us*,' I said. 'I'm not so mad as you think.'

He nodded, and finally he couldn't restrain his grin. 'I did, didn't I?' he said.

'You did,' I answered.

The next afternoon, I summoned the Phoenicians aft. I nodded at the helmsman. 'Paramanos has requested your lives,' I said. 'For myself, I bear no grudge against you – we are at war. But I will only free you for a ransom. Choose among yourselves who will go, and who will stay as surety.'

The eldest nodded. First he embraced Paramanos and then he came back to me. 'I am the richest of these men, and I will stay,' he said.

I could see the hatred in his eyes, but who loves a man who has killed thirty countrymen in cold blood? I didn't need his love.

'Set a price,' I said.

He named a figure in talents of silver. Paramanos approved and Herakleides, the eldest of the Aeolians, gave a curt nod. Herakleides was already serving as an officer, and training with Paramanos to be a helmsman.

'On the beach at Methymna,' I said to the youngest, who was chosen to go. 'Thirty days.' I turned to Idomeneus. 'See to it that he has arms and ten silver owls.'

The eldest Syrian shrugged. 'Land him at Xanthus,' he said. 'We have a factor there.'

And so we did.

When I promised all the rest of the crew shares in the ransom, my status rose again. The four Phoenicians were worth ten times my whole fortune, and I had accounted myself well-off before we fought the battle. Boeotians aren't good at wealth.

The gods were kind. Dolphins sported at our bow and we had the mainsail up by noon of the second day. A kinder east wind stayed at our stern-quarter all the way up the coast of Asia, until we had to turn and row into the magnificent bay at Mytilene. The beach was not as full of ships as it should have been. Indeed, it was as if only a portion of the fleet that had broken the Phoenicians at Amathus had come to the rendezvous. More than a third of the ships had gone home, and at first glance it looked worse. The Cretans were not the only ones to take their loot and go.

I recognized the Athenian cut of the ships on the south end of the beach but not any of the ships themselves – none of them were Aristides', but I saw a black hull that might be Herk's unlovely *Nemesis*, and I turned my ship at the south end of the beach and put the stern in the sand two oar's lengths from the man himself, who stood in the gentle surf laughing and shouting rude suggestions at my oarsmen.

He was the first man to embrace me as I put my feet on the beach.

Miltiades was the second.

# 18

Of course it had been Miltiades advising that rascal Aristagoras – he was the 'Samothracian navarch'. I heard a lot of that story later, and if I have time, I'll answer all your questions about it. But at that point I was simply happy to see someone I knew. I was happy to have someone to be in command. And I was delighted to receive his flattery, which came thick, fast and accurately.

That short sail from south of Cyprus to Lesbos was my first command, and it had taken its toll. I was bone-weary, and the broken ribs hadn't begun to knit, so that every weather change and every jostle caused spikes of pain. I had discovered that commanding men is the very opposite of fighting man to man – what I mean is that when I am fighting, the world falls away and everything is *right there* – the whole circle of the world revealed in a single heartbeat, as Heraclitus used to say. But when you are in command, you have to face the infinite consequences of each action – forward, on and on, until the gods strip the roots of the world away. Is there water? Is there food? Where will you beach tonight? Does that oarsman have a fever? Have you passed three headlands or four?

And it never ends. No sooner were my bare feet in the sand of Lesbos, Miltiades' arms around me, than my men were asking whether we would need the boatsail brought ashore and a hundred more questions.

Miltiades laughed, released my arms and stood back. 'The bronze-smith's son is a trierarch. No surprise to me, allow me to add. You've come right in among my ships – why not camp with me?'

I might have done better, waited for the best offer, but I was so happy to see someone from home – to be honest, when I saw Miltiades, I assumed that the Ionians would win. He always had that effect on me. 'Show me where we can build our fires?' I asked.

He waved and another friend joined me – Agios, now helmsman to Miltiades.

'You have a ship of your own?' he asked, and laughed. 'Poseidon help your oarsmen!'

We walked down the beach and he found me space for fires, a fire for every fifteen men. Then I gathered them all in a big circle and made sure of their mess groups. Eating on the voyage had been a matter of desperation. Now I meant to get them organized.

We mustered ninety-six oarsmen and twenty-one Cretans. I put the Cretans in two mess groups – I didn't expect them to want to stay, and I didn't want their bad attitude to infect the rest. The Aeolians and other Greeks and random Asians who made up the rest of the crew I divided in fifteens. I paid silver out of my own hoard to buy them cook pots, right there on the beach – the local market was huge, and every merchant in Mytilene was selling his wares – or hers. The best of the potters was a middle-aged woman with her hair tied up in a scarf and clay on her hands, and her pots were so much better than her competitors that I agreed to pay her exorbitant rates. Men know when they have the best equipment. I learned that from my father. Even pots are part of morale.

I bought a net full of small tuna, gutted and fresh, and the men fell to, cutting and preparing. I had to pay for firewood and vegetables and bread, and by the time the oarsmen were settled to their first good hot meal of the week, my hoard of silver had diminished by a little under a fifth.

I could not afford to be a trierarch.

When my belly was full of wine and tuna, I caught Idomeneus's eye and picked up my best spear. Ionians follow many of the old ways, and one is that walking with a spear lends a man dignity and formality. I walked over to Miltiades' fires, and found him easily enough. He was seated on an iron stool, the legs digging deeply into the sand. He was telling a tale – an uproarious tale – and the laughter swept higher every few heartbeats as we walked up the beach to-wards him. His red hair burned in the sun, and his head was thrown back to laugh at his own story, and that's one of my favourite ways to remember him. Because he really could tell a story.

'The hero of Amathus!' he called, when I was close enough. He rose and embraced me again.

It was then I discovered just how far my fame had spread. Men gathered around *me*, as if I was Miltiades. And he didn't stint in his praise.

Yet one man's face grew dark. Archilogos turned on his heel and walked away, his servant at his side. I watched them go and the happiness of the moment was marred, like a bad mark in an otherwise perfect helmet, a dimple that you cannot remove.

Miltiades paid no attention – if he even noticed. 'For those of you fine gentlemen who were busy, it was young Arimnestos who defeated their centre – I saw the whole thing from the flagship.' He laughed. 'Oh, how we cheered you, lad. Like men watching the stadion run at the Olympian Games, with heavy wagers on the runner.' He put his arm around my shoulders.

A big man – bigger than me, bigger than Miltiades – came and took my hand. 'I'm Kallikles, brother of Eualcidas.' To the men assembled, he said, 'This man – too old to be a boy – went alone and saved my brother's body from the Medes.'

I accepted his embrace, but then I turned to Idomeneus. 'My hypaspist, Idomeneus. He stood by me that long night, and helped carry the body.'

Kallikles was not too proud to shake a servant's hand. 'May the gods bless you,' he said. 'You were my brother's skeuophoros!'

Idomeneus nodded and shied a step.

'I freed him for his aid,' I said. I hoped that this was within my rights. 'He served like a hero, not a slave.'

'That's my brother all over.' Kallikles smiled, and shook his head. 'Even his bed-warmer is a hero.'

Eualcidas apparently had quite a few admirers even among the Athenians, because Miltiades poured wine from a skin into a broad-bottomed cup and raised a libation to the dead hero's shade, and many men came forward to drink from that cup.

Miltiades stood at my elbow, and one by one the other warriors wandered off, until finally it was just half a dozen. Heraklides was there, and Idomeneus, of course, red with wine and the praise of his betters, Epaphroditos, now a lord of Mytilene, and Lord Pelagius of Chios. If he held my killing of his grandson against me, he hid it well.

'I drink to you, Arimnestos of Plataea,' Miltiades said. And he did. He was looking at me steadily. 'I heard that you were in the front rank – *our* front rank – at the rout at Ephesus. Aristides spoke well of you, and for that sourpuss, it was high praise. And you came off with

Eualcidas's corpse – men will sing that for some years, I can tell you.' He looked at me, with more appraisal than praise. 'But any man has one day's heroism in him. All of us, with the favour of the gods, can rise to it – once.'

Pelagius nodded. 'Too true.'

Miltiades stroked his beard. 'But Amathus sealed the bargain. I watched you clear those triremes, lad. You're the real animal, aren't you?'

'He had one *fucking* good helmsman, too,' Agios added. 'Who was it who cut the Phoenician in half?'

I had to grin. 'Not me,' I admitted.

Heraklides nodded. 'We knew that, lad. With a sword you are a titan come to life. With a ship – you may be good in ten more years.'

'I have an Aegyptian now – took him as a prisoner at Amathus. I'm hoping he'll take service with me. And teach me.' I pointed down the beach, but of course my Nubian was nowhere to be seen. 'But the artist at Amathus was a Cretan fisherman in his first fight, name of Troas.'

Agios laughed aloud. He was a small man, but he had the laugh of a satyr – threw his head back and roared until his chest heaved. 'That for my arrogance!' he laughed. 'I thought you had some veteran, some ship-killer from Aegina or Miletus.'

I kept screwing up my courage to talk to Miltiades, but I didn't want all the praise to end. Who does? I was twenty, and men of thirty-five were singing my praises. Petty matters like money should be beneath a hero. But the Boeotian farmer won out over the heroic.

'I can't afford to run a ship,' I blurted out.

Pelagius turned away, hiding a smile. Agios and Heraklides looked at the sand.

Obviously, I could have done that better.

Epaphroditos shrugged. 'I can,' he said.

Miltiades shook his head. 'No, he's mine.' He looked at me, his head slightly tilted. I think he'd known what I was coming for from the moment he saw me walking with a spear – and he'd pushed me forward as a hero to raise my value.

I blushed. I didn't have a lot of blushing left in me at the age of twenty, but I blushed then. Miltiades laughed.

'Is your city going to make him a citizen?' he asked Epaphroditos, and my friend had the sense to shake his head. 'You going to protect him against fucking Aristagoras, who wants him dead?'

Epaphroditos looked incredulous.

'Oh, yes. Our dear lord and commander wants to see this young pup's head on a spike. There's a rumour . . .' He chuckled, and looked at me. 'Hey, I can keep my mouth shut. Eh, lad?'

Epaphroditos made a noise as if he were strangling. 'He what?'

'Exactly. Whereas I'm a tyrant – I can make him a citizen of the Chersonese this instant. And only I decide who captains my ships. And frankly, Aristagoras can't survive the summer without me.' He turned to me again. 'Come – let's have a look at your ship. He looks like a heavy bastard. One of the Phoenicians you took?'

I nodded. 'Deeper and broader than a Cretan trireme,' I said. All six of us walked back to my ship.

'What's his name?' Lord Pelagius asked.

I shrugged. '*Storm Cutter*,' I said, meaning it as a joke.

'Good name,' Herk said. 'Men give ships the daftest names – gods and tritons. *Storm Cutter* is a real name.'

'I only have half a crew,' I said. I turned to Epaphroditos. 'And most of them are Aeolians. Will they stay with me?'

Miltiades cut him off. 'Doesn't really matter. I'm never short of rowers. Thracians line up outside my palisade to serve for wages.'

My men were forming two neat lines on the sand. Lekthes and Paramanos had the men mustered and ready, and they looked good.

Herakleides was at the right end of the line, and I introduced him to Heraklides – the Aeolian and the Athenian version of a son of Heracles. And then we walked down the rank of men.

'Must have been quite a storm,' Miltiades said. 'These men look like a crew.'

Then he went and looked at the ship. 'Heavy wood,' he said. 'Nice timber.' He nodded. 'What do you think?'

Agios ran a loving hand over the sternposts where they rose in a graceful arc over the helmsman. 'Tyrian. They build well.' He looked at Miltiades. 'This is a heavy ship meant to carry a heavy compliment and twenty marines. He'll be slow, even with a full compliment at the oars, and brutally expensive to maintain.'

Miltiades nodded. To me, he said, 'You have a helmsman?'

I looked at Paramanos. 'I don't know,' I said. 'I can't speak for the man I want.'

'Fair enough. That's a heavy ship. I'll buy her from you and keep you as trierarch, or I'll pay you a wage for her. Herk will work out the details.' He grinned. 'Mostly what I want is you. You're worth fifty spears now.'

I grinned back. 'I believe it, lord. But will your treasurer believe it?'

Herk bargained like a peasant. That was fine with me – I *was* a peasant. We argued like hen-wives, and I finally turned and left him on the beach. He didn't want me to own the ship. His contention was that I had less than half a crew of oarsmen, no deckhands, no marines and no helmsman.

So I tracked Paramanos down to a wine shop – that is, to a blanket awning over a couple of rough stools, with a huge amphora of good Chian wine that was buried in the sand. The shopkeeper charged by the ladleful. The wine was good.

'You have a wife and children,' I said, after asking permission to sit.

He drank some wine. 'I have a pair of daughters. My wife died bearing the second. They live with her sister.'

I nodded. 'What would I have to do to convince you to sail as my helmsman?' I asked.

He put a copper down for another cup of wine. 'Buy me,' he said. 'And aim high.'

I laughed. 'One eighth,' I said. 'That's my opening offer and my final offer.'

He raised both eyebrows.

'You know Miltiades of Athens?' I asked.

He nodded. 'The Pirate King,' he said.

I nodded. 'Exactly. He wants me to serve him. Someday, I imagine he'll stop milking the trade fleets for money and he'll go back to Athens and make himself tyrant there.' I saw a dramatic new vista opening before me – a vista where I was a nobleman, a shipowner, the sort of man who could marry Briseis. 'But I have a mind to spend a year or two making money. I'll give you one eighth of our take – in silver – if you'll serve a whole year.'

He drank more wine. 'Tell me who gets the other eighths,' he said.

'One for me, one for you, one for keeping the ship,' I rhymed off. 'One for the other officers, three divided among all the other men. One in reserve – for a crisis. If there's no crisis, then in a year, we share it out – by eighths.'

He sat back. 'I'm a merchant,' he said, 'not a pirate.'

'Fifty silver owls down,' I said. It was from my own hoard, but I had money coming from Miltiades. I let the sack clink on the table.

'Fifty silver owls bonus,' he countered, and he put his hand on the bag but did not seize it.

Who wants a helmsman who doesn't have a high opinion of himself? I had to smile, because three years earlier I had been a penniless slave in Ephesus. Fifty silver owls was a high price – but I'd seen him in the storm. Yet there was still something about him I did not trust. He was older, and more experienced – I think I assumed that was the problem. And he feared me without respecting me – that was another problem.

But he was Poseidon's own son. 'Done,' I said, and took my hand off the pouch.

He made it vanish. 'I should have asked for more,' he said. He leaned forward. 'So – do you know that two men are following you?'

I went back to Herk with the Nubian at my shoulder, and found him in another wine tent. He was enjoying a massage while drinking. I let him interrogate Paramanos and he was satisfied.

'You found yourself a Phoenician-trained navigator just lying around?' he asked. 'The gods love you.'

'The men dividing the spoils saw him only as a black man,' I said.

'More fool them. So you have a helmsman. And you think that makes the difference – that now I should hire you.' He raised his head and the man kneading his back slapped him down.

I would have laughed, but there was a familiar face peaking at me from a corner of the stall – Kylix the slave boy.

Kylix the slave boy, a foot taller and four fingers broader. He didn't look like a boy any more – he was right on the cusp between boy and man.

He grinned. My promotion from slave to free man to hero hadn't changed much, for Kylix – I'd always been a hero to him.

'Message,' he said, and put a piece of animal skin in my hand. 'And – for your ear,' he said, and I bent down for him.

'That ship of yours is so heavy I wonder if she'll fit through the Bosporus,' Agios was saying, unaware that I was listening to Kylix.

'A friend wants to see you *be* a lord,' Kylix said, handing me a leather sack. It clinked. My surprise must have shown on my face – slaves love to surprise masters. 'It is a free gift, lord.'

'How are you, Kylix?' I asked.

He shrugged. 'Me? I'm a slave.' He laughed, but it was forced. 'Maybe I'll become a sea lord, too.'

'Tell Archi I'll buy you,' I said.

'I wish you could,' he said. He looked around. 'He hates you.'

I nodded. 'I know.'

I clasped Kylix's hand. He frowned, and then looked into my eyes. 'Aristagoras has paid men to kill you,' he said. 'Like Diomedes at home.' He looked at Paramanos, and somehow I thought that he was accusing the man. Then he was gone.

Herk leered. 'Friend of yours? Nice-looking boy.'

'Someone else's slave,' I said.

'Sure.' Herk laughed and made a rude gesture. 'Learned a thing or two from the Cretans, eh?'

I grimaced. And looked in the leather sack. It held gold – dozens of gold darics. Fresh gold darics.

I was holding a small fortune. And as usual, my thoughts showed on my face.

'Good luck? Death of a rich but unloved relative?' Herk asked.

Agios peered at the bag from over my shoulder. 'The slave just gave you his life savings?'

I couldn't imagine why Archi, who spurned me in public, had just sent me so much money. With Ephesus fallen to the Medes, his own fortune must have suffered, or so I thought.

I cocked an eyebrow, though. Oh, how the former slave loves to play the great man. 'I don't think I need to hire out my ship after all,' I said.

'Really?' Herk asked. 'Your friend sent you money for rowers, too?'

How soon the bubble bursts.

'But as you are in funds, I think I can trust you to get rowers. Don't play high and mighty with me, lad – I knew you when you were a slave like yon. I'm not sure I like your Phoenician-trained helmsman and I'm not sure I think you are ready to command a ship. Does that kill our friendship?'

It was a far cry from what I'd heard all afternoon, and a good deal more like straight talk. 'But?' I asked.

'But I'll hire you on for Miltiades, at the usual rate. Two hundred obols a day. That's all found.' He smirked. 'You have to fill up your own compliment of oarsmen.'

'And fifty a day for me?' I asked. 'I assume the average man gets a drachma a day?'

It was Agios, not Herk, who cut in. He frowned. 'I didn't agree to any such foolishness. You pay yourself out of the two hundred a day.'

Now it was my turn to frown. 'That's for aristocrats, friend. They can pass it all to their men and take nothing but political profit.' I shrugged. 'I'll look for another offer. Epaphroditos made a mention—'

'He is lucky to keep command of his ship. The Aeolians are full of tyrannicides.' He smiled. 'It's good to be the officer of an Athenian aristocrat – you get to have a foot in both camps.' He looked around as if he feared interruption. 'Two hundred obols, and five drachmas a day for you.'

'Two and forty,' I said. 'I can't actually serve for less.'

'What did the Cretans do to you, boy?' he asked. 'You used to be a tender morsel. Two and ten. That's it.'

'Two and fifteen,' I said, and held out my hand.

Herk took my hand. 'Fine. But I'm going to charge you two days' pay to get rid of the two twits who have been paid to kill you. They're waiting outside.'

Fifteen drachmas a day was more than I had made with the Cretans – not much more, because the Cretans had bought my bed and board and food and clothes, good clothes, too. But the thought of men waiting to kill me scared me far more than thoughts of spending the summer fighting other men face to face. The more men you kill, the easier you know it is – and the easier you know it will be for some bastard to kill you.

But I'd be commanding a ship with Miltiades, and that was enough for me. 'Done,' I said. We spat and clasped hands. And then I left him to his massage and took my bag of gold to the *Storm Cutter*.

I still couldn't see the two men. But later that afternoon, I saw two heads on spears near Miltiades' ship. There was a board between the spears, and it said 'Thieves'.

Herk pointed them out, as if I hadn't already seen them. 'You owe us,' he said.

Somehow, those words made me feel as if my fate had been sealed.

Paramanos was recruiting, right on the beach. He was shameless – he asked every good-looking oarsman who walked down the beach if he wanted to raise his pay. Shameless twice – he was spending my money. But he'd already engaged a dozen more Aeolians.

When I came up behind him, he was talking to a big man with his back to me, but I knew the man's voice. I darted under his arm and gave him a squeeze, and then he crushed the air out of my lungs.

'Stephanos!' I said. Indeed, I'd all but forgotten the big Chian. 'Why aren't you at home?' Most of the Chian contingent had left to bring in their harvests.

He shrugged. 'I don't want to go back to being a fisherman,' he said. 'I'm a marine with Lord Pelagius.' He was proud. He had a fine quilted-linen corslet that must have come from Cyprus and a beautiful Cretan helmet.

'Well, don't talk to this Nubian too long or you'll be an oarsman on my ship,' I said.

He nodded. 'Lord Pelagius is heading home tomorrow,' he said. 'I'd be – honoured – to serve. That is, as a marine. Not as an oarsman.'

'And your brothers?' I asked. Two of them had been pulling oars. 'And any other Chians?'

In the end there were six of them, five oarsmen and Stephanos. So I went to Lord Pelagius, because that's how the Cretans did things. He was surprised – but pleased – that I'd asked.

'All free men,' he said. 'I can't hold them.' He nodded. 'When you are hailed as the new Achilles, young man, may I brag that I gave you your first award?'

I thought fleetingly of his grandson, Cleisthenes. I forced a smile. 'Yes, my lord.'

Perhaps he was thinking of his grandson, too. He nodded curtly. 'Take good care of Stephanos,' he said. 'He's a good man.'

The addition of Stephanos seemed to change everything for me. I made him my captain of marines, which might have gone to another man's head, but he'd been much talked of among the Ionians, too, and the two of us together in one ship – how many times have I blessed Lord Apollo and the day of the competitions on Chios?

Stephanos and Herakleides got along from the first, and the crew settled down to have a decidedly Aeolian flavour. Paramanos recruited promiscuously, without regard to race, Dorians and Ionians together, Aeolians and mainlanders and Asiatics. But the core was Aeolian, and their lisping, lilting accents could be heard in our camp and on every gangway of the ship.

I forgot the note Kylix had given me until a day had passed, such was the effect of the gold, and when I read it, I was shocked to see that it asked me to a meeting on a beach well around the headland – a meeting whose time had already passed. I looked long and hard at the writing, but it didn't seem familiar – indeed, the ink had scarcely left a mark on the deer-hide and was difficult enough just to read. I tossed it aside, determined to speak to Kylix about it when next we met, and my heart soared at the thought that Archi wanted to see me.

There was fear, too – what if Archi had made the first step towards a reconciliation, and he thought I had spurned it?

But my first command took all my time. I was everywhere, seeing to the underside of the ship, watching Paramanos train the oarsmen, choosing officers and arranging for the Cretans to travel home. I bled gold darics the way a sacrifice jets blood, buying better rigging, paying wages and buying a pair of slaves that Paramanos said were trained oarsmen going cheap. They proved a bargain – I traded them their freedom for a year's rowing without wages, a good deal for both parties, but I still had to pay gold for them up front.

I bought the Cretans a fishing boat, a good hull with a fine sail. Paramanos was teaching me to sail in small boats, a pleasure in itself and a wonderful way to come to understand the sea, and through him I had come in just a week to love the sleek lines of the local fishing craft. The Cretans all felt the same and squabbled about whose boat it would be when they reached home.

'It is for Troas, and his daughter,' I said.

Then Lekthes came to me and asked to go with them. 'I will come back, lord,' he said. 'But my share of the spoils will buy me my bride.'

He was an Italiote, a man from the lovely coast of southern Italy. 'You will settle on Crete?' I asked.

'After I make my fortune with you, I'll take her home to my mother,' he said.

He was one of my best men – but what kind of lord stands between his men and happiness? I let him go. I knew that if he was on the boat, the other men had a better chance of getting home alive. I gave him my second-best helmet and a new bronze thorax and a fine red cloak with a white stripe, so that men would know that he was a man of consequence. Idomeneus surprised me by giving him a fine silver brooch with garnets set in the rivets. 'For the girl,' he said.

So the Cretans sailed away with many salutations and backward looks, and Herk laughed to see them go. He and Paramanos were virtually inseparable now, playing polis in the shade of the beach-edge trees and hunting wild goats together whenever they could, or sailing one of the local fishing boats for sport.

Paramanos shook his head. 'The quality of our crew just improved threefold.'

To be honest, honey, they were happy days. And as usual, I can't remember exactly what happened when – the golden summer of my life is long ago. But I think the Cretans left first, and then I received the message that the Phoenician was waiting at Methymna. Epaphroditos told me – his people held the citadel there.

And that saved my life.

I took Paramanos and his fishing boat, with Herakleides and Stephanos to help guard the Phoenician prisoners. The four of us were enough to work the boat, and we made a party of it – three hundred stades in a fishing boat, and I was beginning to 'learn the ropes', as the fishermen say. I thought that I knew sailing and the sea – until I met Paramanos. He taught me that I didn't even know how much I had to learn, and I'm lucky the lesson didn't cost a lot of men their lives.

At any rate, we had beautiful weather. Even the three Phoenicians seemed to enjoy the trip – at least, they laughed at our jokes and ate our food with gusto.

It was early autumn, and the rain might have fallen on us, but it didn't, and we went around the long point of the islands and kept the mountain of Lepetymnos on our left hands, and before the moon rose on the third day we had the port of Methymna over the bow. I knew it from my visits as a slave, and when I was first a free man sailing with Archi. And I remembered that he had a house here, and a factor.

We beached with the fishing boats, right under the walls of the town, where a spit of rocks makes Poseidon's own natural harbour. There was a Phoenician merchant trireme on the deep beach south of the citadel. I walked up to the guard post, explained my business to the captain of the guard and received his respectful salute. He knew my name. I was flattered, and flattery put me in a good mood, so when I returned to my crew, I thought to do the Phoenicians a favour.

'Any point in waiting?' I asked.

Paramanos shrugged. 'I expect these gentlemen would like to be free,' he said.

I walked them down the beach and left them with Stephanos and Herakleides, right under the wall where the gate-guard could hear us if the Phoenicians decided to take their friends by force.

But of course, the Phoenician captain wasn't aboard. He was up in the town, being hosted by his trading partners. The war hadn't stopped trade – far from it. And Mytilene's loss was Methymna's gain.

But the fourth man – the youngest – was there. He jumped down to the beach, ran past me and threw his arms around his uncle and the other two.

'The ransom is down in the hold,' he said. 'We will sway it up in the morning.' He looked at me, and I didn't like the look. I was getting to be afraid of my own shadow. 'Or you could come and get it right now,' he said, and his smile was forced.

Now, it's hard to tell whether a man hates you because you killed his friends or whether he's just scared or whether he plans to kill you. Best to play safe.

I shook my head. 'That's good,' I said. 'And you can all spend a last night with me, until I see it.'

Then he started away, but I caught him easily, put a knife to his throat while the rest of the Phoenicians muttered angrily. I pushed him off to Herakleides and turned back. 'All four of them are my prisoners until the ransom is paid,' I said. 'I am an honourable man, but don't try me.'

My prisoners were surly now, and I was suspicious. We all slept badly under the hull of our overturned boat. We could hear voices on the Phoenician boat.

Perhaps I should have posted a sentry.

I awoke with the point of a dagger at my throat.

# 19

'You did not come when I summoned you,' Briseis said quietly.

I could see Kylix standing by the embers of our fire.

'You summoned me?' I asked, my head full of sleep. Was that *Briseis*? The arm across my chest felt familiar.

'I brought you a note,' Kylix said. 'Please tell her you received the note.'

Paramanos was awake. I could see that he had a blade in his hand, and he was moving very slowly towards Stephanos.

'I got the note,' I said. I felt like a fool, ten times over. Of course the note was from Briseis. For a man who brags about his intelligence, I can be stupid. I had wanted the note to be from Archi.

'Yet you did not come?' she asked, and her voice was like ice and fire together.

'*You* sent me fifty darics?' I asked. 'I thought that Kylix came from Archi!'

Without moving the knife, she put her mouth down over mine and kissed me.

At some point, the knife vanished and she pushed herself back up and dusted sand from her chiton. 'Walk with me,' she said. 'You still love me. That is all I required to know.'

She looked at Paramanos and he froze. 'My husband is in league with the men you are ransoming,' he said. 'He communicates with the Persians, and the Phoenicians. And he has paid them to kill you.'

Paramanos gave me a look – oh, such a look. The look that older men use when they are laughing at younger men, but when she said *paid them to kill you* he became alert.

'I'll watch,' he said.

I nodded and followed Briseis, and the two of us walked off into the first light of dawn.

She was wearing only a linen chiton – I felt that while she was kissing me. She had light sandals and a wreath of flowers in her hair, the yellow flowers of Lesbos, and she walked with her usual grace, but I could see she was just pregnant.

'Your first?' I asked.

She shrugged. 'Second,' she said. She smiled at me. 'You live!'

'You were closer to killing me than any man since I was a slave,' I joked.

'When you didn't come to meet me, I thought I would kill you.' She stopped, put her hips against a big rock and tossed her head. 'Aristagoras wants you dead. Miltiades made him swear to keep you alive, but he's a liar, and his oaths are worthless.'

'Why does he want me dead?' I asked, and she smiled like the dawn.

'Every time he fucks me, I call your name,' she said. And she laughed.

'But—' Briseis always scared me, as much as I thought that I loved her. 'But you are *married*.'

'Feh!' Her contempt was palpable. 'I am married to *Aristagoras*. If a fart could become a man, it would be Aristagoras.' She looked at me. 'And I thought you were going to kill Diomedes – eh? But he has gone over to the Medes and taken all our property in Ephesus. My brother is all but a pauper.'

I had forgotten what she could be like. Three years had made her more like herself, not less.

'I thought of you – every day,' I said.

She sighed. 'You might benefit from reading Sappho,' she said. '"Some men say a squadron of cavalry is the most beautiful thing, and some say a band of hoplites, and some think that a squadron of ships is the most beautiful."'

'But I say it is whomsoever I love,' I said to her, deliberately warping my Sappho, and she laughed.

'I hear that you are a great hero,' she added, and smiled her approval. 'I hear that you killed more Medes at Amathus than any other Greek. I love to hear men talk of you.' She rose on her toes and kissed me, and pregnant or not, only Kylix's heavy cough stopped us from making love right there. I was hard before her mouth was open and her hands – never mind, ladies.

'There is a party of armed men coming down the beach from the

Phoenician galley,' Kylix said. 'The guard is being summoned in the town.'

I had my sword, and was otherwise naked except for my chiton. My feet were bare. I had been asleep.

'Take your mistress and run,' I said.

'Run where?' Briseis asked. 'There is no entrance to the town from the sea.'

I remember shaking my head. She wanted to stay and see the blood. 'Just run,' I said, and turned back towards my own boat.

'He wants me dead, too,' Briseis said. 'He dares not do it openly, but on a beach, where you can be blamed?'

'And you thrust yourself into this lion's mouth?' I asked.

She laughed. 'You'll save me,' she said. 'Or we'll die together.'

Paramanos wasn't caught napping. As I watched, he bundled the prisoners aboard the fishing boat and put to sea. The Phoenicians came down the beach to find the birds flown.

They were all in armour and I was unarmed, which gave me an advantage – I knew that I could outrun any of them, and they didn't appear to have a bow among them. I hailed Paramanos and he ran the fishing boat down the beach to us. I put my love in the boat and pushed it off, then walked up the beach as if I had nothing to fear.

'You're up early,' I said. 'I'm Arimnestos. Have you come to pay the ransom?'

The two best-armoured men halted the rest, and they formed a small phalanx on the beach.

'The men of the town will be here in the time it takes to sing a hymn,' I called in Persian. 'And they will kill all of you and take your ship.' I pointed up the hill. 'The lord of the town is my friend – any bribe you paid the guards was wasted.'

They were arguing among themselves.

It's a lesson you learn early – plotters never trust anyone. I was nearly certain that the town garrison were going to watch me butchered and not raise a hand – but the Phoenicians didn't know that.

I pointed out to sea. 'My prisoners are out there, in that fishing smack,' I called. 'And if you don't pay up, they'll have their throats slit and be pushed over the side.'

The two men in bronze armour argued, and finally, when I could see the new sun shining on spear points in the town, they turned and went back to their ship. 'We'll pay,' one of the men said. Honey, I've seldom heard those Persian words invested with so much hate.

They stacked bars of silver on the sand.

I ran off down the beach to Paramanos, and I didn't look back.

The exchange went well enough. I rolled the silver and gold in my cloak and carried it to my boat. Then we released all four prisoners, well down the beach, almost as far as the threshing floor where the goats play.

We were gone around the point before the freed men joined their friends. Briseis asked me to take her around to Eresus. How could I refuse?

Eresus is one of the most beautiful places in the world. Briseis had made that fart Aristagoras buy her a house there, on the back side of the acropolis, good land with figs and olives, like a little piece of Boeotia in the desert of eastern Lesbos. The jasmine on the slopes of the acropolis perfumes the air, and the sun is bright on the cliffs over the town.

The people came down to meet us, then Briseis took me up to the acropolis, where I met Sappho's daughter – an old, old woman. She was strong, the lady of the town and still fully in command.

'You are her husband?' she asked.

I shook my head, no, but she smiled.

'You are her true husband,' she said.

She was an odd woman, a priestess of Aphrodite, and the lady of the Aeolian goddess, and a famous teacher. I was a tongue-tied killer in her presence, but I saw another Briseis that day – a witty, educated woman who could sing a lyric as well as an Olympic competitor.

That night we lay together in her house, with the doves cooing and the jasmine smell, and I have never forgotten it. It was the first time we had been together without an element of fear. It was different. She was different. I knew love that night – not the maddened, half-angry love of the young, but the gift of the Cyprian that turns your head for ever.

I would have stayed a second day, but Paramanos came to me, pounding on her door, and his words were hard.

'You are mad!' he said. 'And she is no better.'

And that is what is wrong with the world, thugater. Because I accepted his words. We shared a last drink of wine under her fig tree.

'You are Helen,' I said to her.

'Of course I'm Helen,' she said. 'Why shouldn't Achilles have Helen? Why can't Helen have Achilles?'

'I have to sail away from you for a time,' I said. 'Otherwise, one of us will die, or I'll kill Aristagoras and be an outlaw.'

She put her arms around my neck and it felt like the most natural thing in the world. 'When I've had my way with the world, I'll call you to me and we will make love until the sun stops in the sky,' she said. 'I'll send you a copy of Sappho's epic to pass the time.' She laughed.

I kissed her. 'I love you,' I said.

She laughed. 'How could I have doubted you? Listen, Achilles – when you have a chance, kill my husband. If you don't, I'll have to do it myself, and men will talk.' She laughed again, and ice touched my spine.

There was never anyone like Briseis. And if you know your *Iliad*, you'll know that it was on that very beach that Achilles took her.

She made me feel more alive.

She climbed the cliff while I walked down to the beach, and then she watched us sail away from the top.

I never promised you a happy story.


Miltiades was waiting for me on the beach at Mytilene. I hadn't learned, yet, that he was the greatest spymaster in the west, and knew of every event long before it happened. Indeed, his reach was long.

He embraced me as I stepped ashore, but he was curt. 'Walk with me,' he said.

He was my commander. I walked away with him, thinking of Briseis. I saw the cloud on his face and wondered how I could next see her.

'You had Aristagoras's wife in your boat,' he said.

'The bastard tried to ambush me.' I didn't know what else to say.

'He tried to ambush you when you sneaked off to fuck his wife,' Miltiades said. He turned to face me. 'That's what he's going to say.'

'She's two months pregnant!' I said – which was not, strictly speaking, a denial. 'I went to get my ransoms!'

'What ransoms?' Miltiades asked me, and he was as shrewish as a woman buying fish in the agora.

I hadn't told him, and suddenly I realized that this, not Briseis, was the real matter. 'I had Phoenicians to ransom after the fight at Amathus,' I said.

'You thought to take the money for yourself?' he asked, and his voice was dangerous.

I stopped walking. 'What?'

'The ransom for the Phoenicians,' he said. 'You sought to sneak away? You thought that I wouldn't know?' This was a different Miltiades – a sharper, more dangerous man.

'What?' I asked, foolishly. And then, 'What concern is it of yours?'

'Don't try that on me,' he said. 'Half of anything you take is mine. You expect me to squander political capital to save you from Aristagoras and then you try to steal my money?'

I stepped back. 'Fuck off,' I said. I shook my head. 'Those are my ransoms from Amathus. Nothing to do with you.'

'Half,' he said. 'Half of every penny you take. That is the price of being my man. I pay the wages on your ship. You agreed to the contract.' He spat. 'Don't act like a fucking peasant. You got more than a *talent*.'

I think that my hand went to my sword hilt, because he looked around – suddenly the great Miltiades was afraid to be alone on the beach with me. It wasn't the money, thugater. I am a killer and a lecher, but I have never been a greedy man.

But I thought that he was cozening me, and I can't stand to let other men get the better of me. 'This is my money from before the contract!' I said. 'I've promised part of it to my men!'

'That will have to come from your half, then,' he said. He crossed his arms. He was a little afraid – even then, men saw me as a mad dog. But he was bold, and he must have needed the silver.

If you want to know how great a man truly is, see him talk about money.

I sighed. 'Why didn't you come to me – like a man?' I might have said, *like a friend*, but I had just discovered that pirates have no friends.

'If you ever speak to me that way again, I'll have you killed,' Miltiades said. 'Now pay up your half, and we can forget all about this.' He was shaking with fury, and yet he was above mere insults of manhood. He didn't point at the boat behind me, but he did jut his chin at it. 'You think it's going to be easy to keep you alive after this? *He hates you*. And you come sailing back from a rendezvous with *his wife*.'

Oh, I can be a fool.

I paid. Perhaps you'll think less of me, but Miltiades was the only anchor I had in that world. I had no family and no friends, and I was living far above my birth. So I walked back down the beach, took the rolled cloak out from under the floorboards of my boat and I paid Miltiades half of the ransoms that I had earned without him.

Paramanos watched me do it without a muscle moving on his face, but I knew who the sycophant was by watching. Herakleides wouldn't meet my eye.

I couldn't believe it. He was such an upright man.

But he was an Aeolian, and such men can be bought.

Cheap.

I cursed.

Miltiades counted it out and threw me back a gold bar – an enormous sum of money. 'That's to take the sting out,' he said. 'I'm going to assume you misunderstood. Don't let it happen again, and let's just forget.' He grinned and offered his hand.

I took it and we clasped.

Miltiades looked over his shoulder. Then he looked back. I think he was measuring my value to him. I met his eye.

I trusted Miltiades. As I heard it from him, Aristagoras had plotted to kill her, and me, and that was enough.

Later, he came back and told me. 'I earned every penny of the ransom you tried to hide from me, ungrateful boy,' he said. Then he waved, always the great man. 'Forget it,' he chuckled. 'We're going to have some wonderful times together.'

I never forgot, though, and I assume he didn't either.

He sent me to sea immediately, that evening, with orders to haunt the Asian coast. It should have been a happy autumn, but the politics of the Ionian camp were vicious, and I would have done better to enquire more closely from where my fountain of gold had come. Now that I served Miltiades, I was tied to the faction that favoured the war. There was a peace faction led by none other than the author of the revolt, Aristagoras, who now espoused a peaceful solution. Men said that he had been bought by the Medes with golden darics, and other men said that he feared the Great King.

I discovered, in between short cruises in the Ionian Sea, that Miltiades had informers everywhere, and that being his man did have benefits. He heard of a pair of Phoenician biremes taking a cargo of copper and ivory up the coast of Asia for Heraklea in the Euxine. We took them off the islands – without so much as a fight – and you can be sure that I had Miltiades' half bagged and ready before my stern touched the beach.

Autumn was well-advanced when we heard that the Ionian cities of the Troad had all fallen in two short weeks, as Artaphernes took the Great King's army and besieged and captured them. Our morale plummeted, and men and ships deserted. The last of the Chians sailed away and only the Aeolians remained.

The tyrant of Mytilene demanded that Miltiades leave. Our piracy – that's what he called it – was bringing the city into ill repute. What the bastard meant was that our ongoing commercial war against the Medes was costing his city, which was losing business to Methymna, around the coast of Lesbos.

Salamis, the last free city of Cyprus, fell in late autumn.

Miltiades called his captains to council. It was a fine day, with a stiff west wind blowing. We'd been beach-bound for ten days with bad weather and no targets. The Asians were staying well clear of Lesbos, and the bad feeling between Aristagoras and Miltiades had reached a new height. Men said I was to blame. Some even said that Briseis had had an affair with Miltiades himself – foolishness, as she was eight months pregnant and hundreds of stades around the coast of the island, but that's the sort of wickedness that spreads in a divided camp.

'We're leaving,' he said. That was it – the whole council reduced to a few words. He wasn't much for a lot of talk, unless it was his own.

'Back home?' Heraklides asked.

'What do you call home, Piraean?' Miltiades asked.

'Chersonese,' Herk said. He grinned. 'Don't act the tyrant with us, lord. The wind is fair for the Chersonese and we can lie on our couches with buxom Thracians before the first snow falls.'

One of Miltiades' captains was Cimon, his eldest son. Metiochos, his second son, was his other most trusted captain. That's how the old aristocratic families worked – plenty of sons who could be trusted as war captains. I love to hear men call the Athenians 'democrats' as if any of them ever *wanted* to give power to common men. If Miltiades had had his way, he'd have been lord of the Chersonese first and then tyrant of Athens. He only loved democracy when it packed the phalanx with fighters.

Hah! I'm a fine one to talk. Look at me, lording it in Thrace. There's no hypocrite like an old hypocrite.

At any rate, Cimon was my age, a man just coming into his reputation. I liked him. And he was not afraid of his father. 'We're going back to bad wine and blonde Thracian women because Pater is under sentence of death in Athens!' he said – the first the rest of us had heard of it.

Miltiades' look told me that he hadn't intended the rest of us to know, but Cimon just laughed.

I never knew exactly when and where Miltiades and Aristagoras had started to be allies, and I never knew when they had a falling out, although I suspect that Briseis and I played our part. I still don't know. But Miltiades did all the thinking that won us the Battle of Amathus – in that much, I suppose the bastard deserved a share of my spoils. And I guess that Miltiades had no stomach for peace with the Medes – not that he hated them, but because he made his fortune preying on their ships and he needed that money to make himself tyrant at Athens, or that's how I see it now.

I should have said earlier that by the time Miltiades wanted us to leave, Aristagoras had been supplanted by his former master, Histiaeus of Miletus, who had served the Great King as a general for years and then deserted suddenly. He must have been a great fool – the Ionians were all but beaten when he joined us, and many men thought that he was a double traitor come to betray us into the hands of the Persians. In fact, I suspect he was one of those tragic men who make bad decision after bad decision – his betrayal of the Great King was foolish and dishonourable, and all his subsequent behaviour was of a piece. I only met him once, and that was on the beach at Mytilene. He was haranguing Aristagoras as if the latter was a small boy. I stayed to listen and laugh, and Aristagoras saw me, and the hatred in his eyes made me laugh louder. No one respected him by then. His failure to lead us against the Medes – anywhere – and especially to help the men of the Troad, when our fleet was just a hundred stades away, showed that he was a fool, if not a coward.

At any rate, Histiaeus's arrival was the last straw. I think that Miltiades imagined that he would become the leader of the Ionian Revolt – and eventually the tyrant of all Ionia. And they would have been better for having him, I can tell you, honey. He may have been a bastard about money, but he was a war-leader. Men loved to follow him.

I ramble. Here, mix some of that lovely water from the spring in the bowl, and add apples – by Artemis, girl, do you blush just for the mention of apples? What a delicate flower you must be – thugater, where did you find her? Now pour that in my cup.

We sailed away ahead of the first winter storm, and just as Heraklides predicted, we were soon snug on our couches at Miltiades' great palace at Kallipolis.

Aristagoras took his own retainers and fled to the mainland of Thrace. He had founded a colony there, at Myrcinus, and he abandoned the rebellion, or so Miltiades' informers reported. I wondered where Briseis was. She must be bitter, I thought – from the queen of the Ionian Revolt to the wife of a failed traitor in three short years.

The winter passed quickly enough. I bought a pretty Thracian slave and learned the language from her. I taught the Pyrrhiche to all my oarsmen, and kept them at it through the whole rainy winter, and we went together to celebrate the feast of Demeter, and the return of the sailing season.

I was another year older. I dreamed all winter of ravens, and when the flowers began to bloom I saw a pair rise from a day-old kill and fly away west, and I knew that it was an omen, that I should be going home to Plataea, but there was nothing there for me – I thought. I worried more about my oath to Hipponax and Archilogos, which goes to show what fools men are about fate.

In the spring, Histiaeus declared himself commander of the Ionian Alliance, and set the rendezvous of the fleet at Mytilene again, where he had, over the winter, made himself tyrant. He did it the simple way – his picked men infiltrated the citadel, then he killed the old tyrant with his own hands and every one of his children, too. Soaked in blood, he stepped forward to the applause – the terrified applause, I assume – of the town.

Miltiades told us the tale at dinner, shaking his head with disgust.

'Should have been you,' I said. I didn't mean it as flattery – simple fact. 'Not the killings – the lordship.'

He grinned at me. We were almost friends again – which is to say, he was unchanged, and I had almost forgiven him. Miltiades' land of the Chersonese was the most polyglot kingdom I'd ever seen – Thracians and Asiatics and Greeks and Sakje at every hand, at dinner and in the temples. If Paramanos was the only black man, he was not the only foreigner. He loved the place, and my fear about his loyalties began to relax. At any rate, that afternoon, we had been joined by Olorus, the king of the local Thracians and Miltiades' father-in-law.

He grunted. 'That Aristagoras,' he said. 'I visited him over the winter. He's a greedy fool, and if he keeps taking slaves out of the Bastarnae and the Getae, they'll kill him.'

Miltiades nodded. 'He is a greedy fool,' he said.

'Does he have his wife with him?' I asked, trying to sound un-interested.

He grinned. 'Now, that is a woman!' he said. 'By all the gods, Miltiades – count yourself lucky you didn't marry her. She is all the spine Aristagoras lacks.'

Miltiades shrugged. 'I met her on Lesbos,' he said. 'She is too intel-ligent to be beautiful.' He looked at me.

Heh, honey, that's how men like Miltiades like their women. Dumb. Fear not – I won't marry you to one of those. Miltiades' chief wife – he had several concubines – was Hegesipyle, as beautiful as a dawn and as stupid as a cow tied to a post. Olorus's daughter, in fact. I couldn't stand to talk to her. She had never read anything, never been anywhere – my Thracian slave was better educated. I know, because I taught her Greek letters in exchange for her teaching me Thracian, and then we read Sappho together. And Alcaeus.

Oh, I'm an old man and I tell these stories like a moth darting around a candle flame.

The point of telling you about that dinner is that Miltiades rose and told us that we would not be joining the rebels. 'The Ionian Revolt is only dangerous to the fools who play at it,' he said, and his bitterness was obvious. He was a man who sought constantly for greatness, and greatness kept passing him by.

Cimon was there. He had a lovely girl on his couch, I remember, because she had bright red hair and we all teased him about what her children would look like. Miltiades had red hair, too, remember.

He rose. 'So what will we do to win honour this summer?' he asked.

Miltiades shook his head, and he sounded both bitter and old. 'Win honour? There is no honour in this world. But we'll fill the treasury while old Artaphernes is busy with his rebellion.'

He had a grand plan for a raid down the Asian coast, all the way past Tyre to the harbour of Naucratis. I frowned when I heard it, because I knew the idea must have come from Paramanos.

We sailed after the spring storms seemed to have blown themselves out. We sailed right past the beach at Mytilene. They must have thought we were on our way to join them, but we didn't so much as spend the night. We stayed on Chios instead, and Stephanos gave money to his mother and impressed all his friends with his riches and then sailed away, and I was a little jealous of the ease with which he returned home and left. His sister was married now and had three sons, and I held one on my knee and thought about how quickly the world was changing. And I wondered if Miltiades was right, that there was no more honour to be had.

We fell on the Aegyptian merchants like foxes on geese. All the cities of Cyprus had fallen by then, and they didn't think there was a Greek within a thousand stades. We came out of a grey dawn, five warships, our rowers hard and strong from the trip south, and they didn't have a single trireme to protect them. I didn't even get blood on my sword. Greeks have a name for when a wrestler wins a match without getting his back dirty – we call it a 'dustless' victory. We took those poor bastards and we were dustless.

I took three merchants myself.

When a squadron came out of the port, too late to save their merchants, we scattered.

I ran south, at the advice of Paramanos. I dumped the rowers from the ships we'd taken on the low dunes of Aegypt and kept the gold and bronze and the gigantic eggs of some fabulous animal – Africa is full of monsters, or so I'm told. There was a slave girl, too – ill-use all over her, and a flinch reflex like a beaten dog. I kept her and treated her well, and she brought me luck.

We picked up another pair of Aegyptian merchants just north of Naucratis the day after the raid, ships inbound with no idea of what had happened. More silver and gold, and Cyprian copper. The bilge of *Storm Cutter* was filled so deep that we had a hard time beaching the ship, and rowing was a horror.

I beached again, carefully, fed my crew on stolen goat meat and sent the newly captured crewmen to walk back to Naucratis. Then I went west, to Cyrene. That was for Paramanos. He'd found a girl he fancied in the Chersonese, a free Thracian woman, and he'd decided to pick up his children, which filled me with joy – because that meant that he was committed to me. It was touch and go in Cyrene – the authorities knew us for what we were, but Paramanos was a citizen, and they chose not to tangle with my marines. His sister brought his daughters to the boat, clutching their rag dolls, the poor little things – they wept and wept to be put on a boat full of men, and hard men at that. But some things earn the smiles of the gods, and my Aegyptian slave girl turned out to be a fine dry-nurse. She was ridiculously thankful, now that she found she wasn't to be raped every night. And I have noticed this, honey – animals and people repay good treatment. And the gods see.

We put to sea with a strong south wind coming hot and hard off Africa. We hadn't dared to sell even an ostrich egg out of the hold in Cyrene – they didn't like us, and Paramanos feared that the council would seize the ship. I spent the whole night afraid that he would change his spots and betray us. Which shows that I had something to learn about men.

The wind was fair for Crete. We had a hold full of copper and gold and I knew a good buyer. Besides, I wanted to know how Lekthes was doing, the bastard.

I'm laughing, because most Greek captains thought that it was a great thing just to go down the coast of Asia, or across the deep blue from Cyprus to Crete, but thanks to Paramanos, I sailed the wine-dark as if I owned it, and every night he showed me the stars and how to read them the way the Phoenicians read them.

Good times.

Paramanos was showing off for his daughters and they reciprocated, turning into a pair of little sailors. Ten days at sea and they could climb masts. The elder girl, Niobe, had a trick that scared me spitless every time I saw her do it – when we were under way, rowing full out, she would run along the oar looms, a foot on each oar.

The oarsmen loved her. Every ship needs a brave, funny, athletic eleven-year-old girl.

Probably as part of his showing-off for his girls, Paramanos made a disgustingly accurate landfall on Crete, and was insufferable as a result. We walked up the beach at Gortyn's little port and were welcomed like Homeric heroes – better, in that quite a few of them were murdered. Nearchos embraced me as if he'd forgotten that we weren't lovers, and his father was decidedly warmer than I feared.

'Tell me everything!' Nearchos said. 'Nothing has happened here, of course,' he said, glowering at his father.

So I bragged a little of the raid and I talked of the sea. I was falling in love again – with Poseidon's daughters, as the fisherfolk say. But the sea bored Nearchos – boats were a tool for glory, not an end in themselves.

'You raided Aegypt?' Lord Achilles asked. 'Your Miltiades is a bold rascal. You must be a bold rascal yourself.'

I raised my cup to him and we pledged each other until I stumbled out of the hall into the rose garden and puked up an amphora of good wine. But I gave each of them a cup of beaten gold – half the wages they'd given me, returned in a guest-gift, and then they were my friends for life.

In the morning, I had a hard head, but I went to visit the bronze-smith. He wanted to buy all my copper, as I expected he would. I gave him a good price and we parted with a dozen embraces.

'Any time you want to give up piracy,' he said, 'I could make you a decent smith.'

I waved to him and went down to the fishermen's village and found Troas. He was sitting by his Lesbian boat, mending a net.

'I heard you was back,' he said. He didn't look up. 'She's wed and well wed, and it's your boy she calved first. So don't go making trouble.' Then he looked at me. 'She called him Hipponax,' he said. 'And we all thank you for the boat.'

I'd sold a pair of the eggs and all the copper. I put a bag on the upturned boat hull. 'For the boy, when he's a man,' I said. I had planned a long speech – or perhaps just a blow. I hadn't forgotten how he'd given me a boatload of fools.

But standing there on the beach, by his upturned boat, I had to acknowledge to the gods that his boatload of fools had made me the trierach I was. His hands and the gods had helped make me. Still, I glared at him.

'You nigh on killed me with your cast-off men,' I said.

'I had no reason to send my neighbours and friends with you, boyo,' he said, calmly enough.

'I got them home – even the fools,' I said.

'Aye, you're a better man than some,' Troas said. He nodded, and that was my apology.

'I'd like to see my boy,' I said.

'Nope,' Troas answered. 'My fool of a daughter took quite a shine to you, my young Achilles. She's just about over it now, and settling down to be a prosperous fisherwoman. She almost loves her husband, who's a good man and not a fucking killer.' His eyes held mine, as tough in his way as Eualcidas or Nearchos or Miltiades. Then he nodded. 'On your way, hero,' he said. 'No hard feelings.

Come back in five years, if you're alive, and I'll see to it that you and your boy are friends.'

I felt a rush of – sadness? Rage? And a lump in my throat as big as one of the ostrich eggs.

'Can I give you a piece of advice, lad?' Troas asked.

I slumped against the boat hull. 'I'm listening,' I said.

He nodded. 'You think you're happy as a hero, but you ain't. You're a farm boy. It's not too late to go back to the farm. I saw you play house with my daughter and I didn't figure you'd ever come back. But the fact that you did come back tells a whole different story.' He went back to his net. 'That's all I have for you, son.'

It is odd how quickly you go from the killer of men to the bereft boy. 'I have no home,' I said. I still remember the taste of those words, which slipped past the fence of my teeth against my will.

Troas looked at me then. Really looked at me. 'Don't give me that shit,' he said, but his tone was kind. 'Go and make one.' And he got up and embraced me – Troas, giving me a hug for comfort.

That's the way of youth, honey. One moment you are Achilles risen from the dead, the next an old net-mender feels sorry for you. And each moment is as real as the other.

I got to my feet. I was crying, and I didn't know why.

'Still some human in you, eh, boy?' he said. 'Give me another hug then, and I'll pass it to your son in a few years.' He held me close. 'If you don't leave this life soon, all you'll be is a killer,' he said.

I held him hard, and then I went back down the beach to my ship. Nearchos was waiting, with Lekthes. Lekthes was standing with a sea bag on his shoulder and all his armour nicely shined. His wife held his hand and wept. I kissed her and promised to bring him home, and then I embraced Nearchos.

'I have three ships and all the men to man them,' Nearchos said. 'When you – when you want me, call. We'll come.'

I sailed away with a lump in my throat.

# Part V

## *An Equal Exchange for Fire*

All things are an equal exchange for fire and fire [is an equal exchange] for all things, as goods are for gold and gold for goods.

Heraclitus, fr. 90

It is necessary to know that war is common and right is strife and that all things happen by strife and necessity.

Heraclitus, fr. 80

# 20

We didn't see another ship until we were north of Miletus – the rebels and Miltiades between them had swept the oceans clean. North of Samos we caught a merchantman out of Ephesus – I knew the ship as soon as I saw him on the horizon. It had been Hipponax's pride, a big, long merchant with enough rowers to be a warship. I remembered what Briseis had said, that Diomedes had taken all their wealth, and we ran him down easily enough. They used slave rowers, and slaves will never save your cargo.

With my spear at his throat, the captain admitted that he served Diomedes of Ephesus.

I took the ship as well as the cargo, and all the slaves at the oars, too. But I put the deck crew ashore east of Samos. 'Tell Diomedes that Arimnestos took his ship,' I said. 'Tell him that I'm waiting for him.' I laughed to think how the little shit would react.

And then I took my new ship back to the Chersonese. On the way, I stood in my bow and wondered at what Troas had said, and how I had cried. How could I ever give this up to shovel pig shit? I was a lord of the waves, a killer of men. I laughed, and the gulls cried.

But over on the European coast of the Chersonese, a raven cawed, the raucous sound braying on and on.

Miltiades came down to the docks to meet us, and I laid his share of the take at his feet – every obol – and he shook his head.

'Walk with me,' he said.

We walked down the beach, and I remember the smell of the sea-wrack and the dead fish rotting in the white-hot summer sun.

He put an arm around my shoulder. 'I thought you'd deserted,' he said. 'I apologize. Men will tell you that I said some things about you. But you are weeks overdue.'

'I had a lot of copper in my bilges,' I said. And it was true. 'I went to a port I know in Crete to sell it.'

He wasn't listening. 'Right, right,' he said. 'I have a note for you. From Olorus.' He handed me a small silver tube.

I opened it. It held a scrap of papyrus, and on it someone had written a verse of Sappho.

I smiled.

'I have a big draft of recruits coming in,' he said. 'You planning to crew that Ephesian ship yourself?'

'Planning to return him to his true owner,' I said. 'An old friend of mine. But I paid you your half.'

Miltiades shook his head. 'I told your father once that you were more like an aristocrat than most men I knew,' he said. 'You love this man enough to give him a *ship*?'

I had an idea – a mad idea. I'd thought about it since I'd had Diomedes' captain under the point of my sword. Or perhaps since Troas told me that I should go back to the plough and find a home.

I would need Miltiades' good will, though. So I shrugged and told the truth – always disarming with manipulative men. And women. 'I love Aristagoras's wife,' I said.

It was Miltiades' turn to shrug. 'I know,' he said. 'I've seen her. Even pregnant. And men tell me things. About you, too.'

'It is her ship,' I said.

Miltiades nodded. He turned to face me and he was a different man. He was dealing with me a new way – one warlord to another, maybe. Or one adulterer to another. 'If you send her that ship,' he said, 'her husband will take it – and lose it.'

'I thought that I might just kill her husband,' I said. *And go back to my farm in Boeotia?* I wondered.

'His people would follow you to Thule. To the Hyperboreans.' Miltiades shook his head. 'I hate the bastard, too, but if he goes down, my hand can't be in it, and that goes double for my captains. I feared you might have some such foolishness in mind.'

I turned away.

'Bide your time,' Miltiades said. 'You're young, and she's young. I assume she loves you, too? If she didn't, Aristagoras would hardly hate you the way he does.'

'Does he?' I asked. 'He's pretty dickless.'

Miltiades chuckled. 'It's true – his parts must be fairly small. But he did try to have you murdered on Lesbos,' the Athenian said. 'You'll recall that I saw to it.' He grinned. 'I've been a good friend to you.'

Ah, the delightful customs of the aristocracy.

'There's no rush,' Miltiades said again. 'Listen to me, boy.'

I was getting wiser in the ways of men – hard men. When Paramanos brought his daughters aboard, I knew he was mine – because he'd committed his life to the Chersonese. I liked him – but I *needed* him. And yes, I would have twisted his arm to keep him. The longer I spent with Miltiades, the more like him I would become. That summer, I was the highest earner of all Miltiades' captains. Briseis gave him a hold on me. He knew it, and I knew he knew it. I wasn't going anywhere.

'He looks like a good ship,' Miltiades said cheerfully. 'Crew him up and give him to Paramanos.' He looked at my new acquisition. 'When the time is right, when you need help, I'll see to it you have my aid in getting your girl. My word on it.'

Now, Miltiades was as foxy as his red head proclaimed, subtle, devious and dangerous. He lied, he stole and he would do anything, and I mean anything, for power. But when he gave his word, that was his *word*. He was the very archetype of the kind of Greek the Persians couldn't understand – the kind of man Artaphernes detested, all talk and no honesty, as Persians saw it. But when he gave his word, a thing was done.

'Even if I'm dead,' I said.

He took my hand, and we shook. 'Even if you are dead. Athena Nike, Goddess of Victory, and Ajax my ancestor hear my oath.'

And that was that.


I named the new ship *Briseis* and I kept the newly enfranchised rowers, crewing the deck and marines from Miltiades' men, including all his former slaves. Our new recruits came from Athens, three hundred men. I let Paramanos pick himself a crew from the best of them. Miltiades had an arrangement with the city – it was a secret, or so I reckoned, since even Herk and Cimon were closed-mouthed about it. But the men who came were *thetes*, low-class free men of Athens, and sometimes of Athenian allies like Plataea or Corcyra. The cities were rid of their malcontents and we got motivated men, ready to fight for a new life. Miltiades swore them to service – he was absolute lord in the Chersonese, and he didn't play games with democracy like some tyrants – and made them citizens.

He got aristocrats, too – not many, and most of them down on their luck – but he bought their loyalty with land and rich prizes and they served him as household officers and marines.

The positive side to the arrangement was that new men – former slaves – like Idomeneus and Lekthes – and me – were at home in the Chersonese. The aristocrats needed us and treated us as equals, or near enough.

Miltiades' informants said that the Great King, Darius, was tired of the pirates in the Chersonese, and intended to send a strong naval expedition against us. On the opposite shore of the Bosporus, Artaphernes and his generals, Hymaees and Otanes and Darius's son-in-law, Daurises, campaigned against the Carians. The first battle was a bloody loss for the men of bronze, and they sent to Lesbos for help from their supposed confederates, the men of Aeolis, but the new tyrant ignored them. They fought a second battle to a bloody draw, and though they lost many of their best men, they drove the Medes from Caria – for a time.

We felt like spectators – worse, we felt like truants or deserters. The fighting was so close that we could sometimes see troops moving on the opposite shore. I would train my marines with actual *sparabara*, the elite Persian infantry, visible across the straits.

By midsummer, Miltiades could take no more. He added another pair of triremes to his fleet, purchasing them from Athens, got another draft of new men to crew them, then took us to sea to attack the Phoenician squadron that supported Darius's army.

We had better rowers. Our ships, except mine, were lower and faster under oars, and we could turn faster. Miltiades insisted that we were fighting for profit, not glory, so we were cautious, attacking only when we had overwhelming odds, seizing a store ship here and a Lebanese merchant there.

By the great feast of Heracles, I couldn't stand it any more. My ship was not suited to these tactics and all my crewmen were grumbling because we were snatching at snacks while the other crews feasted.

I wonder now if Miltiades intended that I should revolt.

A great many things happened in the space of a few days, and the course of events is lost to me now. I can only tell this as I remember it. I remember sitting in a wine shop on the quay, drinking good Chian wine with Paramanos and Stephanos. Paramanos had his own ship, the *Briseis*, and he wanted Lekthes as his marine captain.

I shrugged. 'Can't you find your own?' I asked.

He laughed. 'Why not give me all your marines? You don't use them any more.' He chuckled, and I frowned. It was true. My ship was too heavy for the new tactics.

Stephanos shook his head. 'Why don't we go after them where no one can run?' he asked.

Now, it's worth saying that the Phoenician commander, Ba'ales, had a dozen warships at Lampasdis, down the Bosporus towards the Troad. Miltiades had eight ships, all smaller. We always ran when the warships came out. They always ran from us when they were outnumbered.

It was a hard summer for oarsmen on both sides.

I fingered my beard and admired my ship. I loved to sit and look at him while I had a cup of wine. 'Miltiades can't risk it,' I said. 'We only have to lose once and Artaphernes has us. He can lose two or three squadrons and he can always force Tyre to send more.'

Stephanos drank some wine, admired the woman serving it and began to dabble in the spilled wine on the table. 'I just keep thinking of the Aegyptian raid,' he said. 'No risk, no blood and a crippling blow.'

My eyes met Paramanos's over the rims of our wine cups.

'We could catch them on the beach,' he said. I had the same thought in my head.

'They must have lookouts and coast-watchers,' I said. 'All down the strait. Every three or four stades.'

'We certainly do,' Stephanos said, morosely. Indeed, every farmer on our side of the Bosporus reported on ship movements.

We broke up without any decision. But we talked about it every time we were together – catching Ba'ales on the beach, his men asleep.

And some time just after that, while I was arguing with Paramanos on the beach, Cimon brought a man up beside me.

'I can make Lekthes' career,' Paramanos was insisting.

I knew he was right. But Lekthes was closer to me than any of my other men except Stephanos and Idomeneus, and I was loath to give him up. Thugater, there is no argument as harsh as one where you know that you are wrong.

'By Zeus of the waves, you are a thankless bastard. I found you a prisoner and I've made you a captain—' I was spitting mad.

'You? Made me a captain?' Paramanos grew in size. 'Without me, you'd be at the bottom of the ocean three times over. I taught you everything you know. There's no debt between us—'

'My lords?' Cimon asked. He was my own age, of impeccable ancestry and had beautiful manners. He was already a prominent man, not least because he disdained his father's politics. Cimon always wanted to fight. What he wanted was glory – glory for himself and glory for Athens. On that day, he leaned forward, holding his staff, and the only sign that anything was amiss was the trace of a smile on his lips that suggested we were making a spectacle of ourselves.

'Your heart is as black as your skin, you fucking ingrate!' I did say that.

'And which of us is a former slave? I can smell the pig shit on you from here, turd-flinger!' Paramanos pointed a finger at me. 'You are like all dirt-grubbers – you can't stand to see another man succeed. You think it makes you fail! Lekthes deserves—'

Cimon stepped between us. 'My lords?' he said again.

'Keep out of it, Cimon. I'm tired of his poaching my best crewmen.' I was equally tired of how, now that he was an independent captain, Paramanos was the highest earner. It suggested that he was right – he had made me. And that enraged me.

Some friend. Youth is wasted on the young. I knew he was right about Lekthes, and I suspected that he was right about how much I owed him.

'Arimnestos?' asked a voice I knew.

The man standing at Cimon's side was dressed like a peasant, in a dirty hide apron over a stained chiton, with a dog's-head cap on blond curls. The name was said so softly that I wasn't sure I had heard right, and I turned, my tirade draining out of me.

'Arimnestos?' he asked again, and his voice was stronger, happier.

'Hermogenes?' It took me a moment. I hadn't seen him for eight years. He was a man, not a boy. He had a bad scar on his face, a cut that went from the top of his scalp to the top of his nose.

He grinned as if he'd just won the Olympian Games. 'Arimnestos!'

We fell into each other's arms.

Such was my happiness – the instant, life-affirming happiness of rediscovering a friend from home – that I burbled the story of my life in a hundred heartbeats, leaving out everything that mattered, and then turned to Paramanos.

'I'm a fucking idiot,' I said. 'Lekthes needs to go and be an officer. And I do owe you my life.'

That shut him up. Ha! What a tactic. Capitulate utterly. Leaves your opponent with nothing to say. He sputtered, and then he embraced me.

We sat in my favourite wine shop, Hermogenes and me, Lord Cimon, Miltiades' son, and Herk.

'You never came back,' Hermogenes said. He was happy and angry at the same time. 'We waited and waited, and you didn't come back to camp. And then Simonalkes came back and said that you were dead.' He shrugged. 'I searched the battlefield for your corpse and I couldn't find you. I asked everyone – even Miltiades. He knew who you were, and he knew where your father had fallen.' He looked at me. 'You've changed,' he said accusingly. 'You haven't talked to Miltiades about any of this?'

I shrugged. 'No,' I said. 'He doesn't concern himself with petty things.'

'Petty?' Hermogenes asked. 'Petty? Arimnestos, your cousin Simonalkes has married your mother and taken your farm. Is that nothing to you?' He drank down his wine. 'My father sent me – I don't know, three years back? Sent me to Athens to find Miltiades – and you, if your shade was still in your body. Simonalkes always said that you were dead – killed in the last rush of the Eretrians. But there was no body.' He looked at me. 'What happened?'

I felt a rush of memory. It wasn't that I had hidden the memories, it was only that I hadn't thought about them – I hope that makes sense, honey. Young people live in the moment. I had lived in the moment for eight years. Hidden, if you like. Men in stories rush home to avenge their fathers. I had been a slave. I didn't want to go home.

Sometimes, in the silence of my slave cubicle at Hipponax's house, or on my bed in Lord Achilles' palace, I would think of home. Sometimes I would dream of ravens flying west, or I would see a raven and I would think of home – always a home with Pater and my brother. As if they were alive.

But they weren't alive. They were dead. And I knew, as soon as I let myself think about it, that Simonalkes had killed my father. I could see him, turning away from the fighting line, the fucking coward, his sword red at the tip, and Pater falling. Stabbed from behind.

It is like the difference between hearing that your woman is sleeping with your friend and finding them together in your bed. Hermogenes was *there*. It was time to face the facts.

'I was sold into slavery,' I said, slowly. 'I was at Ephesus, as a slave. For years.'

Hermogenes pursed his lips and fingered the scar on his forehead. 'That would have been hard for you, I think,' he said. There spoke a man who had been a slave.

'It was hardest at first,' I said, and I told him about the slave pens. More than I've told you, actually. He was born a slave, and in our family. He was never sold, nor bought.

'That was – terrible,' he said. 'Zeus Soter – I never had to do any of that. Pater did, though. He's told me the story, a dozen times – how he was taken, how he struggled and failed to escape, and how your father bought him.' Hermogenes shrugged. 'Simonalkes tried to re-enslave us, but old Epictetus stuck up for us. Thanks to him, Pater is a citizen now.'

'And you've been looking for me for three years?' I asked.

He shrugged. 'On and off, friend. I had to eat.'

'What did you do?' I asked.

He looked at the wine shop table. 'Things,' he said. 'A little carp-entry. Some gardening.' He took a sip of wine. 'Some theft.'

'By the father of the gods,' I said, 'how did you come here?'

He flexed his shoulders and rubbed his scar again. 'An Athenian magistrate gave me the choice: come here or have an ear cut off.' He smiled. 'Not a hard choice. And then, when I was waiting in a warehouse with a bunch of other lowlifes, I heard a man mention your name – he said we'd be fighting under Miltiades of Athens, and Cimon, and Arimnestos Doru. When I got here, Cimon took me for his crew. He said that you were a Plataean. It seemed too much to hope. But here we are.'

Cimon shook his head. 'What a tale!' He looked at me. 'I take it this man is your friend, as he claimed to me.'

I nodded. 'Absolutely.'

Cimon smiled. 'I shouldn't give him to you. For the things you shouted at Paramanos.'

I hung my head. 'I was in the wrong,' I said.

Cimon shrugged. 'You know what I like about you, Arimnestos? That you can say it – just like that. "I was in the wrong."' He nodded. 'Have your friend, and may your friendship always be blessed. You owe me an oarsman.'

'I'll see to it you get the best I have,' I said. Having Hermogenes sitting by my side was like a drink of clean water on a hot day, for all that his news disturbed me.

'I don't need your best. He may be your friend, but he's a scrawny sewer rat. Send me another and we're quits.' Cimon rose. His eyes grew serious. 'This man Simonalkes really murdered your father, Doru?'

I nodded.

Cimon made a face. 'You *have* to do something about that, don't you?' He shrugged. 'Some day, some bastard – probably an outraged husband – will kill Pater. And then I'll have to kill him, or the furies will haunt me.'

Suddenly, with the clarity of long-delayed realization, I understood the raven dreams. 'Yes,' I said.

Cimon nodded. 'Pater will have a fit if you leave before the sailing season ends,' he said.

He raised an eyebrow and left us alone.

The next day, I took Hermogenes for a sail with Paramanos, Stephanos, Lekthes and Idomeneus. Hermogenes already looked better, cleaner, wearing a new chiton and new sandals. I'd armed him and put silver in his purse. He was two finger's breadths taller when he was clean and dressed. I hadn't had a hypaspist since Idomeneus rose to warrior status, and Hermogenes took the job immediately. It made him laugh to dress so well – it was days before he stopped hiking his chiton to look at the purple stripe.

Paramanos wasn't even angry. He just shrugged. 'Angry men talk shit,' he said with a smile. 'I don't need a picnic on the sand to make it better.'

'You'll want to be at this picnic,' I said.

We had a fishing smack, a light craft, lovingly built, with a single mast. We took turns sailing it, racing along the Bosporus in a way that real fisherman would never risk their rigging or their boat. Hermogenes looked anxious and Stephanos shook his head at what he, a lifelong fisherman, saw as recklessness.

We sailed down the Bosporus for twenty stades and put in at a gravel beach well south of Kallipolis with an old shrine to a hero long forgotten. I sacrificed there sometimes. So I went ashore first, and Hermogenes and I sacrificed a lamb in thanksgiving, and then we all had potted hare and chicken and lamb and lots of wine.

After we ate, Paramanos sat back, poured a libation and we all shared a cup. Then he rose. 'Well?' he said. 'Is this all by way of apology? Or because you've rediscovered your friend?'

I shook my head. 'No. I know how to come at Ba'ales' squadron.'

Paramanos nodded. 'I thought as much. So – tell?'

Instead of telling, I pointed at the upturned hull of our smack.

Paramanos shook his head. 'Brilliant,' he said. He shook his head. 'Why didn't I think of it?'

That was that.

And it was that week, or the next week, that an ambassador came to us from the Carians, begging us to help them. I was invited to hear him, and Paramanos came with me. We lay on couches with Miltiades and his sons, Agios and Heraklides and the other captains, and the Carians asked us to help them with the Persians.

'Anywhere we go, Ba'ales can drop troops behind us on the coast,' the lead Carian insisted. 'You have a great reputation as a lover of freedom. Men say you were the architect of the great victory at Amathus. Can't you defeat Ba'ales?'

Miltiades shook his head. 'No,' he said. 'And I no longer serve the Ionians.' He shrugged. 'I'm a pirate, not a liberator.'

Callicrates, the leader of the embassy, shook his head. 'We thought you might say such a thing.' He handed over a gold-capped ivory scroll tube – the kind that the Great King used. 'We captured this.'

Miltiades took it and unrolled the scroll. He read it by the light of the window, and then handed it to Cimon. Cimon read it with Heraklides and then Herk brought it to me, and Paramanos and I read it together.

It was a set of orders. The orders were to Ba'ales and his subordinates. They were ordered to raise twenty more ships and take Kallipolis and our other ports, and also the Thracian coast, including Aristagoras's town.

'The new ships are almost ready,' Callicrates said.

Miltiades looked angry. 'Why don't I know any of this?'

'There have been rumours,' Cimon said. His brothers nodded.

'Plenty of time to run for Athens,' Miltiades said bitterly. 'I can't fight thirty ships.'

I looked at Paramanos. 'My lord – if I may. I have a way you can knock Ba'ales out of the campaign – for this year, at least. Very little risk – at least, for you.'

Miltiades was leaning on his hands, staring out of the window. He turned. 'Really?' he asked. His voice said that he didn't expect much. Like most arrogant men, Miltiades assumed he'd thought of everything.

'In short, my lord, I propose that we catch Ba'ales at dawn and take or burn his ships while they are beached.' I sat up on my couch.

'No,' Miltiades sounded like a bored schoolteacher talking to stupid children. 'His coast-watchers will see us coming.'

I smiled. 'Fishing boats,' I said.

The story of the boat raid has been told so often that I won't bore you with it. Every fisherman in these waters can tell you how we borrowed their boats, sailed down on the outflow from the Euxine, as the fishing fleet does every evening in summer, and caught Ba'ales on the beach at moonrise.

It was slaughter. We had just two hundred men, all fighters – the pick of Miltiades' men. The only hard part was the last ten stades – when we could see their hulls, black in the moonlight, and we could see their fires, and for all we knew, they were lining the beach ready for us.

They were not. Someone gave the alarm when we were a stade out, but they never got formed. We raced the last stade, rowing our open boats as if they were triremes. My boat went a man's length up the gravel beach when it hit, and I was over the side almost dry-shod, with Stephanos on one side of me and Hermogenes on the other.

Paramanos had one half of the men. Their mission was to secure our retreat by taking the likeliest of the enemy triremes and getting it afloat. My men were to set fire to the rest of the ships and kill as many oarsmen as we could.

Those ships burned like torches. We had fire pots rigged on poles, heavy crockery filled with coals, and we smashed them *inside* the enemy hulls as we went, two pots per hull. They were afire before the enemy recovered, and we were armoured men, formed at the edge of the firelight against the desperation of an unarmed rabble.

The sad truth is we burned too many – we could have taken more. Our two hundred men broke the Phoenicians. Most men fight badly when surprised, and they were no different. Ba'ales died in the first attack, although we didn't know it. I hardly fought – I was too busy giving orders.

By Athena Nike, we drove them! Where they were brave, we

killed them, and where they ran, we reaped them. Hah! That was a victory.

When it became clear that we were masters of the field, we managed to beat out the fires in one of the smallest of the enemy ships still on the beach, and we turned it over in the water, doused the embers and got it afloat too. So we managed to capture two of their dozen hulls, while the rest burned to their keels, and we got away with ten dead and as many wounded. Only Ares knows how many of their oarsmen and marines we left face down on the sand. We rowed, tired but happy, back up the Bosporus, towing the fishing boats in long lines behind us.

It sounds wonderful that way, doesn't it? That's the way a proper singer tells a battle, without mentioning that the ten dead men were dead, and their children were fatherless, their mothers widows, their lives over, perhaps for ever, because Miltiades chose to remain master of the Chersonese. Eh?

And another thing, though it shames me to tell it. I don't always remember men's names. The men who fell there on the beach? Making my reputation and saving Miltiades? I can't remember them. The sad truth, honey, is that some time that summer I stopped learning their names. They died in raids, in little ship fights and of fevers. Men died every week. They came out from Athens, lower-class men with nothing to lose, and most of them brought their deaths with them. Some were too weak. Some never learned to handle their weapons.

We were pirates, thugater. I can coat it in a glaze of honey, set it in epic verse, but we were hard men who lived a hard life, and it wasn't worth my time to learn the new men's names until they'd survived for a while.

Don't mind me. I philosophize.

At any rate, the next morning the Carians ambushed Daurises' columns as he tried to push into the mountains west of the Temple of Zeus of the Army at Labraunda in Caria, and destroyed them, killing Daurises and quite a number of Persians – the first real victory of the whole war. The news went through the Ionians like a bolt from Zeus, and sacrifices appeared on Ares' altars from Miletus to Crete.

I didn't know it at the time, but Pharnakes, who had been my friend, and with whom I had twice crossed swords, died at Labraunda in the ambush.

In the aftermath of these two small victories, we heard that Darius had lost all patience with the revolt, and with Greeks in general. He ordered his satraps to prepare a major armament for the reduction of the Chersonese, and he bragged that he would see Athens destroyed.

That didn't please the democrats in Athens, who were aware that Miltiades was responsible for Darius's anger. But that's not part of my story – just a comment.

As summer gave way to autumn, Miltiades received word from various sources about Darius's preparations. He had ordered fifty ships to be levied from the Syrian towns, and the satrap of Phrygia was to aid Artaphernes in raising an army to destroy Caria and retake Aeolis.

We lay back on our couches and laughed, because that would all happen next summer. There was only six weeks left in the sailing season.

Miltiades toasted me in good Chian wine. 'One stroke,' he said, 'and I am once again master in my own house. You are dear to me, Plataean.'

I frowned. 'Next summer, Darius will come with a vast army.'

Miltiades would not be sober. 'For all your heroism,' he said, 'you have a great deal to learn about fighting the Medes.' He looked at Cimon.

Cimon laughed and spoke up. 'Other provinces will revolt this winter,' he said.

Miltiades nodded. 'You think we hit Naucratis for pure profit?' he asked me. I could see Paramanos grinning. I *had* thought we went there for pure profit.

'Yes,' I said.

Miltiades nodded. 'Not to be spurned, profits. But when we took their ships, we showed the Greek merchants and the Aegyptian priests that their Persian overlords couldn't defend them. And when it appears that we are winning, they will evict their garrisons as they did in my father's time, and Darius will have to bend all his will to Aegypt. And then we will have lovely times!' He laughed. The whole Greek world was speaking of our coup on the beach south of Kallipolis, and Miltiades' name was on every man's lips in Athens, and all was right in the world.

It was a good dream, but we had underestimated Darius, and we had forgotten those twenty ships that were on their way to reinforce Ba'ales.

# 21

That night, I asked Miltiades for permission to go home once the sailing season ended. Miltiades heard me out and nodded. He was a good overlord, and he had a reputation to protect. Besides, I had just put new laurels on his brow.

'Go with Hermes, lad. In fact, I'll see to it that Herk or Paramanos runs you home. Take a couple of men – you'll want to kill the bastard and not take any crap from neighbours.' He nodded. 'Anything you need, you ask. It's as much my fault as anyone's. I knew something was wrong – I didn't give it enough thought. When your father died, I mean.'

He shrugged. I knew what he meant – when the Plataeans helped Athens defeat the Eretrians, Miltiades was done with that part of his busy plotting, and he let his tools drop. That was the sort of man he was. But he was also enough of a gentleman to regret that he had allowed the tools to become damaged when he dropped them.

I spent the next few weeks making arrangements for my absence. I didn't tell Miltiades, but I wasn't sure that I *would* return.

I gave Herakleides one command and Stephanos the other.

Herakleides and his brothers were trusted men by then, and they showed no signs of running back to Aeolis. Both Nestor and Orestes were promising helmsmen, and they had the birth and military train-ing to carry rank.

Stephanos did not. He wasn't an aristocrat, and he didn't have all the command skills that I had learned – nor the enormous, heroic and largely unearned reputation that I had acquired, which grew with every day and vastly exceeded the reality of my accomplishments, even though I was in love with it.

Reputation alone is enough to carry most men – but Stephanos was a fine seaman and a careful, considerate officer. He'd led the marines for a year and they worshipped him. I thought that he was ready.

Idomeneus informed me that he was coming with me. So was Hermogenes. 'You think I came all the way out here just to grab a pot of Persian silver?' Hermogenes asked. 'Pater sent me to find you so that you could restore order. Simonalkes is a bad farmer and a fool. But when he's dead, it will take time to rebuild.'

I found it comic that Hermogenes had spent three years looking for me so that he could get the farm in order.

Paramanos offered to take me home, all the way to Corinth if I wanted, but I had other plans. Plans I'd worked at for a long time.

Miltiades supported me as I moved captains. So Paramanos moved from *Briseis* to the newly rebuilt *Ember*, the ship we'd taken, still smoking from our attempt to burn her, during the boat raid. The smaller ship we'd taken was *Raven's Wing*, and Stephanos had her, and Herakleides took command of *Briseis*. I had *Briseis* stowed for a long voyage, and I gave him his own two brothers as officers – Nestor as the oar master and Orestes as the captain of marines. I spent money like water – I had plenty. And the rowers in that ship still owed me three months of service before wages were due.

I intended to sail that ship into Aristagoras's town at Myrcinus, in Thrace, and take Briseis – or give her the ship and go horseback, overland. It was a foolish plan, a boy's plan, but without it, the next weeks would have been worse. It is a fine example of fate, and how the gods work. Had I left all to chance, I would have died, and many others with me. But I planned carefully. My plans all failed, of course – but among the shards of my broken plans lay the makings of an escape.

The first rain of autumn came and went, and my intentions were set. I sent Briseis a message via the Thracian king, asking her to be ready. Miltiades cautioned me again – directly – against killing Aristagoras. I don't remember what I told him. Perhaps I lied outright. I thought myself tremendously clever. So did Miltiades. The hubris flowed thick and fast, that autumn.

The grain was sheaved in the fields along the Bosporus. The peasants had their harvest festivals, and the sun shone in an autumn that seemed more like summer – when Hymaees descended on the Troad with thirty ships and a thousand marines. The first we knew of his arrival was that our southernmost town was burned and all the inhabitants sold into slavery, and the refugees poured up the one bad road with tales of war and slaughter.

The next day we heard that Hymaees himself was in Caria with twenty thousand men, and the Carians were unable to make a stand. Just like that, the northern arm of the revolt was going down.

The Carians didn't give in without a battle, but we were too busy to help them. Miltiades ordered all the ships manned. We worked night and day to refurbish the two triremes taken in the night attack and with them we had ten hulls. On the first day of the new month, Miltiades led us to sea, down the Bosporus past the still smoking ruins of our town. He had no choice – if we didn't fight, Hymaees would plug the Bosporus like a cork in a bottle and take us, one town at a time. And no one would come to our aid. That's the price of being a pirate.

We sailed down the Bosporus in early morning, and the Phoenicians got their hulls in the water. Then they did the oddest thing. They formed a defensive circle. They outnumbered us, but they pulled all their sterns together, pulled in their oars like a seabird tucking in its wings, and waited for us.

I had never seen anything like it, but Miltiades had. He spat in the sea and leaped from his ship on to my *Storm Cutter*. 'Bastards,' he said. 'All they have to do is *not lose.*' He shook his head.

I nodded. 'Say the word, lord – say the word and I'll go at them.'

Miltiades slapped my armoured shoulder. 'I'll miss you when you leave me, Arimnestos. But there's no point.'

He went back to his own ship, and we spent a fruitless day circling them. Twice, Paramanos tried to lure one of them into an attack by passing so close that his oar tips almost brushed their beaks, but they weren't coming out.

We camped close to them, just four stades up the coast, and the next morning we went for them in the dawn by ship, but they were awake and ready. We threw javelins and they shot bows and I went ashore in the surf and cleared a space on the beach, killing two men in the surf, but Miltiades ordered me back to my boat. I took a pair of prisoners – Phoenicians, of course – and I gave them to Paramanos.

I still think Miltiades was wrong. We had the moral advantage – those Syrians were afraid of us. If we'd landed—

But he was the warlord and he saw it differently.

That night Paramanos called us all together. 'There are ships missing,' he said. 'The two boys that Arimnestos captured say that eight ships went north last week.'

Miltiades was incredulous. 'Eight *more* ships?' he asked.

'Where bound?' I asked.

Paramanos looked at me. 'Myrcinus, in Thrace,' he said. 'They went to get Aristagoras.'

I walked away, calling for my officers.

Miltiades chased me down. 'You are not going,' he said.

I ignored him.

'This is my fleet,' he said.

'I own two ships,' I said, 'perhaps three. I owe you nothing, *lord*. I was leaving anyway. And I am going to Myrcinus.'

He seemed to swell, and in the torchlight, his hair caught fire. He was like a titan come to life – larger than a mere man. 'I give the orders here,' he said.

'Not to me,' I said. 'I have your *word*.'

That took him aback, and he changed tack. 'There's nothing you can do, lad!' he said, his voice suddenly pleading. He was a good rhetorician. 'The town will already be on fire.'

'You don't know that. It rained two days last week. If the storm caught them on the coast, they would have lost days.'

'Give it up!' he said.

I walked away. My men – my trusted men, Lekthes and Idomeneus and Stephanos, Herakleides and Nestor and Orestes, and Hermogenes – got the rowers together and started loading *Storm Cutter* and *Briseis* and *Raven's Wing*.

But Herakleides, always the voice of reason, came up to me out of the dark and wouldn't let me act in anger. 'Miltiades has been a good lord to you, and you owe him better than this,' he said. And he was right, although at the time I growled at him.

Herk fed me a cup of wine, his arm around my shoulders. My men were standing around, waiting for my word, and there was some pushing and shoving at the edges between them and Miltiades' men.

'This won't end well,' Herk insisted. 'Listen to me, boy. I knew you when you were a new free man. A pais. You're a big man now, a captain, lord of five hundred rowers and marines. Every merchant in the Aegean pisses himself when your name is said aloud – but you are nothing without a base and a lord. And if we squabble with Miltiades, who will fight the Medes?'

'I am *not* nothing,' I said. But I knew that he was right. I couldn't keep a crew together by myself – unless I wanted to engage in pure piracy, bloody murder for profit. And I did not. Heraclitus was too strong in me, even then. In fact, what I liked least about Miltiades was his ceaseless search for profit.

I remember sitting there, on a damp rock just above the tide line, my feet in the sea-wrack, when I heard a raven – not a gull, but a raven, cawing in the dark, like Lord Apollo's voice speaking. I held up a hand to silence Herk and I listened, and then I got to my feet and walked off down the beach to where Paramanos and Miltiades were arguing. Herk followed at my heels, clearly afraid I was about to open the breach – but I was not. The god had given me the answer, and I thrust between Paramanos and Miltiades and shouted for them to listen. Their faces were backlit by the big fires we had burning at the sentry posts – we didn't want the Syrians to surprise us, either.

'We should all go,' I said.

That silenced them.

I almost remember what I said. I felt as if Lord Apollo stood at my side, whispering fine words, good arguments, into my ear. Or perhaps Heraclitus, his servant.

'Listen, lord. You think I am blinded by love – perhaps I am. But if the Mede is foolish enough to send eight ships away, we can catch them and destroy them. And then the balance is ours. It might make him hesitate. It will increase our power over the Phoenicians.' I paused. 'If we *take* those ships—'

Honeyed words, Homer calls them. No sooner were they out of my mouth than Paramanos was agreeing. Sometimes, there is a right answer – an answer that suits every man. It took us less time than it takes to heat a beaker of wine to convince our lord that we had a winning strategy, and then he grinned, drank wine and clasped my hand, and we were friends again, instead of rival pirates.

We left in complete darkness. That was the campaign where I learned the value of having *all* my men in high training – the value of making my rowers feel as elite as the hoplites felt. We left that beach like champions. We left our fires burning to deceive the enemy and we raced north under oars, and every man felt as if he was swept along on Nike's wings.

*

We came on Myrcinus as the sun set on the third day. The lower town was afire and the Syrian ships were drawn up on the rocky beach south of the town.

Miltiades summoned me aboard his ship, and I leaped from my helmsman's rail to Paramanos's and then on to the *Ajax*, the black-hulled Athenian trireme that was Miltiades' pride. Cimon and Herk were already there. We never slowed – we were under sail, the wind under our sterns, and our sails must have looked like flowers of fire in the ruddy light.

Miltiades' face was lit as if from within. He was a foot taller than a mortal man, his hair glowed in the sunset as if he was an immortal and his words flowed thick and fast.

'Beach your ships as you find room,' he said. 'Get ashore, get their ships and sweep the beach clean. Paramanos, you and Arimnestos land your full compliment, every man on the beach. Form tight and get between us and the town.' He grinned. 'Once we own those hulls, this campaign is over. Their commander is a fool.'

'Or it is a trap,' his younger son said. He shrugged.

Cimon, the older son, shook his head. 'Don't be a stubborn ass, little brother. There's no trap because they shouldn't know we could even *be* here!'

Miltiades nodded his approval of his older son's thinking. 'Even if it is a trap,' he said, 'there's not much they can do to us if we keep our ships manned and only land our marines. You two can cover us on the beach – if we have to run, your crews are fast.' He laughed. 'Oh, I can feel the power of the gods, companions! We are about to burn the Great King's beard!'

We were five stades off the beach when I leaped back to Paramanos's ship. The Medes and the Syrians could see us coming, and men were running down from the burning town to form on the beach. Most of them were Greeks – I could see from their arms. In the centre was a knot of Persians, but their line wasn't long enough to cover the whole length of the beach, even two deep.

But there were other men – Thracians. Some of them came down from the town in clumps, like thick honey dripping from the comb. Others hung back.

The enemy commander had hired Thracians. It probably wasn't hard, because from all we heard, the locals detested Aristagoras as much as we did. I had never faced them, but I heard that they were titans, big, tough men with no fear of death. I always doubted such tales, but the men I could see in the red light of sunset had tattoos like black slashes on their faces and around their arms, and they held heavy swords and long spears.

'I'm going for the town as soon as we break their line,' I said to Paramanos. 'I know that you don't have to follow me.' I looked at him.

He shrugged. 'No,' he said. 'I don't.' He pointed at the Thracians – there were more of them every heartbeat. 'You think we can break that?'

We were three stades out from the beach. I got up on the rail where it rose to protect the helmsman and balanced there, waiting for the rise of the wave. 'Watch me,' I boasted, and jumped.

I landed on my own deck. 'Bow first!' I said. 'Marines aft! Empty the first ten benches forward and send all those men aft!' I waved at my deck master. 'Sails down! Then masts!'

The other ships were starting to turn, because they intended to beach stern first – a necessary precaution to prevent their ram-bows from digging so deep into the sand and gravel that the ship was damaged – or worse, could never be brought off.

I caught a stay and swung up on the rail. 'Stephanos!' I called. He was behind me in line, in the smaller *Raven's Wing*. I had to wait while he came forward – precious time, while my bow rowers ran back, dragging their cushions, unsure what they were supposed to do – while the deck crew swarmed over the masts, caught in the midst of arming, and the marines clustered by the helmsman's bench. Hermogenes was in full armour, and Idomeneus looked like a hero in a solid bronze thorax with silver work and a fine helmet with a towering crest shaped like a heron.

'My lord?' Stephanos called back.

'Into the port!' I said. 'Land your full crew and take the Thracians from behind! See?'

Indeed, the little port itself was covered by a mole. There were two ships moored to the mole, and no defenders – because the lower town had been lost, so there was no longer any point in holding the harbour. Before the lower walls fell, there had no doubt been a garrison on the mole. I had seen this and Miltiades had not. If *Raven's Wing* could get into the harbour, her marines would be *behind* the enemy line.

Stephanos turned away, already calling orders, and his ship turned, went to ramming speed and sprinted for the mole.

'On me!' I shouted, and ran forward as far as the amidships command station at the foot of the mast. 'Get that mast down!' I called to the deck crew – who looked like hoplites. Pirates are always better-armed than other men, with the pick of many dead men's gear to plunder, and I dare say that my sailors had better armour than the front rank of many a city.

The deck crew let the mast down on to the central gangplank, with all the marines and thirty rowers to speed things along.

We passed the other ships, who were all still turning or backing ashore. The smaller *Ember* was already halfway around.

I had just time to line up the marines and sailors and rowers behind me. They filled the central catwalk all the way aft to the helmsman, and filled the small deck around him, pushing the stern down in the water and raising the bronze-tipped bow. The weight of the mast and the sail helped, too. I pushed the men farther back, and again, pushing against them with my shield to pack them tight in the stern.

'When we beach,' I roared, 'every man follow me! We will form under the bow and cut our way up the beach! Our war cry is "Heracles!"' I looked aft and raised my spear, and my voice filled my chest like the sound of a god. '*Are you ready?*' I shouted, and the oar master shouted 'Oars in! Brace!' and we struck.

Our bow went right up the beach. I was too far aft to see it, but I'm told that our ram actually broke their line, scattering men to the right and left.

'Follow me!' I called and raced forward between the oar benches, along the catwalk, over the bow, and I jumped without breaking stride into a clump of Ionian Greeks still shocked by the arrival of the ship.

They had no order, and I got my feet under me and my spear licked out and ripped the back of a man's knee behind his greave. Blood spurted, red as red in the dying sunlight, and then I looked at a second man, my eyes locking with his under the bronze brows of our helmets, and my spear shot out and caught *another* man – oldest trick in the world – caught him between his thorax and his helmet, ripping up his chest and plunging deep into his neck, stealing his life. He fell off the spear point and I reversed my spear, thrusting underarm with the butt-spike. I thrust deliberately into the aspis of a fourth man. He was trying to retreat – under my feet, the sand thumped as other men came off the *Storm Cutter*'s bow. I knew that in a fight like that, I had to attack – attack and keep attacking until my arm failed me, because as soon as they recovered from the shock, they'd turn back into warriors and kill me.

My butt-spike stuck in the bronze face of his shield. I ripped it out and thrust again, knocking him back and off balance by attacking his shield. I could *feel* Idomeneus behind me, so I pushed forward, thrust into my opponent's shield and when the tip stuck I used it as a lever and prised his aspis to the right. Idomeneus killed him with a quick thrust over my shoulder.

All my marines were on the beach, and my deck crew was pouring in behind them, the shield wall forming, hardening the way bronze hardens when you pour the molten stuff on a slate floor to make a sheet, and even as the wall solidified we pressed forward up the beach.

The Ionian Greeks I had been fighting were in flight, and I risked a look – pushed my helmet back on my brow and looked left and right. To the left, the town burned, throwing an evil light on the beach. On the road from the town were two hundred or more Thracians. Their leader was inciting them to deeds of valour, or simply promising them loot – I didn't understand a word of his language, but I knew what that body language and those gestures meant.

The other ships were landing. *Briseis* was stern to stern with my *Storm Cutter* and Herakleides was sending his marines right down *Storm Cutter*, over the bow and onto the beach, leading his men himself. Oh, I loved him like a brother that hour.

To my right, the big knot of Persians and Phoenician marines was wheeling towards me, intent on pushing me off the beach before the other ships were ashore.

My men were like the runners in the fight at the pass. We were drawing all the enemy to us, while the other ships got their marines ashore. I knew the game. I roared defiance at them. I *was* Ares. I raised my spear over my head and told them they were all dead men, in Persian.

I had no intention of awaiting the onset of the enemy. If I waited, the Persians and the Thracians would hit me together – and each of them outnumbered me. On the other hand, my rowers were coming over the sides now, and every breath put three more men in the rear ranks.

'The Persians!' I shouted, and I ran forward a few paces and held my spear parallel to the enemy line. 'On me!'

We'd been together all summer. My crew knew what I wanted,

and they were beside me in three long breaths, more than a hundred men. A ship's length to my right, I saw Herakleides' black horsetail and I knew his big aspis was locked into the line.

'Heracles!' I roared.

'HERACLES!' came the response like the thousand-fold voice of the god, and we were off up the beach. The Phoenicians had no bows, and the handful of Persian officers got off one volley – I know that I got an arrow in my shield – and then we were into them.

That was hard fighting, no quarter given, and the sun was set low enough that skill was replaced by luck. Twice I caught heavy blows on my sword arm – one bent my vambrace without cutting through into my arm and a second blow was the flat of an axe and not the blade, thank the gods, or my life would have spurted out of my arm. Even so, I dropped my spear and Idomeneus stepped past me while I fell on my knees. A blow that hard unmans you – I thought I was finished for a long heartbeat, then my eyes told me that my sword hand was intact, my arm ached but was not broken, and again the vambrace had held and saved my life.

But while I was on my knees, a Mede in a gold helmet and bronze aventail cut at my head with his short *akinakes*. His blow landed, and my ears rang. But Hermogenes stood by me, and he made clumsy parries with his spear over my shoulder.

When you are in a real fight, your world is a tunnel formed by the walls of your helmet and the width of the eye slits. I had no idea whether we were winning or losing, but even with my ears ringing and my arm afire, I knew that having their heroic captain on his knees in the sand was not going to help my men win their way up the beach.

I exploded to my feet, pushing with my Boeotian shield just as Hermogenes blocked another cut. I got the bronze spine in the Persian's face, trapped his sword arm high, dug my feet in the sand and pushed. He landed another blow, but it sheered my horsehair crest without connecting with my head, and I shook it off and pushed again. He tripped and fell. I punched him with the rim of my shield, the rim an extension of my fist. A Boeotian shield lacks the weight and authority of an aspis, but the rim is a weapon in a way that an aspis's rim can never be. I broke his nose with my first left-handed blow, broke his sword arm with the second and crushed his throat with the third as he tried to cover himself with his arms.

I had time to flex my numb hand once, and then I drew my sword from under my arm, fumbled it and dropped it. I remember looking at it lying in the sand and thinking – now I'm a dead man.

But the Phoenician marines gave ground, backed away from us ten paces and rallied. They were magnificent fighters, those men – they didn't lose heart, just backed off to give the Thracians time to take us in the flank. But their retreat showed them that all their officers were down, and that rattled them. I could see it in the movement of their shields in the fiery light.

Idomeneus was ahead of me, lithe limbs flashing. He harried their retreat and the best of my marines followed him, so that our taxis lost cohesion. The better men were willing to keep fighting; the others hung back, pleased to have beaten the Phoenicians and the Medes, and wanting a rest from terror. That's how it always is.

'Thracians!' one of my rowers shouted, just before he leaped from the ship's rail into the surf and ran to join us.

The Thracians were still hesitating, and their hesitation had already cost them the battle. But they might still wreck my men with their charge.

I could hear Miltiades calling his battle cry – 'AJAX!' – to my right, and I knew that the rest of our men would be coming ashore now, and in the time it took to beach a ship, the fight would be over. But there was plenty of time for things to go wrong.

I had to go forward.

'Stephanos is behind the Thracians!' I shouted. 'Follow me!' I stooped and picked up my sword – just about. I remember well how little grip I had. But a Greek cannot lead from the second rank. No one would follow such a warrior. So I pushed forward and bellowed 'Heracles!' like an angry bull, trying to get the daimon of combat to fill me and carry me up the beach.

Idomeneus was on his knees when I came up, using his big shield to cover his body against two Phoenician marines with axes. I ran full tilt over one man and his axe bit through my shield. The bronze plate over my left arm turned the blade and I hacked at him with my nerveless sword hand like any green ephebe who doesn't know how to hold a sword.

Sometimes, as Heraclitus says, when skill fails, passion must suffice.

Hermogenes took the second man. The man with the axe swung and for a long heartbeat I thought he was gone, but the shaft, not the blade, bit into his shield. Hermogenes had an aspis, and the tough face turned the shaft with a hollow boom and Hermogenes was on the man, stabbing wildly with his spear. What he lacked in accuracy he made up in ferocity.

Now that we had cleared the ground around Idomeneus struggled to his feet. We shamed the rest of our line forward. The Phoenicians might have rallied then – but they didn't. They hesitated for a moment – they were brave men, and they knew what the loss of their ships would mean. But they decided that retreat was the wiser option, and they went up the beach, still cohesive enough to drag their wounded and one of their leaders with them.

The sun had set and the only light was the red autumn sky and the fires of the town. The Thracians still outnumbered us, but they were retreating, flowing up the hillside like a herd of deer, and Stephanos was harrying them from the left, his best runners trying to outrun the Thracians to the crest of the long hill above the town.

I flexed my hand. Some feeling was returning.

At that point, Aristagoras elected to bring his men out of the citadel in a sortie. It was typical of the bastard – too late to help win the victory, too soon to come out in safety. His sortie caught the Thracians in the flank, though, and suddenly they had to turn or be eaten by the new threat and by Stephanos's crew nipping at their heels like a hunting pack.

I could see it all happening in the red light on the hillside above me. It was unreal – I have never seen such light again, red as blood – and I knew that Ares himself was watching us, that we were on his dance floor, and he would judge us.

I could see the swan on Aristagoras's helmet and I knew who he was. And thanks to the folds in the hill, I could see what neither he nor Stephanos could see – there was another contingent of Thracians behind a parallel crest.

And I was already tired.

Too bad. I wanted Aristagoras dead, and I would never have a better chance than now.

I've made all this seem to last a long time, but in truth, Miltiades' marines were still coming off his stern and some of our ships were just coming ashore – it had all happened that fast. But if you want to know what fatigue is, fight for your life for three or four hundred heartbeats, then run up a rocky hillside at dusk with a hundred men baying at your heels. My scale shirt felt as if it weighed as much as my body, and my helmet sat on my head like the weight of the world on

Atlas's shoulders. Who am I to complain? Many of my rear-rankers had rowed all day.

Up we went, and the Thracians stood against us. I think they were shocked – appalled, even – that they were being charged. They weren't men who stood in a line to fight, they were wild tribesmen who killed with the ferocity of their charge. I think they stood only because they knew that their allies were in position to take us in the flank. But my men overlapped their flank, so that my own flank files were bound to push right up into their ambush. I didn't have to plan it that way – there was no other way it could happen. The hillside wasn't that wide, and its seaside edge was a cliff that rose above the beach.

Paramanos's men were pouring ashore from his ship, which was beached beside mine. Turning his ship hadn't taken long – yet in that time my crew had broken the Phoenicians, killed the Ionians and run up the hill, and now his men were eager to come up and get their share of the loot.

Thracians were famous for having gold.

My men slowed as we came up to the Thracians. I couldn't blame them – there is no such thing as a ferocious charge *uphill*, at least not on a hill that steep.

'Form tight!' I called, and the men pressed in.

Sorry, honey – I should explain. There's no phalanx in a fight like that. No order. We didn't form by rank and file on the beach, nor yet going up the hill. In a fight like that, you are a mob. But my mob had been together in fifty fights, and we didn't need a lot of orders. So when I roared 'Get tight', all the boys in the front rank crowded in on me, and all the rest pushed, and we made a shield wall in less time than it takes to tell it.

The Thracians threw spears and javelins with the whole weight of the hill behind them, and men fell. A spear came right through my torn Boeotian and the scale shirt turned the wicked point. Ares' hand had turned death aside – again.

The right end of my line was lapping over their shield wall and then extending further as Paramanos's men came up. I could hear his voice and his Cyrenian Greek as he ordered them into line.

'All together!' I sang. My voice held, steady and high. If you want an order to carry in a storm or on a battlefield, you sing.

My Boeotian shield was flapping in pieces. I used it to bat another javelin out of the air and the spine snapped.

'Shield!' I roared.

An oarsman behind me passed his forward and Hermogenes held it for me. I dropped the useless corpse of a shield off my arm and thrust my left hand into the leather porpax of the cheap aspis, and then I was ready.

'All together!' I called again.

'*Heracles!*' they called back. It wasn't the god's own roar of the first shout, but it was sufficient to get us forward, and we went up the rocky ground. Someone started the Paean, and our voices rose like sacred incense to Ares, and he must have smiled on us.

Thracians fight with ferocity, but they are not competitors in an athletic event, the way Greek warriors are, and they don't practise together, dancing the war dances and measuring the swing of their weapons. They stand too far apart to have a solid line, and their crescent-shaped shields are too small to use in a close fight, where men to the left and right – and men in the rear ranks – can all take a thrust at you when your tunnel-vision is turned on a single opponent.

They hit us hard with javelins as we started forward, though, and men fell. Gaps were opened in our wall and we weren't deep enough for those holes to close naturally. So the fight that resulted was sheer deadly chaos, and the carnage was grotesque. Skill in arms counted for little – it was too dark. But we had the burning town behind us, and they were above us, and we could see them much better than they could see us, and in that fight, a minute advantage of vision was sufficient.

And we sang. That's what I remember – the red light of the dying sun, and the Paean of Apollo.

It was no pushover. In the first contact, men fell like weeds cut by a housewife in the garden. I got three men so fast that when my borrowed spear fouled in the third, the first still hadn't given up his life and fallen on his face. I dropped my spear shaft and pulled my sword again. The marines who should have been either side of me were gone, and Idomeneus was in the front rank, and Herk, of all men, his scarlet plume nodding, pushed in beside me.

'Aren't you supposed to be on the beach?' I asked.

He laughed. 'Fuck that!' he shouted.

We all felt the impact as the Thracian charge struck Paramanos's end of the line. The Thracian sub-chief hadn't waited for Paramanos to come over the crest at him. He must have been wise enough to figure that we knew he was there.

I didn't see it, but I've heard the tale often enough. Paramanos went down – knocked from his feet by a barbarian – and Lekthes stood over his body until he rose. Lekthes died there, like a hero. He took three thrusts, but he didn't fall until Paramanos was back on his feet.

I didn't know it, but Lekthes' moment of heroism steadied the whole line.

Paramanos's men turned, unwilling to abandon their commander, and they stood where they might have broken. Even then, we felt the shock and our line bent back.

But Stephanos was on their *other* flank with Aristagoras and his sally, and the fortunes of the Thracians began to ebb like the tide from a salt flat when fishermen go into the surf to collect the catch. Their line disintegrated the way an old linen sail rips when the rope-edge is lashed to the mast and the wind begins to tear at a weakened corner, so that each gust rips a little more of the sail, and then the sail goes, faster and faster, the rip wider and the *rate* of the tear faster with every gust, and then with the noise of a thunderclap, the whole sail rips out of its harness of rope and flutters away into the storm. Just like that, the Thracian line tore asunder.

Towards the end, their centre gave way – or died. I began to kill men with every cut of my arm. My hand was growing *better* as I cut, and my opponents' eyes were elsewhere – looking up the hill and behind them, where Stephanos's men had climbed the ridge and now came back down on their left flank from above. Every cut and every thrust took another man down, and then none of them would stand against me. I killed twenty men, I think.

Yet even as they ran, they fought. Thracians are never more dangerous than when they run – men will turn and throw spears, and they can form again as soon as they think you have lost your order. And my rowers had no stomach to follow them – nor could I blame them.

So we pushed left, trapping their left wing in a pocket formed of the three forces – the sally from the town, Stephanos's marines and my own left wing. My right separated from me, going up the hill with Paramanos, so that Herk and Idomeneus were the end men of our part of the line.

I couldn't see whether the Thracians were rallying in the trees beyond the crest or not.

One of their chieftains commanded their left, and he must have known that the end was on him. A handful of his men threw themselves at us – there were three of them, and there was still a gap between Herk and Stephanos as he came down the hill to close the circle. But I put my cheap shield into the face of one and knocked him flat, and his falling fouled the other two, then we put them down in less time than it takes to tell it, Herk thrusting hard past my shield with his spear and Hermogenes giving me a rap on the helmet in his haste to kill the third one over my shoulder.

It was clear to all that the Thracians were going to die. The chieftain had a scale shirt, a double-bitted hunting axe and a tall helmet of scales crowned with a boar's head in gold. He was bellowing challenges, but neither Stephanos nor Aristagoras intended that we would fight him man to man, and the circle tightened.

I had other plans. I ran at him – two paces, all the space that the dying mêlée allowed. His axe went up and I gave him the edge of my aspis and he split it, gashing my shoulder so that I saw white. But I had his axe trapped in my shield, and my good sword thrust into his face as if of its own accord. I stabbed him twice, but I think he was dead after the first.

And then I was helmet to helmet with Aristagoras. He was trying to claim my kill, and he cut at me, probably because his vision was blurred and it was dark – or because he knew me and hated me.

Now, I keep promising that I will be honest. I want to tell you that we duelled at the edge of the dark, me the hero and he the villain. But, in fact, I had lost the crest of my helm and had a rower's shield, and unless he knew me by my scale shirt, he had no idea who I was. But by the gods, I knew him. The last of the Thracians were dying noisily, and I had him all to myself.

I was a little above him on the hill and I had my shield fouled by the dead chieftain's axe. It was split and my shoulder was gushing blood, and I couldn't spin fully to face Aristagoras. So I rotated on my rear foot, pulling my left arm clear of the porpax as I spun and taking a second blow from Aristagoras on the reinforced shoulder of my scale thorax as I turned, so that I just managed to keep my footing.

Aristagoras thrust at me a third time, and his blade slid off my scales and down my thighs, cutting me. But I paid no heed. Instead, I completed my rotation, clear at last of the wreck of my shield – the gods must have decreed that shields would be my bane that day – and I cut at him, a long overhand blow that caught him behind the shield because I had spun so fast. I sheared through his swan and my blade rang on his helmet. I powered my right foot forward and lifted my blade with my right arm, catching it under the rim of the cheekpiece of his helmet and cutting into his throat – an ugly blow, no skill to it, but I had my blade inside his shield and I wasn't going to let him go.

I saw his eyes then, and he knew he was a dead man. He would have run, but I'd cut the artery in the neck. He wasn't dead, but he let his limbs go loose – a final cowardice. He might have cut me one more time, but he gave up.

I like to think he knew it was me. But I don't know that for certain.

My sword glanced off his neck guard, where the yoke of his corslet rose to cover his back, and I lifted it high in the 'Harmodius Blow', an overhand back cut with the legs reversed and the whole weight of a man's body and hips behind it, and I cut his head right off his body – no easy feat with a short sword. Try it the next time you sacrifice a calf.

The stump of his neck jetted blood like a newborn volcano, and he fell.

I won't lie. It was a sweet moment.

Herk caught my wounded left shoulder, and the pain brought me to my senses. 'Well done, lad!' he said. 'Now get out of here, before one of his men fingers you for it.'

The fighting was fading away. It was the ugly part of a fight – when the brave men find how bad their wounds are, and the cowards push forward and bloody their weapons on dead and wounded men, as if anyone can be fooled by such stuff. I had a dozen cuts, and my arms were both hurt.

Hermogenes had to prise the vambrace off my arm. It was twisted, the cut that had numbed my arm had deformed the surface, and he had to deform the metal to get it off me, putting the flat of his eating knife against my skin and using it like a crowbar. But my right hand and arm felt better immediately.

My left arm wasn't so easily fixed. I had four different cuts, and Hermogenes pulled his old chiton out of his pack, ripped it in four pieces and used one of them to wrap my arm. 'This is no life for a man,' he said, out of nowhere. 'Your friend Lekthes is dead.'

That was the first I'd heard, although I've already told you the manner of his passing.

Idomeneus had as many cuts as I had, and a deep gash on the outside of his thigh that wrapped around his hip and on to his buttock. You could see white at the bottom of the wound, where the deep fat was.

'That's not good,' Idomeneus said, looking at his hip, and fainted.

Hermogenes shook his head. 'This is no life for a man,' he repeated. 'Look at yourselves. And this for gold? Who needs fucking gold?' He laid out his leather bag, lit a lamp – he was a monster of efficiency, our Hermogenes, even then – and wrapped Idomeneus, even stitching his arse, which woke the poor bastard. He woke with a scream, but by then Herakleides and Nestor had his arms and he fainted again.

Herk came back with Agios and a wineskin, attracted by the lamp. There was no breeze, and the wounded were calling for water, and the night things were coming.

He handed me a cup of wine, but Hermogenes intercepted it and drank it. Fair enough – he was the one doing all the work.

'Still Thracians in the town,' Herk said. 'Miltiades is anxious to get off.'

Paramanos came up with Stephanos. Paramanos had a bandage around his head, and he sighed and pushed the wineskin away. 'One drink and I'll be out,' he said. 'I owe Lekthes' widow,' he said. 'He traded his life for mine.'

'He was a good man,' I said. The wine cup had come to me, and I poured a libation to his shade. 'Apollo light him to Elysium.'

'Aye, he went down like Achilles,' Herk said.

I handed the cup back to Hermogenes. 'I'm going for the town,' I said. Stephanos stepped forward and I shook my head. 'You gather up the wounded,' I said to him. 'Make sure men go aboard the right ships. Herakleides – I'll bring Briseis to her namesake. Be ready.'

I embraced them all, one by one. 'I don't know if I'll be back,' I said.

They all embraced me again, and then I headed downhill, to the sally port from which Aristagoras had come.

Paramanos came with me. When I turned to look at him in the moonlight, his eyes sparkled. 'You need a keeper,' he said.

A party of Aristagoras's men was carrying his body through the gate. A young man had his shield over his shoulder. We followed them.

If there were Thracians, we didn't see them, although we could hear screams and occasional sounds of fighting from lower in the town. We followed the body up two narrow alleys and a long staircase set into an outer wall, and then we were at a torch-lit gate. It was a small place, compared with Kallipolis. There were two sentries, and they were too young and raw to have gone with the sortie.

I don't know what I expected, honey. I think that I thought that she would throw herself into my arms and weep. It wasn't that way at all, of course.

The hall was small, and she was waiting to receive the body. Her handmaidens were around her, and they took his body – the man I'd beheaded an hour before – and they washed it. She caught my eye and started. She raised an eyebrow – that was all the greeting I got – and then went back to her task. Her role. Like a priestess, she had her part to play, and she played it well.

An old woman sewed the head back on. While that happened, I stepped up next to Briseis. She bowed.

'Lord Arimnestos,' she said. 'We are honoured.'

She bowed to me – imagine, Briseis the untouchable bowing to Doru the slave. It was all like a dream.

'I am a poor hostess,' she said, and led the way out of the hall, on to a balcony over the sea.

I still expected an embrace.

'I killed him,' I said quietly, and I think I smiled.

She nodded. 'I know that,' she said. 'And I thank you. Now – go. You should not be here.'

'But—' I couldn't believe it. She was pregnant again, I could tell – about three months. But her beauty was unchanged, and her power over me. 'But I came – to rescue you.'

Such things, once said, sound very weak indeed.

'Why do you think I need rescuing?' she asked. Then she laughed. She stood on tiptoe and kissed me. He tongue darted in and out of my mouth, and then she stepped back and licked her lips. 'Blood in your mouth and all over you,' she said and she smiled. 'Achilles. Now be gone, before people talk. I'm a widow and my reputation will matter.'

'I don't care,' I said. 'I'm your next husband.'

Then she looked – hurt. Not proud, and not angry, and not sad, but as if some deep pain had touched her. She reached out and touched my bloody right hand. 'No, my love,' she said. 'I will not marry you.'

She shook her head. 'I have children to protect – beautiful children. And where would we go?'

I felt as if the Persian's axe had got me. 'I want to take you home,' I said.

'To Ephesus?' she asked.

'To Plataea,' I said. 'To my farm.'

She smiled then, and I knew that my dreams were foolish. The gods must have laughed at me all autumn.

'Listen, my love,' she said gently. 'I am not called Helen by other men for nothing. It is not my fate to be a farm-wife in Boeotia, wherever that may be.' Her smile became bitter – the bitterness of self-knowledge. 'That is not my fate. Nor would I want it. I will be the lady of a great lord.' Her hand remained on mine. 'I love you, but you are a killer. A pirate. A thief of lives.'

'You seem to need me from time to time,' I said, and my bitterness was too close to the surface.

She looked past me, into the room where her husband's body was being washed. She had things that she needed to be doing, she said with her eyes. 'Be glorious, so that I may hear of you often, Achilles,' she said softly.

'Come with me,' I pleaded.

She shook her head.

Well, I had my pride, too – and that was my foolishness. When Archi walked away from me, I should have wrestled him to the ground, and when Briseis chose another life, I should have put her over my shoulder and taken her. We'd both have been happier.

But I was proud.

'In the harbour, there will be a ship in ten days,' I said. 'Unless Poseidon takes him. His name is your name, and he is your ship. I took him from Diomedes of Ephesus. The rowers are yours until the end of autumn.'

Then she threw her arms around my neck. 'Oh, thank you!' she said. 'Now I am truly free.'

I turned to leave – but then it struck me. 'You will marry Miltiades!' I said, and there was death in my tone.

Her lip curled in disgust. 'You are worth ten of him,' she said. 'And if it were my fate to be a pirate queen, I would be yours.'

'Who then?' I asked. 'I could protect your children.'

'And make them tyrants of Miletus?' she asked. 'Lords of Ephesus?' She came and put her arms around my neck, and I had no hatred for her in my body. 'Go! Let me hear of you in songs of praise, and perhaps we will meet again.'

We kissed. It cannot have helped her reputation much, since every woman in that hall could see us, but it did me a world of good. That kiss had to hold me for many years.

# Part VI
## *Justice*

Citizens must fight to defend the law as if fighting to hold the city wall.

Heraclitus, fr. 44

For gods on the one hand, all things are beautiful, good, and just; but men, on the other, suppose some things to be just and others to be unjust.

Heraclitus, fr. 102

# 22

I had almost recovered from my wounds when I stepped wearily off my own gangplank like an old man and limped up the beach at Piraeus. The red wounds were closed and the bruises had faded, but the black hole where my guts had been was never going to close.

Herakleides landed me from *Briseis*, and he embraced me like a brother. To be honest, I'd never really forgiven him for selling the information of the value of our ransoms to Miltiades, but in his way he'd done me a favour, showing me who I worked for and what a life I'd come to. So when I limped down the plank, I turned and took his hand.

'Take this ship back to its owner, and she'll keep you as captain,' I said. 'You are too good a man to spend your life as a pirate and die face down on the sand. And you're not good enough with the bronze and iron to stay alive. Do you hear me, friend?'

He nodded.

'Take this ship to Briseis and we're quits, you and me – no blood price over a certain matter back on Lesbos. Fail to deliver, and I'll find you. Am I clear?' Behind me, Hermogenes and Idomeneus and a pair of Thracian slaves – men I'd taken as part of the booty – were carrying my goods down off the ship.

'Aye, lord,' he said. 'I swear it by all the gods, and may the furies track me down and rip my guts from me—'

'Stop!' I said. 'You're hurting me. And never, ever swear by the furies.'

And so it was done. I embraced him, and he sailed away.

Idomeneus and I watched that ship until it vanished around the great promontory.

He had tears in his eyes.

I laughed bitterly. 'I didn't ask you to come with me,' I said.

Hermogenes grunted. 'Some people would be nostalgic about torture,' he said. 'I'm going to hire a wagon. You can afford it, *lord*.' He had a wicked glint in his eye. 'Best forget about anyone calling you that – ever again.'

I traded some silver for copper and tin in the city at Athens, and got bitten by bedbugs in a horrible tavern, lower than anything I'd seen since I had become a slave. And then we started walking home.

A day on the roads of Attica, and I remembered all too well – Greece, land of farmers. Every man was equal and surly farmers cared nothing for swagger. I could put my hand on my sword hilt and they would just glower the more. We came to Oinoe, and I looked up at the tower in the sunset. We camped within easy walk of the place where my father and his friends had stopped the Spartans. Hermogenes and I told the story to Idomeneus – and the two slaves, who were already becoming part of the household. They were decent men, not too smart, tough as nails. I told how my brother died.

That night I wept. Look at me – even now, I blubber.

Listen, honey. May you never know the loss of love. But you will. I loved Pater, for all his ways, and he died. And my brother. And those losses will never be redeemed. You will lose me, and your mother, and your brothers, too. And if the gods don't favour you, you will lose a child. No – I don't mean to be cruel. But that night, with the watch tower at our backs, while I sat watching our cart, I wept for Briseis, and for Pater, and for Archi, and for Hipponax, and for Lekthes. I wept for the man who I killed in the dark on the battle-field at Ephesus. Most of all, like most people, I wept for myself.

When I walked away from the ship in Piraeus, I walked away from myself – my reputation, my riches. All gone. I was going home to avenge my father's killing against a man whose face I couldn't hold in my mind. Not because I wanted to, but because I could think of nothing else to do.

I think it was the loss of Briseis most of all. I think that I had been certain I would have her – that I would bring her up this pass to the foot of Cithaeron, lie with her in the grass by Leitos's tomb and carry her over the threshold into my father's stone house.

Without her, it seemed an empty exercise. I cared *nothing*.

I promised when I started this story that I would tell the truth. So here's a truth for you – I didn't care much about avenging my father. Oh – I see the shock. Listen, honey – listen, all of you. When you are young, and you listen to the poet, you take in the rules of life – the laws of all Hellenes. Oaths, gods, laws of gods and men.

When I sat with my back to the stone fort at Oinoe, I had probably killed a hundred men. My love had chosen another life over me, and I had turned my back on the only calling I had ever felt.

Every time you kill a man, the doubt grows. Every time you take a ship, empty it of valuables and enrich yourself with the blood and sweat of other men, every time you make another man a slave, every time you buy a woman for sex and discard her when she's pregnant, you have to wonder – are there any laws? Are there any gods?

There weren't any laws for me just then. No rules. Perhaps no gods. Nothing mattered.

The darkness of that night is absolute, even in memory, and I was afraid to go to sleep.

I don't remember much more than that, until we came to the foot of Cithaeron. The next day, I hadn't slept, and I was morose and ill-tempered, and yet curiously happy to be walking the southern slopes where I could see my home mountain. Cithaeron is an old god, and he reached out to me and touched the blackness.

The cart slowed us, and it was nightfall when we came to Pedeis.

Pedeis was the typical border town, with high prices and crap for wine. Dionysus first preached just over the mountains at Eleutherai, and the grape grew there first, and my money says that his worship *never* spread to Pedeis. The girls were ugly and there was a wooden Temple of Demeter that was a disgrace to gods and men. I snarled at my men to keep moving, and we rolled through the streets and camped in the stony fields north of town.

The border garrison, if they existed, were so slipshod that we passed without a road tax, almost without comment. We climbed the pass to Eleutherai, up and up in switchbacks, and our cart filled the road so that the faster traffic of men walking and men with packs on donkeys ended up in a long queue behind us like the baggage train of an army. Men chatted to Idomeneus or Hermogenes. I walked on in silence.

We found the body near the summit of the pass. The corpse was that of a young boy, probably a slave, about twelve years old. He'd been killed in a bad way, with a series of hacks to his face and neck from a dull, heavy knife. He lay in his own blood in the middle of the wide space near the summit where wagons turn to begin the descent, and where polite men pull to the side to let the faster traffic pass. There are deep ruts in the rock where the old men cut a road for their chariots, and he lay across the stone tracks like a botched sacrifice.

He looked so pitiful. He was just about the age I had been when I stood in the phalanx for the first time. Frankly, from the ripe old age of twenty-two, he looked too small to have died by violence. Had he tried to fight? I would have.

I was already low, and the sight of the dead boy almost moved me to tears again. I knelt by him and cursed because his sticky blood got on my chiton. But I determined to bury him – no idea why, either. In general, I leave corpses for the ravens.

I got him on my sea cloak, which had seen worse than blood, and men from the rest of the caravan behind our slow wagon came up and joined me, quite spontaneously. In fact, my opinion of men went up, right there. I was reminded of why Greeks *are* good men. We cleared a space, and every man, slave and free, gathered rocks, and we built a cairn as fast as you can tell the story. I put coins on his eyes and another man poured wine over the grave. More and more men came up – they must have been cursing my wagon all the way up the pass – and every one joined in.

There was a small man, a pot-mender, and he had a pair of donkeys and a young slave of his own. He came up when the cairn was half-finished. He looked more angry than sad. I caught his eye, and he looked away.

'You know him?' I asked. A pair of korai from Thebes who were travelling to the Temple of Artemis at Athens were washing his face under their mother's direction. They were good girls, conscious of so many men around them and yet aware of their duties as women.

He shrugged. 'He looks like the pais of Empedocles, the chief priest of the smith god.' He made the sign automatically – even a pot-mender is at least an initiate.

I gave him my sign – it was the Cretan version, and probably a little different, but he knew that I was an initiate and more, and he stepped closer. 'I know Empedocles,' I said. It was like remembering another life. Empedocles the priest, and his magic lens. I looked at the pot-mender. 'You sure?' I asked.

He nodded and swallowed. But he wasn't afraid of me or much else – no travelling man can afford to be scared on the road, and he called out to the other men. 'Anyone heard of thieves in this pass?'

Other men nodded – a farmer, and a wool merchant, and a man with a load of fine wine, still in cheap amphorae used at sea, loaded carefully on a big wagon. He wasn't the owner but a trusted slave, and his manner suggested that he used this route often.

'There's a gang of them,' he said, 'off towards the east.'

'Took the priest for ransom?' I asked.

The slave spat. 'Who knows what they want? They're killers. They're like animals.'

An old peddler with a leather sack full of goods put his sack down and rubbed his chin. 'I heard they were west of Eleutherai,' he said. 'Always best to just give them the money,' he said, to no one in particular.

We finished the cairn, covered the boy's face and sang a hymn to Demeter, the girls' voices carrying sweet and high. I wept again, although I wasn't sure why. And then we let the other men pass, and we waited while another caravan coming up out of Boeotia climbed past the turn-around. The tinker and the peddler waited with us. The tinker's name was Tiraeus, and he was shifty and unwashed but not, I think, a bad man. The peddler was Laertes.

He looked wistfully at my entourage. 'You are a rich man,' he said.

'Hmmm,' I said, sounding too much like Pater for my own peace of mind. But I had the lapis and gold necklace from Sardis at my throat and a belt of heavy gold links around my waist under my chiton – in my experience, that's the safest way to carry a fortune. 'I have money,' I said.

He shrugged. 'It never sticks to me,' he said. 'Thanks for the wine.'

Tiraeus, the tinker, was emboldened by the peddler. 'You a smith?' he asked suddenly. 'You don't – look like a smith,' he said. 'Apologies, master. Too often, I say what comes into my head.'

I shrugged. 'I can bang out a good flat sheet,' I said. 'I can repair a helmet. I make a nice simple cup.' I grinned, thinking of my latest attempt at a helmet in Hephaestion's shop on Crete – my first grin in a day, I think.

'Looking for an apprentice?' he asked eagerly, mistaking my statement of fact for false modesty.

'No,' I said. 'But if you help get the wagon down the pass, I'll stand you both a good dinner.'

He shrugged. Laertes grinned wolfishly. I gathered that he lived life a day at a time. 'Deal!' he said.

And we turned the wagon, yoked the pair of oxen backwards and started down, the six of us braking the wagon, leaving the new grave under the afternoon sun.

Sweaty, back-breaking work, but many hands made it lighter, and my mood had changed. So I made jokes, praised the two Thracians when they worked, and we were a different crew entering Eleutherai than we had been at Pedeis. We were faster, too, and there was still plenty of light in the sky. Eleutherai is in Boeotia, honey. Men speak the right way there, and women look right and the barley is sweeter. What can I say? I'm a Boeotian, honey. Eleutherai felt like home, and my mood rose again. Men told us that Eleutherai was so named because runaway slaves from Boeotia were free when they got there – and I felt like a freer man, drinking the wine. If I'd been a slave close to home, instead of across the ocean in Asia, I like to think I'd have run the first night I wasn't watched.

I took the seven of us into the biggest taverna, summoned the owner and put a gold daric on the table. Then I used my sword to split it in two and gave him half. 'I want a dinner,' I said. 'A really good dinner, and wine that's not like cow piss, and sweet almonds with honey. I want clean straw, food for my beasts and no crap.'

Half a gold daric should have bought his whole village, but it did get us a passable meal, a pretty girl to wait on us and some seriously obsequious service. And the wine was the wine of home – not the wonders of Chian wine, but good, strong stuff. The tinker was thankful and pleasant, but the peddler was sullen. I didn't like him.

My gold half-daric brought the basileus in the morning. He was an old man, and not really the power of the town – the Athenians owned Eleutherai to all intents and purposes by then, and he was a puppet.

He was an old aristocrat, and he was waiting for us in the courtyard of the wine shop. He looked me over, saw the blood stains on my chiton and drew the wrong conclusions. 'Where do you come from?' he demanded. He had two men with him, and they had spears.

I shrugged. 'Here and there, sir,' I said.

'Answer,' he demanded.

He made me angry and I liked that, because the blackness had been so heavy. 'I serve Miltiades,' I said. 'Does that mean anything to you?'

It certainly did. His whole demeanour changed. He stepped forward and offered his hand, and we clasped. 'My apologies, sir,' he said. 'I have a plague of bandits to deal with.' He pointed to the blood stains on my chiton. 'I thought—'

I nodded. 'A boy was killed by bandits in the pass yesterday,' I said, and told him what I knew. Tiraeus added what he knew and the basileus shook his head. 'They are bad men,' he said. 'Old soldiers, or so I hear.' He looked at my men, then at the two fellow travellers, and then at my necklace – I could see him taking it all in. 'Are you a local man, sir?' he asked politely.

Suddenly, I thought that I knew just where the bandits would be. But I held my tongue, only glancing at the two travellers with sudden interest. And the old basileus disconcerted me. I'd been away for ten years and my first day in Boeotia, an aristocrat mistook me for one of his own.

'Plataea,' I said.

'Ah!' he said, as if a mystery was solved. 'And these bandits are operating from south of Plataea. You are going to deal with them? Miltiades sent you?' His relief was palpable. A problem passed on is a problem solved, and all that.

Idomeneus brightened. The prospect of violence restored his faith in the logos, or whatever passed for the logos in the Cretan's world.

You know, thugater, sometimes the fates speak loudly, and sometimes we have to be the men that other men expect us to be. And Old Empedocles – if indeed it was he – deserved something from me.

Frankly, it was good to have a simple mission. It allowed me to put off going home for another day or two.

Even Hermogenes nodded. Bandits were bandits.

'Yes,' I said. 'That is, it is not what I'm here for, but I'll deal with the bandits.'

Everyone smiled, except the tinker, who looked confused, and the peddler, but sullen was pretty much his only mood.

We got our oxen hitched and started up the long road to Plataea. There's a short road, down the valley of Asopus, and a long road up along the skirts of the mountain. The long road would pass the hero's shrine and come down past my father's farm. The short road was faster. I wasn't surprised when both of the other travellers stuck with us at the fork towards the mountain, however. Not surprised at all.

'You said that you were a smith!' the tinker said when we were clear of Eleutherai.

'Yes,' I said.

'But he thinks you're some sort of aristocrat,' the peddler said, as if I was intentionally deceiving him.

'Hmm,' I said. We crossed the Asopus in silence, and started up the long ridge towards the hero's shrine. When we reached the first copse of big oaks, I pulled the wagon off to the side.

'Arm,' I said to Idomeneus and Hermogenes.

The tinker watched us as if we were performing a miracle play, his eyes as wide as a young girl's. The two Thracians were slaves, of course. But I took them aside, handed each of them a heavy knife and a javelin. 'Stand by me, and you will be that much closer to being free men.' It's easy with Thracians – they arm their own slaves, and a bold slave can expect to be freed faster than one who hangs back. They took the weapons as if they were going to a party.

'Swords in your belt, spears in the top of the wagon and a cloak over everything,' I said.

I went over to the peddler and the tinker. 'You two might want to walk away,' I said. I looked pointedly at the peddler. 'You especially.'

He wouldn't meet my eye. 'Oh – I can look after myself,' he said.

'Hmm,' I said. I turned to Tiraeus the tinker.

He looked around. 'You'll – let me go?'

I remember laughing. We must have been a grim band when we changed into our armour, because he was terrified. 'We're not the thieves,' I said. And then it hit me – we weren't the thieves *here*. It actually took my breath away. These thieves – these men on Cithaeron who stole from travellers – were only doing what we'd been doing to Phoenician ships for years.

Except that they preyed on their own, and they weren't very good at it.

Tiraeus watched me.

I must have made a face, because he flinched. But then I opened my hands. 'I intend to rescue the old priest and rid the pass of thieves,' I said.

The peddler made a noise.

Tiraeus opened his chlamys and revealed a short sword, or a long knife. 'I am a servant of the god,' he said. 'And – perhaps it will change my luck.'

Maybe he had decided that following me might get him a job.

'Everyone made up his mind?' I said.

We went up the road, the oxen plodding along. The sky went from blue to leaden grey in the time it took to climb half the ridge, and it began to rain, a slow, cold rain.

'What if they have bows?' Idomeneus asked. 'I should scout ahead.'

I shook my head. 'They won't have bows,' I said. 'That boy was hacked down by a kopis.' I shrugged. 'They're mercenaries. They're using the old shrine as a headquarters, because all the hard men used to come there when Calchas was priest.' In my head, the rule of law was reasserting itself, and the gods themselves, and I thought that it must have been too long since the hero had had his sacrifice.

Since Oinoe, I had thought about the logos. How Heraclitus said that men could only come to wisdom through fire. How strife was the master of all, and change was the way. But most of all, I thought of what he said to me when he chided me for beating Diomedes.

*'If you would master the killer in you, you must accept that you are not truly free. You must submit to the mastery of the laws of men and gods.'*

So I trudged through the ever-increasing rain, and I thought about fire.

Hermogenes stepped up beside me. 'What are we going to do?' he asked.

'Find the bandits and teach them some philosophy,' I said.

Idomeneus laughed.

I shook my head. I had a Boeotian cap, a heavy felt one purchased that morning from a stall, and it was more like a sponge than a hat, so I pulled it off and wrung it out. 'I mean it,' I said.

'You are *mad*,' Idomeneus said. He laughed again. 'Let's hear the bronze sing!' he shouted. 'Who gives a fuck about *philosophy*?'

'You are the mad one,' I said, and went back to the road.

We climbed and climbed. I wasn't worried that they would attack us on the hillside. Bandits are lazy men. They would want the wagon at the top, and I knew this mountain like I knew the calluses on my sword hand. There was the crest of the road and then a slight dip that would be full of mud and water in late autumn, and they would be in the big trees around the sinkhole.

Just short of the top, I stopped the wagon like a man who was too tired to go on. My sandals were full of mud and the oxen looked as miserable as we all felt.

Idomeneus made a face. 'I wouldn't rob anyone on a day like this,' he said. 'I'd be on a nice soft couch with a cup of wine in my hand.'

Hermogenes chucked him with an elbow. 'Why aren't you, then? Eh? I know why I'm here, and I know why Arimnestos is here. And I don't think the slaves have any choice. And the tinker thinks there's a meal in it. You, you mad Cretan?'

'Arimnestos is my *lord*,' the Cretan proclaimed. 'Besides – wherever he goes, there's blood, oceans of it. Never a dull moment. You'll see. I doubted it the first days out of Athens – but here we are.'

I winced at his description of me.

But I recognized it.

'Leave the wagon now,' I said. I turned to the tinker. 'Stay here with the beasts. We'll do the work.'

The peddler was looking at Idomeneus. I put my fist in the peddler's ear and he fell like a sacrifice.

You see it, don't you, thugater?

The tinker turned white, put his back to a tree, and drew his sword.

'Don't fret,' I said. I took the peddler's pack and dumped it. It was full of rags and nothing else. 'He's the spotter for the bandits,' I said. 'Tie him, and don't let him go. We'll be back.'

He didn't protest, and I led my little band off the road, uphill. The slope increases above the road and we took our time. The deer trails had changed, of course, but I got us up to the little meadow where Calchas had once killed a wolf, and cocked an ear for sounds from below. The only real weak point in my plan was the tinker and our wagon.

From above, we could see the ambushers, even through the rain. The gods love irony, and in the best tradition of their laughter, the wagon and the ambushers were only a stade apart or less, so that we could see Tiraeus pacing nervously and we could see the bandits in the trees, waiting for a wagon that was not coming.

'I'll go right down the hillside,' I said. 'You drive them.'

Perhaps it seems foolish that I was going to take on all the bandits myself, using my men as beaters. I was in an odd place – I wanted the fight. I told myself that I'd let this make my decision for me – thief against thief, so to speak. If I fell, that was that.

Another voice said that in fact there was no need for gods, because there were few men in Greece who could stand before me. Perhaps none.

And as I began to kick down the hill, the wet leaves flying from under my boots, I felt old Calchas at my side. How many times had we raced through these woods together, he and I, in pursuit of some quarry?

The bandits saw Idomeneus first, as I had intended. They took too long to realize that this wasn't a chance-met farmer – this was real. The end man rose from his concealment and called a warning and then he was down, his agony a better warning than his shouts.

Hermogenes appeared from behind a boulder, running hard, and he threw a javelin.

Then I was on them. The bandit closest to me was a fool and he neither saw me nor heard me, his whole attention on the crisis at the other end of the ambush.

They had no armour, and they looked more like escaped slaves than mercenaries, although the line between the two can be faint. I put my spear point between his kidneys and ran on.

The whole band broke from cover then. There were about a dozen of them, and they ran for the road, just as a frightened deer might, but I was on the road first, between them and the wagon, and the two Thracians were on the other side of the road. We were five against twelve, but the issue was never in doubt.

When two more of them were dead on my spear, they fell back into the mud-filled hollow where they had intended to take my wagon.

I stopped and wiped my spear blade on a scrap of oily cloth from my pouch. 'Surrender,' I said. 'Surrender, or I'll kill all of you.'

'You can't kill us all,' one scarred wretch said. He had a proper sword – a kopis.

'You're right,' I said. 'My friends would have to kill a couple of you.'

They trembled like sheep.

'Surrender!' I said. 'I am Arimnestos of Plataea. If you drop your weapons, I will spare your lives, by Zeus Soter.'

The man with the kopis threw his spear at Hermogenes and bolted, running right up the face of the dip and away downhill. Hermogenes ducked the spearhead but got the tumbling shaft across his temple and went down. Another bandit broke downhill, but the nearest Thracian speared him like a fisherman on a Thracian river, and the rest dropped their weapons.

'Hold them here,' I said. Calchas was in my head, and I knew what was going to happen as if I had read it on a scroll.

I ran downhill after the man with the sword. He had a long start.

But I knew where he was going, and I wanted him to get there.

I ran easily, following the contour of Cithaeron, staying high on the hillside, and after two stades of bush-running, I came to the trail I had used to climb the mountain as a child, and I ran down it, swifter than an eagle.

It was odd, but at first I felt Calchas beside me, and then I felt him *in* me. I *was* Calchas. Or perhaps I had become Calchas.

I passed the cabin, running silently on the leaf-mould, and I had just time to slow at the verge of the tomb when my prey burst out of the woods in front of me, eyes wild with panic from whatever ghosts rode him through the woods – I hope that boy was on him. And the panic on his face exploded like a hot rock drenched in water when he saw me. He raised the sword – the same sword he'd used to kill the boy at the top of the pass – and cut at me. I parried high and refused to give ground, so that he slammed into my hip – I turned him, our bodies pressed close by his momentum, and my hip pushed him ever so slightly, and he went sprawling across the stones of the precinct of the hero's tomb. His head hit a stone and his sword hand hit another so hard that the kopis fell from his hand, as if taken by the hero himself.

He tried to rise, coming up on all fours like a beast, and I caught his greasy hair in my left fist and sacrificed him, cutting his throat so that his life flushed out across the cool wet stones, and the hero drank his blood as he had with every bad man that Calchas sent into the dark.

I wiped my sword on his chiton and went to the cabin, such as it was. The years had not been kind, and the bandits had slaughtered a deer badly and left the hanging carcass to rot by the window of horn, the fools.

The wreck of a door was open. Inside, there were two women clinging to the priest. They flinched away from me.

'Empedocles?' I asked gently. And then, when he still looked wild and afraid, I tried a smile. 'It's a rescue,' I said.

'They took my cup,' he said weakly, and fainted.

We were quite a crowd by the time the rain stopped. We had nine prisoners and six of us, the two women and the priest. He wasn't in a good way – he had a fever and they had abused him – he had burns – but he was a strong man and he smiled at me.

'Come a long way, eh, apprentice?' he said, when I gave him the sign of the journeyman. He was lying on the cot. We had cleaned the cabin and I had found his cup – the fine cup my father had made him – in the leather bag of the leader. The Thracians were amusing themselves rebuilding the door while Hermogenes and Idomeneus hunted for meat. He frowned. 'Where did you learn that sign?'

I knelt by him. 'Crete, father,' I said.

He coughed. 'Crete? By the gods, boy – you'd have done better in Thebes!' He coughed again. 'Here – give me your hand. That's the sign for Boeotia.'

Then he lay still so long I thought he was asleep, or dead. But when I threw my cloak over him, he managed a smile. 'I saw you,' he said.

'Father?' I asked.

'Sacrificed the bastard,' he said. 'Zeus, you frightened me, son.'

We fed the lot of them on deer meat and barley from our wagon. I let the prisoners stew in their fear. The tinker stayed with me and was enough of a help that I wanted him to stay.

I left the body of their leader across the threshold of the precinct, so that his end was clear to all of them. Let them wonder how it had happened. Divine justice takes many forms. I had just learned that lesson, and it was steadying me; the blackness of three days before was already a memory. And seeing Empedocles – even older, and badly hurt – was a tonic. It reminded me that this life – Boeotia, a world with ordered harvests and strong farmers, a cycle of feasts, a local shrine – it was real. It was not a dream of youth.

Idomeneus wanted to kill the lot of them. Of course, that's what we'd have done at sea. My reluctance puzzled him.

'Different places have different rules,' I told him.

He nodded, happy that there was some reason. 'Wasn't much of a fight,' he said.

'I'm not here to fight,' I said. 'I may go back to smithing. And farming.'

He had finished his deer meat, and we were sharing wine from his *mastos* cup. He winced, as if I had cut him. 'That's not you, lord,' he said. 'You're no farmer! You are the Spear! Arimnestos the Spear! Men shit themselves rather than face you. You can't be a smith!'

'I'm tired of killing,' I said.

In the morning, I sat on a log with all the prisoners. They were a use-less lot, beaten men in every way, but they'd behaved like animals when they had the chance – raping the women they'd taken, burning Empedocles, and only the gods knew how many more victims were in the shallow graves behind the tomb.

'You are broken men,' I said.

They stared at me dully, waiting for death.

'I will try to fix you,' I said.

One man, a dirty blond, smiled. 'What will you have us do?' he asked, already aiming to ingratiate with the conqueror.

'We'll start with work,' I said. 'If you displease or disobey, the punishment will be death. There will be no other punishment. Do you understand?'

'Will you feed us, master?' another man said.

'Yes,' I said. They were ugly, those men. As far from the virtue that Heraclitus taught as Briseis was from an old hag in Piraeus. But I understood that the principal difference between us was that my hand still held a sword.

Their first task was to dig up all the shallow graves. There were fifteen – ten men and five women. None of the corpses was very old, and the task horrified them. That pleased me.

We made a pyre and purified the bodies, and then we sent their spirits to the underworld avenged, the old way, at least in Boeotia, and their ashes went into the hero's tomb, where they could share in the criminal's blood, or that's how I understood it from Calchas. The women wept as we poured the oil we had over the bodies. The two who survived had known some of the others.

I didn't ask them any questions.

It took us three days to restore the cabin and to dispose of the victims. We raked the yard, and we cut firewood, and we cleaned the tomb. I poured wine on Calchas's grave each day.

Each night, I lay awake, thinking.

On the third day, Empedocles' fever broke and he began to re-cover quickly.

That night, Hermogenes came and sat by me as I looked at the stars shining down into the clearing by the tomb.

'I understand,' he said.

I put my hand on his. 'Thanks,' I said.

'But it has to be done,' he said.

'I had to put my own house in order,' I said, 'before I go to my father's.'

'This is not your house,' he said. Hermogenes lived in a very literal world.

'Yes,' I said. 'This is my house.'

The two women had been farm slaves across the river. After some conversation, and some halting answers, I set on a course of action with Hermogenes.

I left Idomeneus at the shrine. Ah, thugater, you smile. Well might you smile. I left him with the Thracians as helpers, and I told the Thracians that they were halfway to their freedom. They both nodded like the serious men they were. Tiraeus came – he was already oikia by then. One of mine.

I left my armour and all my weapons, except my good spear. A serious man in Boeotia may walk abroad with a spear. I wore a good wool chiton, and my only concession to my recent life was the necklace.

We put Empedocles in the wagon with the two women and walked down the mountain, across the valley and up the hill.

I stopped at the fork where one lane ran up the hill – the lane of my childhood. And another ran down and away, into the flat lands by the river – Epictetus's lane. Even alone, or with Hermogenes, I knew I could go up that golden lane to my father's house, drench it in blood and make it mine in an hour. I stood there long enough, despite my resolve, that Hermogenes cleared his throat nervously, and I found that I was standing with my hand on my sword hilt.

Then I turned my back on my father's lane and walked downhill.

Coming into Epictetus's farmyard, I felt remarkably like Odysseus, especially when a farm dog came and smelled my hand, turned and gave a friendly bark – not a cry of joy, but a bark of acceptance.

Peneleos – the old man's younger son – came down into the courtyard from the women's balcony. His face was reserved. He admitted later that he had no idea who I was. But he knew Hermogenes.

'There's a friend!' he called. I saw a bow move in another window, and I realized that the bandits must have preyed on all these farms. I can be a fool.

'Peneleos!' I called. 'It's me – Arimnestos.'

He started as if he'd seen a ghost, then we embraced, although we'd never been that close. And his brothers came to the yard, the eldest carrying a bow.

'You're alive!' he said. 'Your sister will go wild!'

And then the old man himself came into the yard. 'They don't sound like thieves!' he said in an old man's voice.

It was hard to see Epictetus as an old man. Of course, I'd thought that he was older than dirt as a child, but I'd seen differently at Oinoe. He was starting to bend at the waist, and he had a heavy staff, but his back straightened when he saw me, and the arms he put around me were strong. 'You came back,' he said, as if he'd just made a hard bargain, but a good one. He reached up and fingered my necklace. 'Huh,' he said. But he gave me the lower half of a grin to take the sting out of the grunt. 'What kept you?' he asked.

'I was taken as a slave,' I said.

'Huh!' he said in a different voice. He had started as a slave. Then he put his head over the edge of the wagon bed. 'Say!' he said.

'We broke the bandits,' Hermogenes said. He was still being embraced, now by a bevy of Boeotian maidens – Epictetus's daughters. The eldest, who had once been offered to me, was a matron of five years' marriage to Draco's eldest, and she had a fair-haired boy just five years old and a daughter of four.

Looking at her stopped me in my tracks, because seeing her was like living another life. Not that I'd ever *loved* her – simply that in another one of Heraclitus's infinite worlds, I might have wed her, and those would have been my children, and I would have had no more blood on my sword than I got at the yearly sacrifice. That other world seemed real when I looked at her, and her children.

Epictetus the Younger, now a tall man with a heavy beard, lifted the two slaves down from the wagon.

'Thera's,' he said. 'The bandits killed her and took all her women – and her slaves joined them.' He looked at me. 'I guess they're yours, now.'

That stopped all conversation.

'Simon has my father's farm,' I said into the silence.

'Aye,' Epictetus the Elder said.

I nodded. 'He killed my father,' I said. 'A blade in the back while you fought the men of Eretria.'

All the men present winced. The silence stretched on and on, and then old Epictetus nodded.

'Thought so,' he said, and spat.

'What're you going to do?' Peneleos asked.

'*You* broke the bandits?' Epictetus the Younger asked. 'You and – who?'

His father understood. 'You going to kill him?' he asked. Epictetus didn't even care where I'd been, how we'd broken the bandits – none of that mattered. He had my right hand in his, and the calluses on my palm told him all he needed to know.

His question returned the courtyard to silence.

I helped his son lift the priest down from the wagon. 'I came to talk to you about that,' I said.

'You want to call him before the assembly?' Epictetus asked later, over bean soup.

I nodded.

Hermogenes shrugged. 'I thought we were just going to kill him,' he said apologetically.

'And then what?' I asked. 'Start a bandit gang? This is Boeotia, not Ionia. What would the archon say if I butchered him and moved into the farm. And hasn't he married my mother? He has sons – do I kill them all?'

'Yes,' Peneleos said. 'Bastards every one. Sorry, Ma.'

I shook my head. 'Law,' I said.

Empedocles was sitting up and taking broth. He saw through me as if I was a pane of horn. 'You could do it,' he said. 'Buy a few judges with that trinket around your neck. Men around here remember you and your father. He died fighting for the city – everyone knows that. Hades, I'm from *Thebes* and I know it. Kill the bastard – and his brood, if you must. No one will hold it against you.'

I was stunned. 'You're the *philosopher*.'

Empedocles shook his head. 'I'm interested in how the world works,' he said. 'And heed the words of Pythagoras – *there are no laws but these, to do good for your friends and to do harm to your enemies.*'

Epictetus the Elder looked at me as if I was a good milk cow on the auction block. 'You plan to live here?' he asked. 'Or will you go away again?'

'Live here,' I said.

He nodded. 'Assembly, then.' He looked around his table, absolute master in his own house. 'No talk of this until the assembly. I'll arrange it. The archon was your father's friend, after all.'

'Myron?' I asked.

Epictetus nodded. 'His son is married to my second,' he said. He looked at Peneleos, and the young man flushed.

'Of course I'll go,' he said. His father drafted a message in heavy-fisted letters, and Peneleos was off across the fields in the fading light.

'You really going to stay?' Epictetus asked as we watched his son run.

'Of course he is,' Hermogenes said.

Myron summoned the assembly on the pretence – really the truth – that there was news from Athens. In a city with fewer than four thousand citizens, you can summon the assembly before sunset and expect the majority of your citizens to be standing under the walls in the old olive orchard when the sun rises.

I didn't sleep much, and when I did, Calchas visited me from the dead and told me in a raven's voice that I was no farmer.

I knew that.

I woke in the chilly time before dawn, plucked my face carefully by lamplight with a woman's mirror and took Hermogenes over the hill. We waited among the olive trees by the fork, as we had as children, and we waited until we saw his father come down the hill, alone, walking quickly with a staff. And then behind him, raucous as crows following a raven, came Simon and his sons, four of them.

I risked my whole future by laughing aloud. How much easier it would have been, having crushed the bandits, to cross the valley, slaughter this foul crow and all his people, and blame the criminals? Men might have suspected the truth – men would have known it for vengeance.

But, *'If you would master the killer in you, you must accept that you are not truly free. You must submit to the mastery of the laws of men and gods.'* Heraclitus said it to me. It took me a few years to see it. I didn't want to be a landless man or a pirate king.

And yet I remember thinking – *even now, I could leave them in a heap before the sun rises another finger's breadth.*

Simon started at the sound of the laugh, but then he kept walking to town and for the first time I hated him as deeply as he deserved to be hated. He had killed my father, and he walked like a man who has a hard life. The useless bastard.

We let them lead us by a couple of stades, and then we followed them. I wanted to make sure that they were at the assembly. I rehearsed my speech as I walked and I feasted my revenge on the sight of Simon's back.

Someone had talked. I know that, because by the time I reached the assembly, most of the men of Plataea were already there, and the silence was like a living thing. I was closer behind Simon as he and his sons trudged up the acropolis to the meeting place. The sun was up, and the world was beautiful with autumn splendor. Demeter and Hera had made a perfect day, the sky was blue and justice was close to my hand.

Myron was dressed in white, and he stood on the little rise where the archon always stood. He waited until Simon walked into the crowd. Even Simon noticed that the crowd parted around him, and no man went to stand close to him. But he was a surly man, he had few friends, and perhaps he expected no more. He crossed his arms and his loutish sons stood around him.

I remember that there was one voice that went on and on – Draco. He was trying to sell a man a wagon, and he hadn't noticed the silence. He was hidden by the crowd, but after a while, he understood, or perhaps a neighbour caught him with an elbow.

I meant to be the last, and I waited by a cowshed, watching the latecomers, some hurrying down from the heights through the gated wall, others trotting up the lanes from outlying farms. Myron's sons were both late, still chewing bread. And then Epictetus and his sons came in a group, with Empedocles on a litter. I fell in with them, and we walked into the middle of the assembly and stood before the archon.

Men looked at me, because I had a spear. Perhaps five other men in the crowd had spears, and they were over sixty. And my spear was fine – in a way that farmers seldom decorate a weapon.

A murmur started.

Myron raised his arms, and silence returned. And then, with two other men, priests, he sacrificed a ram.

'You owe me for that,' Epictetus said in a hoarse whisper.

Then the archon raised his hands, wiped the blood and faced the assembly. 'Men of Plataea!' he said. 'I call you to order, the assembly of the men of the city, to make law.'

We gave him three short cheers, and then the whole assembly sang the Paean.

I had imagined that my moment would come immediately, but however long you wait for revenge, there's always delay. In this case, an existing boundary dispute had to be read into the record. I didn't even know the men involved.

While old Myron's voice droned on, I saw Bion spot his son. I saw the change come to his face. And then I saw him look at me.

His grin was wide enough to split his face. He looked away, hiding his reaction from Simon who was not far from him, and then he began to move through the crowd – not towards us, but to stand *behind* Simon.

Simon took no notice, but other men had marked Bion – he was a popular man – and they followed his eyes, and men began to point and stare, first at Hermogenes – and then at me.

Draco saw me. He threw back his head and laughed.

Myron got to the end of his boundary dispute. 'New business,' he said. 'News from Athens.' He looked out over the assembly. 'Where is the messenger?'

I stepped forward, and men cleared a path for me.

'I have come from Athens,' I said. 'And before that, from Asia, where I was a slave. I have come to accuse Simon son of Simon of the murder of my father – and of selling me into slavery.' I turned, and pointed my spear at Simon, and a path cleared from me to him.

'What can the punishment be,' I asked into the silence, 'for a man who stole my father's farm, his land, his tools and his wife? After stabbing him from behind *in the face of the enemy*?'

Simon was so surprised that one of his hands clawed the air, as if to push away the words I said.

'Who here does not know Simon the Coward? How many of you stood against the Spartans when my brother died at Oinoe? Who was it who ran from the rear of the phalanx? And when we went against the Thebans? Who shirked, and stood in the rear? Is there a man here who remembers Simon standing his ground? And when we faced the Eretrians – I *saw* him stab Pater. I *saw* it.'

'You!' he spluttered. It was nigh on the worst thing he could have said, because his shock and his guilt were writ on his face.

'I am Arimnestos of Plataea!' I roared in my storm-cutter voice. 'I accuse this man of murder!'

He lost his case there, before he opened his mouth to plead.

Mind you, the law doesn't work like an avenging titan. The assembly voted to hear the case, and appointed a jury. And on the spot we argued our cases – this wasn't Athens, and we had no paid orators.

Nor did we have a prison, or guards, or Scythians to take a man and bind him.

The jurors heard our evidence. I had some – and I was determined to use what I had learned in Ephesus and from Miltiades, so I summoned witnesses about Pater's courage and Simon's cowardice, and Simon writhed and his sons glowered. But when the sun began to set in the sky, the jurors went to their dinners and the crowd wandered away, and Simon and his sons headed back up the road to the farm.

I followed them. All of Epictetus's sons were with me, and Hermogenes and his father, and Myron's sons. In every way but the decision of the jurors, the trial was over. We followed them up the road, and hounded them until they reached my lane.

'Stop,' I said.

They cringed.

'Simon,' I said, and he turned. He was shaking. His sons stood away from him – I think in revulsion.

'Take your chattels and go,' I said. 'Or the law will kill you.'

He turned away from me, a shadow of the angry man he'd once been in my father's andron. Honey, I think what he had done had eaten him, until he had nothing left but an angry shell, like the outside of a thorn apple eaten by worms.

And this is the lesson. Remember that I said, when I sat at Oinoe, that I had learned that you could kill, and rape, and force others to your will?

Perhaps you can, for a time. But the gods are there. They do watch. Simonalkes needed no punishment from me. He wore his failure, his cowardice, his alienation, on his face. He was no Plataean, though he had occupied my house while I was a slave. And I – I was welcome back. He lived an exile in his own house – and if I was a poet, I might say that I'd carried Plataea with me wherever I wandered.

I would submit to the mastery of the laws of men and gods.

I went back to Epictetus's house, and slept well.

In the morning, none of Simon's Corvaxae came to the trial. The jurors sent two men to find them.

They came back to say that Simon was hanging by a leather rope from the rafters of the bronze shop, and the sons were gone, and my mother was too drunk to speak.

And so, about noon, on a beautiful day, I walked up that long hill, past the olive trees, past the byres and the grape vines. Bion and Hermogenes walked with me, and Empedocles, moving slowly, and Epictetus, and their sons, and Myron and his sons, and Draco and his sons.

I could hear the swarm of flies on the corpse in the shop.

I was numb.

But the men around me held me up, the way men do in the phalanx when you are wounded. The shields of their friendship covered me. The spears of their humour kept the furies at bay. They were there – the furies, baying for his blood, revelling in the accomplishment of their task – I could feel them on the air.

We walked up into the yard, and then my sister was in my arms, saying my name over and over.

I held Pen a long time, and then I put her down.

'You are all my neighbours and my friends,' I said. 'But I need to clean my own house.'

Every man there nodded, even the youngest. Some things you have to do yourself.

I never promised you a happy story, Honey. It has glad parts, and sad parts, like life.

I went upstairs to Mater. She was drunk – but she knew me. She had a knife – a good bronze knife. Pater's work. She'd tried it on her wrists a few times, and there was blood on her linen and on her arms and, incongruously, some on her feet. Her skin was old, and the blood found folds to run in.

She burst into tears when she saw me.

'Oh!' she wailed. 'I meant to be dead when you came, and now I am a coward as well as everything else.'

I took the knife from her, my strength against her weakness. And then I took the water from her table and washed her, and I bound up the slashes – the inadequate slices – on her wrists.

'He killed Pater,' I said.

'I know,' she said. She raised her head, and a touch of her pride came back. 'I never let them have Pen,' she said. Not an excuse. Just a statement.

So many types of strength, and so many types of weakness, too.

When she was clean, I got Pen to help me get her dressed, and then I went to my next task.

I went into the shop, and I climbed the rafters alone and cut Simon down. He smelled like a new-killed deer, all blood and meat and ordure. It was the smell of hunting and battlefields. The smell that attracts ravens.

I took the corpse to the wagon, and I drove it – scarcely a thought in my head, to tell the truth – across the valley and up the ridge. I spent that night at the tomb, with Idomeneus. In the morning, we burned Simon on the pyre with the dead thief, and sprinkled their ashes across the tomb. Broken men, sacrificed. But what broke them?

Later, Idomeneus had the criminals scrubbing the tomb's round stones with brushes he had them make themselves. I fed my oxen and turned both wagons for home.

A man came up the road from Eleutherai with an aspis on his back and a beaten Thracian cap on his head. I didn't know him, but I knew the look. He came up the hill like a man doing a serious job, and when he reached the tomb, he took a canteen from under his arm and poured a libation. Then he hung his aspis on the great oak tree by the cabin.

'Is the priest here?' he asked. His eyes were a little wild. His hands shook a little.

I let the oxen stand. I sat him on the cabin's step and fed him some wine.

He was still telling about the campaign in Caria when Idomeneus came and sat with us. The mercenary's name was Ajax, and he'd known Cyrus and Pharnakes. He told us how Pharnakes died, and his hands shook. He'd served with the Medes against the Carians. Sitting at the hero's tomb in Boeotia, that didn't matter a fart. We were brothers, all of us, in an ugly brotherhood of spilt blood and terror.

When I left, they were weeping together. Neither cared when the oxen clumped out of the clearing. I took the wagon over Asopus, and when I reached the fork, I stopped and just breathed.

I took my time going up the hill. Over our gate was a wreath of laurel, and there were men in the courtyard, and there was a fire outside the smithy, and the old priest stood with Pen and Peneleos.

I laughed. 'I'm home,' I said.

# Epilogue

My voice is gone, and I've talked enough – your stylus hand must hurt like a swordsman's after a long fight, lad. And you, lady – I must have run you out of blushes by now. And you, honey – you've yawned more than a child at lessons. Although you were kind enough to weep for your grandmother.

Aye, there's more. Come again after the feast of Demeter, and I'll tell you of how I next met Briseis – how I lost the farm, and won it back – how the men of Plataea stood against the Medes at Marathon.

Now there's a story.

# Acknowledgements

On 1 April 1990, I was in the back right seat of an S-3B Viking, flying a routine anti-submarine warfare flight off the USS *Dwight D. Eisenhower*. But we were not just anywhere. We were off the coast of Turkey, and in one flight we passed Troy, or rather, Hisarlik, Anatolia. Later that afternoon, we passed down the coast of Lesbos and all along the coast of what Herodotus thought of as Asia. Back in my stateroom, on the top bunk (my bunk, as the most junior officer), was an open copy of the *Iliad*.

I will never forget that day, because there's a picture on my wall of the Sovremenny-class destroyer *Okrylennyy* broadside on to the mock harpoon missile I fired on her from well over the horizon using our superb ISAR radar. Of course, there was no Homeric deed of arms – the Cold War was dying, or even dead – but there was professional triumph in that hour, and the photo of the ship, framed against the distant haze of the same coastline that saw battles at Mycale and Troy, will decorate my walls until my shade goes down to the underworld.

I think that *Killer of Men* was born there. I love the Greek and Turkish Aegean, and the history of it. Before Saddam Hussein wrecked it in August, my carrier battle group had a near perfect summer, cruising the wine-dark sea where the Greeks and Persians fought.

But it may have been born when talking to various Vietnam veterans, returning from that war – a war that may not have been worse than any other war, but loomed large in my young consciousness of conflict. My grandfather and my father and my uncle – all veterans – said things, when they thought I wasn't around, that led me to suspect that while many men can be brave, some men are far more dangerous in combat than others.

Still later, I was privileged to serve with various men from the

Special Operations world, and I came to know that even among them – the snake-eaters – there were only a few who were the killers. I listened to them talk, and I wondered what kind of a man Achilles really was. Or Hector. And I began to wonder what made them, and what kept them at it, and the thought stayed with me while I flew and served in Africa and saw various conflicts and the effects that those conflicts have on all the participants, from the first Gulf War to Rwanda and Zaire.

*Killer of Men* is my attempt to understand the inside of such men.

This book was both very easy and very hard to write. I have thought about *Killer of Men* since 1990 in some way or other; when I sat down to put my thoughts into the computer, the book seemed to write itself, and even now, when I type these final words, I am amazed at how much of it seemed to be waiting, prewritten, inside my head. But the devil is still in the details, and my acknowledgements are all about the investigation and research of those details.

The broad sweep of the history of the Ionian Revolt is really known to us only from Herodotus and, to a vastly lesser extent, from Thucydides. I have followed Herodotus in almost every respect, except for the details of how the tiny city-state of Plataea came to involve herself with Athens. That, to be frank, I made up – although it is based on a theory evolved over a hundred conversations with amateur and professional historians. First and foremost, I have to acknowledge the contribution of Nicolas Cioran, who cheerfully discussed Plataea's odd status every day as we worked out in a gymnasium, and sometimes fought sword to sword. My trainer and constant sparring partner John Beck deserves my thanks – both for a vastly improved physique, and for helping give me a sense of what real training for a life of violence might have been like in the ancient world. And my partner in the reinvention of ancient Greek xiphos fighting, Aurora Simmons, deserves at least equal thanks.

Among professional historians, I was assisted by Paul McDonnell-Staff and Paul Bardunias, by the entire brother- and sisterhood of RomanArmyTalk.com and the web community there, and by the staff of the Royal Ontario Museum (who possess and cheerfully shared the only surviving helmet attributable to the Battle of Marathon), as well as the staff of the Antikenmuseum Basel und Sammlung Ludwig, who possess the best-preserved ancient aspis and provided me with superb photos to use in recreating it. I also received help from the library staff of the University of Toronto, where, when I'm rich enough, I'm a student, and from Toronto's superb Metro Reference Library. Every novelist needs to live in a city where universal access to JSTOR is free and on his library card. The staff of the Walters Art Gallery in Baltimore, Maryland – just across the street from my mother's apartment, conveniently – were cheerful and helpful, even when I came back to look at the same helmet for the sixth time. And James Davidson, whose superb book, *Greeks and Greek Love* helped me think about the thorny issues of ancient Greek sexuality, was also useful to a novelist with too many questions.

Excellent as professional historians are – and my version of the Persian Wars owes a great deal to many of them, not least Hans Van Wees and Victor Davis Hanson – my greatest praise and thanks have to go to the amateur historians we call reenactors. Giannis Kadoglou of Thessaloniki volunteered to spend two full days driving around the Greek countryside, from Athens to Plataea and back, charming my five-year-old daughter and my wife while translating everything in sight and being as delighted with the ancient town of Plataea as I was myself. I met him on RomanArmyTalk, and this would be a very different book without his passion for the subject and relentless desire to correct my errors.

But Giannis is hardly alone, and there is – literally – a phalanx of Greek reenactors who helped me. Here in my part of North America, we have a group called the Plataeans – this is, trust me, not a coincidence – and we work hard on recreating the very time period and city-state so prominent in these books, from weapons, armour and combat to cooking, crafts and dance. If the reader feels that these books put flesh and blood on the bare bones of history – in so far as I've succeeded in doing that – it is because of the efforts of the men and women who reenact with me and show me, every time we're together, all the things I haven't thought of, who do their own research, their own kit-building and their own training. Thanks to all of you, Plataeans. And to all the other Ancient Greek reenactors who helped me find things, make things or build things.

Thanks are also due to the people of Lesbos and Athens and Plataea – I can't name all of you, but I was entertained, informed and supported constantly in three trips to Greece, and the person who I can name is Aliki Hamosfakidou of Dolphin Hellas Travel for her care, interest and support through many hundreds of emails and some meetings.

In a professional line, I would like to acknowledge the debt I owe to Mr Tim Waller, my copy-editor, whose knowledge of language – both this one and Ancient Greek – always makes me feel humble. He's pretty good at east and west, too. Thanks to him, this book is better than it would ever have been without him.

Bill Massey, my editor at Orion, found the two biggest errors in this story and made me fix them, and again, it is a better book for his work. A much better book. Oh, and he found a lot of other errors, too, but let's not mention them. I have had a few editors. Working with Bill is wonderful. Come on, authors – how many of you get to say that?

My agent, Shelley Power, contributed more directly to this book than to any other – first, as an agent, in all the usual ways, and then later, coming to Greece and taking part in all the excitement of seeing Lesbos and Athens and taking us to Archaeon Gefsis, a restaurant that attempts to take the customer back to the ancient world. Thanks for everything, Shelley, and the dinner not the least!

I'm lucky that my friends still volunteer to read my manuscripts and criticize them: Robert Sulentic, Rebecca Jordan (who also maintains the websites at www.hippeis.com and www.plataians.org), Jenny Carrier, Matt Heppe, Aurora Simmons and Kate Boggs. Thanks to you, this is a better book.

Christine Szego and the staff and management of my local bookstore, Bakka-Phoenix of Toronto, also deserve my thanks, as I tend to walk in and spout fifteen minutes' worth of plot, character, dialogue or just news – writing can be lonely work, and it is good to have people to talk to. And they throw a great book launch.

As usual, this book was written, almost every word, at the Luna Café in Toronto, where I sit at my table, take up another table with Barrington's Classical Atlas, and despite that, get served superb coffee, good humour and excellent food all day.

It is odd, isn't it, that authors always save their families for last? Really, it's the done thing. So I'll do it, too, even though my wife should get mentioned at every stage – after all, she's a reenactor, too, she had useful observations on all kinds of things we both read (Athenian textiles is what really comes to mind, though) and, in addition, more than even Ms Szego, Sarah has to listen to the endless enthusiasms I develop about history while writing (the words 'did you know' probably cause her more horror than anything else you can think of). My daughter, Beatrice, is also a reenactor, and her ability to portray the life of a real child is amazing. My father, Kenneth Cameron, taught me most of what I know about writing, and continues to provide excellent advice – and to listen to my complaints about the process, which may be the greater service.

Having said all that, it's hard to say what exactly I can lay claim to, if you like this book. I had a great deal of help, and I appreciate it. Thanks. And when you find misspelled words, sailing directions reversed and historical errors – why, then you'll know that I, too, had something to add. Because all the errors are solely mine.

Toronto, March 2010

# About the Author

Christian Cameron is a writer and military historian. He is a veteran of the United States Navy, where he served as both an aviator and an intelligence officer. He lives in Toronto where he is currently writing his next novel while working on a Masters in Classics.

To learn more, visit www.hippeis.com and join the online agora, or visit our reenactment group website at www.plataians.org and look through the photo gallery. Or join and come to the 2500th anniversary of Marathon!